BREAKNECK

Also by Marc Cameron

The Arliss Cutter Series
BREAKNECK
COLD SNAP
BONE RATTLE
STONE CROSS
OPEN CARRY

The Jericho Quinn Series
ACTIVE MEASURES
THE TRIPLE FRONTIER
DEAD DROP
FIELD OF FIRE
BRUTE FORCE
DAY ZERO
TIME OF ATTACK
STATE OF EMERGENCY
ACT OF TERROR
NATIONAL SECURITY

The Jack Ryan Series
TOM CLANCY: RED WINTER
TOM CLANCY: CHAIN OF COMMAND
TOM CLANCY: SHADOW OF A DRAGON
TOM CLANCY: CODE OF HONOR
TOM CLANCY: OATH OF OFFICE
TOM CLANCY: POWER AND EMPIRE

BREAKNECK

MARC CAMERON

KENSINGTON
PUBLISHING CORP.

www.kensingtonbooks.com

KENSINGTON BOOKS are published by

Kensington Publishing Corp.
119 West 40th Street
New York, NY 10018

All Kensington titles, imprints, and distributed lines are available at special quantity discounts for bulk purchases for sales promotion, premiums, fund-raising, educational, or institutional use. Special book excerpts or customized printings can also be created to fit specific needs. For details, write or phone the office of the Kensington Special Sales Manager: Attn. Special Sales Department. Kensington Publishing Corp, 119 West 40th Street, New York, NY 10018. Phone: 1-800-221-2647.

Library of Congress Card Catalogue Number: 2022950827

The K with book logo Reg. US Pat. & TM Off.

ISBN: 978-1-4967-3761-8

First Kensington Hardcover Edition: May 2023

ISBN: 978-1-4967-3762-5 (e-book)

10 9 8 7 6 5 4 3 2 1

Printed in the United States of America

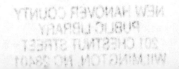

For
Odis—
my Grumpy

"O, from this time forth,
My thoughts be bloody, or be nothing worth!"

—William Shakespeare, Hamlet

PROLOGUE

Alaska

*G*ladys Tomaganak's husband, Pete, was the one who decided they should all go upriver to catch ducks—and she would never forgive him for it.

It was June, *Kaugun* in Gladys's native Yupik, when fish would soon be so plentiful you could hit them with a stick. The ice had gone off the main Yukon just the week before with much destruction and shrieking.

Gladys made almost as much noise when she spied the new hickey on her fifteen-year-old son's neck. That damned downriver girl, Agnes Polty, was the culprit. Gladys called her *utngucegnaq*—one who looks like a wart.

Pete assured her Emmett was just going through a phase. Boys would be boys. When Gladys pointed out that those same boys were already cozying up to their twelve-year-old Winnie, Pete started getting the boat ready for duck camp.

Emmett took care of the shotguns and the .270 Winchester rifle—Gladys's camp gun. There were bound to be bears about. Winnie helped pack their basic supplies—flour, oil, salt, sugar, coffee, and a gallon baggie full of smoked salmon strips—the last of the previous year's harvest. Two dark blue boxes of Sailor Boy Pilot Bread went on top of everything. More of a hard cracker than bread, each piece was the diameter of a hockey puck—and good with everything, from peanut butter to seal oil. It was a staple in bush Alaska.

All chubby cheeks and smiles, baby Martha enjoyed the ride up and down the riverbank swaddled in soft cotton in the back of Gladys's summer *kuspuk.*

Moose camp, berry camp, fish camp, or duck camp, the Tomaganaks were pros, and they had the boat loaded in no time. Gladys's worries began to melt away from the first growl of the propellor biting the turbid brown waters of the mighty Yukon. The river was wide here, swollen by spring floods to almost a mile across. Sandbars had popped up in new places since last summer and rafts of ice floated by like killer torpedoes.

The mouth of the main Andreafsky was less than two miles upriver, just around the corner. St. Mary's, a couple of miles north of that. A series of crescent sloughs and side channels, the East Fork of the Andreafsky snaked between the main river and the Chuilnak, meandering south and east before turning northward through the low Nulato Hills. It was called *Qukaqlik* in Yupik—the Middle One.

Pete pulled the tiller toward him, avoiding a sandbar as he cut up the channel. A grayling leaped on the sun-dazzled surface, biting at some unseen insect or bit of fluff. The sight of it filled Gladys with hope for a good supper.

The normally clear waters churned and frothed, swollen and cloudy with silt. Jagged rafts of old ice grew more plentiful as the little boat motored upstream. Pete wove his way carefully, keeping well clear of the bergy bits. His dad had died falling through rotten ice and he harbored a healthy respect for it.

Two hours after the Tomaganaks departed Pitka's Point, their little boat nosed around the protected bend they all knew so well. Gladys marveled at how much of the bank had simply vanished. Thick cottonwoods that she'd known for decades were gone, sheared off during breakup and taken downriver. What had once been a gentle slope had been gouged into a steep muddy cliff, five feet high.

Emmett gave his sister a stiff elbow and called dibs on any fossilized mammoth teeth or ivory they might find in the newly exposed earth. Gladys clapped her hands, elated when she saw the plywood shelter was still intact. Pete reversed the prop for a short burst and then lifted the motor out of the water. Momentum carried them in.

Skunk cabbage and purple sedge sprouted on the wet bank amid patches of ice and snow. Twenty feet upriver, an otter zipped down a mud chute and slipped beneath the surface with a squeak.

Emmett and Winnie crowded into the bow, their bulky life jackets fighting for the best spot. Winnie grabbed the bow rope, the sleeves of her purple hoodie pushed up on her little forearms, ready for work, and scrambled over the side the minute they scraped gravel. She sloshed up the bank to take a loop around a cottonwood that had survived the ice dams. Emmett gripped the bow with both hands and threw his weight backward, tugging the boat closer to the bank so his mother wouldn't get her feet wet.

The grunt of winging ducks drew everyone's attention upward. If there was a more beautiful duck than the strikingly black-and-white eider, Gladys had never seen it. Pete stood at the sight, teetering the aluminum hull against the gravel. Never much of a talker, he turned his head to follow the winging birds.

Gladys smiled, happy her husband was such a good hunter. "You boys catch us dinner," she said. "Me and Winnie will unload the boat."

Pete raised both eyebrows. In other parts of the world the expression might convey amusement or surprise, but to Gladys's people, who might have to sit silently for hours waiting to catch their food, it was a quiet way to say "good idea."

Baby in the back of her *kuspuk*, Gladys trudged up the hill to the little cabin. It was a shack, really, with a blue tarp roof, weathered plywood walls, and one long window Pete had salvaged from the rear of an old Ford pickup truck. The door was unlocked—a thief would just break it down—and someone caught in a blizzard might need shelter.

"Teapot's been moved," Gladys said as soon as she stepped inside.

Winnie crowded around her mother and surveyed the sixteen-by-sixteen interior. There was plenty of light thanks to Pete's pickup-cab window.

"Did they take stuff?"

Gladys scrunched her nose. *No.*

The furnishings were sparse—four metal folding chairs, a set of bunk beds built from two-by-fours, a similar crib, and a double bed with a rusted metal frame. A plywood shelf ran along the wall beneath the truck window. Spattered grease stains marked the spot where she would put her two-burner camp stove. The Coleman lantern was still hanging from a wire on the center two-by-four rafter—right where they'd left it.

Gladys took the lid off a blue metal bear barrel in the corner and peeked inside.

"They mighta took some tea . . ." she said, the hushed clucks of a mother hen. "Probably hunters who'd needed to warm up. That's okay . . ."

A half hour later, the beds were laid out, a fire snapped in the woodstove, and the baby snored softly in her crib.

Winnie reached into her daypack for a paperback copy of *The Hunger Games* she'd gotten from the Trooper book-boat.

Gladys held out a five-gallon bucket.

"Fill this up. Then you can read."

Winnie went out the door, book in one hand, bucket in her other.

It took fifteen minutes before Gladys started to worry. She opened the door and called out, cupping her hand so as not to wake the baby. No answer but wind and water.

She was probably lost in her book.

Gladys called again.

Nothing.

Exasperated, she scooped up the startled baby and stomped down the hill, .270 rifle in hand.

Only minutes before, the river had brought her so much joy; now it took on a sinister gulping sound—as if it were hungry.

Heart in her throat, Gladys searched up and down the bank, bending willows, parting grass, looking for any sign or track.

Then a cake of dirty ice, the size of a car door, slammed into the mud exactly where Winnie would have been getting water. Seconds later, a huge log came around the bend. It caught the same eddy and gouged a furrow in the bank before spinning back into the current.

All the blood drained from Gladys's face. If Winnie had been reading and shown the river her back . . .

Beyond panicked, Gladys set the baby on a patch of grass and fired three shots into the air. She worked the bolt quickly, screaming all the while for her missing child. The baby flinched at the gunfire, and began to wail along with her mother.

It seemed like forever before Pete and Emmett crashed through the willows. Emmett carried not only his shotgun, but a yellow five-gallon bucket.

"I found this floating downriver," he said. "Mom? What's—"

"Winnie's missing . . ." Gladys pointed at the churning brown water. Her knees buckled and she had to grab her husband to keep her feet.

Emmett scuffed at the bank with his boot. He looked up at his father.

"Here's one of her tracks."

Gladys clutched the baby to her chest.

"Look at this, Dad," the boy said. "She's facing away from the water, leaving. We shoulda passed her when we came up."

Pete wheeled. "Come on. She might be hung up in a sweeper, or some willows." He stopped abruptly, turning back to Gladys, his bronze face twisted with the worry of a man who'd lost his father to the river. "How long's she been gone?"

Gladys told him.

"Come, come." Pete flicked his hand at Emmett.

"Hold on, Dad," the boy said. "This track . . . It's different."

Pete glanced at the mud. "Probably when we were unloading the boat. Now come!"

"I don't think so," Emmett said. "Different heel—"

Pete cuffed his son on the shoulder. "I told you, let's go! Dirt's too tore up to see anything for sure." He crashed into the thick brush with Emmett on his heels, both shouting Winnie's name.

Gladys waded knee-deep into the water beside their skiff, screaming for her little girl until her voice cracked.

In her haste she missed the fresh boot track in the mud.

Russia

Fifteen hundred miles to the east of Alaska, a man with feral eyes and a hatchet face held court from a tufted leather booth in the back of Ogon' i Led—which meant Fire and Ice—his back-alley nightclub off Primorskaya Street in the Russian city of Petropavlovsk. A hint of rotting seaweed from nearby Avacha Bay muddled with the pungent body odor and eye-watering perfumes of the three women crammed into the booth with the man. Low, moaning music throbbed in time with pulsing lights, illuminating three cages and, more important, the nubile dancers inside them. Two dozen men sat at low tables around the stage, all entranced, swaying, drinking the hatchet-faced man's booze, and throwing wads of cash at his women.

When Maxim Volkov was a boy, his friends had called him *"Toporok,"* (in English, it would have been "Little Axe")—and not only for the severe angles of his face. He was a fighter, prone to fits of rage. The tail of a black-dolphin tattoo the size of his thumb peeked above the rat's nest of gunmetal chest hair spilling from the open collar of his silk shirt. The ink was a memento of another time when the air smelled, not like the sea, but of misery and urine and fear. In Penal Colony Number 6 he'd earned another nickname: *Kostolom* (Bone Breaker).

Volkov's lieutenant, a handsome silver-haired man, with a pencil-thin mustache, stood at the end of the booth, with a phone pressed to his ear. He pulled the device away and gave a slow shake of his head.

"No answer, boss," he said. The music made lipreading a necessity.

At forty-six, five years Volkov's junior, Ilia Lipin had earned tattoos in the Black Dolphin Prison as well. All had been applied with a jury-rigged electric razor motor, plastic from a melted toothbrush, and a straightened staple from a fat book in the prison library. Ink was made of boot polish and piss, preferably from the person getting the tat. Volkov had decided early in their acquaintance that Lipin's handsome face and prematurely silver hair made him perfect for politics or the cinema. Even in prison he advised the man to keep the tattoos concealed under his clothes, mindful of a time when they might wish to blend with the world.

"No answer?" Volkov muttered, as if the notion was inconceivable.

Lipin shook his head, his mouth pinched in a frown, demonstrating to his boss that he was disappointed at the current situation too.

The tendons in Volkov's neck thrummed as if carrying high voltage. People, he could bend to his will. Phone lines, satellites, undersea cables—those did not care that he was a feared leader of the *bratva*, known as the Russian mafia or mob in the West.

One of Volkov's many mistresses, a raven-haired waif named Kira, cuddled up beside him. Even she was not sure how old she was, but Volkov put her at around sixteen, if he happened to think about her age at all.

He gave a nod to Lipin to try the call again and then turned his attention to the pudgy naval officer standing before his table. The man kept his head up, shoulders back, but rubbed his sweating hands at his waist like a housefly—at once, nervous and defiant.

"It is Bukin, correct?"

"Yes," the man said. "Gennady Arkadyevich Bukin."

Volkov toyed with an empty vodka glass, turning it back and forth as if grinding something against the table. "Captain of the third rank," he noted. "Stationed across the bay at Rybachiy Naval Base aboard special mission submarine BS-64 Podmoskovye—"

"This . . . This is sensitive information," the captain stammered. "How did you come by—"

Volkov cut him off. "You owe me money, Gennady."

"And I will pay," the captain said. "I only need—"

"You have money to spend at my competitor down the street."

"That was an error in judgment," the man said. "It will not—"

Volkov pushed the glass away and sat back on the soft leather between his women. "I am curious," he said. "The Russian Navy is very strong . . ."

The captain squirmed. When no question came his way, he said, "Yes?"

"Stronger than me, do you suppose?"

"The navy is . . . is larger . . ."

Volkov nodded, considering this. "I am not large," he said. "Does that mean I am not strong?"

Bukin flinched like he'd been slapped when Volkov snatched up a mother of pearl spoon and slathered a blin with caviar from a large bowl in the center of his table. The mafia boss eyed the younger man while he chewed.

Then, out of nowhere, Volkov grabbed young Kira by her face and squeezed hard, grinding hollow cheeks against her teeth. The girl hung there in his grip, sobbing quietly, obediently. She was startled, but not at all surprised. Bloody saliva trickled from her pursed lips. Volkov held her for a time, his nose inches from hers, face canted to one side as if puzzled.

He pushed her away just as suddenly as he'd grabbed her. She collapsed into the booth beside him, rubbing her face, obviously too terrified to run or make a sound.

"And there you have it, Captain Gennady Arkadyevich Bukin." Volkov used a linen napkin to wipe the girl's tears and spittle off his fingers before popping another bite of caviar into his mouth. "That"—he nodded sideways to the quivering girl—"that was for nothing. Can you imagine what I would do to her if she had done something . . ."

The captain trembled more than the girl now. Volkov studied him for a moment and then glanced at Lipin.

"Still, no answer?"

The mob lieutenant shook his head.

Ignoring the navy man, Volkov snatched the phone away and pressed the button to redial, cursing the fast busy signal.

"I told the boy to expect my call," he said, drawing a nod from the stoic Lipin. Finally, on Volkov's third attempt, a male voice crackled over the line, an American speaking barely passable Russian.

"Sashenka!" he said, using the informal diminutive for Alexander. He wished the boy's Russian was better, but that would be remedied soon enough. For now, Volkov spoke English, getting straight to the point. "It is your father."

"Papa!" the boy said. "I was hoping you would call. Do you have any newspaper clippings about grandfath—"

"I need you."

"I'm on a fishing boat," the boy said. "We should be in Kodiak—"

"Not Kodiak!" Volkov snapped. "I thought your boat berths in Homer. I expected you would come to Anchorage from there."

"Wait!" Alex said, suddenly more animated. "You're in Anchorage?"

"Soon," Volkov said. "And I want my son there to meet me. We have much to discuss. When do you arrive in Homer?"

"I don't know," the boy said. "Four days, maybe five or six. We only left Dutch Harbor yesterday."

"No, no, no," Volkov said. "Why five or six days? It should not take you this long, even all the way from Dutch Harbor."

"I already told you," Alex said, sounding flippant—far too much like his mother. "The skipper wants to stop in Kodiak for a few days."

Volkov rubbed a hand across his jaw and barked an order to Lipin, who took another phone from his pocket.

"Very well," Volkov said to his son. "I will make you reservations to fly from Kodiak to Anchorage—"

Lipin looked up from his phone and shook his head.

"Flights full for the next five days," he said.

"I'm not surprised," Alex said, hearing Lipin's end of the conversation. "Weather's been bad in the Gulf for a week. Kodiak flights get canceled all the time for fog. Backs everything up like crazy. Don't worry. I'll be in Homer in a week, tops."

"*Nyet!*" Volkov snapped. The girl beside him jerked, fearing he might grab her face. "A week does me no good. No good at all. Tell your captain he must sail directly to Homer."

"You don't really *tell* this skipper anything," the boy said. "He's kind of a—"

"Talk less." Volkov cut him off. "Listen more."

"Okay . . ."

Volkov closed his eyes, forcing himself to calm. "You are my son, Sasha," he said. "Inform the captain you have a family emergency. You must stress to him that you have no choice."

Alex chuckled. He not only had his mother's laugh, which was galling enough, but her glib nature as well. "What's so important? It's just a couple of extra days."

Had any of Volkov's men spoken to him this way, he would have cut off their balls with a carpet knife, one by one, so they would have time to think on their behavior.

The *bratva* boss took a deep breath and then said, "I must see to someone personally. I want you by my side."

The boy was uncharacteristically silent for a time. "Okay . . . When you say 'see to someone,' you usually mean—"

"Correct."

"And you want me to help you?"

"No!" Volkov said, harsher than he intended to be. "And yes. Explanations will come. For now, convince your captain."

"I'll try," the boy said. "Can I ask you something?"

"Of course."

"I need proof about grandfather. The crew doesn't believe—"

"Focus, Alexander!" Volkov chided. "Call Uncle Lev when you have a time of arrival in Homer. He will work out transport to Anchorage. Then we will discuss your grandfather."

Volkov ended the call and slipped the phone in his pocket.

He glanced at the navy man. "You are still here."

"I thought . . . you wanted me to stay—"

"I did," Volkov said. "We could spend an endless amount of time on this . . ."

"I—"

"Do you want to know what I think?"

The captain ran a trembling tongue across his lips. It was clear that he did not want to know at all, but he gave a tentative squeaky "Yes . . ."

"I think that you believe your military rank gives you a certain latitude. You believe because you work aboard a secret nuclear submarine your debts should—"

"N . . . no," Bukin stammered. "I promise—"

At a nod from their boss Lipin and a young man named Gavrill grabbed the captain by both arms. Gavrill was around Alexander's age, dark and handsome, with a Superman curl on his forehead. He drove a boot into the side of the navy man's knee, causing him to double over in pain.

The crowd drew back, heavy with anticipation and dread. They knew what was coming. Volkov's men pushed a terrified Bukin to his knees, and then forced him facedown so his head was on the step of the booth while his body trailed downward at an angle to the carpeted floor.

Gennady Arkadyevich Bukin, captain of the third rank in the Russian Navy, painted the floor with tears, begging forgiveness for his debt. Music throbbed. Dancers writhed in their cages. Kira, the sweating waif on whom Maxim Volkov had recently demonstrated his cruelty, passed her employer a heavy wooden walking stick. He shooed her out of his way and rose from the booth to place the thick mahogany against the base of the wailing navy man's skull.

The wooden stick was nothing ornate. Bland, in fact, like a table leg. But it held great sentimental value to Maxim Volkov, its frequent use providing his Bone Breaker nickname.

Gennady Bukin gurgled and pleaded, his hand flopping against the carpet like a pallid fish.

The girls in the cages stopped dancing. The bartender climbed up on a stool to get a better view. Lipin had the houselights raised and Volkov waited a beat so everyone's eyes could adjust. Sometimes men needed to be killed in private, but an audience was exponentially more powerful at driving home his point.

"I have no time to discuss." He put his full weight on the stick. "I must see to someone in America."

Washington, DC

Depending on the case before the United States Supreme Court, half the country loved Associate Justice Charlotte Morehouse. The other half wanted to see her hanged from a gibbet. Those halves swapped sides on a frighteningly regular basis.

She'd learned long ago—and was still trying to teach her teenage daughter—not to fret over what people thought. Do the right thing because it was right, not because one side of the argument screamed the loudest.

At forty-five, Morehouse was the youngest and, according to *Rolling Stone* magazine, the "most handsome" justice on the Court. She stood five feet ten inches tall, and the days she wasn't on the Court's basketball court, she spent an hour in the gym reading on the treadmill or stair climber. Shoulder-length hair fell somewhere between dun and silver. Her late husband had called it grulla. She considered her hair the most interesting thing about her. He'd always said it was on his list, but had a few other ideas.

John Morehouse had passed away a month before the president appointed her to the Court—just over a year ago. She missed him terribly, but saw his eyes every day when she looked at their fifteen-year-old daughter.

Morehouse pushed away from the desk and stood at the same moment her clerk—also a Duke alum—breezed in with a stack of folders, each containing briefs for pending cases.

"Good morning, Libby." Morehouse strode to her chambers' window and looked out toward the Library of Congress.

"Good morning, Madam Justice." The clerk set the briefs on the corner of her desk. Libby Weems wore a dark A-line skirt and smart silk blouse—like a thousand other young lawyers working inside the Beltway. Her brow was knitted, clearly concerned. "Apparently, one of your hosts, US District Judge Markham, would like to show you around Alaska after your speech at the Fairbanks conference. He's taken the liberty of planning a couple of extra excursions."

"Excursions?"

"He described them as 'wilderness excursions.' "

"Sounds—"

"Terrifying?"

"I was going to say *exciting*." Morehouse paced to the other side of her chambers—much more commodious than the ones she'd had as a district court judge. She'd always been a walker, especially when deep in thought. By now, Weems and the rest of her staff estimated the carpet *might* last two years if they were lucky.

Weems nodded, lips pursed as if she'd sucked on a lemon.

"What?" Morehouse said. "You mean you don't love a good adventure? Feast your young eyes on this idea of Judge Markham's." She moved to her desk and brought up the image of a blue-and-yellow Alaska Railroad locomotive winding its way along a section of track between sea and endless snowcapped mountains. "Ramona is super stoked."

"Wait." Weems pulled up short. "Your daughter's going?"

"We notified the Marshals Service this morning." Still standing, Morehouse scrolled the photos. "You can't tell me that a rail journey through this supremely wild place wouldn't be amazing."

"Honestly, ma'am," the law clerk said. "My idea of wild adventure is a foreign film with subtitles. What if something were to happen? You're going to be . . . I don't know, a million miles from the nearest big hospital."

"Pffft," Morehouse chided. "Alaska has hospitals."

Weems leaned in, as if confiding a secret. "Did you know that there are twice as many people inside the Beltway as there are in the entire state of Alaska? I checked."

"So, you're saying you'd like to come?"

Weems blanched. "No. I mean, of course, I'd go if you—"

"Relax, Libby," Morehouse said. "I won't drag you along."

"You should watch a couple of episodes of *Alaska State Troopers*," the clerk said, slightly breathless. "Volcanoes, earthquakes, plane crashes, not to mention ten-foot grizzly bears and ginormous moose that all want to stomp you to death. And . . . ."

Her voice trailed.

"Spill it," Morehouse said. "What else?"

"With all due respect, ma'am," Weems said, "you have a way of . . ." She paused, chewing on her lip, holding back the words.

Morehouse narrowed her gaze, chiding. "Libby . . ."

"The marshals say you can be a bit too . . . spontaneous," Weems said. "Like you're not worried about your own safety."

"I'm not," Morehouse scoffed. "That's *their* job."

CHAPTER 1

Supervisory Deputy US Marshal Arliss Cutter didn't see anyone along the banks of the Andreafsky River, but his gut told him someone was there. It made perfect sense. Prey—smart prey, anyway—kept its head up, ever on the lookout for hunters—and Cutter was hunting.

Six-three, with a healthy fighting weight of 240 pounds, Cutter took up most of the real estate in the bow. One of three in the boat, he was dressed for the bush—wool shirt, which was black-and-green plaid, brown Fjällräven pants, and rubber XtraTuf boots. He'd taken off his desert tan boonie hat and clipped it to his pack, revealing a thick mop of unruly blond hair. It wasn't that he was averse to combing it. The thought just rarely occurred to him.

A twelve-gauge Remington 870 with a bird's-head grip and a remarkably maneuverable eleven-inch barrel—called a WitSec shotgun in the Marshals Service—rested in a scabbard secured to the waterproof daypack at his feet.

Cutter's partner, a twentysomething Polynesian deputy named Lola Teariki, hunkered amidships, trying in vain to smash a biting moose fly that buzzed around her face. George Polty, a Village Public Safety officer, sat on an overturned plastic bucket working tiller on the outboard, torn between chuckling at Lola's antics and watching out for sandbars.

Cutter scanned the wood line, wondering if their target was in the shadows, watching.

Forty-two-year-old Lamar Wayne Jacobi was wanted on a federal warrant for mail fraud, a relatively innocuous white-collar crime, but a history of a violent assault on his ex-wife put the deputies on guard. The Oregon judge who'd presided over the assault case eight months earlier hadn't viewed smacking someone in the shoulder with a ball-peen hammer as bad enough to hold Jacobi in custody pending trial. The judge had ruled that if the accused had wanted to kill the victim, he would have struck her in the head. Apparently, it never occurred to His Honor that the defendant might simply have missed his ex-wife's noggin during the attack.

Cutter had long since given up on trying to make sense of judicial fiat, focusing instead on recapturing the pukes that courts insisted on releasing back on the street. Those releases occurred with slightly less frequency in federal court, but they still happened enough that Cutter and his team had, as they say, a target-rich environment.

Jacobi legged it the same day he made bond for the hammer assault, precisely one month before a federal grand jury in Dallas indicted him for defrauding two elderly women out of their life savings with a roofing scam. Local law enforcement didn't have the resources to spend much time chasing fugitive con artists, and they were all too happy to pass the case to the United States Marshals Service, once federal paper was involved. Deputies from both the North Texas Fugitive Task Force and Pacific Northwest Violent Offenders Task Force worked the case. Jacobi moved around the country like a Whac-A-Mole popping up all over the place. Other than some flimsy intel that he'd fled to Alaska, there wasn't much to go on. The case literally fell farther and farther down the stack, beneath sexier, more pressing warrants that landed every day. It would have languished for months, had a Yupik duck hunter not posted on YouTube footage of his trip along a tributary of the Yukon River and shots of a mysterious white man. Even then, with over 800 million videos on the platform, seven seconds of GoPro footage would have gone unpursued, but for the fact that Jacobi was wanted as a material witness in the murder of a prominent Texas state legislator. A Dallas County DA investigator, aware of the slim possibility that Jacobi might be in Alaska—and interested in duck hunting, anyway—stumbled on the YouTube footage during a lunch break. The image was distant and only lasted a few seconds, but facial recognition software put the odds at better than 75 percent that it was Jacobi.

The district attorney was up for reelection, and with a high-profile murder trial looming, his office made a formal request for the US Marshals Service to turn up the heat on Jacobi's fugitive case.

As it turned out, an upcoming election, not trying to clobber your ex-wife with a ball-peen hammer, provided the best grease for the wheels of justice. The chief deputy US marshal for the Northern District of Texas reached out to District of Alaska Chief Jill Phillips—and Lamar Wayne Jacobi's powder-blue warrant folder shot to the top of Arliss Cutter's stack.

Eighteen hours after Chief Phillips received the collateral request, Cutter and Teariki found themselves climbing out of a thirty-seat Ravn Air Dash 8 in the Yupik village of St. Mary's—over four hundred miles from the road system. Two hours later, they were in VPSO George Polty's boat, motoring up the Andreafsky.

The Alaska State Trooper lieutenant in Bethel had tasked the two troopers stationed in St. Mary's to assist, but as usual, they were up to their eyeballs in work when the deputies arrived. This time it was a death investigation involving an ATV driver and a utility pole. Cutter and Teariki found themselves in the capable, if unarmed, hands of a Village Public Safety officer who would be their boat driver and guide. VPSOs had powers of arrest, but most carried no sidearm, relying instead on a Taser, pepper spray, and their wits. George Polty had grown up sixty miles down the Yukon River in the village of Alakanuk—which he pronounced with a clicky wet throat that sounded very much like the cry of a raven and reinforced to Cutter that he would never come close to learning the language.

The troopers assured Cutter they'd be right along if nothing else popped up. That meant the deputies and Polty were on their own. In bush Alaska, something always popped up.

The thirty-horse Tohatsu outboard pushed the skiff up the river at a respectable pace. Runoff from melting ice and snow put the Yukon at flood stage, giving them a backward current of almost two miles an hour when they'd left St. Mary's. Even now, some fifteen miles upstream, turbid water eddied and swirled as if it didn't quite know which way to flow.

Perched in the center of the skiff, Lola Teariki knocked a thick strand of ebony hair out of her customary high bun as she swatted at the moose flies. It now trailed across her cheek, pasted there by periodic rain. Five years as a deputy US marshal added to her natural swagger and ability to turn her Polynesian princess face into a fearsome scowl—which she now used to little effect on the moose flies.

George Polty took a small metal tin from the pocket of his exterior ballistic vest and offered it to Teariki.

"Yarrow salve," he said. "Helps keep the bugs away."

A chilly rain pocked the surface of the river, hard enough to make a jacket necessary but not enough to chase away the clouds of mosquitoes and no-see-ums.

Lola waved her hand through the morphing cloud. "Yarrow? Like the weed?" Willing to try anything, she leaned in and took it.

"Don't work quite as good as DEET," Polty said. "Smells better, though. I save the DEET for when the bugs are really bad."

Lola grimaced. "You don't call this really bad?"

"Nah," Polty said. "Bad is when you're camping and the inside of your tent looks like fur 'cause so many mosquito noses are poking through the net tryin' to get at you—"

His head suddenly snapped toward the tree line.

Cutter followed his gaze.

Polty crinkled his nose—an unspoken *"no"* in Yupik culture—and then translated by shaking his head for Cutter's benefit.

"I don't *see* anything," the VPSO said. "But I can feel it lookin' at me."

Lola cursed at the bugs, slapping her own face while she scanned the wood line. "A bear, maybe," she said. "Aren't the salmon beginning to run?" Another swat knocked more hair out of her bun. "This is so stuffed . . ."

Polty gave a somber nod. "Could be a bear, I guess, but I don't think they're too thick yet. Fish been comin' in later and later the last couple of years, if they come at all."

The two moose flies circled Teariki's head like biplanes buzzing King Kong. One got through her defenses and zapped her on the upper lip, incising a tiny hunk of flesh before she could react. Like their southern horsefly cousins, moose flies were resilient little beasts, capable of withstanding a solid flat-handed swat and still coming back for more.

Lola killed one, grimacing at the movement of a recently cracked rib. She flicked her non–gun hand to keep the remaining fly at bay.

"Talk to me, Cutter. What are you thinking?" Of Cook Island Maori descent, her Kiwi accent tended to clip her Rs, making "Cutter" sound like "Cuttah."

"Just a feeling," he said.

Polty stretched his arm over the water. "This part of the river is bad news. Not good . . . not good at all." He shot a quick glance at Cutter, then Lola, eyes wide. "You guys ever been to Hooper Bay?"

"A couple of years ago," Lola said. "Why?"

Cutter shook his head. At one fifth the size of the contiguous United States, there was still a lot of Alaska he'd yet to visit.

"A girl died in the school," he said. "*Ukka tamani* . . . long, long ago . . ."

"How'd she die?" Lola asked.

"I'm not even sure," Polty said. "But it must have been brutal. People see her ghost hangin' around all the time."

Lola gave him a side-eye. "What do you mean all the time?"

"That's pretty much it," the VPSO said, earnest as a church deacon. "They see her all around the school—library, halls, peeking out the windows—teachers, students, lots of folks."

"Okay," Cutter said. "Hooper Bay's, what, a hundred miles away? What's that got to—"

Polty jammed his index finger at the aluminum siderail, shaking his head as if his reasoning was all so obvious. "This stretch of river killed little Winnie Tomaganak." He shivered, checked the tree line again, and then wiped a hand over the top of his head to steady his nerves. "She disappeared just a week ago. Poof. Vanished off the bank. We searched every snag and sandbar." He stared over the side of the boat into the water, eyes glazed. "You ever see the big treble hooks they use to drag the water for a body?"

Cutter nodded.

"Horrible thing, draggin' a river," Polty said over the roaring motor. "Hoping you find something . . . then hoping you don't . . . I'll tell you that much." His index finger went back to poking the gunnel, punctuating his words. "We looked for that poor kid for three days solid. River ice musta taken her out to sea. It can sneak up and eat you alive if you're not lookin'."

Lola finally nabbed the surviving moose fly and flicked it into the water. A fat grayling rose from the depths and gulped it down with a burbling splash.

"You're telling me you feel the ghost of a dead child watching you from the woods? I'm a good Christian girl. I don't believe in that shit."

The way she eyed the bank said she obviously did.

"That's a tragic story," Cutter said, meaning it. "But no. I don't think there's a ghost in the woods."

Polty shrugged. "Something's out there, Marshal. Winnie's body wasn't ever found. A bad death like that, I bet her little spirit is just wanderin' the banks, trying to find a door to the other side—"

Lola banged her fist on the gunnel and made a futile attempt at chasing away the cloud of mosquitoes with the other.

"How about some speed, George? Get us away from these mozzies. And knock off this shittery about ghosts. You're creepin' the hell outta me."

Polty grunted, giving a little shrug like he knew better, and then rolled on more throttle. The added speed did little good. Mosquitoes and tiny biting midges the locals called "no-seem-ums" followed the boat in great black clouds, pulsing and morphing like specters on unseen currents of chilly air.

Lola slapped herself on the neck. "That footage that's supposed to be Jacobi," she yelled above the sound of chattering water. "Where was that taken?"

"A half mile upriver," Polty shouted back. "Near as I can tell, he was fishing." He hooked a thumb toward the bank and then caught his ballcap before it blew off. "There's a derelict camp in the woods not far from here."

Lola dabbed at the fly bite on her lip. "What sort of camp?"

"A bunch of end-of-days whack jobs followed their prophet out here in the late nineties." Polty let up on the gas, slowing a hair so they could hear each other better. "Ten or twelve of 'em pretty much invaded, preppin' for the shit to hit the fan on Y2K. This is all Native corporation land, so they had to have some connection. I think one of the main dude's disciples was half Yupik. The place was a going concern for a while, chickens, greenhouses, some goats, a commune, if you want to call it that. Folks from St. Mary's would trade for fresh eggs and such—"

"What happened?" Lola asked.

"Not a damned thing," Polty said. "The earth kept spinnin' on Y2K plus one. I guess the prophet got sick of the bugs and went back to his dental practice in Chicago. The entire group evaporated as quick as they'd come."

"But they left the cabins intact?" Cutter mused, waving away a fly.

"Yep," Polty said. "Good place to spend the winter if you're running from the law. Kids used to go out there, but everybody says it's haunted now."

"Jacobi's file says he's spent plenty of time in the woods," Cutter pondered. "He's enough of an outdoorsman to survive if push came to shove."

"Hmmm," Polty said. "This is a push-comes-to-shove kind of place."

"You got that right," Lola said, more relaxed now that she'd dispatched the moose flies and only had to deal with 2 million other biting bugs. "I'll bet ninety percent of my Academy classmates are sitting in court right now or serving civil papers—" She froze, eyes locked on the far bank some seventy-five yards upriver on the left.

"What have you got?" Cutter whispered.

Lola shot him a glance, turned back to the bank. "You didn't see that?"

"Jacobi?"

"No," she said, still peering at the trees. "A Native girl."

The VPSO smacked the side of his boat. "I told you!"

"It wasn't a ghost," Lola said.

"A kid from one of the fish camps, maybe," Cutter mused.

Polty shook his head. "Nobody's out at fish camp yet. What'd she look like? This Native girl?"

"Young," Lola said. "Dark hair, ten, twelve years old."

"Purple hoodie?"

Lola nodded. "I thought you didn't see her."

"I didn't," Polty said. "Winnie Tomaganak was wearin' a purple hoodie when the river got her."

CHAPTER 2

*C*utter shrugged on his daypack, while Polty gunned the throttle, coaxing the little boat up on step.

"Get on the sat phone," he shouted to Lola. "Let the Troopers know where we are and what we've got."

Lola wedged herself beside the rail and unfolded the satellite phone's antenna. She plugged one ear with her free hand while she spoke. All the while, she stared so hard at the trees, Cutter imagined they might burst into flames. He liked that kind of focus. It reminded him of himself.

Polty threw the outboard into reverse as he neared the bank, slowing. The bow scraped bottom at the same moment Lola ended her phone call.

"Troopers are an hour and a half out," Lola said, hushing her voice in the abrupt absence of the deafening outboard. "They want George to stay with the boat."

"Screw that!" Polty said. He'd gotten past the idea that Lola had seen a ghost. "I was the one who had to look Gladys Tomaganak in the eye and tell her we were callin' off the search for her daughter. No way I'm waitin' by the damned boat."

"No worries, George." She gave him a wink. "I told 'em we needed you as a guide." M4 carbine in hand, she nodded to Cutter, letting him know she was ready. One of the first things he'd taught her was that a sidearm was for emergencies. If chances were good there might actually be a gunfight, you took a long gun. That went double in the bush, miles or even days from any backup.

Cutter jumped out of the boat first, tying the bow line to the base of a stout spruce, while Lola covered the woods, rifle at the ready. The VPSO took a quick moment to detach the black rubber fuel hose that connected the outboard to the plastic tank and hid it behind a clump of willows. The last thing they wanted was to be stranded by someone who decided to borrow their skiff.

The muddy ground along the bank was a perfect track-trap. He found the girl's trail almost immediately and followed it into the trees. Twenty feet inside the forest, he paused, stooping low to study the tracks more closely. Lola provided overwatch, scanning the shadows, rifle up to her shoulder. The muzzle went where she looked.

Rain began to fall in earnest, pattering the carpet of dead leaves that littered the forest floor.

"Talk to me, boss." Lola kept her voice low. She chanced a quick glance at the ground, then got back on the rifle. "Whatcha got?"

"New set of tracks," Cutter said. "Large. Over top of the girl's."

"Over top? That means . . ."

"Yep. He's behind her." Cutter stood. "Did she make eye contact with you?"

"I don't think so," Lola said. "Looked as though she might have heard the boat and was coming out to wave us down. She was turned sideways, though, looking into the trees. You think she's running from Jacobi?"

"She's running from someone." Cutter nodded at the tracks. "If this is Jacobi, then . . ."

Lola glanced over her shoulder at the VPSO. "Our guy's got no history of resisting arrest, but he's obviously dangerous, and he doesn't want to be found. I'm a little concerned about you being out here with no gun if things go sideways."

"Don't you worry about me," Polty said. "I'll be fine."

Cutter wiped the rain off his face. "I have an extra pistol if it comes to that."

He carried his grandfather's Colt Python, as well as a small Glock 27. The .357 Magnum made more sense in the bush, but the Glock kept him in line with Marshals Service firearms policy. He gave the trees ahead a nod. "The abandoned Y2K camp is through here?"

Polty looked around, then back toward the river, getting his bearings. "We passed it already, maybe a half mile back from where we first saw the girl."

The three fell into a plodding rhythm. Cutter worked the ground, while Lola and Polty served, respectively, as overwatch and rear guard. There was a strong possibility that they weren't dealing with a lone fugitive. If it was Jacobi, someone had to have dropped him off and brought him supplies. As this was all Native corporation land, Cutter guessed that someone might even live nearby.

Individual tracks became harder to discern the farther they got from the river. Birch and poplar leaves carpeted the spongy ground. Mottled and slimy with rot, they'd spent the past winter under several feet of snow and now let off the sickly-sweet odor of decay. Here and there, patches of ground had obviously been turned from a traveling foot, but it was often difficult to tell if the creature that foot belonged to had two legs or four. The girl's movements zigged and zagged, cutting around trees, even back-tracking a few times to start off in an entirely new direction. The way the ground was kicked up suggested that she was running most of the time—as was the man behind her.

A stream, some three feet wide, crossed their path a hundred yards in from the river, providing a natural funnel, as well as a few yards of mud for more distinct tracks. Mostly moose and wolf, but human tracks too. Water flowed into the impressions as Cutter studied them, indicating that they'd only recently been made.

He hopped over the stream, taking care not to disturb any tracks or slip in the snotty leaves, then stopped to read the ground on the other side.

Lola cleared the water with an easy leap and came up behind him. "What is it?" A cloud of vapor blossomed from her lips on the chilly air. A raindrop hung from the tip of her nose.

Cutter pointed to a clear line of the larger set of prints that were relatively free of leaves and forest litter. "His left foot pivots slightly and leans in . . . here . . ."

"Checking over his shoulder?" Lola offered.

"That's right," Cutter said. "But look. He takes two more steps and—"

"The tracks turn," Lola said, cutting him off. "He spun around completely and walked backward a couple of strides." She glanced ahead and then checked the tracks again. "You think he has a rifle."

"That's my guess," Cutter said.

Lola quickly explained their exchange to a puzzled George Polty. "Ever notice how when you look behind you when you're carrying a long gun, you almost always turn all the way around and walk backward for a step or two, as opposed to just glancing over your shoulder, like you do when you're unarmed?"

The VPSO mulled it over. "I never thought about it. But I guess that's true. You want the gun to go where you're looking."

Cutter was already moving again, bounding quickly to the next visible track, confirming he was on the right line, then repeating the process. If this girl was on the run, he wanted to close the distance before Jacobi caught up with her.

Lola trotted behind him. "So our guy has a gun and knows he's being followed. He can't be that far . . ." She paused, hissing to get Cutter's attention. "Smell that?"

Cutter took a deep breath, then pointed the same direction the tracks were going. "Woodsmoke. Wind's in our faces, so—"

A hoarse voice from the shadows to the left caused Cutter to freeze. He resisted the urge to raise the short shotgun, not wanting to escalate the situation into something worse than it was—which was already bad enough. He had no target—yet.

"Damn right the wind is in your face," the voice said, rough, like rusted barbed wire—or someone who rarely spoke. "While you focus on a whiff of woodsmoke, I creep up from downwind—"

"And?" Teariki's Kiwi accent came through, making it sound like "ind."

"What . . . what do you mean?" the voice asked, more than a little bewildered at the sudden challenge. He sounded too old to be their fugitive.

"What do *you* mean?" Lola asked. "You creep up from downwind and do what? What is your plan exactly?"

The voice mumbled, "Don't you worry about *my* plan. I'm telling you now, leave that little girl alone."

"We need to talk to a man named Jacobi," Cutter said. "But if it's the missing Tomaganak girl you're talking about—"

"So, you're not friends with that bald guy?"

"Bald guy?" Lola said.

"The one chasin' the kid."

"We are not," Cutter said, gritting his teeth. "Listen—"

"You troopers?" the voice demanded, growing more agitated by the moment.

"US Marshals," Cutter said.

"You looking for me?"

"Your name Jacobi?"

"It is not."

"Then we are not," Cutter said. "Now knock it off and show yourself! I've got no time for this."

Pattering rain and the distant churning of the river made it impossible to pinpoint where the voice was coming from.

"Put your weapons on the ground," the voice said.

"Yeah." Cutter shook his head. "We're not doing that." He turned slowly to peer into the dense foliage. Nothing.

"What's your name?" Lola asked, friendly, like they'd just met on the trail.

"Capt . . . Tom . . . Tom Walker . . ."

"Hey," Polty said. "I've heard of you!" He turned to Cutter. "Captain Walker was a soldier at Fort Wainwright. Came out here and disappeared into the woods." He turned and addressed the bushes. "People said you died a couple of winters ago—"

"They were mistaken—"

"Listen up, Tom," Cutter said. "We have a child in trouble. Get out here and tell us what you know. If you've got a weapon, don't point it our way."

The brush rustled a scant fifteen yards to Cutter's ten o'clock. A gaunt man wearing faded Carhartt coveralls and a backward ballcap stepped out of the scrub. The rifle clutched in his hands looked like an ancient military Mauser—the kind the Spanish used against the Rough Riders from the San Juan Heights. Cutter had taken fire from more than one such rifle in Afghanistan, and knew from experience that the old ones were plenty deadly. He guessed Tom Walker to be in his early fifties, but his eyes shone with a fierce intensity that made him seem younger than he probably was. Living rough had weathered his bronze skin, giving it the shiny, varnished look common to those exposed to long hours of wind. A fly-away gray beard stuck out in all directions, like he didn't own a mirror or didn't give a damn. He clutched the rifle down by his thigh, forward of the action, his finger well away from the trigger. Even so, Cutter gestured with the shorty shotgun, hurrying things along.

"Set your gun on the ground."

"Why? I'm not your guy. The VPSO just told you he's heard of me."

"He's right," Polty said. "Captain Tom Walker's kinda famous in this area. We can trust him."

"I'm not in the trusting business." Cutter kept his voice low. He stood completely still. "Put down the rifle. Do it now."

The man complied. Lola moved in and cleared it, popping out the rounds and shoving them in the pocket of her rain jacket. The chamber had been empty, a good sign. She brought the rifle with her when she rejoined Cutter, and then leaned it against a tree behind them, before turning to watch the woods behind them.

"Captain?" Cutter gave a curt nod. He wanted to get moving, but had to deal with one problem at a time.

Walker gave a groaning nod. "14th Cav scout. 172nd SBCT."

"Ranger Regiment," Cutter said, introducing himself as he eyed the man. "I did a fair amount of work with cavalry scouts in Afghanistan."

"Iraq," Walker said, leaving it at that.

"When?"

"Oh-five through oh-six."

Cutter knew the 172nd had seen a year-and-a-half deployment in 2005 through 2006, with twenty-six killed in action and over three hundred wounded.

He changed the subject. "You described the man who came through here as bald. What else?"

Walker shrugged. "Heavy, especially for living out here as long as he has."

Cutter and Lola exchanged a glance.

"Maybe Jacobi shaved his head," she said.

"How tall would you say he is?" Cutter asked.

"Shorter than me," Walker said. "A few inches shy of six feet."

"That's not Jacobi," Lola said.

"Where would the girl have gone?" Cutter asked. "Since she was running."

Walker slumped. "He's already got her. I assumed you were friends of his."

"Let's go," Lola fumed through clenched teeth. "I don't give a shit who he is."

"Agreed." Cutter scanned the ground, a familiar worry roiling his gut. He looked up at Walker. "Did this bald guy see you?"

"No. He grabbed the kid and just kept going. Dragged her into the trees. I was about to challenge him, when I heard y'all coming up the trail. He either didn't care that you were behind him or didn't realize it. I thought I could . . . Anyway, it seemed smarter to stay hidden and work out a plan to save her than get myself shot and leave her to that guy."

"Which way did he take her?"

Walker pointed south. "Toward his camp. An old compound."

"The Y2K cabins," Polty said.

"That's right," Walker said. "I used it as a winter place for years, until the new guy turned up last fall and claimed it. He's bad news, that one. Hangs monofilament with fishhooks around his compound. Son of a bitch nearly blinded me."

Cutter rubbed the rain out of his face with a forearm and studied the ground again, letting it tell him as much of the story as possible as he came up with the bones of a plan.

"You ever see him with a gun?"

"First time I saw him at all was today," Walker said. "And yeah, he has a rifle. I've heard him shooting it for a couple of months. A big bore from the sounds of it. None of my business. I leave people alone. They leave me alone."

Cutter searched the trail until he found a clear impression of one of the larger tracks. He stooped beside it, leaving Lola and the VPSO to watch Walker.

"I don't get it," Lola said. "This guy's been around for months, and you've never made contact with him?"

Walker gave a resigned shake of his head. "I left Fairbanks to be by myself. Got no use for people—less so for those who try to gouge my eyes out with fishhooks."

"But you've seen the girl before today?" Lola asked.

"She stole some of my supplies a couple of days ago. I tried to talk to her—"

Polty looked as though he'd been slapped. "There were search parties banging up and down this river. You didn't think to flag down a boat?"

Walker glared, not accustomed to conversation at all, let alone being grilled. "I'm a hermit, not a moron. Kids from the fish camps skulk around back here every year to get out of pickin' nets with their parents. I only realized today this particular kid was on the run. I tried to help her, but she just took off. Then I heard the big guy calling for her to 'come back.'" He softened, face twisting as if he might begin to cry.

"Wait," Lola said. "Those were his words? 'Come back'?"

Walker gave a slow nod.

Polty groaned. "He must have snatched Winnie from her parents' camp, but then she got away from him."

"And now he's got her again," Lola said. "We should get going, boss."

"Hold up a second," Cutter said. "I need to check something." He followed the trail into the trees for another twenty yards before he found the answer to the niggling question that had crept into his mind. He stooped beside the tracks, studied them quickly, and then rose, trotting back to the others. He looked Walker up and down, trying to get a measure of the man.

"Lift your boot so I can see the bottom."

The hermit turned, balancing on one leg as he kicked up a foot.

Cutter checked it, then turned to Lola. "Give him back his rifle."

"Bullets too?"

"Yep," Cutter said. "He could have shot us when we came up. Instead, he told us to leave the girl alone."

Walker eyed him suspiciously as he took his gun back. "I thought you weren't in the trusting business."

"I'm not," Cutter said. "I'm in the hunting-bad-men business—and from the looks of things there are at least two of them out there. We could use your help."

Lola and Polty perked up at the revelation.

"I swear I only saw the bald one," Walker said.

"The tracks tell me to believe you." Cutter pointed toward the woods. "The girl and the man you saw went that way. But there's another set of tracks coming to meet them. This new set was made by someone with a larger foot and they overlay the others, meaning they were definitely made after, by a different person."

"Jacobi?" Lola said.

"That's my guess." Cutter shrugged. "Not sure how we're going to do this, but we'll flesh out the plan, once we get a better look at that compound."

He looked the VPSO in the eye. "George, with the child in the mix, I'm not inclined to wait for the troopers before we make our move. According to Walker, we were right behind the bald guy when he grabbed her. That means they're still on the move, probably just getting back to their cabin as we speak. I'd rather not allow them time to settle in and fortify any more than they already have."

"I'm with you there," Polty said.

Cutter gave the dark woods around him another look while he thought, listening to the rain and wind and the hushed sounds of the river a few dozen yards away.

"We are miles away from reinforcements," he said. "If we get into a gunfight, it's just us."

Lola held up a closed fist in solidarity. "Justice."

Cutter shook his head. *"Just us . . ."*

Tom Walker suppressed a smile at Lola's exuberance, despite the situation. "What do you want me to do?"

"Use your Cav scout skills to help us," Cutter said. "We'll decide exactly how, after we get there, but I'm open to suggestions."

Polty smashed a fist into his open hand. "Speed, surprise, and violence of action."

"Sounds like somebody I know." Lola glanced at Cutter. "Okay, boss," she said. "There's a kid involved. Dial it back a notch. You know how you get. I don't want you crashing in and shooting everyone who's not Winnie Tomaganak."

"Sounds like a good plan to me," Walker said.

"Me too," Polty said.

Cutter turned and followed the tracks into the woods. *Justice.* He liked the sound of that.

CHAPTER 3

"*H*e did what?" Maxim Volkov's red-faced shout caused the flight attendant on the chartered business jet to turn her head away. Some things were better not to witness.

The rich baritone voice of Lev Rudenko, Volkov's trusted friend and former cellmate, poured from the satellite phone. In most circumstances, the sound of it would have calmed Volkov. Now he wanted to kick a hole in the aircraft, or, in lieu of that, stomp someone to death.

"Forgive me for saying so, boss," Rudenko said. "But your blood runs in his veins. The boy has your passions. Your tendencies. The tendencies, I might add, that have served you well."

Rudenko was one of the few men who could speak so freely. They'd been through much together, too much.

Volkov lowered his voice. "Are we ruined?"

"I do not think so, boss," Rudenko said. "Certainly, the deaths will cause a stir—"

"I do not give one shit about the deaths," Volkov said. "Is Alex likely to be captured? Found out? He is young and has not been trained. The bodies—"

"He took care of that," Rudenko said. "Not to worry. I will help him disappear the boat."

"He will have to show identification to fly," Volkov said. "Even between Homer and Anchorage. That is too great a risk after this."

"I know someone," Rudenko said.

"Ah," Volkov said. "But can we trust this someone with my son's freedom?"

"A Russian," Rudenko said. "He knows your reputation."

"You have done too much already, my friend," Volkov said. "I am afraid this will disturb your retirement. It would be good to see you, but I understand the danger."

"Do not worry about me, boss," Rudenko said. "I will take care of everything here and send your son to you. You have my word."

"I cannot believe he would be so rash," Volkov said.

At the other end of the line Lev Rudenko gave a quiet chuckle. "Forgive me, boss, but you should not be surprised. You should be proud."

CHAPTER 4

*L*eonard Jukes would be the last to die.

Shortly after coming to work aboard the fishing vessel *Esther Marie,* Alex made the mistake of telling his crewmates that his paternal grandfather had been killed and eaten by a Siberian tiger. None of the men believed him; Jukes, the boat's electrician and first mate, egged them on.

The bastard.

It made what he did next all the easier.

Alex was eleven when he'd first seen his father kill a man. He'd never personally taken anyone's life—but it turned out not to be nearly as difficult as it looked.

At nineteen, he was the youngest member of the crew by almost a decade. He had his father's pinched face, but was tall and blue-eyed like his American mother. Unfortunately, he'd also inherited Maureen Preston's pale complexion. Even after he spent weeks on deck in the sun and in the wind, his skin remained as white as a peeled potato.

At his father's insistence he'd practically begged Captain Hannigan to bypass Kodiak and go straight to Homer. The skipper, a stooped man with a white ponytail and an unlit briar pipe perpetually clenched between his teeth, actually offered to pay airfare from Kodiak to Anchorage. A quick check online showed what Alex already knew. Low clouds had canceled multiple flights—no seats available for well over a week. There may have been some charter flights, but they were expensive and the captain was not that sympathetic. Hannigan explained that he didn't intend to stay long in Kodiak, and, to be blunt, didn't quite believe the boy even had an emergency, "what with his tall tales about Siberian tigers."

None of the crew would have known he had any ties to Russia, had he not told them about his grandfather. But from that point on, everyone began calling Alex "comrade" and butchering what few Russian phrases they'd learned trying to hook up with Russian women online. Butch, the captain's son, had learned a garbled pronunciation of *boleye boyepripasy*—more ammunition—and, for whatever reason, blurted it out every time he got within earshot of Alex. Jukes growled like a tiger whenever they were on deck pulling crab pots.

They were dead men walking—and Alex was the only one on the boat that knew it. There was tremendous satisfaction in that.

He happened on just how to go about it while working in the wheelhouse with Jukes and the captain—and it was audacious as hell. Chiginigak Bay lay off the beam to the west. The captain planned to keep to the inside, sailing between the island and the mainland and then cutting east below Raspberry and Whale to reach the city of Kodiak. Boat traffic would increase exponentially, the closer they got to the island. If he was going to make his move, he needed to do it now.

The other three crewmen were on deck, tending crab pots and other gear during the run home from the Bering Sea. Jukes lay on his back, buried up to his waist under a bulkhead cabinet, chasing one of the many electronic glitches that plagued boats that spent their lives in freezing salt water.

Low man on the crew, Alex stood at the electrician's feet and handed him tools.

An eerie calm fell on the boy when he saw Hannigan's short shotgun under the counter, with a Tupperware container of shells. He passed Jukes a pair of wire strippers and casually asked the captain if he kept the shotgun loaded.

Hannigan nodded, concentrating on the quartering waves.

The electrician thrust an oily fist out from beneath the cabinet, opening and closing bony fingers. "Small flathead!" he demanded. Then added, "An unloaded shotgun wouldn't do us a hell of a lot of good, comrade."

Alex considered driving the point of the screwdriver through the hand on behalf of all the sons and helpers who'd chased the moving hands of impatient fathers and bosses. Control of another man's destiny brought a powerful sense of euphoria. Alex held all the cards, so he decided to give Jukes one last chance for a quick and merciful death.

"My uncle says that when you catch your first glimpse of a tiger, it's already been watching you for an hour."

Jukes gave a condescending chuckle from beneath the counter.

Grinning, the captain muttered around his pipe, "I think I read that about tigers."

Alex pushed on, studying the men's reactions. "My uncle says it's better to get eaten by a tiger than a brown bear. He says tigers crush your neck and it's pretty much lights out. A bear, though." Alex shook his head for effect. "A bear might leave you alive while it chows down on your kidneys." The boy tossed a roll of electrician's tape into the air, caught it with one hand, then sighed. "Bears apparently love kidneys. My uncle says wolves are the worst, though. They drag you down and start eating from the ass end—"

Jukes's muffled voice came from inside the cabinet. "Your uncle knows a shitload about getting eaten by wild animals."

Alex dropped the tape into the bag, eyes on the shotgun. "Guess so. He's a hunter."

Jukes bumped his head on something, cursed, then finished off his oaths with a chuckle. "Didn't I hear you say your grandfather lived in Okhotsk."

"Yeah . . ." Alex paused, wary. "He's really from a little place called Ayan, about two hundred fifty miles down the coast. I always say Okhotsk because even Russians don't know Ayan."

Jukes shimmied out from under the bulkhead and sat up, arms resting on his knees, grinning, pointing at Alex with the screwdriver. "That is where you get it wrong, kid. Assuming you can spout these little villages like there's no Internet to check. I found an article online about Russian cops chasing a tiger around Vladi-

vostok. But Ayan's too far north for you to set your lie." He flipped
the screwdriver in the air, caught it by the end, and then dropped it
in the bag. "No tigers that far up."

The boy gazed out the window at the gathering waves. "Someone
should tell that to the one that ate my grandfather . . ."

Captain Hannigan half turned from the wheel. "It's still a good
story, kid. And you tell it masterfully, I'll give you that. You make a
person pay attention."

"Yeah, like watching a train plow into a school bus," Jukes said—
a breath before Alex shot him in the left hip.

Alex took down the captain like a tiger—quick, a single shotgun
blast to the neck.

Meanwhile, Jukes collapsed, screaming, eyes flashing between
angry to astonished. He teetered there for a long moment before a
swell slammed him on his ass in a pool of blood.

"Be right back," Alex said, and went to take care of the others.

The shotgun was fast and efficient, leaving no time for begging
or the pithy sayings people made in the movies.

For all his bullying bravado, Leonard Jukes did nothing but moan
when Alex dragged him to the deck and leaned him against the
gunnel beside his dead crewmates.

The captain's body took two trips.

Low clouds obscured the horizon and much of Kodiak Island off
the starboard rail. A quick check of the radar showed no nearby
vessels.

Jukes had his eyes closed when Alex returned to the deck.

"Hey!" Alex snapped, putting a boot to the man's ribs. "You can't
die yet."

Jukes squinted upward, as if looking into a bright sun even
though it was overcast.

Certain now that he had the man's attention, Alex began stuffing the bodies into crab pots. They weighed something like eight
hundred pounds empty and could hold two bodies each if Alex
loaded them right. The davit and winch took care of lifting them
onto the launch chute.

The captain and Butch went into the first pot. It seemed like the right thing to do. Alex pulled the lever that sent father and son torpedoing into the sea, where the pot settled quickly and disappeared, cut from its customary line and retrieval buoy.

Alex shot a glance at Jukes to be certain he was getting an eyeful of his future. "Wouldn't want to leave any of this evidence just floating around for some fisherman to find," he said. "Sounder shows us around three hundred feet. Sea lice and shrimp will pick you all down to bones in a day or two . . ."

Alex worked quickly to launch the remaining bodies. The deck around Leonard Jukes was mopped with blood. No way he was going to last much longer and Alex wanted him awake for his ride over the side.

"Ever been to Siberia?" Alex asked.

"No," Jukes said through a shuddering grimace, eyes closed. "I . . . have not."

"It's like Alaska," Alex chuckled. "Only with tigers."

He used the winch to lift the heavy lid on the third steel-and-mesh prison. When he turned, Jukes had somehow mustered the energy to push himself into a standing position on his working leg.

He leaned against the rail with one arm trailing over the side, supporting most of his weight. His eyes blazed with the inexplicable fire of defiance. Words came between panting breaths, low, measured, much too calm for someone about to slide three hundred feet to the seafloor.

"You're . . . doin' all this . . . because I didn't believe your shit about the tiger?" A coughing fit turned his distorted face purple. "Hell, nobody . . . believed that story."

"It's true," Alex said.

Jukes wiped a forearm across his face, smearing it with gore. "So?" He panted harder now, swaying in place. "I'm . . . I'm not gettin' in that pot."

Alex laughed. "You can't even stand up and now you're gonna kick my ass?"

Jukes closed his eyes. "Nope," he said. The boat hit a deep trough and he used the falling motion to haul himself over the side. The *Esther Marie* left him bobbing in the silver waters of her wake, making a steady thirteen knots north.

Alex considered going back and shooting the bastard, but decided it was pointless. The frigid water would kill him in minutes, if
he didn't bleed to death first. There were sharks here too.

"Well, Papa," the boy said under his breath, "you wanted me to
see to things . . . I think I did a damned fine job."

A wave broke over the bow and washed across the deck, draining
out the scuppers with the snotty tendrils of Leonard Jukes's blood.

CHAPTER 5

Arliss Cutter was not in the habit of trusting strangers—or much of anyone, for that matter, but bush Alaska was a wild place and he needed something to help even the odds.

He put Tom Walker beside him, with Lola next in line—just in case this was a monumental error in judgment. The VPSO brought up the rear, watching their back trail.

Walker proved stealthier than anyone Cutter had ever seen. He moved like a bear, each step falling careful, quietly—but at a steady ground-covering pace. The former cavalry scout had been living in the woods for the better part of fourteen years, isolated but for his yearly supply drops and the infrequent hunter who stumbled on his camp. When they ran across him, local Yupik children told their friends they'd seen Arulataq—He Who Makes a Bellowing Cry—Alaska's version of a sasquatch. Tom Walker did little to dissuade them of this notion.

He had, he said, grown too weary to associate with mankind.

Cutter understood how he felt.

Walker came to an abrupt stop as the trees began to thin, pointing out a line of fishhooks dangling at eye level on strings of transparent monofilament. At a nod from Cutter, Polty used his knife to remove the vicious booby trap. The hushed sigh of moving water drifted through the trees from the river, mixing with the patter of rain.

Another dozen steps brought a weathered plywood cabin into view. Fifty meters away and streaked with peeling white paint, it was nearest of a half-dozen other visible cabins, sheds, and dilapidated animal pens. Raised log beds that had once served as gardens were now choked with alder and devil's club. No smoke rose from the metal stovepipe of the nearest white cabin, but Cutter caught a glimpse of a man with a dark beard in the window. Jacobi. He'd yet to see the girl or the bald man, but the tracks told him everyone was there.

Cutter squatted behind a thick clump of scrub and studied the faint trails that led from the water toward the cabin. Steady rain rattled through the poplar foliage above them.

Lola lay belly-down in the wet leaves, scanning over the top of her rifle. Ever the teacher, Cutter got her attention with a hiss.

"What do we know about booby traps?"

"They hurt like hell?" she whispered, her voice muffled against the moist ground.

"Where there is one," Cutter said, "there are more." He turned his head slowly, moving with his eyes so as not to miss anything. It didn't take long to find what he was after. "And there you go . . ."

Walker gave a knowing nod. Lola and Polty looked on in astonishment as Cutter used a length of willow to push back a thick mat of leaf litter to expose a spruce log that had been rough-hewn with an axe into a two-by-four about a foot in length. One end was split lengthwise, forming a Y. Parachute cord wrapped the middle to keep it from splitting completely when the two arms of the Y were pried open, allowing them to snap almost closed if released. A ten-penny nail had been driven upward through the lower arm, into the open space. Drilled into the upper arm was a hole into which a twelve-gauge shotgun shell had been inserted. The business end of the shell aimed skyward. Downward pressure from anyone unfortunate enough to step on the contraption pushed the upper split arm of wood into the lower, driving the primer into the point of the nail and detonating the shotgun shell with catastrophic effect on the foot and leg above.

Lola rolled half up on her side, her lip pulled back into what she labeled her "Maori warrior face."

"You're tellin' me there are more of these hidden around here?"

Cutter's jaw tensed at the idea of a child like Winnie Tomaganak stepping on the improvised explosive. "I'd bet on it. This is a natural funnel, where he expected someone to step. He'll have others on approaches he thinks people would use."

"So we go where he doesn't expect us," Lola said.

"Might be using other kinds of trap too," Walker mused. "Depending on the terrain. This guy ever serve?"

"No," Cutter said. "Fishhooks and shotgun mines seem more like a poacher than former operator."

Walker grunted. "True enough."

"Sick bastard," Polty said. "Kids play in these woods. What's this guy expect will happen?"

"He expects to hear someone's foot getting shot off if they try to slip up on him." Cutter set the homemade land mine against the base of a tree and then passed George Polty the shorty shotgun. "We're going to let him think that's exactly what he's hearing. Lola and I will circle around to get a better view of the door. Give us five minutes and then fire a round against one of these trees. Aim away so it sounds muffled. Screaming and thrashing around in the brush would help sell the ruse, but whatever you do, stay out of sight. Remember, Walker has heard shooting. They have at least one long gun and don't appear worried about who they maim."

"What do you want me to do?" Walker asked, laser focused on the cabin.

Cutter eyed the man's rifle. It had no scope, relying instead on the same ladder-style iron sights from when it had been manufactured over a century before.

"That Mauser still shoot straight?"

"It does," Walker said. "As do I. Just give me the rules of engagement."

Cutter rubbed his face. The words he spoke next might well come back and haunt him.

"Tom," he said. "If the men inside run, just let them run. I can't really tell you to do anything. But if you see them try to hurt the little girl, I'd appreciate it if you put a stop to it. I'll back your play. You have my word."

"What about you and Deputy Teariki?"

"We'll take care of ourselves," Cutter said.

Still on her belly, Lola gave a hoarse whisper without looking up.

"For what it's worth, Tom, if one of those assholes tries to hurt me, I'd be perfectly happy if you put a stop to that too."

Cutter led the way, moving quickly but purposefully through the brush, staying just outside what he hoped Jacobi considered his perimeter for improvised explosives. They made it three-quarters of the way around the cabin at the three-minute mark, bringing a dilapidated outhouse into view. Cutter gave the area a quick scan and then tapped Lola on her elbow.

"Set up here," he whispered. "I'm going to work my way up so I'm waiting when they come out."

"What about booby traps?" Lola hissed.

"I'll be careful, but it's not likely he'd lay explosives between his front door and the shitter."

He moved out with a minute and a half to get into position, keeping a weather eye out for tripwires, fishhooks, and anything else that would ruin his day. It was getting dark, or as dark as it would get this far north in June. Still light enough to see silhouettes, but fishhooks would be a problem.

Cutter had just reached the corner of the cabin when a shotgun blast shattered the stillness of the clearing. He drew the Colt Python, holding it low but ready.

The scrape of shuffling furniture on a wood floor came from inside the cabin, followed by muffled voices.

In the dark woods to the northeast George Polty screamed like a man who'd just lost a foot, giving an Oscar-worthy performance.

The door creaked open and the smell of fried food rolled into rainy night air. Cutter caught the hiss of a gas camp stove.

It was all he could do to keep from crashing in, but he didn't want to bottle up two armed men inside with the girl.

A hushed voice carried out the open door. "You're such a dick for grabbing that kid. You've stayed off the radar for months just fine, and now, when things are finally quieting down at home, you risk this. You knew we were coming to pick you up. Do you realize how quick the shit would have rained down on us if she'd made it to that boat? It's not like there are a million ways out of here."

"Gets lonely," another voice said, this one deeper with a distinct UP Michigan accent. Jacobi.

Cutter held his breath when he heard a third voice.

"You knew we were comin' to get you. You put us all in danger."

"Cut me a break." Jacobi again. "A man's got to take advantage of the opportunities nature affords him. You know that. Wasn't my fault she was just standing there on the river when I came by. Anyway, the troopers quit lookin' for her days ago. Those screams out there are from that shitheel hermit, Captain Bob or whatever. I shoulda taken care of him last winter."

"Either way," the first voice said, "one of us gotta go finish him before that boat comes back downriver and hears his racket—"

"Go ahead," Jacobi said. "The kid'll have us some bannocks fried up by the time you get back."

The first man cursed and then strode out the door, rifle in hand, directly into Lola Teariki's sights.

Colt up and aimed, Cutter gave a soft, almost inaudible cluck, the sound he would have used to get a horse to step out.

"Police!" A whispered snarl. "On the ground."

Instead of stopping, or even uttering a word, the bald man dropped the rifle and bolted for the river. Cutter stayed focused on the cabin. There was little that Lola or Walker could do, but watch the man go, probably toward a boat he'd stashed in the willows. That couldn't be helped. He was unarmed and Winnie Tomaganak was the primary mission.

"Joey?" the third man called, more annoyed than worried. "What the hell's going on with y . . ." He stuck his head out, shining a flashlight on the ground, cursing when the beam crossed his friend's abandoned rifle.

Any man who'd go along with kidnapping a twelve-year-old was bought and paid for in Cutter's book. It looked cool in the movies—and Cutter had to admit, he'd done it before, but smacking someone in the head with a revolver was a good way to earn your exit ticket from the Marshals Service, not to mention unintentionally shooting that person in the face (no matter how bad you wanted to). Instead, Cutter snatched the man's metal flashlight out of his hand. He brought it down and around in a quick circle, coming up under the man's chin, smashing his teeth together—all while he was still trying to figure out what was going on.

Jacobi slammed the door, abandoning his stunned partner to Cutter, who put a boot to the side of his knee while, at the same time, he growled, "US Marshals! On the ground!" as if it were all one word.

Pain and gravity helped with compliance.

"Lola," Cutter yelled. "If he moves, shoot him in the head."

"Roger that!" Lola shouted back, along with some orders of her own that left no doubt she meant to follow through.

A half a breath later, a high-pitched screaming rose from inside the cabin.

Colt Python up, Cutter booted the door, intent on shooting Jacobi where he stood. Inside, he found the man on his back, writhing in pain, clawing at his blistered face. A steaming lump of half-cooked fry bread lay beside his shoulder on the filthy wood floor. A small Native girl in a stained purple hoodie stood trembling in front of a Coleman camp stove, an empty frying pan clutched in her hands. She brandished the pan in front of her like a shield.

Cutter checked Jacobi for a weapon, and then holstered the Colt. He pulled back his rain jacket, tapping the silver star on his belt. "Police," he said softly. "It's okay. We're here to help you."

She gave a shuddering nod, suddenly worried that Cutter might think she was the aggressor. "He's a bad man—"

"Yes, he is," Cutter said.

She was so small, it brought tears to Cutter's eyes. He squatted to make a more thorough weapons check, hoping to make himself look less imposing.

"You're Winnie, right?"

She gave a trembling nod.

"Well, Winnie," he said, "you are a smart young lady to be your own rescue."

Jacobi howled and cursed when Cutter rolled him none too gently onto his belly and cuffed his hands behind his back. Outside, a second shotgun blast shook the darkness.

The girl cringed at the noise.

Cutter gave her what he hoped was a reassuring smile and rose quickly to his feet. He drew the Colt and stepped to, but not out, the door, half expecting to hear the staccato pop of Lola's M4.

Silence.

"We're secure inside!" he shouted.

A pitiful wailing rose from the direction of the river.

"We're all right-as, boss!" Lola shouted. "Coming your way."

Cutter whistled to Polty. "You good?"

"All good," the VPSO yelled back. "Looks like your runner didn't know about all the booby traps."

Lola crossed the open ground quickly, using her flashlight now to watch for improvised explosives and fishhooks. She handcuffed the man outside and dragged him in. Cutter was pleased to see he'd knocked out two of the man's front teeth with the flashlight. His name turned out to be Rollie Turpin. One-eighth Yupik, he was from Anchorage, but his auntie lived in Mountain Village.

Winnie Tomaganak was tundra tough, but she'd been through more than any twelve-year-old should have to bear. Lola's easy smile and boisterous presence calmed her at once. The two were joined at the hip from the moment Lola breezed into the cabin and threw back the hood of her rain jacket.

"We got these pukes, boss," Lola said. "Go ahead if you need to go check on the others." She unfolded the satellite phone and looked down her nose at Jacobi as she pointed the antenna out the open door.

Winnie's aim with the boiling oil had been spot on. His face was covered in a mass of weeping blisters, and his right eyelid was ruined, if not gone completely. Much of the beard on that side had sloughed away from the flesh. Cooked. His words came on ragged breaths. "I . . . need . . . doctor . . ."

"Soon," Cutter said, brimming with rage each time he looked at the girl. Tough as she was, her experience at the hands of these filthy men had surely given her ghosts she'd carry for the rest of her life. Cutter envisioned beating both men to death, but for the time being, better angels prevailed. Instead, he squatted beside the prisoners, keeping his voice low and steady. "Help's on the way, Mr.

Jacobi. Too many of us to fit you in the little boat we came in on. My partner's on the phone with the Alaska State Troopers now, so we'll know something soon. In the meantime I need you to draw me a map of all the exploding surprises you've got hidden around this place."

"Wait one damned minute," Turpin said. "This is Jacobi's deal. I don't know what you're talkin' about. Exploding surprises, my ass."

"I'm sure you're pure as the driven snow," Cutter said. "How about I just walk around with you for a bit? See what we stumble onto?"

"Draw him what he needs," Turpin groused.

"I can't see," Jacobi sobbed. "How do you expect me to draw any—"

"You best figure it out, mate," Lola said, folding the sat phone. "Your buddy just blew his foot off with one of your contraptions. If he dies, I reckon the Troopers'll charge you both with his murder—"

"Hello, the house!" Tom Walker called from outside, smart enough to make sure he didn't catch a friendly bullet in the face by sneaking up unannounced. He was alone.

Lola's brow shot skyward. "What about George?"

"I thought I'd come to see if y'all needed help," Walker said. "Polty stayed with the bald guy. We got a tourniquet on him, so I don't think he'll bleed to death, but his foot is shot to ribbons. I'm thinking the leg is toast from the knee down."

Lola gave Jacobi a reassuring pat on the shoulder. "There you go, you're only looking at aggravated assault instead of murder. Lucky day, you piece of shit."

The outlaw threw his head back and howled.

Tom Walker dug what looked like a snuff tin from his jacket pocket and held it up in the lantern light. "Balm of Gilead," he said. "Make it myself with the resin from balsam poplar buds along the river. Good for burns."

"You're pretty kindhearted for a guy who hates people," Lola said.

"People are tiresome," Walker said. "Didn't say I hated them."

It was all Cutter could do to dredge up a shred of sympathy, but the former scout sniper gently applied his homemade concoction to the burns of the man who only minutes before had wished him dead. Walker sensed Cutter was looking at him and glanced up, a dab of yellow salve on his fingertip.

"I'm not doing this for him," he said. "I'm doing it for the kid. She's seen enough cruelty to last ten lifetimes. Good for her to witness a little humanity. Don't you think?"

Cutter nodded. Better angels indeed. He shot a glance at Lola. "Are the Troopers bringing in the boat or a chopper?"

"Boat," Lola said, inciting another round of wails and moans from Jacobi. "Chopper's held up in Fairbanks, but they're sending a plane with medical staff to meet us in Saint Mary's."

"Dandy," Cutter said, feeling the exhaustion that fell over him when a long fugitive hunt came to an end. "Just dandy." He gave Jacobi a hearty smack on the shoulder, resigning himself to the fact that he was not nearly as good a man as Tom Walker. He looked from Jacobi to Rollie Turpin. "I don't care who does the drawing, but I'm going to have a map of booby traps in the next five minutes if I have to use pieces of you to draw it."

Rain pelted the cabin in sheets by the time two state troopers and a nurse radioed their arrival forty minutes later. Walker went to check on George Polty and the wounded prisoner, while Cutter and Lola walked Jacobi and Turpin to the river. Winnie Tomaganak stayed glued to Lola's hip. Cutter tried to give her his raincoat, but she found a black plastic trash bag in the cabin and cut a hole in the top to make her own poncho.

Hood thrown back to keep an eye on the prisoners, Cutter was soaked by the time they reached the river. The troopers recognized Turpin and shook their heads as if his presence was not the least bit surprising. The junior of the two took the map with the locations of Jacobi's improvised explosives and made his way back to the cabin to wait for daylight and an ordinance disposal team. The remaining trooper, a fortysomething sergeant named Allen, would give Cutter, his team, and the girl a ride back to Polty's boat. They didn't want her to spend any more time than was absolutely necessary with her former captors.

Word spread quickly via VHF radio that Winnie Tomaganak had been found alive. Tundra drums, they called it. Her elated parents would meet them on the river, unable to contain themselves and wait until she reached St. Mary's.

Cutter had his prisoners settled on the Trooper boat before he realized Walker was nowhere to be seen.

He nudged George Polty when he walked by. "Where'd Tom run off to?"

The VPSO shrugged. "Gone."

"What do you mean, *gone*?"

"He just turned around and walked into the woods," Polty said. "We didn't need him for anything, did we?"

Cutter thought for a moment, peering into the darkness. "Nope," he said. "No, we do not."

"Envious?" Lola said, following Cutter's gaze.

"I am," Cutter said. "A little bit."

She grinned. Wide and sly. "You'd miss me, boss."

"I would," he said. "A little bit."

CHAPTER 6

A pod of Dall's porpoises spouted off the Esther Marie's port rail, startling Alex Volkov awake from dreams of blood and bone and Siberian tigers.

His arms shot out defensively from where he'd slumped in the captain's chair, and then settled into a long, jittery stretch when he realized where he was. A toxic soup of coffee and energy drinks sloshed in his gut. He rubbed his eyes with the sleeve of his hoodie— a newish, semi-clean gray one he'd put on after the killings. Like a good sailor, he checked the position and shape of his vessel first thing.

The sun had disappeared, leaving Russian Point and the twinkling lights of the tiny Native village of Nanwalek along the rocky shore two miles away at his two o'clock off his starboard rail. Following seas pushed the *Esther Marie* into Kachemak Bay at a solid twelve knots. Fourteen miles an hour.

He arched his back, stretched out the last of his shakes, and then walked to the door, hanging on to each side of the jamb as he leaned into the chilly sea breeze to survey the purple blue evening—and to brace himself awake. Hidden rocks and shoals were strewn all along the coast, especially where he was going.

He pushed up the frayed cuff of his hoodie and checked his watch, nodding to himself through another long, shuddering yawn that showed the fillings in his back teeth. Five minutes past eleven p.m. He'd been out for almost an hour, unconscious really. He was lucky he hadn't run aground or crossed the path of an inquisitive skipper—or, worse yet, the Coast Guard Cutter Mustang that prowled the Gulf of Alaska.

The sun had dipped below the horizon, but only just. Soon it would sink low enough to bring nautical twilight, that time of evening when sailors could navigate with the stars, but the horizon was still visible. Alex made sure his running lights were on. Kodiak was well behind him. Homer lay almost thirty miles ahead, but Seldovia—and a bed—was just around the next point. Alex didn't care if the bed was soft, or even clean. Hell, he would sleep on a concrete slab, as long as it was horizontal, dry, and didn't roll with the waves.

He did his best to blink away the cobwebs from the insufficient nap.

The porpoises shot back and forth, their black-and-white bodies looked like stubby baby orca flashing in the silver bow wake, matching the boat's speed. "Workhorse" by All Them Witches thrummed loud and broody over the deck speakers. That was supposed to have kept him awake too, but fading adrenaline after sudden violence combined with the gentle rolling of the swells had the opposite effect.

Alex turned down the music and popped open another energy drink.

Red lights in the wheelhouse protected his night vision and turned the stains and smears of dried blood black. The spot where he'd shot the skipper looked like someone had let their dog loose with a gallon of ink. Breaking waves had washed most of the carnage off the deck, but the cabin looked like the massacre scene it was. Alex had kicked the worst bits of flesh and gore out the hatch, but it was impossible to track down all the blood. Sodden carpet, hairline cracks in the flooring, bulkhead seams, the authorities would find a mountain of evidence with even a half-assed search—if they ever got on board.

An aluminum purse seiner approached on his port side heading south. Fortunately for them, they kept going. Alex had resolved to kill anyone who got in his way. At this point he had absolutely nothing to lose.

Slowing the vessel to six knots, Alex stayed well offshore as he took the boat around Russian Point, eyes peeled for any pleasure boats that might be at anchor in the shallows—unlikely because of the scattered rocky shoals.

A light flashed ahead. Alex was able to make out a small runabout bobbing just south of a series of hidden rocks known as Bird Reef.

Alex eased back the throttles, feeling the wake catch up and shove the *Esther Marie* from behind as he slowed to a crawl. He flicked his running lights, red and green, on and off, gasping with pent-up relief when the man on the runabout flashed a light three times in return.

The water averaged twenty fathoms deep here, 120 feet. Alex had already identified the through-hulls that would let in water the quickest. Even if someone happened by and saw her going down, the boat would be awash by the time they got close.

Fifty meters off the runabout, Alex threw the *Esther Marie* into reverse, bringing her to a full stop. After days of constant thrumming, the absence of the noisy diesel allowed the hushed whispers of a nearby waterfall to wash into the wheelhouse.

Alex started immediately removing the hoses on the thru-hulls—the intake on the toilet, the cooling system on the motor, every possible avenue for seawater to flood the boat. He wanted to step from the sinking boat to the runabout—though he would have taken a swim if that's what his father had told him to do. The things he did for that man would probably kill him one day. But there was no other choice. When Maxim Volkov wanted something seen to, you saw to it. Even—*especially*—if you were his son.

Alex's mother hated the man, but for some unknown reason, she'd allowed Alex yearly trips to Russia from the time he was seven, the year after the divorce. Never more than two weeks, the trips were always far too short to Alex's way of thinking. He and his cousin Gavrill did everything together—from go-carts when they were boys to sports cars when they got older. Maxim had given the boys their first women when Gavrill turned fifteen. Alex was a year younger, and benefited from his cousin's age.

Maxim coddled him, gave him sweets and pocketknives, and let him throw hand grenades in the hills above Petropavlovsk.

His father terrified and mystified the boy. Cruel, benevolent, brooding, or hilariously funny, those in his orbit never knew which

Bone Breaker they were going to meet. But to Alex, he was always the nurturing father. "The world is cruel," he would say, "and so am I—but never to you, my Sasha. Never to you."

Oh, but he was cruel to others, especially women. To Maxim Volkov, there were only two types of females—mothers and whores.

Simply bearing children did not set one firmly in the "mother" side of the equation. A woman, Maxim said, if she had the wrong attitude, could give birth and still be a whore. On the other hand, one could have no offspring and still qualify as a mother figure. The notion had made little sense to twelve-year-old Alex, other than the fact that his father had spoken the words, so they were true on their face. They had to be.

A mother must be respected, he'd explained, even if she was not to be trusted. Whores, while useful in their own way, were disposable. They were like candies in a Pez dispenser—a new one popping up behind the last one. One did not need to think ill of them. It was simply a waste of energy to think of them at all, unless they were needed to serve a purpose of the moment. Maxim left it up to Alex to decide which women fell into which category. His own mother, for instance, was not given a classification during the lesson.

A banging on the hull brought him out of his memories. He shook his head, loopy, sleep deprived, then waved over the rail at Lev Rudenko. His father called the man "Uncle Lev," but he was no relation. He was closer. Rudenko had worked for Alex's father in Petropavlovsk for as long as he could remember. They'd done time together in Penal Colony Number 6, the infamous Black Dolphin Prison. Something had happened there, something to make Lev owe his life to the Bone Breaker.

He'd disappeared three years earlier. At the time Maxim had explained that Lev was wanted by the Russian Police and had to flee the country. He'd ended up in Alaska working as a fisherman and living in Seldovia under the name Lev Russel.

He was big, a head taller than Alex's six feet, with massive hands and biceps that were larger than most men's legs. He spoke mainly in grunts, doing what needed to be done, but deferring to Alex as the boss's son and pretending like he was happy to be sinking a bloodstained boat, instead of remaining safe at home with his American wife.

Under the big Russian's guidance, the *Esther Marie* went down quickly, gurgling and spewing as seawater filled her holds.

Rudenko gunned the throttle and brought the runabout on step the instant Alex stepped aboard, unwilling to spend a moment longer than he had to near the ill-fated crabbing vessel.

"I'm glad you're here," Alex said, stifling a yawn as they sped north. "My ass is ready for a bed."

Rudenko gave a forced smile that looked as though it hurt his face. "Sleep is long way off, my young boss," he said.

Alex's head snapped up when they passed Seldovia Bay. "We're not going to your house?"

"Yes," Rudenko said, shaking his massive head. "We are not." The smile was gone now. "It would not be good for my wife to see you. She is good woman, but is . . . How do you say it? Problematic . . ."

"Where, then?" Alex groaned. His body felt as if it had been rubbed with sandpaper. "I thought I was supposed to meet my father tomorrow."

"You are," the big Russian said, coughing into the crook of his elbow. "But first we get you vehicle."

"Get a vehicle?" Alex caught the smell of a menthol cough drop in the air. "You don't have one?"

"I have motorcycle," the Russian said. "But the engine is not so good to make the long ride to Anchorage. A man I know will meet us at China Poot. He has clean car."

"*Clean?*"

"Not connected to anyone we know, not reported stolen."

"Whatever." Alex yawned and tried to settle into the hard seats on the bouncing runabout. He woke an hour later to the slowing boat and Lev Rudenko's vehement mix of cough and curse.

"What?" Alex arched his back in a futile attempt to get the kinks out of his spine.

"The little shit is not here!" the big Russian spat. He dug another lozenge from the pocket of his overalls. "I knew there was problem with this one."

"What problem?"

"*Suka!*" Rudenko spat. "Now we must go up mountain to Voznesenka."

Alex groaned. "The Old Believers?"

"Yes," Rudenko said. "His family are good people, but Pavel Gurin is boil on my ass."

"The boil who was supposed to provide a car?"

Rudenko nodded. "I spoke to him earlier today. He agreed, but was . . . How do you say? Cagey." Rudenko pounded the side of his boat, considering their next move. "He has only been married one month. Women make men stop thinking."

"You know what else makes men stop thinking?" Alex said. "Lack of sleep. Let's go back to your place and catch a few hours. I'll sleep on the floor, I don't care."

"I wish was so easy, young boss," Rudenko groaned. "We are on a schedule. Your father say to get you car tonight, so I get you car tonight." He tapped the little red-handled Victorinox paring knife on his belt. Less than ten bucks at the hardware store, this "Vicky" was disposable and razor sharp, perfect for letting enough blood out and enough air in to take care of business. "If Pavel will not come to us," Rudenko said, "then we go to Pavel."

"This clean car is twenty miles up the mountain?"

"I do not know where car is!" Rudenko yelled over the outboard. "But Pavel is in Voznesenka. We take motorcycle up mountain and tell the little puke your father sent us."

Alex didn't give a shit about Pavel or his pretty wife. Lev Rudenko could carve them both to pieces with the little red paring knife if that's what he wanted to do, but he'd better be quick about it. Alex needed to sleep.

CHAPTER 7

*R*udenko made the five-mile crossing of Kachemak Bay quickly and tied up in a transient slip alongside a float. Alex trudged up the floating metal ramp—a steep incline now because of the extremely low tide—to a squat lighthouse and log cabin affair called the Salty Dog Saloon. The place was dark, closing every day at eight p.m.—odd for a bar in a town that was often described as "a quaint little drinking village with a fishing problem."

The big Russian stood in the shadows for a time, digging in his pocket. He muttered and cursed to himself when he couldn't find what he was looking for, and then, after a moment of subdued panic, he pulled out a single key wrapped in a wad of cough drop wrappers. He used the key to unlock the doors to a wooden shed adjacent to the Salty Dog parking lot, and then rolled out a rangy Kawasaki KLR650 that had been painted rattle-can primer green. Spartan, to begin with, and missing a front fender and headlight cowling, the motorcycle looked like something the Soviet military might have ridden into battle.

Rudenko topped off the fuel tank from the red jug inside the shed and the bike started immediately.

The road to the Old Believers' village wound up the bluffs above Homer, rough and uneven. Riding pillion, Alex had to wrap his arms around Rudenko to keep from tumbling off the back. The big Russian's coat reeked of cough drops and a forgotten bait box, but Alex had to bury his face against the man's back to make it work. He didn't quite know what to do with his hands. To make matters worse, his toes dragged the ground if he wasn't careful—and he was much too exhausted to be careful. The noxious stench notwithstanding, he dozed almost immediately after he nestled against the other man's coat, and nearly fell off three times before they were two miles out of town.

Rudenko skidded to a halt in the gravel, planting his boots to turn around and peered over his shoulder. He breathed heavily, hair plastered to his scalp. His blocky jaw tensed as if trying to keep words he would regret from escaping his teeth. He was subservient when he finally spoke, but it was clear that he would have been all too happy to pound Alex into halibut chum if not for his father. Even then, Rudenko threatened to stab the boy in his hand with the red-handled Vicky to wake him up "for his own safety" if he continued to fall asleep. Incurring Maxim Volkov's wrath for driving a blade through his son's hand was certain to be less dangerous than if he allowed the boy to fall off a moving motorbike and break his neck.

The chilly drizzle and the Russian's very real threat gave Alex enough of an adrenaline shot to keep him awake—if not necessarily alert—for a time. He was just about to nod off again, when Rudenko cut the motorcycle's engine and coasted to a stop in front of a thick line of alder trees alongside the road. A gravel drive disappeared into the darkness to their right. He parked the bike and led the way silently down the drive. Through the foliage Alex could vaguely make out the outline of a house, but it was completely dark, absent any security lighting or glow of a television through the windows.

Rudenko stopped abruptly, coughing and cursing the way he had when he couldn't find his motorcycle key.

"He is not here."

"Pavel?" Alex shook his head, dizzy with fatigue, sounding drunk even to himself. "How do you know? Maybe he's asleep."

"No car." The Russian trudged back to the Kawasaki and threw a leg over, bracing the handlebars so Alex could climb aboard. "I know where he is, but this is problem. There will be witnesses. I had thought to take care of this myself, but I now need your help."

"Help?" Alex said, too exhausted to comprehend.

"Your father was clear on the matter," Rudenko said. "No witnesses."

Alex gave a slow nod, understanding. Wide awake. In his father's world there was always someone who needed seeing to.

Five minutes later, Rudenko stashed the motorcycle in the trees.

Alex had come to Homer many times on trips with friends, camping on the gravel spit and drinking and trying to hook up with the girls who'd come to Alaska for summer jobs. He'd spent several days here before the *Esther Marie* embarked for the crabbing grounds of the Bering Sea. He knew about the Russians, the Old Believers. It was impossible to miss them in town. Some of the girls might have been cute if they'd bothered to put on a dab of makeup.

Women dressed in traditional, colorful dresses they sewed themselves and kept their heads scarved if they were married. Men wore baggie Russian shirts and beards. Alex had always associated the group with Mennonites or Amish or other religious separatists. But Old Believers had cars and trucks and electricity. Some even had televisions in their homes. Children attended school, but special attention was paid to reading Scripture and practical knowledge for the family business, which was often fishing or building boats. Every effort was made to keep children in the community. Youth who strayed too far from the community had a tendency to fall away from their system of beliefs.

The forebearers of these Old Believers had arrived in Alaska by a circuitous route. They'd split from the Russian Orthodox Church in the mid 1600s after a disagreement over changes in, among other things, the number of fingers used to make the sign of the cross. Old Believers felt that not only did these changes go against their canonized traditions, but that they were arbitrary and made without any consultation. Unfortunately, the Russian government sided with the Orthodox Church. Old Believers were arrested, tortured, and even martyred. Survivors hid, and when they were able, they eventually fled communist Russia to China, then communist China to Brazil. The Kennedy administration paved the way for them to emigrate from Brazil to Oregon. Many stayed in the Pacific

Northwest, but a handful of hearty souls, wanting to get even far-ther from society, came north, founding villages on the Kenai Penin-sula. Voznesenka, which was one of them, was twenty miles east of Homer on the bluffs a thousand feet above Kachemak Bay.

The literal end of the road.

Some forty homes clustered on gravel streets around a commu-nity center, a consolidated school, and, of course, the onion-dome church that was the center of Voznesenka village life.

Rudenko stopped abruptly in front of a gray house with a fenced yard and newer model all-wheel-drive Toyota Tundra pickup truck.

"You think the keys are in it?" Alex asked.

"This is not clean car," Rudenko said. "Too many people have seen it." He handed the razor-sharp Vicky to Alex.

Rudenko unclipped his overalls and then rolled them to the waist, peeling off the sweatshirt beneath, presumably to keep from getting blood on his clothes. The eight-point stars of a *bratva* lieu-tenant were tattooed on each shoulder adjacent to his collarbones. It was no small testament to Maxim Volkov's power that a man as fearsome as Lev Rudenko would find himself in the man's debt while they were in prison.

Rudenko pulled a six-inch Benchmade folding knife from his pocket and flicked it open. "Pavel is young and strong. I will see to him. May take him moment to tell me where vehicle is."

"Who else is in there?"

"Agafya," Rudenko said. "Pavel's pretty wife." The Russian's mas-sive face tilted to one side in the midnight twilight, studying Alex. "This work is tricky with small blade."

"I know what to do." Alex followed suit and took off his own shirt, stashing it in the bushes beside the pickup. His hairless torso was so pale it appeared to glow in the darkness.

"Very well," the Russian said. "But take care. She will be handful."

Alex gave a soft chuckle. "So . . . she's a big-boned girl?"

"Strong, yes," Rudenko said. "But she is . . . *svernut' sheu*—a twister of necks. Quite beautiful." He frowned. "I am glad there are no children to see to. I would not enjoy that."

The Russian coughed and gave a little shrug, as if he might very well enjoy the rest of it.

Alex supposed that some in this business, most really, planned their violence, discussing tactics, route, egress. But Rudenko's plan was simple enough. Find out where Pavel had stashed the clean vehicle and then be certain the young man and his wife were dead. Apart from warning Alex of Agafya's beauty, Rudenko simply whispered, "Let's go," and booted the door.

The Russian had evidently been in the house before and knew the way to the bedroom, even in the dark.

Pavel Gurin bounded out of his bed, startled awake by the crash. He shouted to wake his wife. Rudenko met him at the bedroom door, driving him backward and making a path for Alex. It was impossible to tell much about the man in the dark, but from the way he crumpled, it was apparent that he was no match for monstrous Uncle Lev.

The big Russian's questions came machine-gun fast amid kicks and cuffs from boots and fists.

Alex didn't have time to listen.

Agafya was, as Rudenko described her, incredible to look at in her nightdress, flaxen hair flowing over the pillow, eyes wide in terror. None of it slowed Alex down.

Pavel coughed up answers to Rudenko's questions as fast as he could ask them, mistakenly thinking it would help him survive the night. Lying on her back, pretty Agafya thrust out her hand, attempting to defend herself. Her severed finger struck Alex in the cheek before falling back to the pillow beside her. Her eyes opened wide, as if studying Alex's face.

He stepped deftly to the side as he used the blade, avoiding "the painting," as his father called it.

These were not the frenzied psychotic stabs of passion, but quick surgical slashes, severing the femoral arteries, and a finishing stroke across the throat to keep the couple from disturbing the neighbors. The little blades did the job. Agafya Gurin did not utter a single intelligible word.

Rudenko spat on the dying man, apparently unworried about DNA. "*Suka!* You should have come to the boat like you promised!" He wiped his blade on a clean portion of sheet at the foot of the bed, lumbered into the kitchen, where he rummaged through a ceramic dish beside the microwave until he found a set of keys.

Outside, Alex held up the red-handled knife when they reached the motorcycle. "May I keep this?"

"It is yours," Rudenko said.

"We should just take the truck."

The Russian held up the keys he'd taken from the ceramic dish. "Clean van is hidden in boat shed halfway down mountain. I know this place. Is not far." He reached down to wipe a drop of blood off the boy's face with his thumb, smiling a crooked smile. "You did good, young boss."

Inside the Gurin house, sixteen-year-old Efrosinia Basenkov cowered on the floor beside the couch, where she'd been sleeping. Shaking knees held tight against her chest, she chewed on the high collar of her cotton nightgown, holding her breath until she heard the sound of a motorcycle speeding away. She stared wide-eyed through the darkness at the open door of her sister and brother-in-law's bedroom, frozen with fear.

The men had barged right past where she slept. Decorative sheets blended with the floral pattern on the couch, camouflaging her presence.

Efrosinia was not particularly well-read, compared to girls her age who lived down the mountain. She had little contact with the outside world, nor did she want to. But she knew enough about Russia to recognize the big man's tattoos in the light of the microwave clock.

He was *bratva*, a thief . . . and a murderer.

She choked back a sob and then stopped, holding her breath again, straining to hear a new noise.

From the darkness of the bedroom her sister gave a faint mewling cry.

CHAPTER 8

*C*utter and Teariki made it downriver to the village of St. Mary's at two thirty in the morning. Troopers took custody of Rollie Turpin. A responding medical aircraft flew the wounded prisoners to the Yukon-Kuskokwim Regional Hospital in the hub village of Bethel, a hundred miles south. Doctors there would get them stabilized prior to transport to one of the trauma centers in Anchorage.

Cutter's head didn't hit the pillow until ten after three. This far north, the sun skipped along just beneath the horizon all night and was already blushing a line of clear sky between tundra and a layer of grouchy gray clouds. Heavy rain pelted the metal roof of his room, one of a half-dozen converted walk-in freezers across from the St. Mary's airport. Cutter had hung his wet clothes in every available spot around the small enclosure, filling the air with essence of wet wool and gun oil that reminded him of his grandfather. Cozy and warm, the room boasted a set of twin beds, a lamp, and a framed photograph of a bull caribou that looked to have been cut out of a *National Geographic* magazine. A single window with a set of frilly curtains over miniblinds did a passable job of keeping out the midnight sun. The communal bathroom was down the connecting hall near Lola's freezer/room.

Exhausted to the point of loopiness, Cutter reached across the nightstand to set the alarm on his phone and saw he'd missed a text from his widowed sister-in-law, Mim, while he was in the shower.

She'd covered half a night shift for a coworker in the Emergency Department and was just getting home.

Cutter beat his head against the pillow, debating whether or not he was awake enough to keep from making a fool of himself if he called her back—not an easy thing to do considering how he felt.

He'd known her since they were both sixteen years old when she'd worked in a little bait shop on Manasota Key, near where the boys liked to fish and hunt shark teeth. Then as now, she was the most fascinatingly beautiful human he'd ever seen. Unfortunately, his older brother, Ethan, had swooped in and swept her off her feet before he could make his move. It remained one of the very few times in his life he'd been truly angry with his brother. Now Ethan was dead, killed in the oil fields of the North Slope—in a pump explosion that might not have been an accident. Johnson, Benham, and Murphy Engineering, or JBM Engineering, the firm Ethan had worked for, contested the death payout, insisting that the incident had been a fault in Ethan's design. Arliss had been promoted to supervisor, the most thankless job in the Marshals Service—except possibly for criminal clerk—and transferred to Alaska to help. He became a financial helper, stand-in father, and confidant—but not a husband.

He rolled over on his side and stared at his phone. All his fretting about calling her back was probably a moot point. The text had come in a half hour ago. She was surely in bed by now. He texted her good night—to be polite. The phone buzzed almost immediately. He stifled a grin when he saw it was FaceTime. It was an irony of bush Alaska that there were places with no doctors, no restaurants, and no roads, but cell reception was good enough he could lay entombed in his converted meat freezer and have a video chat with the woman he'd loved since his youth.

He put on a pair of reading glasses so he'd be able to see her face better and nestled against his pillow, still on his side when the call connected.

Mim was in bed too, wearing a dark blue T-shirt with a silver District of Alaska US Marshals star over the left breast pocket. She was on her side as well, straw-colored hair across a stack of pillows tall enough to give Cutter a crick in his neck.

"Hey," he said through a long yawn, trying not to sound bored or, worse yet, creepy. He smiled when he saw the shirt.

She pulled at the collar. "Hope you don't mind that I stole this out of your room. Constance conveniently forgot to do laundry, so all my stuff is dirty."

"Of course not," he said. "You should keep it. You wear it better than I do."

She laughed, apparently unbothered by the light flirting. She had, after all, snooped through his room to find a shirt. He noticed a tiny mustard stain below the neck, just a smudge really, from a trip to the reindeer-dog cart in downtown Achorage with his twin nephews the weekend before. She'd chosen a shirt he'd already worn. There were clean ones in his dresser, and the idea that she might want something that smelled like him made him a little dizzy. He chalked up the feeling to fatigue and kept the observation to himself. FaceTime chats while he was away were far more intimate than the two of them ever were in person—both in bed, face-to-face, sharing important news of the day. The whole thing made his stomach ache—in a good way.

"Long night?" he asked, trying in vain to clear his thoughts.

"Not as long as yours," she said. "I'm assuming since you actually made it to bed that there was no gunplay."

"You'd be half right," Cutter said. "Bad guy shot his own foot off and we saved a little girl who'd been missing for a week." He left out the part about knocking out Rollie Turpin's teeth—something he definitely would have told Grumpy.

Mim pressed an incredibly smooth cheek against the pillow, scrunching her lips up in a half smile. "Like I said, my day was nowhere near as exciting as yours."

"Excitement is overrated," Cutter said.

"Maybe so . . ." She sighed, batting her eyes like she might drift off at any moment. "You coming home tomorrow?" She craned her head to glance at the bedside clock. "I mean *today*."

"That's the plan."

They were quiet for a long time, just looking at each other, thinking. Grumpy, the paternal grandfather who'd raised Arliss and Ethan, had often talked about how he could sit with "Nana" Cutter for hours, with neither of them saying a word. Lofty goal,

Cutter thought. Mim stirred, looking like she was about to end the call.

Instead, she adjusted her grip on the phone and closed her eyes as if she had hard news. "So, you think you'll be home for a couple of days before they send you off to hunt more fugitives?"

"I imagine," Cutter said, narrowing his eyes. "Why do you ask? What's up?"

Mim exhaled hard, sticking out her bottom lip to blow a lock of hair out of her eyes.

"SSM got back with me," she said.

Cutter rubbed his eyes, doing a poor job of hiding his concern when he realized what she meant. SSM was Samuel Simmonds Memorial.

"The hospital in Utqiagvik?"

"That's the one," Mim said. "I didn't expect to hear from them for a while, but the administrator called today. They're ready for a traveling nurse right now. Arliss, a week in bush Alaska would give me some good practicum hours toward nurse practitioner."

"Still," Cutter said, "Utqiagvik is a hell of a long way away from . . . well, from anywhere . . ."

Formerly known as Barrow, the Iñupiat village of Utqiagvik was the northernmost city in the United States. Samuel Simmonds Hospital served the population of over four thousand, as well as surrounding villages in roughly the top third of Alaska, an area above the Brooks Range known colloquially as "The Slope." Other than a monthlong barge trip when the ice pack was open during summer months, the only way in or out was by plane.

"I told them I could only stay a week," Mim continued. "Get a feel for the area, you know. See what I can learn."

"JBM Engineering has a satellite office there, don't they?" Cutter said, knowing the answer before he asked the question. "This is more about talking to someone there than anything to do with your nurse practitioner program."

She darkened. "Of course, it's about Ethan. The notion that your spouse might have been murdered sort of takes over a person's life."

Cutter shook his head, wishing he hadn't as soon as he did so. He paused a beat, then unable to stop himself, said, "Utqiagvik is a—"

"I know," she cut him off. "A long way from anywhere. You said that already. Can't you come up with some new material to lord over me?"

Cutter closed his eyes, then, with what he hoped sounded calmer than he felt, said, "If Ethan's death was not an accident, then more than a few people had to work in concert to cover it up. The closer we get to any one of those people means the more danger to everyone involved."

"I can take care of myself," she said. "Don't you worry about that. I'm not some fragile clay pot." Ever since Arliss had known her, she'd slipped into a heavy Florida drawl when she was angry—and at the moment, she'd gone what Ethan called "full-on grits and fried green tomatoes."

Cutter started to speak, but she cut him off. "I'm sick of sitting on my ass in Anchorage."

Cutter took another deep breath, this time holding it for a slow count of five.

"Don't you dare do that combat breathing with me, Arliss Cutter. It's not fair that you get to stay calm while I'm this pissed off."

"Hey, I'm pissed too," Cutter said honestly. "I'd march into the chief's office and resign the second I get off the plane if I thought it would help. Quitting would give me the time to go the places I need to go and talk to the people I need to talk to, but I'd be doing it without a badge, and, for that matter, without a paycheck to finance the travel. I'm not saying I'll use my badge to leverage an investigation, but it greases the skids with other departments when I have it."

"Come on, Arliss." Mim sighed, throwing her head back on the pillow. "I don't want you to quit your job. I just want to do something too."

"I know," Cutter said, thinking he'd rather be in a running gun battle than get in Mim's way when she was this determined. Her plans were reckless and fraught with danger, but he had plenty of experience with that himself.

"Anyway," she said, softening, "you'll still need a job after we get to the bottom of this mess. I'm happy to have a gun-toting deputy US marshal ready to come save me if I bite off more than I can chew in Utqiagvik."

"Mim—"

"Seriously, Arliss, I'll be fine. I wish you'd give me a little credit about staying out of trouble."

"Yeah," Cutter said. "I'm sorry—"

"Me too," Mim said. "Listen, it's late and we're both one yawn away from saying something incredibly stupid. How about we talk about this tonight after dinner."

Cutter brightened and she saw it in his face—a downside of FaceTime.

"I'm still going," Mim said. "But we can talk, make a plan, so to speak. I'd be happy for some investigative guidance. If it makes you feel better, you can teach me a few self-defense and wrestling moves . . ."

Cutter started to respond, but thought better of it.

They said good night, and she ended the call, abruptly. As a nurse, she was skilled at ripping off Band-Aids.

CHAPTER 9

1989
Port Charlotte, Florida

Middle school was awful enough, to begin with, but assholes like Ray Thornton, nicknamed Ray T, and his sneering gang of thugs made it harder on everyone, including themselves.

Twelve-year-old Arliss Cutter was shorter than all the girls in his seventh-grade class, except for Lana Green. Worse than that, he was scrawny. There was no other way to put it. Every year on his birthday when Grumpy measured him on the kitchen wall, his mark was at least an inch shorter than Ethan's at the same age. Arliss must have gotten all the genes for bony knees and elbows.

Both boys wore thrift shop clothes and brought their lunches from home every day—usually leftovers from something they cooked the evening before. The younger brother, Arliss, got hand-me-down clothes from Ethan. As long as he had a pair of shorts and a beach to play on, he didn't care what he wore to school.

Arliss didn't remember much about his mother. He knew she'd run off amid some scandal that Arliss only ever heard about in hushed whispers among his aunts and Grumpy. Ethan acted like he knew, but wasn't spilling any of the details. Evidently, you had to be *this* tall to know the Cutter family secrets, and Arliss wasn't there yet. Whatever happened, their father got sick and died not even a year after. When he talked about it, which was seldom, Grumpy made a face like he wanted to spit.

With their parents out of the picture, the business of raising the Cutter boys fell to Grumpy—their paternal grandfather, who was a Florida Marine Patrol officer out of Port Charlotte.

Grumpy worked hard, but made a public servant's wage, often forgoing extra shifts in favor of spending time with his grandsons. "Ends need to meet," he'd often say. "They don't need to overlap."

Nice clothes or new guns weren't nearly as important as opportunities to model behaviors the boys needed in order to become stalwart men. Grumpy liked to employ dusty-book words like *stalwart* and *forthright* and *chivalrous*.

Arliss relished the lessons, internalizing his grandfather's "Man-Rules" and living up to them as strict articles of faith.

"A man should stand when he shakes hands or when a woman comes into the room or leaves the table. Even more important, a man should stand up for someone who can't stand up for themselves."

You didn't need to be big to do that.

Arliss had just passed the eighth-grade lockers on his way to Ms. Palmer's social studies class, shouldering his way through the crowd of kids, when he heard a tight gasp from Pammyann Griffith. It would have been impossible to tell anything was wrong in the crowded hallway, but Pammyann was Ethan's sometimes girlfriend, who lived next door. She was upset about something—mad or scared. Arliss couldn't tell for sure over the racket. Probably both.

Another girl made a sort of half yelp. Ray T's sneering laugh cut through the crowd. Then his friends followed suit, cackling like a bunch of hyenas.

Small as he was, Arliss shoved his way through the other kids just as Ray T grabbed Shelly Newsome's skirt and lifted it over her head as she came down the hall, oblivious to what was going on.

Ray Thornton was fourteen, held back a grade for reasons that were obvious to anyone who spent ten seconds around him. Dark hair was parted in the middle and feathered like he was in the movies or something. His perpetual sidekick was an eighth grader named Ray Conklin—known to everyone at Port Charlotte Middle School as "Ray C" or simply "C." C was only thirteen, but every bit as big as Thornton. Both Rays had a good six inches, probably fifty pounds, on Arliss—and most every other boy in school, for that matter. The principal had already warned them both to start shaving every day.

The Rays ruled the school, swatting food trays in the cafeteria, stuffing sixth graders into lockers, whatever they could think of to cause misery. C once hid a centerfold picture of a naked woman inside Ms. Palmer's wall maps so everyone got an eyeful when she rolled them down during a lesson. Arliss had to admit that was pretty funny, but the rest of it pissed him off.

"It's Dress-Up Day!" Ray T sneered. Ray C and the other kids laughed, some giddy, some nervous, like they didn't quite know what to do.

Shelly jerked away and smoothed her skirt.

Pammyann huddled along the wall, mother-henning a girl named Roxie, who'd started to cry.

Ray T scanned the hall, hunting for someone else to torment.

"Knock it off!" Arliss yelled, too furious at what he saw to think it through. His voice cracked, sounding anything but threatening.

The two Rays wheeled in unison, laughing, backed by three more sneering eighth graders, who were almost as big.

"Well, hey there, Little Arl-ass," Ray T parroted Arliss's cracking voice. The other boy crowded forward, closing the distance so he was less than three feet away. "Baby boy like you probably doesn't get to see many panties—"

Pammyann glared. "Shut up, Ray."

Thornton wagged his head, mocking her now. "You shut up." He reached for her skirt. "It's not my fault you decided to wear old-lady panties on Dress-Up D—"

Arliss dropped his books and lunged.

Some behaviors should not be tolerated.

Ever.

Somehow Arliss knew that threats or posturing would be a waste of words and time. Worse yet, stalling was a terrible tactic against boys so much larger than he was.

His first punch caught Ray T by surprise, connecting to the startled boy's nose before the books hit the floor. Thornton back-pedaled into his friends, blood pouring from his nose. Ray C took a half step forward, cursing, threatening, chockful of bluster, but uncertain as to what to do next. Arliss meted out a second punch, this one connecting under the boy's eye. Stunned, Ray C just stood there, so Arliss hit him again. Twice.

Pammyann yelled a warning an instant before Ray T shoved him hard between the shoulder blades, knocking him headfirst into the lockers. Arliss spun instinctively. Ray C had recovered enough to smack him in the jaw, but it hurt far less than Arliss thought it would. He drew back to retaliate, but something caught him hard behind the ear, sending up a geyser of lights. He thought he might puke. Another blow knocked him sideways, rattling his teeth. He covered his head with both arms and fell to the floor under a volley of fists and feet.

Pammyann screamed for them to stop.

Through the haze Arliss heard a muffled yell, then what sounded like the growl of an attacking dog. Ray T flew backward in a blur, crashing against the lockers. Ray C, who was bent over Arliss with an arm pulled back midpunch, took a crepe-soled chukka boot from Ethan Cutter directly to the face. Arliss scrambled to his feet and stood back-to-back with his brother, his fists clenched, blood spraying from a gap in the bridge of his nose with each fuming breath.

Ms. Palmer shrieked when she ran out of her classroom, sending kids running like roaches in all directions. The principal appeared out of nowhere, followed by big-armed Coach Mason, the PE teacher. The men grabbed Ethan and the Rays by the scruff of their necks. Ms. Palmer took Arliss's elbow and marched him behind the others down the hall toward the office. He was certain she was giving him some sort of chastisement as they walked, but he couldn't understand a word of it over the ringing in his ears.

"A three-day suspension," Grumpy mused, light from the back-yard firepit dancing in his blue eyes. He'd been home less than five minutes and still wore his slate-gray Florida Marine Patrol uniform. His patrol boat bobbed alongside the wooden dock like it was eager to make another run into Gasparilla Sound on the outbound tide. The sun had long since set out over the Gulf beyond the gut known as Little Alligator Creek.

Grumpy pushed Arliss's unruly bangs aside to study his injuries. He was particularly interested in the horizontal split at the top of the boy's nose between his eyes.

"I'd surmise that to be a four-stitch wound," Grumpy said, squinting a little like he always did when he was working through a decision. "I should get my suture kit."

"I don't think I'd like gettin' stitches very much," Arliss said.

"Oh, is that right?" Grumpy said, like what Arliss thought didn't make a hill of beans when it came to medical care. "I suppose it's already startin' to knit, anyway . . . You still breathin' all right?"

"Yes, sir," Arliss said. He demonstrated by closing his mouth and taking a couple of quick breaths. Getting smacked in a fight was one thing. He wasn't keen on the idea of getting a needle in his nose.

Thankfully, Grumpy moved on with his exam, tilting the boy forward to run a hand over the large goose egg behind his ear. "We'll have to watch this knot," he said. "How's it feel?"

"Tight," Arliss said. He was still so dizzy he could hardly keep his feet, but he kept that to himself.

"You'll want to avoid getting knocked in the brain as much as possible," the old man said. "Good way to end up with the blind staggers."

Arliss dabbed tentatively at the goose egg. "No kidding."

"Got an appetite?"

"Yes, sir," Arliss said.

"Good sign," Grumpy said. Apparently convinced Arliss didn't need to see a doc, he shifted his gaze to the firepit.

The old man often made it home later than the boys, leaving them to take care of dinner. Tonight it was hobo meals—Polish kielbasa with sliced onion, potatoes, and carrots, sandwiched between cabbage leaves. The whole shebang was wrapped in aluminum foil and placed on the coals of the fire Ethan built while Arliss assembled the meals. Grumpy preferred a seasoned hamburger patty, but the sausage was more forgiving to being undercooked, which was a distinct possibility with the boys doing the campfire cooking.

They topped it off with Doritos and leftover refried beans

Grumpy had made the Sunday before. They were so creamy and rich, the boys called them "dessert beans."

Ethan used a folding shovel to flip the foil pouches on the coals. "Five more minutes," he said.

Smooth and social to Arliss's quiet awkwardness, Ethan was darker and almost six inches taller. He'd turned fourteen a month before.

Grumpy squatted to poke at the fire with a willow switch he found on the grass. "Let's have it then. What happened?"

Ethan did most of the talking.

Grumpy was a masterful listener. He didn't look up at the boys, but focused on the periodic flames leaping from what was mostly a bed of breathing coals. "Cowboy TV," he called it.

Everyone knew the elder Cutter as Grumpy, a name that stuck when as a baby Arliss had been unable to pronounce the word *Grandpa*. It suited the old lawman, who, like Arliss, didn't seem to have the right muscles in his face to do much smiling. The mean mug worked well for Grumpy, prowling the rivers, muddy guts, and glades looking for bad guys. Strong both physically and in swagger, Grumpy Cutter was barely five foot seven, but he was a giant in Arliss's eyes. His badge and nickel-plated Colt Python revolver were the most wondrous totems the boy had ever seen.

The old man watched the end of his willow switch burn after Ethan had given him a blow-by-blow description of the fight and the events leading up to it. "So . . . these Rays were messing with the neighbor girl . . ."

"Yes, sir," Arliss said. "Pammyann. And some other girls too. Lifted their dresses right up over their heads."

"And nobody else stepped in?"

"Pammyann was about to do something," Arliss said, thinking back on the look in her eyes.

"And you waded in among how many of these Rays?"

"Two," Arliss said.

"There were five boys," Ethan said. "Ray Thornton runs in a pack, the prick."

Grumpy raised a brow, but didn't look up. "That's enough of that kind of talk."

"Sorry," Ethan said. "Anyway, when I got there, Arliss was down. Both Rays and three of their friends were kicking the shi . . . kicking him while he was down. Five against one, and all of 'em way, way, way bigger than he is."

Grumpy gave a slow nod, jabbing harder at the coals now. "All right, then, I reckon they *are* pricks." He glanced up at Ethan. "Did *you* see them mess with the girls?"

"No, sir," Ethan said. "Arliss was already on the ground when I came up."

"Did anybody tell your principal what these Rays were doing?"

Ethan gave an emphatic nod. "Pammyann told him exactly what happened. A bunch of kids did. But both the Rays swore they were just goofin' around and didn't mean any harm. Ms. Palmer seemed like she was on our side, but Mr. Hunt and Coach Mason laughed it all off and said boys were gonna be boys. They thought the Dress-Up Day thing was pretty funny." Ethan stared into the glowing coals. "Arliss broke Ray T's nose, so that didn't help our case. Mr. Hunt decided Arliss was the primary aggressor. He said it was my responsibility to pull my little brother away, instead of joining the fight. He says I'm just as guilty, if not more so."

Grumpy pitched the willow switch into the fire and stood with a groan. He checked Arliss's cuts and knots again, clucking under his breath.

"You'll heal," he said. "But tell me if anything gets worse."

"Yes, sir." Arliss dabbed at the spot behind his ear again. "Mr. Hunt said I should have tried to talk it out."

"Did you?"

Grumpy was all about law and order, a man who followed the rules.

Arliss chewed his lip. "I saw them liftin' up the girls' dresses and how much it upset Pammyann. I told them to knock it off. Ray T tried to do it again, and then he squared off like he was gonna fight me."

Grumpy shrugged. "Well, men, your principal is not wrong when he says it's best to talk things out. That *is* the preferred method—when it's possible. But I'd lay odds Mr. Hunt hasn't ever had his bell rung by a person who is past talking. I'm sorry you have to learn this so young, but some people just aren't civilized. That's a fact. The outcome to this whole deal is dirty, mighty dirty, but sometimes you get punished for doing the right thing. Cutters don't look to fight, but when one comes knockin', we knock back."

The willow switch smoldering on the coals burst into flames, bathing their faces in firelight.

Grumpy gave Arliss a slow nod, as if pondering how best to put his words.

"It was awful brave of you to go up against a bunch of punks who are bigger than you."

Arliss knew better. All the emotions of the day crashed down around his scrawny shoulders. He swallowed hard, trying desperately not to cry in front of his hero. In front of Ethan. "I . . . wasn't . . ."

"Nah," Ethan said, seeing his kid brother's distress. "You knew Ray T could beat your ass, but you went up against him, anyway—and you busted his nose too."

The corners of Grumpy's mouth perked ever so slightly. "That's what bravery is, son." Then the old man did what he usually did when he was making a point and quoted some moldering poet. Arliss recognized this one as Emerson, one of Grumpy's favorites. "'A hero is no braver than an ordinary man, but he is brave five minutes longer.'"

Ethan threw an arm around his little brother's neck and pulled him sideways into an awkward hug. It hurt like hell, but Arliss didn't care.

"That hall was packed with other kids," Ethan said. "According to Pammyann, Arliss wasn't brave *longer* than anyone. He was the only one."

Shadows danced on Grumpy's craggy face, glinting off his badge and the metal nameplate on his uniform as the willow switch burned itself out. "You stuck together," the old man said. "As you should. It's important for the world to know, you fight one Cutter, you fight us all."

CHAPTER 10

*E*frosinia Basenkov hovered near the row of hospital waiting-room chairs, too nervous to sit, but so exhausted she teetered on her feet. Her fleece jacket did little to hide the huge bloodstains that covered the front of her nightgown—her sister's blood. The biting antiseptic odors of the hospital made her want to vomit. Hot soup, strong tea, those were the smells that healed the body. This place . . . this place reeked of sharp blades and bad omens—and she'd seen far too much of those.

Two policemen, a man and a woman, stood just inside the hospital entrance. The man spoke to a nurse. The female officer turned away, talking in hushed tones on her cell phone. When Efrosinia asked about her brother-in-law, the female officer assured her a state trooper was on the way from the crime scene. He would give her the details.

Like a rat in a cage, the Russian girl paced in the small alcove outside the surgery center. Her head jerked toward double doors with a start each time she heard the click/buzz that signaled they were about to open. So far this morning the doors had disgorged nothing but nurses and orderlies, no one who'd looked like a doctor. The sun was up, but low clouds made it impossible to see where it was in the sky. It could be six in the morning or eight o'clock at night. Completely drained, she would not have been surprised if an entire day had passed.

In truth, it was just after five thirty a.m. Agafaya had been in surgery more than an hour. She'd survived—for the time being,

anyway—because of two coincidences. An Air Force trauma surgeon from Joint Base Elmendorf-Richardson happened to be in
Homer providing training to the South Peninsula Hospital Emergency Department, where the Guardian Flight crew happened to
be overnighting with their helicopter. An ambulance ride down the
mountain—half an hour on a good day—would have killed her,
not to mention the wait for an ambulance to arrive.

Those who lived in Alaska's isolated places were, above all
things, hardy or they didn't live there very long. Sometimes they
didn't live at all. Period. Bad things happened: horrible accidents
with chain saws, boat motors, or wild animals. In addition to steely
constitutions, it was essential to possess some knowledge of self-
care. Help was miles, and more often than not, hours away.

Efrosinia had called her father moments after she heard the intruders ride away on the motorcycle. He'd contacted 911 while she
switched on the bedroom light and dropped to her knees beside
her butchered sister. Blood, so much blood, soaked Agafya's once-
white nightdress. Her eyes were closed. Short, panting breaths escaped barely parted lips. When she tried to speak, it was to check
on her husband, who lay still as a stone at the foot of the bed.

The lace collar of Agafya's gown was severed, probably having
redirected the blade away from important veins and arteries during the attack. Blood poured, but it did not gush as it did when
Papa slaughtered a lamb. This was not the case on Agafya's leg. A
pulsing fountain shot from a gaping wound above her right knee,
inside the thigh. Again, the cotton gown had robbed the cut of
some of the power, but not nearly enough.

Efrosinia had pressed her hand against her sister's wounds and
prayed harder than she'd ever prayed. Her mother and father arrived and the three of them worked and prayed together. Her father called on help from his neighbors. They stood outside in the
rainy darkness and directed the Guardian helicopter to an adjacent field clear of overhead wires and large enough to land in.

All three of the Basenkovs were baptized in blood by the time
the medical crew hustled into the house. It seemed impossible, but
Agafya still breathed.

Now Efrosinia's mother sat in the corner of the hospital waiting
room beside her two cousins, the three women wearing head-

scarves and long woolen coats over traditional dresses that seemed much too colorful for the moment. They muttered prayers and words of encouragement, and then wept and prayed some more.

Sergei, the Basenkov patriarch, was a quiet man, prone to smoking his pipe and staring out at the sea in the rare moments when he wasn't working his fingers to the bone. He loved his family, his Church, and his vocation, in that order. A good pipe of tobacco came in a close fourth.

A long black beard was beginning to show streaks of gray. He wore dark slacks and a teal-colored shirt with blousy sleeves and three buttons in the front. His wife made all their clothes—even Agafya's bloodstained nightdress.

Sergei patted his daughter's arm with a rough hand.

"She will be all right," he said in accented English. "If it is God's will." Efrosinia was certain her father would rather have spoken Slavic, but the younger generations were not quite fluent. He must have sensed she was in no mood to search her exhausted brain for the right words. He patted her arm again. "What will you tell the troopers?"

"I . . . I will tell them what I saw, of course," the girl said, taken aback at the question. She'd already been over every horrifying detail with him, the awful words spilling out before they'd even left Agafya's house.

Sergei took his pipe from a coat pocket and rubbed the side of the bowl with a trembling thumb. A passing nurse gave him a hard look and he raised an open hand to show he knew the rules. "Perhaps we should think about what you witnessed," he whispered to his daughter. "Tell me once more."

Sergei folded his arms across his chest, pipe in hand, breathing deeply as Efrosinia rehearsed yet again what had happened.

When she finished, he closed his eyes and leaned back against the wall. "I am going to share with you something, my *rybka*." For as long as she could remember, little fish was his endearment for her. "It is true that your sister loved Pavel Gurin very much, but it is also true that he was involved in—how to put this—very shady business."

"Shady?"

Sergei gave a slow nod. "I hesitate to speak ill of him at this moment, but . . . I am sorry to say his murder comes as no surprise."

Efrosinia gasped. "Papa!"

He put a hand on her arm to shush her, his eyes shifting around the waiting room to be certain no one heard. "You yourself told me the house was dark. You cannot be certain of what you saw."

Efrosinia spoke through clenched teeth, beside herself. "Papa, I saw the tattoos. Those men were Russian mafia—"

Sergei shushed her again, then gave a long groan, choosing his words carefully. "This I know, my *rybka*," he said. "And that is the heart of what worries me." He scooted to the edge of his seat, nervously bouncing the pipe. "You say the big one had stars on his shoulders?"

She nodded, sniffing back tears. "By his collarbones, something else on his shoulders, like stripes. I cannot be sure."

"You are correct that this one is *bratva*," Sergei mused, his voice low, the words barely making it past the nest of his great beard. "But it is much worse than that. This man you saw is a . . . a boss of sorts."

"Then don't you see, Papa?" She twisted in her seat, catching a glimpse of hope for even a little justice. "If this man is high up in the *bratva*, we must—"

Sergei held up his hand, his face slack, stricken. "Shhh."

She lowered her voice and continued. "If he *is* Russian mafia, then maybe the troopers will be able to figure out his name—"

"I know his name!" Sergei snapped. "And he will kill us all." Sergei swallowed, and then put a hand on his daughter's arm, pleading. "Perhaps you did not see what you—"

"I am not mistaken, Papa," she said. "Think of what these men did. Agafya is your daughter!"

"Yes," Sergei said, closing his eyes again. "And so are you. I know exactly who this man is. He was *sovietnik* for a very powerful man."

"Sovietnik?"

Sergei threw his head back again. "A trusted counselor. Very high up. If these men learn of a witness, then no place on God's earth will be safe—for either of my daughters . . . or anyone in our family."

"But, Papa—"

The doors from the parking lot slid open and a state trooper strode in, imposing in his bristle-brush mustache and blue Stetson. Sergei stroked the back of Efrosinia's hand. "Think of your mother," he said. "She would not survive losing you both."

"You are right, Papa," Efrosinia whispered as the trooper walked toward them. "It *was* dark."

CHAPTER 11

Two hours earlier

Alex woke to Lev Rudenko banging on the steering wheel, cursing violently. They'd found Pavel Gurin's "clean" Toyota van with no problem and stashed the motorcycle in the woods. Rudenko glimpsed the two approaching Alaska State Trooper SUVs when they were on a bend in the road below, giving him time to kill the headlights and swerve down a side road behind a thick stand of devil's club.

The AST vehicles roared past with a singular focus, their red and blue lights bouncing off the trees as they continued up the mountain toward the bloody mess awaiting them in Voznesenka.

The killings came to light much sooner than either man anticipated. Troublesome, but not the end of the world. No one had seen them. Alex felt certain of that. Pavel had done a good job of concealing the van, and he was too scared of Maxim Volkov to get them anything that had been reported stolen. That only left the two corpses.

"You think Pavel had a fishing appointment?" Alex asked.

"Who can know?" The big Russian cleared his throat and popped another cough drop in his mouth. "More likely, we missed some babushka who stopped to make certain her granddaughter did not forget to attend early services. These Old Believers, they go to church at all hours. Two in the morning is not out of question." He craned his head out the window, checking for more troopers before venturing out from behind the devil's club. He kept his headlights off, a frightening prospect on the steep mountain road.

"So," Alex said, "Pavel was supposed to meet us at China Poot and take me to the van?"

"Correct."

"That means you were not planning to come to Anchorage with me. You're out, living with a wife in Alaska. Why would you get involved again?"

Rudenko chuckled. "You know what this means: *'Progulka s drugom v temnote luchshe, chem hodit' v odinochku pri svete?'*"

Alex shrugged. "'In the dark with friend, alone in the light . . .'"

"'Is better in dark with friends,'" Rudenko said, "'than alone in light.' Your father is—how to put—he is more than friend . . . I need you stay awake, young boss. Help keep watch for more troopers."

Alex yawned, planting his feet against the floorboard to stretch. "Okay . . ."

He woke almost three hours later when Rudenko pulled off the road at a rest stop at Cooper Landing, along the milky emerald waters of the Kenai River.

"Sorry 'bout that," Alex said, yawning again.

Rudenko grunted something unintelligible. He didn't appear to be angry, but it was hard to tell with him. He would hardly even blink while he cut another man's throat—for an offense far less egregious than going to sleep on guard duty.

They took turns in the outhouse, pungent from frequent use by summer tourists.

"Next time we go in trees," Rudenko said as he climbed back behind the wheel. "My clothes now smell like bubble gum and shit . . ."

"You think this van is really clean?" Alex asked, awake enough now to worry.

"I passed two Homer PD cars and Trooper car from the Soldotna post," the Russian said. "Not one gave us second look. They not search for van."

"Good to hear." Alex's stomach began to growl. He leaned sideways to check the gas gauge. "We'll need fuel in Girdwood. Let's grab a hot dog or something."

"That idiot, Pavel, left the van on E," Rudenko said. "I stopped for fuel in Stirling while you sleep. Your father expects us before noon."

" '*Kostoprav,*' " Alex said, bouncing his fist on the console between him and the big Russian.

"What?" Rudenko shot him a quizzical look

" '*Kostoprav,*' " Alex repeated. "The 'Bone Crusher.' It is what they call my father. I looked it up."

" '*Kostolom,*' " Rudenko said, shaking his head, chuckling. "We call him '*Kostolom,*' 'Bone Crusher' or 'Bone Breaker.' What you say . . . '*Kostoprav*' . . . that mean *chiropractor*. I do not think big boss would like that name."

Alex woke with a start to the van door sliding open. He tensed, started to lash out, but the web of sleep cleared just in time to see the outline of his father standing in a hotel parking lot. Two bodyguards stood behind him, their own backs guarded by a stand of birch trees. These were his *byki*—figuratively, his bulls. These men were not stereotypical musclebound goons, but wiry, pig-eyed killers who would not hesitate to gut a member of their own family if the boss ordered it. Alex recognized one, Ilia Lipin, a goateed man with news anchor good looks. The other was Yegon Zhuk, the younger brother of Nina Zhuk, the woman Maxim had married after Alex's mother had divorced him. Zhuk had a wide, puff-adder-like face and very little hair. Powerful hands hung at the end of cable-like arms that looked accustomed to hard physical labor. The muscles must have been genetic, because as far as Alex knew, the closest thing the man he called "Uncle Yegon" did to a workout was beat the shit out of people who crossed Maxim Volkov. Neither Lipin nor Zhuk had visible tattoos around the neck or hands—as Maxim Volkov liked his men to be able to move freely in social circles without arousing suspicion.

Maxim Volkov all but dragged Alex out of the van, smothering him in a tight bear hug against his chest. Ruthless killer that he was, those he loved, he loved deeply. Genuine tears streamed down his hollow cheeks.

"Thank you, my son." He sniffed. "Thank you, thank you. I would not have asked you to come if this were not so important." He held Alex away by the shoulders, looking him up and down. "How you have grown in the short months since your last visit home."

And you have shrunk, Alex thought, but kept it to himself.

A float plane buzzed low overhead, descending toward Lake Hood, helping Alex figure out they were somewhere on Spenard Road, an area of Anchorage sometimes known for its by-the-hour hotels.

Maxim turned to Lev Rudenko and embraced him as well, kissing him on both cheeks. "I am sorry to do this to you, my old friend." He pushed the big Russian away to look him over too, and then drew him back close to kiss his cheeks again. "Welcome back into our circle of brothers."

"It is good to be back, boss," Rudenko said.

"You know Ilia Gregorovich Lipin," Maxim said, then nodded to the puff-adder-faced man. "And Yegon, of course. With you here I have my *bratskaya semyorka*—my most trusted brotherhood of seven—"

A door slammed beyond the birch trees, sounding enough like gunfire that they all froze, like rabbits at the overhead screech of a hawk.

A friendly voice came through the foliage and footsteps padded quickly down the concrete steps of the motel's second floor.

Alex's twenty-year-old cousin, Gavrill Pogodin, stepped from the trees beside his father, Oleg. The older man's face was passive, very Russian, but his son's green eyes laughed.

"Sasha!" He took Alex's head and pulled him into a backslapping brotherhood hug. "It has been many months."

"Gavrik." Alex used his cousin's pet name. Out of context, the nickname meant something similar to Punk Kid, but Gavrill was so far from a punk that he didn't take offense. Bronze to Alex's pale complexion, Gavrill was tall, well-muscled, and had kind eyes that perpetually snared him his choice of girls. A year older than Alex, he'd been a fierce protector and guide on the yearly trips to Petropavlovsk for as long as Alex could remember.

Gavrill gave his cousin a mischievous half grin. "What was that redheaded beauty's name?"

"Anna," Alex said.

"Ah, yes," Gavrill said. "Well, your Anoushka pined away for three whole days after you left last year."

"Perhaps I was the only one in the club with skin paler than her—"

Maxim banged a fist on the car door. "Come, Sasha," he said to Alex, barely concealing a jealous glare directed at his nephew. "We have much to do. One may travel freely in America without some asshole policeman demanding to see your papers . . . unless you happen to be behind the wheel of a vehicle. I need you and Lev to drive."

"Of course, Father." Alex yawned. "Where are we going?"

"Do you have a gun?"

"No," Alex said. "I do not."

Maxim gave a sullen grunt. "We are going to get you one," he said. "In fact, we all need guns."

"I will ride with you, cousin," Gavrill said, starting for the minivan.

Maxim shook his head. "You and Yegon go with Lev in the SUV."

"Of course, Uncle," Gavrill said.

"Buying guns?" Alex mused. "That could be tricky . . ."

Maxim scoffed. "Buy them . . . The people we go to see have many—and they will not need them anymore."

"I can imagine not," Alex said, knowing his father's penchant for bloodshed. "When will you tell me your plans?"

"My plan is simple," Maxim said. "Kill the bitch judge who let my Nina die—on camera for all the world to see." He waved a hand in front of him. "All of this, what I do, it is for Nina."

Lev Rudenko looked at Volkov with an amused glint in his eye. "You are my friend," he said. "And you are certainly your son's father."

CHAPTER 12

With the injured prisoners under guard in the Bethel hospital and Rollie Turpin turned over to the custody of the Alaska State Troopers, Cutter and Teariki were free to grab the last two seats on the afternoon Ravn Air flight out of St. Mary's. Overhead bins on the Dash 8 were nowhere near large enough to accommodate their carry-ons, so they made the two-hour trip to Anchorage with daypacks on their laps. Lola, certainly exhausted from her early-morning workout in the Troopers' office gym, promptly conked out, listing sideways onto Cutter's shoulder to avoid putting pressure on her bruised ribs.

She thrummed with energy even when she was asleep, making her seem to take up more space than she actually did. Cutter didn't mind. Even with her sometimes-annoying perkiness, this vivacious Polynesian had proven herself time and time again. He'd come to think of her as a kid sister of sorts and, though she was technically his subordinate, a partner.

Both deputies' phones pinged with text messages the moment they took them out of airplane mode at touchdown.

Lola arched her back against the seat in a long, groaning stretch. Cutter had to lean half into the aisle to keep her out of his lap.

She read the text and then turned the screen so he could read it. "'All hands meeting in the conference room,'" she said aloud. "I bet it's the Supreme," Lola said glumly. "Mark my words. Chief's going to put us on the protection detail. Federal judges are bad enough, but the Supremes . . . This one is new. Maybe she's not ruined yet . . ."

Chief Jill Phillips postponed the meeting until operational deputy US marshals, or DUSMs, returned from the evening jail run—dropping prisoners who'd had court appearances that day back at Anchorage Correctional. Cutter and Teariki arrived in the Federal Building underground parking garage at the same time that the caged prisoner van pulled in. DUSMs Dave Dillard and Paige Hart joined them in the prisoner elevator sallyport. Hart, a short, petitely built African-American woman served three years with the Dallas Police Department before coming aboard the Marshals Service. The District of Alaska was her first duty station. With no rank or specialty, she was affectionately known as a POD, or plain old deputy. Hart's conservative business suit fit her perfectly, concealing the Glock pistol, extra magazines, handcuffs, and Taser that crowded together on the heavy leather belt on her smallish waist. Her clothing was so clean and pressed that Cutter half expected to see a price tag hanging off a sleeve. She'd been out of the training academy a grand total of three months and still had the dazed look of a deputy to whom every assignment was completely new and fraught with danger.

DUSM Dave Dillard was at the opposite end of the spectrum. Fifty-six, he was just months from mandatory retirement, and reminded everyone within earshot on a daily basis that he'd been around longer than anyone in the district. The buttons on his cream-colored shirt strained under the pressure of his gut. A striped polyester tie bore a chili stain that had likely been there for the lion's share of his career.

"Hey, Paige." Lola gave Hart a convivial fist bump. "Dave regaling you with tales of the glory days before we had Glocks and cell phones?"

"Damn right," Dillard said. "Wheel guns and pagers, baby."

Cutter gave a nod of approval. "Amen to that, brother."

The inner workings of the elevator clanged and popped as it made its way down to them. As usual, when more than two deputies got together, talk turned quickly to district gossip.

Hart, who was known to tape a business card to the steering wheel of her G-car so she could see her name next to the silver star, looked to Lola.

"I heard the chief's going to headquarters next month," she said, still breathless about anything to do with Marshals Service lore or politics. "The deputy director is supposed to be grooming her for an AD position."

ADs, or assistant directors, ran each division of the Service. Cutter had heard the rumor as well.

Dillard's eyes fell from the lighted numbers above the elevator to land on Cutter. "You lobbying to get the acting-chief job while she's out of district?" He winked, quoting the old saw the brass always used when they wanted a deputy to do something unpleasant. "The experience would be good for your promotion package."

"Promoting to chief is the last thing on my mind," Cutter said.

"Scott Keen is gunnin' hard for that acting spot." Lola pretended to gag at the thought.

"Would Keen not be good?" Hart asked.

Lola sucked her breath through her teeth. "He's . . . er . . ."

"He's a capable supervisor," Cutter said. "He'd be—"

Dillard cut him off. "The honest answer, Paige, is yes. Scott Keen would *not* be a good chief. The only reason he took the supervisor job is because he knew he needed it to reach more lofty climes. He's perfectly capable of managing programs, but he's got too much ego to supervise live humans."

"Yeah," Lola said. "Scott and leadership are chalk and cheese. A bad fit. He's all too happy to take credit for other people's work. Cutter's the better choice by far."

The elevator arrived and Cutter shot Deputy Hart a warning glance. "Don't pay them any mind, Paige. If you're going to pass judgment on Scotty Keen, base it on what *you* see, not other people's opinions of him." He paused, and then, having had his own issues with Keen, added, "That said, it doesn't hurt to document every interaction with the guy."

The four of them crowded into the cramped elevator. Hart, the "baby" deputy, had to stand sideways against the sliding screen gate that normally separated prisoners and deputies.

Crammed cheek to jowl, Lola glanced at Dillard. "When did you come aboard again, Dave?"

"Eighty-nine," he said.

She whistled under her breath. "Eighteen eighty-nine . . . Service must have been somethin'."

"You bet it was," Dillard said, unfazed by the jibe. "We had the world by the nuts in those days."

Dillard might look like he slept in his clothes, but he would carry a shitload of savvy and institutional knowledge out the door when he rode into that retirement sunset.

Deputy Hart piped up; her voice was so eager and earnest that it was almost painful to hear. "Any of y'all ever work with Justice Morehouse before?"

The elevator opened into the secure hallway outside the cell-block, facing a large ballistic glass window. Cutter gave the court security officers in the control room a nod before turning to the right.

"Madame Justice leans a little too far left for my taste," Dillard said. "I expect she looks down her nose at us knuckle-dragging gun carriers."

"I've been on details for a couple of others," Lola said. "Not her."

"Judges, justices, they're all special souls," Dillard said, ever the teacher for his younger acolyte. He chuckled, shooting a side-eye at Lola as they walked. "I had a judge in the Eastern District of Texas take a shine to me when I was about your age. Made me her pet deputy, so to speak. She demanded that *I* be the one assigned to her court when we had in-custody hearings. Any threats came down the pike, it was me who had to chauffeur her honorable ass around. In any other occupation she mighta been called a badge bunny and sent packing. As a right honorable United States district judge, she got whatever the hell she asked for." Dillard batted his eyes. "Of course, I was prettier and had more hair then . . . Anyway, Her Honor had these two humongous German shepherds she treated like they were her kids. Had more photos of them in her office than she did of any humans. Every day at lunch she would dispatch me to her house to grill up a big fat rib eye steak for those beloved shepherds."

Lola winced. "The judge made you go home and feed her dogs? Every day? That's some bullshit right there, Dave. Didn't you complain to your chief?"

Dillard shrugged. "We didn't do much complaining back then." He shot a furtive look up and down the hall. "Truth is, I knew those dogs couldn't snitch on me, so they got a daily can of Alpo and I enjoyed a well-marbled rib eye every day for lunch . . . I think my cholesterol went up a hundred points that year." He raised his eyebrows up and down. "Federal judges. God love 'em . . ."

CHAPTER 13

*D*eputy Gil Brady came out of the kitchen with a cup of coffee as Cutter and the others approached the conference room at the end of the hall past the admin offices. Almost as much of a gym rat as Teariki, Brady was assigned to the FBI Safe Streets Task Force. He only darkened the doors of Marshals Service office space when he absolutely had to, afraid of being snared to work court or, heaven forbid, a judicial protection detail. Sean Blodgett, the bulldog of a deputy who served with Lola full-time on the fugitive task force, hobbled out of the kitchen behind Brady. He wore a knee brace, limping into the conference room ahead of Cutter with a chocolate muffin in hand. Like most of the deputies there, Blodgett wore no jacket, leaving his pistol exposed. This was home. Everyone here was family. No reason to dress up or cover up.

Newly promoted operations supervisor, or ops soup, Scott Keen was camped out with a pile of important-looking file folders, seated beneath a rug made from the skin of a huge brown bear on the far wall.

Eleven deputies sat around the long oval table that took up most of the conference room, seven men and four women. The walls were decorated in the fashion of US Marshals offices across the country, but with a decidedly Alaskan flair. Along with a two-foot circle-star badge, the ubiquitous Tommy Lee Jones *Fugitive* and John Wayne *Cahill* posters hung there as well. Beyond that, near the head of the table, was a painting of a Tlingit Native chief draped in a Chilkat blanket. Two bearskin rugs—the massive brownie behind Scott Keen, and a large black bear, flanked a mounted walrus skull, long ivory tusks scrimshawed with scenes from an Arctic hunt, likely the one where this particular walrus met his end. Inside the door a half-dozen eight-by-ten black-and-white photos displayed district history: fur-clad deputy marshals doing their job when Alaska was a territory—posing in front of whalebones, moving a prisoner by dogsled, and standing on the deck of a US Customs ship making the rounds from Seattle. It was a wild country then. In Cutter's experience it still was.

Chief Phillips stood at the head of the table in front of a large whiteboard. Short mouse-brown hair framed eyes that looked like they would judge fairly, if not always kindly. An avid hiker with her husband and toddler, her face looked perpetually nipped by sun and wind.

"I know it's late and y'all want to go home," she said, her Kentucky drawl loud and proud. "So let's get the show on the road."

"Let me guess," Mitch Billings said. "Our visiting Supreme decided not to show." Billings had almost as much tenure as Dave Dillard, all of it in Alaska. The difference was, people would actually be sorry to see Dillard go when the time came. Losing Billings would be like gaining two new deputies.

Phillips's jaw tensed, just slightly, but Cutter knew she was biting her tongue. "As a matter of fact," she said, "Justice Morehouse has decided to extend her stay by three days. Fly-fishing, a train ride out to Spencer Glacier, and a trip to see brown bears."

"Ain't that just peachy," Sean Blodgett groused. "Thousand-pound brown bears and Supreme Court justices make for the perfect little picnic."

"Chief," Dave Dillard said. "I'd like to recommend Sean for that detail." He gave a nod to Blodgett's knee brace. "That way, in the event of a bear attack, Madam Justice only has to outrun him."

Phillips ignored the banter and moved on with her meeting. If she paid attention to every smart-ass comment, they'd be here all night. "Morehouse will be wheels-down in Fairbanks day after tomorrow at two fifteen p.m. Senior Inspector Nicki Sloan of Judicial Security will link up with her on her layover in Sea-Tac."

Lola shot a glance at Cutter at the mention of Sloan's name.

Dillard gave his nod of approval. "Nicki Sloan is good people."

"That she is," Phillips said. "More important, she's got experience with each of the Supremes, their idiosyncrasies and the like."

"*Idiosyncrasies,*" Dillard muttered. "That's putting it mildly."

"Morehouse is relatively new," the chief said. "But she's apparently a little naïve about safety."

"That's every judge I ever met," Brady said. "Right up until the moment some asshole climbs over the bench and tries to gouge their eye out with a pencil."

"You're not wrong," Phillips said. "Just something to be aware of. Follow Inspector Sloan's lead." She turned to Keen. "As our former Judicial Security inspector, Scott is going to be the primary liaison between Morehouse and the folks at the Alaska Bar Association who are running the conference. Scott, go ahead and give us a rundown of the threats we're looking at."

Cutter opened his BattleBoard to take notes.

SCOTUS had its own police force that saw to the safety and security of the facility and the justices while they were in DC. When they traveled outside the Capital Beltway, protective duties fell to the Marshals Service. Both agencies kept extensive threat files on each justice and the institution itself.

It was a testament to the impartiality of Charlotte Morehouse's rulings that she'd managed to garner bitter enemies on both ends of the spectrum during her career on the federal bench. White Supremacists from a group called The New Front posted photoshopped images of her face on a naked body hanging from a lamppost after she ruled against them in a civil dispute. Environmental activists sent a box of cow shit when she sided with ranchers along the Texas border. Most of these communications were veiled in such a way that made them hard to prosecute. But a few were more candid, like an unemployed mathematics professor who provided descriptions of how he planned to "saw off the bitch judge's ears and burn out her eyes with a flaming poker." Included in his meticulously hand-printed seventeen-page manifesto were several startlingly detailed pencil drawings of other things he planned to do with the flaming poker. The professor was presently in the federal medical facility in Springfield, Missouri, and not considered a threat for the time being.

The quiet ones were the real worry. They made no noise, hiding instead to strike without warning, with package bomb, bullet, or deadly white powder sent through the mail. Because they rarely tipped their hand, it was up to the Marshals Service to pay attention to judicial rulings and suss out who might be pissed off enough to cause harm. This meant a great deal of interaction with one of the few positions in the US that resembled a British peerage. Federal judges and justices were appointed for life. This kept them from being beholden to any electorate, but it also allowed them, as some deputies called it, to "turn purple" or believe their own bullshit and think of themselves as royalty.

By and large, the men and women of the federal bench whom Cutter had worked with were fair-minded souls. But, when an asshole happened to know a United States senator well enough to get a judgeship, they could slip through the cracks. Over time these began to realize the scope of their power. They just could not help themselves—like the pompous woman who'd sent Deputy Dillard to feed her dogs every day. It was human nature, Cutter supposed, to get a little quirky when everyone laughed at your jokes, begged permission to speak in your presence, and routinely addressed you as Your Honor.

Beyond manifesto writers the Supreme Court police passed along photographs and rap sheets of seven people they considered possible threats to any justice when they traveled. Keen provided information packets on all of them.

But there was a dirty little secret to the dignitary protection racket. In order to keep your principal safe, you had to be right all the time. An attacker only had to get it right once. Most bullets missed. Anthrax letters got caught by vigilant mail clerks, and package bombs often failed.

But once in a while, something got through.

Cutter let his mind drift, half listening as Keen described shotgun-wielding guards while Morehouse visited Alaska's coastal brown bears. A US Coast Guard cutter would loiter offshore if she went out on a boat . . . There would be an ambulance standing by at the venue in Fairbanks . . .

". . . so heads on swivels," Keen said, sounding less tactical than he probably thought he did.

Chief Phillips took the lead again.

"All but one judge from Anchorage will attend the conference," she said. "Billings and I will stay in Anchorage to work any court that pops up. Most of you already have your travel scheduled, and that's good, but here's the kicker. Justice Morehouse has decided to bring her fifteen-year-old daughter. This necessitates some changes in staffing. I've spoken with Inspector Sloan about the daughter . . . Ramona. Seems she's extremely vivacious and loves to exercise . . ."

All eyes fell on Teariki.

"So . . . I'm going to Fairbanks," Lola said.

"Yep," Phillips said, popping the P.

"No worries, Chief," Lola said, frowning just a little as she thought through the logistics of rearranging her life at a moment's notice—a vital skill for a deputy US marshal.

"Arliss, I'd like you to go too," Phillips said. This drew a disgusted look from Scott Keen. "You and Lola can help Gutierrez advance any venues prior to the justice's arrival." Paul Gutierrez was the lone deputy in Fairbanks, until his new partner graduated the Alaska State Trooper Academy.

"We have all the advances covered, Chief," Keen sputtered. He'd expected to be the only supervisor at the conference and guarded his turf like a jealous dog. "There's no need to—"

"Suit yourself, Scott," Phillips said. "If you don't need him."

"No," Keen said. "I think we're good to go without him."

"All right," Phillips said, turning to Cutter. "I still want your boots on the ground, Arliss. The more eyes running countersurveillance, the better. I'm sure you have a warrant or two you can work on in Fairbanks."

"Roger that," Cutter said, happy not to spend the week alone in the house while Mim was off risking her neck in Utqiagvik.

"Very well," Phillips said, pushing off the table with both hands. She winced a little as she got to her feet. "Everyone get some rest. These conferences make for long nights."

Lola stood, turning toward the black-and-white photos on the wall. She tapped the one that showed a deputy with a prisoner bundled up in the basket of a dogsled. The shack behind the deputy read US POST OFFICE, TELLER, ALASKA. A team of mismatched dogs stood in harness, ready to hit the trail.

"This guy sure looks like you, Scott," she said. "Your grandpa ever live in Nome?"

Keen glanced up from the open operational plan in front of him, sneering. "My grandpa wasn't a deputy."

"I'm talking about the prisoner in the dogsled," Lola said. "Damn, if he's not your spittin' image."

Cutter moved in closer to Phillips. "You okay, chief?" he asked in a whisper. "You're moving like you're hurt."

"My hip's just a little outta whack," Phillips said, giving him a wink like he was more peer than subordinate. "We're workin' on another baby. Muncy can get carried away—"

"Okay . . ." Cutter felt his face go red. "Say no more."

Phillips gave him a wry smile. "It's fine. I'm just not as limber—"

"No, really, Chief," Cutter said. "Say no more."

Phillips gave him an energetic thumbs-up, twisting her hips just enough to bring another wince.

Keen, apparently put out that Cutter was getting individual face time with the boss, carried his ops plan to the end of the table. "Okay, Cutter, if you're going to be there, anyway, you might as well—"

"No, no," Phillips said, raising an open hand. "You made your point, Scott. I don't want to muck up the works, as you have them in place. Arliss doesn't need to get in your way. I'm sure he'll find something to occupy his time until the justice and her daughter arrive."

CHAPTER 14

*L*ev Rudenko left the *bratva* life behind when he'd fled Russian authorities across the Bering Sea to Alaska, but old habits die hard, and he'd kept his finger on the pulse of things going down in his new home state. Maxim's plan—which he'd yet to divulge in any detail—required guns, lots of them. Rudenko suggested they target a private game room specializing in a video gambling game called *Fish.* Players sat around each table feeding money into their respective stations buying ammo to shoot at various fish. The more difficult the target, the more money it paid out.

Rudenko knew of two such *Fish* game rooms. The most likely was tucked into an industrial area off Arctic Boulevard in Midtown Anchorage, relatively close to their hotel. The Polynesians who ran this operation were rumored to have gang affiliations out of Los Angeles, but that didn't matter to the Russians. Where there was gambling, there would be a great deal of money, and where there was money, there were guns to guard it.

The place was essentially an industrial strip mall—five units, four of them defunct—a surveyor, a geologist, one with no sign, and offices for a shipping company—all shuttered and vacant. Black plastic garbage bags covered the windows and glass door of the center unit.

Alex followed in the minivan while Rudenko made the block several times in the SUV, scoping the place out, looking for sentries or, worse yet, cops who might have chosen today of all days to enforce gambling laws in Anchorage. The Russians checked the windows of surrounding buildings, paid special attention to rooftops, and scanned the sky for loitering drones.

They found a half-dozen cameras by looking where they would put them if this had been their criminal enterprise, but no suspicious box vans or unmarked cars, with bored officers scrolling social media on their phones or making excuses to an impatient spouse.

Satisfied that they were the only predators in this part of the jungle, Maxim sent Ilia and Gavrill inside the game room to play and get a feel for security. They were the least imposing members of his crew, the best at hiding their true natures.

The rest of them waited, pissing in Gatorade bottles and sitting in silence. Maxim, though exuberant in his welcome to Alex, now gazed out the window at his own reflection. In years past he'd been given to boisterous stories of women, adventure, and violence. Heady stuff for a growing boy. Now he'd slid into a funk that made him seem all the more dangerous. Something was wrong. Alex just couldn't figure out what it was.

Finally, after almost two hours, Ilia and Gavrill exited the frosted glass doors and returned to the van to report. They'd made a show inside of being a couple of car salesmen who'd had a recent run of good fortune.

"I told them I was going to go and get more money," Lipin said.

Gavrill went on to describe the interior of the arcade in detail.

The front doors were locked, with customers having to be buzzed in electronically *after* a very large Samoan stationed inside the door to the right assessed them on video. Weapons, even small pocketknives, were forbidden. Two more large men scanned everyone with a metal-detecting wand as soon as the big dude buzzed them through. A middle-aged woman sat behind a table positioned near the left wall. She handled the money that the bank used to pay out winnings. Two goons flanked her, maybe her sons, maybe watching her so she didn't run off with the dough—maybe a bit of both. According to Lipin, the woman looked like she might be quicker on the trigger than anyone else in the place.

There were four *Fish* games, each about the size of an air hockey table, with stations for ten players around the edges. Play wouldn't kick into high gear until after eight, and as of now, there were only two customers.

The Polynesians inside looked ready to protect their business if threatened. Some surely had trigger time—but it was unlikely any one of them had ever met a black-eyed killer like Maxim Volkov.

All the men inside were armed, and probably the mama too: Glocks, at least one Draco—a short-barreled AK pistol. The plan was simple and, as Maxim preferred all his plans to be, audacious.

Ilia and Gavrill would return for more play. Ilia would drop his leather jacket in the doorway to block it open, allowing the rest of the crew to pour in, swarm the doormen, grab their weapons, and then kill everyone. Robbery could be problematic, Maxim explained to his son. Too many variables. Murder, on the other hand, was often the simplest thing in the world. When a man was dead, what he had owned, you now owned—including his weapons.

The tar in the honey—the fly in the ointment—was what appeared to be an office door in the back of the game room. It was impossible to know who or how many were behind the door, but they needed the guns, so they would soon find out.

Alex was relegated to the van, the equivalent of holding the horses.

"I cannot risk you." Maxim slammed the door, leaving no room for argument.

A light rain fell on the windshield as Alex watched the adventure unfold from down the street. His father and the other men trotted quickly to the far edge of the building, careful to stay out of view of any exterior security cameras. They'd just gotten into place when a monstrous dude stepped out the front doors and lit a cigarette. He wore a baggy flannel shirt and a pissed-off sneer.

Angry and bored out of his mind, Alex turned on the FM radio, catching the end of *Alaska News Nightly*. The final story mentioned Voznesenka.

Voznesenka.

Alex kept his eyes glued to the giant in front of the game room doors, but nudged the volume up a hair. His stomach fell away as he listened. Alaska State Troopers were looking for any leads related to a murder in the Russian village above Homer. One man had been killed and his wife was in serious condition. No word yet if she was able to identify her attacker.

Alex was still reeling when the commentator segued directly into a story about the mysterious case of the *Esther Marie,* a fishing vessel that had been found half submerged in Kachemak Bay. Divers had found none of the crew on board and it was feared that all had been lost. Authorities were attempting to refloat the vessel at the time of the newscast. Officials with the Alaska State Troopers and the US Coast Guard planned to have it towed into Homer, where the investigation would continue . . .

Alex threw his head backward against the seat.

"Well, shit—"

A flash of movement in the rearview mirror yanked him back to the here and now. An oncoming car, a little over a block away.

He glanced toward the game room. The smoker had gone back inside. Gavrill and Ilia made their move. Maxim led the others, hot on their heels. The Russians boiled through the doors.

Gunfire cracked inside. Pistols, Alex thought, followed by the sharper report of rifles. AKs. Alex imagined his father's men gaining control of some weapons and chasing their prey around the video tables, dead-checking each of them with shots to the head.

He pounded the steering wheel, cursing to himself and thinking of the girl in Voznesenka. He should have dead-checked her—

A white Dodge Charger drove past, stereo bass rattling the windows. It pulled into the parking lot and rolled to a stop directly in front of the building. Two large Polynesian men got out, apparently in the middle of a heated conversation—until they heard the gunfire. Both men drew pistols from beneath baggy football jerseys. The driver pulled a set of keys with his non–gun hand. He wasn't going to wait for anyone to buzz him in.

Alex started the van and threw it into gear, stomping on the gas. The sudden movement jerked the newcomers' attention away from the firefight. They spun to face the oncoming threat. For a fleeting moment Alex considered plowing straight into them and continuing through the glass doors into the building. He let up at the last second. A van with that much damage was sure to draw attention, if it worked at all.

The front bumper caught both newcomers above the knees, slapping them backward into the concrete walkway.

Alex bailed out of the van to finish the threat. One was out for the count, but the other had rolled over and was attempting to crawl to his feet. Alex kicked him hard between the shoulder blades. Even wounded, this guy was like booting a stone wall. Alex sprang for the other one's gun, but the game room door swung open and Rudenko stepped out. He put a round from a Draco AK pistol into the wobbly man's chest, before anchoring the other one with a shot to the head.

He flicked his free hand at Alex. "Come, come, young boss." One foot held open the door while he craned his head to look up and down the street for any more threats. "Hurry!"

The scene inside looked like something out of a slasher movie. Bodies littered the game room, slumped behind chairs or sprawled over video tables, horrific wounds illuminated by the colorful video screens. The money woman pitched forward onto her table, blood and gore spilling from what remained of her head.

Maxim leaned against the back wall beside an open door that was riddled with bullet holes. He panted as if he'd just run a race. A black CZ Scorpion 9mm pistol hung from a nylon sling around his neck. The fact that it was not in his hands told Alex all the threats inside the office had been neutralized.

He beckoned Alex to the door, mussing his hair when he got close enough. "You are wet from the rain, Sasha, my boy. You could catch a cold."

Alex smiled, relieved to be near his father again. He leaned to get a peek inside the office, almost running headlong into Ilia Lipin coming out with two Glock pistols stuffed down his belt. The smell of gunpowder and gore was stifling. Maxim and his men obviously fired through the door before going in. An older man lay on the ground beside an overturned office chair, his arm thrown over the body of a young girl of maybe ten or eleven, whom he'd apparently been trying to shield.

Maxim clapped his hands. "Quickly now." He used a handkerchief to slide open a desk drawer. "Is anyone hurt?"

Alex had once been with his father when one of his men was cut horizontally across the belly. The poor soul had no idea he'd been

wounded until his guts spilled into his hands. It was then that Alex
had learned two things. His father was a tremendous leader who
cared deeply for those in his brotherhood, and that intestines
looked a great deal like chewed bubble gum.

"Touch only what you plan to carry with you," Maxim said. "We
must assume that someone heard our gunfire." He flung open another drawer, oblivious to the dead girl at his feet. She was not his
child, so she was of no consequence.

CHAPTER 15

"Kenny Robertson snores," nine-year-old Matthew said.

He stood on a kitchen chair wielding a nine-inch fillet knife against a fresh chunk of halibut. Cutter stood beside him, dish towel over one shoulder, clucking periodically to make sure the boy kept his fingers out of the path of the blade. As they all pursued their kitchen projects, Cutter knew that teaching the twins to be good men was far more important than getting perfectly cut portions of fish. The younger of Cutter's nephews by twelve minutes, Matthew had perpetually mussed blond hair, like Arliss's. The boy looked up at his mother, who sat at the kitchen table, poring over a chemistry quiz on her laptop.

"How long do you have to be gone?"

"Just a week," Mim said. "It'll be fun. Think of it as a long sleepover."

Michael, the elder twin, dark like his father, rolled a thick wooden pin back and forth over a gallon Ziploc bag full of Ritz Crackers, glaring down at them as if they owed him money.

"What about Uncle Arliss? How come he can't watch us?"

Mim's sixteen-year-old daughter, Constance, hovered over a pot of hot oil, slotted spoon in hand like a club. Notoriously prickly, she rarely graced them with her presence in the kitchen, but a recent near-nuclear blowup with her mother had started a healing process of sorts. Her friends were picking her up in less than an hour for a long-planned trip to Seattle, but she stepped in to help with dinner—as if she might actually enjoy being around her little brothers. It reminded Cutter of the old days, before her father was killed.

Though she'd grown slightly more sociable, her holey jeans and baggy mechanic's shirt were still a fusion of Goth and I-don't-give-a-shit style. She pushed a sullen flap of bottle-black hair out of her eyes and shot a laser look at Cutter.

"Yeah, Uncle Arliss, why is it that the twins have to vacate the house tonight, if you're not going out of town until tomorrow?"

From the table Mim said, "Because I have to leave for the airport at four a.m. and your uncle could get called out. You are welcome to postpone your trip to Seattle if you want and stay home and babysit."

"You are high-larious, Mother," Constance said, deadpan. "Becca's mom has been planning this for months."

"It's good for all involved," Mim said. "I'll sleep better knowing the boys are at the Robertsons' while I'm away."

"I won't sleep better," Matthew said, eyes on his blade, like Cutter had taught him. "And you wouldn't either if you had to listen to Kenny snore. I wish you'd just stay home."

"Okay, men," Cutter said, changing the subject—though he happened to agree. "Remember our process?"

"We dunk a hunk of halibut in the egg," Michael said. "Shake it in the smushed crackers, then drop into hot oil." He waved his hand in a little flourish. "And—ooh la la!"

"It's *voilà*, little bro," Constance whispered, letting her nurturing side peek out.

"I remember Grumpy using Ritz Crackers to fry snook," Mim offered.

"*Snook!*" Matthew laughed. "That's not even a real fish."

Mim gave a low groan. "I swear, y'all are forgetting your Southern roots."

"I like halibut," Michael said.

"Me too," Arliss said. "So let's get to cooking it before your mama moves you all back to Florida."

The boys scooted their chairs closer to the stove, each with a metal spoon, entranced by the pot of sizzling fish.

Constance lifted out the first batch when the nuggets turned golden brown.

"Ooh la la," Michael said.

The twins wolfed down their dinner, oblivious to how lucky they were to be eating halibut that had been swimming in the bottom of Prince William Sound less than a week before—and then headed off to spend the week listening to their friend snore. Constance's friends showed up early, conveniently rescuing her from having to help with the dishes. She gave Cutter a stern look, but went out the door, without making any overly snide remarks.

"I'm calling that progress," Mim said after she'd gone.

An hour later, the two of them stood at the backyard firepit that Ethan had built out of round stones he'd picked up along the Matanuska River. Mim stared hard at the flames, her arms folded tight across the chest of a garnet FLORIDA sweatshirt, hands drawn up in the cuffs. The fire was mostly split birch, but Cutter had added a couple of pieces of spruce that cracked and popped, sending orange sparks into the chilly evening air.

"I like this," Mim said, breathy, distant. "That snap reminds me of the cedar fires Grumpy used to build in his backyard." Dancing flames bathed her face, highlighting a peaches and cream complexion with a splash of orange across her cheeks. Her hair hung loose, still damp from a quick after-dinner shower.

They stood close, shoulders just touching if either of them breathed deeply or swayed just right. It was a hair after nine. The sun wouldn't set for two more hours, but three days of rain had cooled things off and the warmth of a fire drew them close.

"Ethan had a theory," Mim said. She followed a spark upward with her gaze, blowing out a blossom of vapor.

Cutter waited a beat, and then said, "A theory?" to show that he was paying attention.

"He always thought Grumpy liked you more."

Cutter gave a contemplative chuckle. "That's not true. Grumpy paid more attention to me. I think because I required more care and feeding . . . more maintenance. Ethan was the bright one, studious, rarely let his emotions get the better of him—except when it came to you. He thought ahead and saw the consequences of his actions. I was writing checks my ass couldn't cash from the time I was a sprout."

Mim warmed her hands over the fire, smiling. "Ethan would have agreed with most of that."

"I think Grumpy felt sorry for me because I was the most like him." Cutter poked the coals with a long piece of alder.

"Untamed?"

"I suppose you could say that."

"Yeah," Mim said. "I always saw Grumpy as a bit of a tortured soul. He told me once that there was a piece of him missing after his wife passed."

"I never knew Nana Cutter," he said. "Wish I had."

"She must have been something to keep Grumpy corralled."

"I expect so," Cutter said.

They were quiet for a time; then out of the blue, Mim said, "Constance thinks you and I need a chaperone."

Cutter laughed out loud, still poking the fire. "You are one of maybe three people in this world who can startle me." He looked sideways at her. "Seriously, a *chaperone?*"

"Being alone at home together like this," Mim said. "She's certain you and I planned it so we could have some adult time."

Cutter thought of a dozen things to say, but made do with turning a piece of smoldering birch so it caught fire again.

"It's true," Mim said softly, prodding him to look at her. "I'd never admit it to my teenage daughter, but I did plan to get the kids out of the house for the evening—to talk. You've been beyond wonderful coming up to help after Ethan was killed. But we've never . . . you know, talked about . . . that thing we don't talk about. We dance around it, but I know that's not the way you do things."

"Oh, I don't know," he said. "Maybe it's best that way."

"I know it hurt you when I married Ethan," she said.

"Okay," Cutter said. "Straight to the heart."

"I wish I could tell you that I was stupid and that I should have chosen—"

He touched her arm, gently, but enough to get her to stop speaking. "You don't have to explain anything. I'm here and I'll be here as long as you need me."

She pushed on. "It would have been so much easier if you were a dick about it all, but you were just . . . sad."

"Mim," Cutter said, touching her arm again. "Please let's not—"

"I was so glad when you married that first time," she said. "Truth be told, I was more than a little jealous. I mean, I know I had no right to be, but I was. It was a load off my conscience too. I know that marriage didn't work out—"

"Or the next one." Cutter sighed. "Or the next one . . ."

"But Barbara was great," Mim said. "Right?"

"Yes. Barbara was terrific."

"The point is, you moved on—"

"Nope." Cutter tossed his stick into the fire. If they were going to play this game . . . "You know, when you and Ethan got really serious, I told myself you'd eventually come around. I was sure it was only a matter of time before you realized *I* was the better choice. It took a while, but it finally dawned on me that you had chosen the right man for you. Hell of a thing to swallow. I quit college, joined the army, and fought like a berserker in Afghanistan. Married a series of four different women over the years. The last one, I actually loved . . ." He glanced up and looked Mim dead in the eye. "But don't you, for one minute, think I ever moved on."

For a moment he thought she might say something important, something life changing, but in the end she sighed and glanced at her watch. "I have to get up in four hours to catch my plane."

"About that—"

"No, Arliss." Mim stomped her foot. "Don't ruin this moment with your overprotective bullshit."

Both his hands came up. "You're going. I get that. It's just that . . . you're liable to uncover some really awful things."

"Like my husband, the father of my children, was blown to pieces by some bastard who has yet to see a pinch of justice?"

Cutter closed his eyes.

"I took Barbara to see this movie once, right after she'd gotten her cancer diagnosis. Some violent flick with a lot of death and vengeance. You know, the kind of movies Ethan and I liked to watch. Anyway, I thought it might get her mind off her illness, but the images really shook her. One of the biggest regrets of my life is *not* walking out of that theater, instead of sitting there and subjecting my wife to that awful shit. It piles up, you know. I just want to protect you from it."

"Well, you can't," Mim said. "That awful shit has already piled on me."

"You're going to hear things about Ethan," he said. "The rumors aren't true, but some of these people have a vested interest in making him look bad."

"What do you think I'm going to find?"

"I have no idea. The things we already know about could well be the tip of the berg. And you really do need to be careful."

"I know," she said. "Don't trust anybody."

"Oh," Cutter said, "you can trust them. You just have to trust them to try and hurt you if you stumble onto something. That's what I'm saying. This is serious business, Mim. If someone murdered Ethan, then they would have no problem making you disappear—"

"You are one hundred ten percent correct," she said. "And you know what? To quote you, 'I do not give a pinch of shit.' Aren't you the one who's always telling the boys they have to stomp their own snakes? Well, I can't just sit back and wait for someone else to do the work, even if that someone is you."

"Mim—"

"I'd like to be able to call and compare notes, leverage your expertise, but I'll wing it alone if you're going to lambast me with guilt every time we talk."

"It won't be like—"

"I need to get to sleep."

She turned and strode to the house, fuming, breathless. She paused at the door, then turned again to stomp back toward Cutter until she was again in the light of the fire.

"Families can be pissed at each other and still be close, right?"

"Yep," Cutter said, more than a little dizzy.

"Good." She wheeled and walked to the house without another word, leaving him alone with the dying fire.

CHAPTER 16

*T*he rain had stopped by the time Lola Teariki and Joe Bill Brackett walked out of the Beartooth Theater and Pub into the eerie glow of the midnight sun. The movie, the newest Bond flick, had started later than expected, putting them behind schedule. They'd both seen the movie before, of course, and considered leaving early, but with their jobs constantly conspiring to keep them apart, it was just too damned pleasant to sit in the dark theater and eat salmon quesadillas while they sipped wine and watched 007 save the world. The meals and atmosphere at the Beartooth made pretty much any movie worthwhile.

Lola liked to keep her gun hand free, as did Brackett, a patrol officer with Anchorage PD. That meant they walked close to one another, but didn't actually hold hands—most of the time. They'd planned to grab dinner and a movie the following night, but her sudden trip to Fairbanks to babysit the justice's daughter had pushed up the timeline. Brackett understood all too well about volatile schedules. He worked midshift and often worked late or got called in on his day off. He'd taken the night off so they could spend a few more hours together.

"I still have to pack," she said.

He swayed closer so his shoulder brushed hers. She liked that. "What time is . . ." his voice trailed off. Normally one to mosey, anyway, his pace now slowed to a crawl.

She followed his gaze to the parking lot across Twenty-Seventh Street.

"You seeing this?" he whispered.

It was late enough that all the stores in the strip mall to the west were closed, but the lot was relatively full of patrons visiting the Bear Tooth and a restaurant across the way.

"What am I looking at?" Lola caught movement in front of the scuba shop.

"Gray Silverado," Brackett said.

"Got it," Lola said. "Two people, dark hoodies, working the door."

"The tall one goes by 'Fuzzy,'" Bracket said. "We should call it in."

"Okay . . ." Lola said, unconvinced.

"You're right. They'll be gone by the time anyone gets here. Anyway, my badge isn't broken just because I'm off duty. Right?"

Lola grinned. "Wouldn't know. I'm never off duty."

"Okay, 'BAF,'" Brackett said. He often called her "Bad Ass Fed." "You're carrying?"

She scoffed. "Joe Bill."

"Right," he said. "Of course, you are. We'll cross together, then split up like we're going to different cars. Fuzzy's not the type to run unless he thinks we're onto him."

Lola took Brackett's left hand and started walking. They chatted quietly, like any other couple coming out of a movie.

Nothing to see here. Go ahead and keep stealing your truck.

Fuzzy and his partner had already smashed the side window and stopped to loiter beside it, less than a hundred feet across the parking lot.

Lola paused beside a dusty Ford Taurus, directly across from the Silverado, and grabbed Brackett by the butt, genuinely startling him. Laughing, she leaned sideways, resting her head on his arm, nuzzling. He shuddered, despite the situation.

"Hurry up, poppy," she said, loud enough Fuzzy and his friend surely heard. "I got some things to show you back at my place . . ."

She threw her arms around his neck and drew him into a passionate kiss.

"Screw it," Brackett mumbled, lips buzzing against hers. "I say we let them steal the damned thing."

Lola grabbed a handful of ass again, nibbling Brackett's neck, giving the car thieves a great show. "You follow me," she said sotto voce; then, nibbling Brackett's ear, she added, "Keep walking, mister."

Brackett stole one more kiss, and then trudged away as if going to a different vehicle. Lola stood by the Ford and watched him go.

Thirty feet away, Bracket spun, sprinting for Fuzzy and the Silverado pickup.

"Anchorage Police! On the ground now!"

Fuzzy dropped a screwdriver and turned to run, but froze when he saw Lola coming toward him.

"US Marshals! On your face!"

Blocked by the scuba shop behind them and pinched between the oncoming officers, the men gave up and wilted to their knees.

Lola handcuffed the nearest one, a skinny tweaker named Lopez she'd seen on the street before, but had never arrested. Brackett took care of Fuzzy, aka Andrew Furbush.

Brackett called Dispatch and asked for a couple of marked units to come for transport. He picked up a half a brick while they were waiting and toed the bits of broken glass in the parking lot.

He pitched the brick in the air and shook his head at Fuzzy. "Every time I see you, there's Mountain View mineral on the ground. I don't get it. Why not just jimmy the door so you don't drive around with a broken window?"

Furbush spit on the pavement, sneering. "I wasn't stealin' that truck."

"Well," Brackett said, smiling, "we'll see what the court thinks about that."

Furbush spit again, then wagged his head derisively. "You might get me on burglary, but you got nothin' that says I was stealing anything."

"He's not wrong," Lola said as two APD marked units rolled into the parking lot. Her face screwed into a puzzled frown. "What's this about Mountain View mineral?"

Brackett laughed. "Glass, spent shell casings, you know, naturally occurring resources in Mountain View and Spenard. Spenard mineral just sounds lame—"

Sandra Jackson, an APD officer in her late twenties, took custody of Furbush. She had a couple of years on Lola and a couple of inches too. Dirty-blond hair and pale skin—aka an Alaska tan, because it was so prevalent—stood out against the dark blue uniform. Lola thought they could have been friends, were it not for their mutual affection for Brackett.

He seemed oblivious to how she felt about him, but Lola felt the spines come out the first time they'd met.

"Thanks for coming, Sandy," he said.

She opened the trunk of her marked Impala and retrieved a couple of evidence bags for the screwdriver and brick. "Not a problem," she said.

Lola noted a plastic bin in the truck with at least a dozen evidence bags that appeared to be full.

"Busy night?" she said, hoping to sound congenial.

Jackson nodded, but spoke to Brackett. "You must have had your phone turned off."

"What do you mean?"

"Swing shift got clobbered. I came in early to help with the crime scene. I've been over there for the last three hours. Just cleared, when Dispatch sent me here."

She gave them a down-and-dirty brief of the murders at a *Fish* game room off Arctic.

"Holy shit!" Brackett said as Jackson finished her description. "Nine dead? I'm surprised they didn't call everyone in."

"'Jeans-police' are out in force," Jackson said, referring to Vice, Narcotics, Investigative Support, and any other plainclothes units. "SWAT's spooled up, but so far, it looks like a done deal. There's no reason to call them out after the fact."

"You need the task force?" Lola asked.

Jackson looked like she might say something flip, but took a deep breath, keeping it professional. "Above my pay grade. But probably not yet. Patrol's canvassing for witnesses, but it's an industrial area. Hardly any security cameras."

Brackett chewed on his bottom lip, the way he did when he was in deep thought about something. Lola couldn't help but wonder if Sandy Jackson knew that about him.

"Nine dead," he said again, his voice hollow.

"That'll make the news," Lola said. "Any leads?"

Jackson stepped away from her patrol car, making sure Furbush couldn't hear her through the window.

"There was an older guy counting money in the back office with his granddaughter," she said. "Detectives talk like he was the business owner. Sounds like he got a call out to his son. Said they were under attack. Apparently, he heard someone speaking in Russian."

"A lot of money changes hands in those *Fish* games," Brackett mused. "That would be a pretty lucrative haul."

"Did they find guns?" Lola asked.

Jackson gave her a wary side-eye, like maybe she wasn't comfortable talking to a Fed. "Nope. A couple of half-empty boxes of nine-millimeter ammo. You make of that what you want, but I'm thinking what guns there were went out with the money. Whoever this was, they took everything."

Lola rubbed her face with both hands, suddenly overwhelmed with fatigue. "And then murdered everyone—even the kid."

"About the size of it."

"Any prints?" Brackett asked.

"Nothing promising. I bagged a couple of hairs from the floor by the office, but those could belong to anyone. Game rooms aren't exactly known for how often they vacuum the rugs."

Brackett glanced over to make sure Furbush wasn't trying to worm his way out of the patrol car, then turned back to Jackson. "Inside cameras?"

"Destroyed," she said. "According to his nephew, the owner was about to make the switch to a web-based system, but hadn't pulled the trigger yet . . ."

"Interesting about them speaking Russian," Brackett said, half to himself.

"Could be nothing," Jackson said. "One of the deceased customers has a Russian surname. Could have been scared shitless, screaming at their killers. Anyway, Homicide is running point now. Nakamura heard I was on my way to assist you with this call. He made a point of having me tell you he'd better not see your face around his crime scene. You got a rep, son."

Officer Jackson excused herself, giving Brackett a sad smile and all but ignoring Lola.

They walked back to Brackett's truck in silence, still coming down from the adrenaline dump of the arrest. He opened her door—quaint, and kind of sweet. Steeped in a world of testosterone-drenched type-A deputy marshals, a little chivalry wasn't something she was going to argue about.

Brackett trotted quickly around to the driver's side and hauled himself into his truck.

"Russians shoot up a video gambling joint," he said once he'd started the engine.

Lola reached around for her seat belt. "You sound like me, leaping to conclusions in a single bound. The Russian might be the customer Sandy mentioned. For all we know, one of the *Fish* games is programmed in Russian . . ." She changed tacks. "What is the deal with that woman, anyway?"

"What woman?"

She snapped her fingers in front of his face. "Stay with me, Joe Bill. When is Sandy Jackson going to get over the fact that you and I are dating? She looked like she wanted to cook me for dinner."

Bracket put the truck in gear and pulled out of the parking lot onto Twenty-Seventh Street. He turned to Lola and batted his lashes. "I'm pretty hard to get over."

"I can see that."

"Anyhow," Brackett said, squirming, "do you really believe it was the *Fish* machines speaking Russian?"

"Phshh," she scoffed. "I told you, I jump to conclusions too. Nine people massacred. Chicago and Detroit are gonna start calling *us* 'Murderville.'"

"Have you ever been in one of those game rooms?"

She widened her eyes, looking down her nose at him. Her *haka* face. "Why? Because I'm Polynesian?"

"I . . . No."

She punched him softly in the arm. "I'm just messin' with you, Joe Bill."

He breathed out slowly, relieved. "You know you're terrifying when you do that?" He shook his head. "Anyway, those game rooms are crawling with armed security. Sounds like organized crime to me."

"Yeah," Lola said, playing devil's advocate. "But *Russian* organized crime?"

"You know about the murder in Homer?"

"Today?"

He nodded. "In the last twenty-four hours."

Lola groaned, the long day catching up to her. "Who got killed down there?"

"A twenty-six-year-old man from the Old Believers' village of Voznesenka."

"Are you kidding me?"

Bracket turned south on Spenard, toward the airport and Lola's condo, and told her what he knew about the murder. Which wasn't much. "His wife's out of surgery, but touch and go. They have her in a medically induced coma."

"The victims are Russians?"

"Yep," he said smugly. "Russians. Think about th—"

Lola cut him off. "You're tellin' me there's more?"

"There has to be," he said. "We just haven't figured out what it is yet."

"A couple of intrepid investigators like you and me . . ." Lola leaned sideways, reaching across the center console and ran her fingers over the back of his hand. "You staying over?"

"Hell yeah," Brackett said. Both hands on the wheel, he shot her a glance. "If I'm invited."

"I still have to pack for Fairbanks."

"No worries."

"And I still have to work out," Lola said.

Brackett turned, studying her for a long moment before putting his eyes back on the road. "Cardio?"

She shook her head. "Leg day."

"Crap," he said, hangdog. "Your leg days can render a dude incapable of . . . pretty much anything."

"It doesn't have to be tonight. I'll get up early." She ran a finger along his bicep. "You sure know how to plan an interesting evening, Joe Bill Brackett."

"That was, by far, the best date I've ever been on." He chuckled. "Movie and an arrest. Those idiots had no idea until we were right on top of them. You're pretty damned good at role-playing." He glanced sideways again. "That ass grab was a nice touch."

"What can I say, Joe Bill?" She winked, her Kiwi accent coming on strong. "It's a fight-or-flirt response."

CHAPTER 17

Alaska State Trooper Sam Benjamin tapped the brakes on his blue-and-white Ford Explorer. He was the only vehicle on this portion of the George Parks Highway, the two-lane thoroughfare between Anchorage and Fairbanks. A lone cross fox stopped mid-stride, frozen in the glare of his headlights at the edge of the pavement, black from recent rain. Temperatures dipped into the low forties this time of night, and the fox still retained a thick winter coat of smoke blue and rust red. Forepaw raised, almost feline face cocked to one side, the animal paused for the space of just a few heartbeats, apparently trying to decide if it could beat the oncoming SUV, and then turned to melt into the fireweed and scrub willows.

Trooper Benjamin didn't believe in omens, but if he had, seeing a cross fox on the Parks Highway would have been a good one.

He picked up his speed again, fiddling with the buttons on his good-time radio, trying to find an AM station that didn't spew conspiracy theories, a tall order at two thirty in the morning.

He yawned, settling in. A thermos of coffee lay in the passenger seat beside his Stetson. The iconic blue campaign hat was a symbol of his position in the Alaska State Troopers. He was one of fewer than four hundred men and women who enforced the laws of the largest state in the Union, often single-handedly responsible for geographic areas larger than entire states in the lower forty-eight.

By and large, the Alaska State Troopers left urban law enforcement to the city kitties. APD could have the hotels and shopping malls and bar crawls, thank you very much. Alaska was primarily a rural state and the AST was a rural force, with much of a trooper's work in places that were accessible only by air or river—the Bush.

Sam Benjamin had grown up in the far north, hunting and fishing with his family from the time he was old enough to sit on a blanket beside the campfire. When he was ten, a trooper had landed a Super Cub at the family hunting camp along the Yentna River. The trooper had been wearing a helmet when he landed, but as soon as his boots hit the gravel, he leaned back inside the rear seat of his airplane and retrieved a blue Stetson, which he'd set on the awestruck boy's head.

Cool hat, gun belt, not to mention the bush plane—Sam Benjamin's future had been written in stone during that ten-minute chat between his father and the trooper with a bristle-brush mustache.

He checked his watch, then eyed the thermos of coffee again. His house was just over five miles to the southeast . . . but the swamps and braids and sandbars of the Susitna River blocked his way. He still had to drive south, and then north again, for a total of over thirty miles in order to get home, or, at least, the place where he was staying for the next two weeks—Talkeetna, a quirky little town with a cat for a mayor and a good base for the work Benjamin had been assigned.

He was stationed on Prince of Wales, an island in Southeast Alaska. It was the perfect post, far from his bosses in Ketchikan, and even farther from the flagpole at HQ. It was the best of all worlds, miles of paved roads, even more logging roads, mountains, deer, fish, hidden coves to explore—and just enough people to make law enforcement necessary without being overwhelming. He planned to live out the rest of his career there, forgoing promotion in favor of duty station.

But it was against some unwritten rule for AST brass to let their troopers grow too content—and Sam Benjamin was sent on special assignment on the road system, augmenting the three troopers and one sergeant of B Detachment's Criminal Suppression Unit. His specific duty: night patrol of the many trailheads along the Parks

Highway, where hikers and ATV riders parked their vehicles. Thieves took everything, from Ray-Bans left in glove boxes to catalytic converters. All-terrain vehicle trailers were favorite targets.

Trooper Benjamin chalked up the assignment on the road system as a chance to stop by Costco and Sportsman's Warehouse. He'd briefly considered calling Lola Teariki. They'd met when she'd come to Prince of Wales, hunting a fugitive. Things had heated up for a time—he got chills every time he thought about it—but distance and careers had clubbed the relationship to death. They were still friends, but she was seeing some APD guy now, so . . . In truth, he'd not dated anyone after Lola. It was a little too soon to—

A pair of headlights cut the twilight a couple hundred yards ahead, playing across the wet highway as the vehicle turned north out of the parking area for the East-West Express Trail. It was a large lot, surrounded by trees, and since it wasn't visible from the highway, it was a favorite target of vehicle burglars and trailer thieves.

Brake lights flared as the older model Toyota minivan passed him, heading north, the driver surely noticing the prominent blue stripe and golden bear Trooper badge on the Explorer's door.

The driveway to a State DOT maintenance site lay a few hundred feet to the south, and Trooper Benjamin used it to flip a quick one-eighty. Seconds later, a new set of headlights appeared behind him. He thought for a moment that they had come out of the trailhead parking lot too, but surely he would have seen that. They'd probably just rounded a curve or crested one of the numerous bumps and swells along the Parks Highway. Cars appeared out of nowhere all the time out here, contributing to more than a few accidents when motorists pulled over to gawk at bears or moose or cross foxes.

Ahead, the van driver picked up his speed, slightly, but enough to notice. Headlights filled the trooper's rearview mirror as the second vehicle overtook him, blinker flashing in the night. Normally, it was something of a cardinal sin to pass a trooper, but Benjamin was happy to let this guy get by, so he could initiate his stop on the van.

Benjamin grabbed the mic from his dash, trying to make out the plate number before he activated his red and blues.

He never got the chance.

Ten minutes earlier, Alex Volkov turned the van into a secluded parking lot on the east side of the Parks Highway, hidden among the trees. It was something of a badge of honor with Maxim Volkov that his whores had given him everything from trich to gonorrhea, too many times to count. He made no secret that he had probably given as much or more than he'd received, so he did not really blame the girls, so long as they continued to work. Frequent rounds of antibiotics had stemmed the worst of his infections, but they had taken their toll—and when Maxim Volkov needed to piss, he needed to piss right now!

Rudenko had been around the boss long enough to know what was happening and rolled up in the Expedition a few moments later. All the men took advantage of the stop to off-load some of the coffee and Red Bulls they'd been swilling for the past several hours. They were only a quarter of the way to Fairbanks and none of them wanted to be the reason they had to pull over again. You pissed when the boss did, or you went in a bottle in the car.

Alex stood by Gavrill while both boys relieved themselves into the bushes. He'd been looking for a moment to catch up, out from under his father's nose.

"How have you been, cousin?"

"Good." Gavrill nodded, shrugged, then nodded again, as if he couldn't make up his mind. "Busy. The boss has been planning this for some weeks now."

"So it would seem," Alex said. He shot a glance over his shoulder, making sure his father was still occupied. "I see him for a few weeks, once a year, but you are around him all the time. I know he loved Nina Zhuk, but . . . this seems on the extreme side, even for him."

"Uncle Maxim loves who he loves, and hates who he hates, with a great passion." Gavrill shrugged again. "The rest of us follow his lead."

"Still—"

"Did you ever know Nina?"

Alex shook his head. "We were kids," he said. "What, fourteen or fifteen? I had other girls to occupy my mind. I didn't think much about my father's wife. And, anyway, I don't understand why he's doing all this for a woman who left him for a New Jersey gangster."

Gavrill's whisper was barely audible over the pattering rain. "I will tell you this. Nina Zhuk is much safer now that she is dead. I am quite certain Uncle Maxim would have snapped her pretty neck with a broomstick for leaving him if he'd had the opportunity. Perhaps a measure of his hate for Charlotte Morehouse is really leftover emotion for his Nina. He blames Nina for betraying him. He blames himself for being the sort of man whom she would betray, and he blames the judge for keeping his Nina in prison when she became ill. The only one he can do anything about is the judge. He plans to livestream her death, to make a big splash of it."

"An enigma, all right," Alex said.

"Anyway," Gavrill said, "we are all along for the ride. Yegon is Nina's brother. Lev and Ilia owe your father from prison, and, well, your father and I are blood. Your father's passions, his fights, are as good a reason as any to fight."

The men stood where they were, not wanting to make the boss look bad, since it usually took him a full two minutes to finish, and that was after numerous stops and starts. Finally he zipped his trousers and walked to the front of the van, putting one foot on the tire so he could stretch his hips.

Alex moved closer, keys in hand. If anything, the talk with his cousin had made him even more confused. Like the others, he waited for orders.

His father must have seen it in his face. "I wanted you here, Sasha," he said. "But you must not be directly involved in any of the funny business."

Alex bit his lip at that. *Funny business* . . . an apt description.

Maxim looked skyward, mouth open, letting the raindrops hit his tongue. At length he sighed and clapped his hands together in front of his waist. "It is time I told you. I am sick."

Alex perked up at the news. Lev Rudenko went pale.

Maxim Volkov might get the clap, but he was never "sick," certainly not bad enough to mention it.

Both the big Russian and the boy took a half step forward. Rudenko shook his head, slack-jawed. "Surely, your doctors—"

His father raised a hand to stop him. "No," he said. "They can do nothing but make me sicker while prolonging the inevitable. I had no idea I even had a pancreas, or what it did, until the doctors told me mine had decided to kill me."

Alex could not have been more stunned if his father had pulled out a gun and shot him. Maxim Volkov was as immortal as the volcanoes overlooking Petropavlovsk.

"Boss . . ." Rudenko said.

"How . . . how long do you have?" the boy stammered.

His father turned to stretch his hips again. "Let us just say, when all this is over, I will be dead. One way or another. So long as the bitch who killed your aunt Nina is dead as well, I do not mind going a little earlier than the doctors predict."

"But—"

"No buts, *zaychik*," Maxim said.

Alex bit his lip, grateful for the twilight so no one could see him tearing up. His father had not used this endearment—little rabbit—since Alex was eight years old.

"You have your Russian passport still?"

"Yes, Father." Alex grunted to cover the catch in his voice.

"Good," Maxim said. "Your uncle Oleg will see that you settle into your new role in the family business. Lev has agreed to return to Russia, as a favor to me, to make sure you are not challenged."

Alex turned to Oleg Pogodin. "You would be a much better candidate to lead."

"This is what I say to that!" Oleg loosed a proud fart. He laughed. "No, no, no, nephew. Heavy is the crown . . . I enjoy my status as it is."

Lev Rudenko touched Volkov's arm with a huge hand. "Your sickness, boss," he said. "It is not because of—"

"Not at all, my friend," Volkov said.

Gavrill gave Alex's shoulder a friendly smack. "We are here for your father, and we will be here for you."

"Enough with all this emotion," Maxim said. "You act like a bunch of old women. If we stand here too long, you will have me in the ground before I finish what I came here to do."

Maxim Volkov was not one to give an order twice, even when he was dying. Less than a minute later, Alex pulled the minivan north onto the Parks Highway, straight into the crosshairs of a state trooper.

The Russians had stayed several hundred meters apart from the time they left Anchorage. This would give Rudenko, behind the wheel of the big Ford, time to run interference if the need arose. As long as they remained within a basic line of sight, they were able to communicate over a pair of cheap FRS walkie-talkie they'd picked up from Walmart. They kept to obscure channels on the little walkie-talkies and spoke in code—usually.

"Kill your lights!" Maxim barked into his radio the moment he realized the oncoming car was law enforcement. He leaned sideways toward Alex. "Accelerate slowly, but do not give the impression you are running."

Rain began to fall in earnest, making windshield wipers a necessity.

Alex gripped the steering wheel, keenly aware of the Glock pistol shoved under the tail of his shirt. Carrying a concealed handgun wasn't illegal in Alaska, but you had to let the cop know you had it.

"*Suka!*" Maxim spat when the trooper whipped around to fall in behind them. He spoke into the radio again, using rapid Russian to communicate with Rudenko in the Ford. Alex understood most of it. "He must not be allowed to call in our license plate." Then, to Alex, still in Russian: "Accelerate slightly, but activate your turn signal, as if you plan to pull over."

Alex nodded and said, "Yes," showing he'd heard the order.

A second set of headlights loomed behind the trooper vehicle.

Maxim patted his son on the knee, his voice calm, steady. "This is important, Sasha. When you see Rudenko pull out beside the policeman, you must press the accelerator all the way to the floor. Do you understand?"

Alex barely had time to comply, let alone answer.

The world seemed to move in slow motion as Rudenko moved over as if to pass the speeding AST SUV, bringing the two sets of headlights side by side. Alex punched it. The little van shuddered, and then began to pull away, ever so slowly.

Behind them, in the rearview mirror, the two sets of headlights careened together like billiard balls, sending the smaller Trooper vehicle spinning off the roadway. Facing south again, the driver's-side wheels dropped off the shoulder, causing the SUV to flip onto its side before coming to a halt. Rudenko sped past, but slowed as soon as he could without losing control. He flipped a quick U-turn, putting him back next to the Trooper vehicle before all the debris had settled.

Maxim pounded the dash. "Pull over," he said. "But do not go back just yet."

Alex did as he was instructed, turning to watch Rudenko and Lipin swarm the overturned SUV. Rudenko's large silhouette was unmistakable as he vaulted onto the side of the vehicle and put a boot through the front passenger window, dropping inside. Flashes of gunfire cut through the gray-blue twilight.

Moments later, Rudenko's voice came over the radio. "Done."

"Was he able to call in?" Maxim asked.

"I am not certain," Rudenko said.

"I suppose it is too late to ask him?"

"Yes, boss," Rudenko said. "Sorry about that."

Uncle Oleg was out of the Ford too, and all three men began to push on the AST vehicle.

"Now we go back," Maxim said, patting the dash again.

Rudenko and the others had the Explorer on its wheels by the time Alex turned and made it to them.

Maxim rolled down his window and issued orders from the passenger seat. He had Alex remain in the van with him, in case they saw another vehicle and had to drive away.

"Get his phone," the mafia boss said. "Give it to me."

Lipin leaned into the vehicle, next to the lifeless form of the trooper, digging around until he came up with the mobile phone. He handed Maxim the portable radio off the trooper's belt as well. "No one is calling to check on him yet, boss," Lipin said. "That is a good sign he did not have a chance to call in."

"True," Maxim said. "Does he have a laptop computer?"

Lipin nodded. "He does, attached to a terminal in the car."

"Destroy it," Maxim said. "In case they are able to use it to track his whereabouts."

Rudenko pounded lightly on the van's hood, while Lipin did as he was told. The big Russian looked up and down the deserted highway. "You should go, boss, before someone comes along and sees you."

"Your plan for the car?" Maxim asked.

"We passed a trail into the woods a hundred meters or so past where we took our piss break. We'll drive it in, under some trees, and cover it with brush. Should keep it invisible, even from the air, unless they know where to start looking."

Maxim held up the trooper's phone. "I will help with that." He leaned out the window, an open hand shielding his eyes from the rain as he surveyed the scene along the road. "There is quite a lot of debris," he said. "The light bar from on top of his vehicle . . ."

Rudenko held up a mud-covered thermos. "His door must have flown open when the car flipped. Fortunately, the glass did not break. I believe we have gotten everything."

"Be sure," Volkov said. "Then join us as quickly as you can." He nodded at Alex, who put the van in gear.

The men had dragged the trooper into the passenger seat by the time Alex turned back to the north. Lipin now sat behind the marked vehicle's wheel, heading south.

"I have to say," Alex all but gushed, "that was a very smooth operation."

He smiled. "Maxim's Law of Force Dynamics, Sashenka. 'Audacity plus brutality equals victory.'" He shook his head in disgust. "Mercy amounts to failure."

"What will you do with the mobile phone?"

Maxim clicked on the visor light.

"Do you remember Federal'naya Sluzhba Bezopasnosti?" he asked while he studied a map.

"Yes," Alex said. "Russian Security Service."

"Exactly," Maxim said. "We have learned the hard way that the FSB can track the trail we leave with our mobile phones. I see no reason to doubt the police in the United States will do so with even more precision."

Alex eyed the phone. "I am sure they can. We should not have—"

"Easy, Sasha," Maxim said. "No one knows anything is amiss. We *want* them to see that the phone is traveling north, so when they realize the trooper is missing, they will begin their search there, instead of where we left him. There are many lakes to choose from along the road. I will make a call on the phone, to be certain there is a record once we have gone forty miles or so, then both the phone and the trooper radio will go in the water. That will expand their search considerably. By the time they find the trooper, you will be on your way to the motherland, and the Morehouse bitch will be dead in a very public way."

CHAPTER 18

*C*utter heard the shower come on at a quarter past three a.m. He was awake, anyway, so he threw on a pair of sweats and a T-shirt reading: SOUTHERN DISTRICT OF FLORIDA MARSHALS SERVICE.

Mim's shower ran long. Hopefully, she'd gotten more sleep than he had. Some scrambled eggs would be good medicine. He'd taught the twins how to make sourdough bread the weekend before and there was just enough left for toast if he ate the heel—which he preferred, anyway.

Mim walked into the kitchen about the same time the toaster popped.

Damp hair mopped the collar of a pink flannel shirt.

Cutter threw a cup towel over his shoulder and took the eggs off the heat.

"Good mornin'," he said. The first words he'd said to her since their disagreement the night before—a minefield of emotion.

"Smells good." Mim covered a yawn with the back of her hand. "I'm surprised my stomach's awake, but it is."

"You happen to check the weather in Utqiagvik?"

"I did." She looked at her watch before stepping past Arliss to grab two plates from the cupboard. A whiff of her shampoo hit him in the face, wobbling him.

"Thirty-four degrees on this balmy June morning," she said on her way to set the table. "It's supposed to get up to thirty-nine, so I'm good to go."

Cutter took a deep breath, thinking there was no convenient time to say what he was about to say.

"I'm sorry about yesterday."

Mim situated the plates and turned, leaning back against her hands on the edge of the table.

"I'm the one who should apologize." She tilted her head slightly, hair falling to one shoulder. "You're worried about my safety. That should make me happy, not piss me off." He started to say something, but she raised an open hand. "I'm still going north, though."

Cutter gave a crooked grin. "Hence the creamy scrambled eggs and toast. You need a breakfast that sticks to your ribs where you're going."

"There it is," she whispered.

"There what is?"

"Earning a smile from Arliss Cutter means something," she said. "They're scarce as . . . What did Grumpy used to say?"

"Could have been anything. 'Hen's teeth,' 'honest politicians,' 'whores in church.' Grumpy's metaphors reflected the moment." Cutter chuckled at the memory of his grandfather. "He wasn't much of a smiler either."

"But you were at one time," she said. "Even after I . . . You know what I mean."

"Why, I have no earthly idea," he said, Southern and stone-faced.

She groaned and threw back her head to stare at the ceiling. "You know, I spent most of the night thinking about you . . ."

"That hurts," Cutter said. "Not all night?"

"You're always so good about looking after me. I wish you'd let me return the favor."

"You're letting me make you eggs," he said. "That's not nothing."

"I think you're trying to change the subject."

He shook his head. "No, ma'am. I'm trying to keep you from changing the subject."

"I wish you'd talk to me."

"I think we're having some damned fine talks."

"I don't want to pry," she said. "It's just that . . . you seem so angry sometimes . . . I want to be there for you, the way you're here for me."

"You were," Cutter said. "Both you and Ethan kept me afloat when Barbara died."

"So," Mim said. "Let me be here for you now."

"What if you find out some truth about me, and then you pee down your leg and run off screaming in disgust?"

She shook her head, eyes sparkling. "If that's the bar you're setting, then I think we're good."

"It's not a short conversation," Cutter said. "How about we wait until you don't have to catch a plane."

"Okay," she said grudgingly. She eyed him hard, still leaning against the table.

"Call me tonight," he said. "After we're settled."

"Arliss . . . think about what I said."

"Mim, you're *all* I'm going to think about."

"And not getting shot," she said.

"Yeah," Cutter said. "That too."

CHAPTER 19

*L*ola tapped her bare foot on the carpet, scanning the mountain of gear spread out on her side of the bed as she ticked through her mental checklist. She'd barely had time to unpack from the St. Mary's trip and now she was going out again.

In truth, the frenzied pinball schedule of the Marshals Service suited Teariki's personality. On any given day she might find herself en route to the airport for a Witness Security assignment in LA, only to get a call from Cutter or the chief redirecting her to track down a bunch of fugitives in the Virgin Islands after a hurricane blew the walls of their prison down.

A loose MARSHALS SERVICE tank top revealed just enough side boob and panties to show Joe Bill she wasn't ignoring him while she packed. He lay on top of the sheets on the far side of the bed, wearing gym shorts, his hands folded on the pillow behind his head.

Her phone screen lit up on the bedside table. She'd missed a three a.m. call from Sam Benjamin, a trooper she'd dated . . . It seemed so long ago. He'd called in the middle of the night, but hadn't left a voice mail. She suspected he'd noticed the butt-dial and this was an apology text.

Nope. Just the damn phone telling her that her screen time was up 27 percent from the week before. Judgy little bastard. It wasn't her fault she'd spent half the last five days sitting in airports waiting on bush planes.

She returned the phone to its charger and kept packing.

Her condo was small, to begin with, making it difficult to distinguish the bedroom from a closet. She'd been in sailboats that had more room to walk around the bed. Her mother had come the year before to help her decorate. Despite her Japanese heritage she stayed mostly with the South Pacific theme of Lola's father's side of the family. On the wall nearest the bathroom she had hung a toothed spear, five feet long and made from the heavy red wood of the ironwood tree. Maori used the same word *toa* for the tree and for warrior. A signed Judith Kunzle drawing—a shapely Cook Island dancer, facing away, flower *ei* on her head, lithe arms outstretched, full hips moving a grass skirt—hung beside the spear. The energy was so evident in the sepia lines that Lola often fell asleep to the sound of wooden drums in the dim glow of her bathroom night-light. A small statue of Tangaroa, the fierce and extremely well-endowed Maori god of the sea, stood guard on top of her dresser. The figure was a joke from her three brothers to scare away all the runty white guys.

It didn't bother Joe Bill Brackett.

He glanced up from his phone. "I'm guessing it wasn't him?"

Lola had been open about Sam's earlier call.

"Nah," she said. "He was never the sort to call in the middle of the night."

"Probably a butt-dial. Like you said."

"Yeah," Lola said. "Probably." She fell forward on the bed, landing on top of her folded T-shirts so her face was next to Brackett's. "You don't seem too worried about a call from an old boyfriend."

He set the phone on his chest. "Should I be?"

"Not as long as you don't whinge about it."

"I love the words you use."

She ran a finger down the center of his chest. "Are you sad I have to go?"

He nodded. "Very. But I get it. Life of a federal lawwoman and all. I figure it's okay to be upset that you're leaving, but not mad that you go."

"You're, like, the perfect boyfriend."

She kissed him and then pushed away before they both got worked up again and wrecked all her folded clothes.

"He'll be here in an hour," Lola said.

"There are two dozen cars in your parking lot." Brackett banged the back of his head against the pillow. "I doubt he even knows what my pickup looks like."

"Cutter. Knows. All. Full stop."

Brackett gave a long growl of frustration. "Okay. I'll leave as soon as I'm able to walk again. That leg workout you put us through was . . . The best I can come up with is *horrible*."

"*Horribly* good." She set the charger for her handheld radio in an open suitcase. "Weighted lunges, squats, quad raises . . . yum."

Bracket stared down at his feet, chin to chest. "I've always had decent triceps," he said.

"Among other things," she added.

"But I think my legs owe the rest of my body an apology."

"Your legs work just fine, Mr. Brackett," she said, stuffing items in her suitcase willy-nilly now, knowing that if she looked up, she'd get distracted. Cutter really would be there in an hour.

She wedged two boxes of .40-caliber ammunition next to the radio charger, held in place with some sports bras, two pairs of khakis, and a couple of rolled polo shirts. Protective work could require everything from formal wear to fishing waders, but her primary responsibility on this assignment was the teenage daughter, so she usually went with business casual.

"Care if I check the news for a minute before I go?"

"I don't want you to go," she said. "I just want you to be ready for Cutter to go full batshit-crazy-uncle mode if he happens to be in a pissy mood."

Brackett laughed. "How could you tell with that guy? He always seems to be in a pissy mood."

"Believe me," Lola said, "you'd be able to tell."

"You gotta be kidding me!" Brackett said, sitting up straighter in bed.

"News?"

"You could say that. I don't know how I missed this. Early yesterday morning some guys in an inflatable Zodiac found a sixty-five-foot fishing boat partially sunk across Kachemak Bay from Homer."

"Partially?"

Brackett scanned the article on his phone. "Air pocket kept it from sinking. Ocean's only about two hundred feet deep in that spot, but if it had gone down, no one would have found it, not for a while at least."

"A Russian vessel?"

"Can't be that lucky," Brackett said, reading as he talked. "A crab boat called the *Esther Marie*. Looks like she'd been in the Bering Sea working the opelio fishery for the past two weeks. Was due in, anytime."

"And the crew?"

He looked up, wide-eyed, and pantomimed a little explosion beside his face. "Vanished."

Lola whistled, low and long, tossing over the possibilities in her mind. "I'm not seeing how a missing crab boat would have anything to do with some Russian dude's murder or the slaughter at a video gambling room?"

"Maybe it doesn't," Brackett said. "But if it does . . ."

Loaded like a pack mule, she rolled a Pelican rifle case across the parking lot with one hand and dragged a suitcase with the other. A large desert-tan duffel balanced on top. Her daypack was slung over her shoulders. She stopped in her tracks when she saw Cutter with his palm on the hood of Joe Bill Brackett's pickup.

"Stone cold," he said, patting the hood hard enough that it thumped. "It's been here awhile."

"Yep," she said.

He raised a brow, the rest of his expression as cool as the truck. "Need some help?"

"Why in the world would I need help, Cutter? Brackett's a good man. The last thing I need is for you to waltz in and—"

"I meant with your bags."

"Oh . . . yes." She took a sheepish breath and pushed the suitcase out in front of her. "You can take this one . . ."

Cutter rolled it to his G-ride, a little Ford Escape, and shoved it on top of his own bags.

"You get a call from Sam last night?"

She stopped again. "That's a weird thing to ask."

They'd both worked the fugitive and kidnapping case with Benjamin on Prince of Wales Island. Cutter had done several dives with him for evidence, though she doubted the two men had kept in touch for anything but professional matters.

"So, you did?"

"Yep," she said. "A butt-dial, I reckon. How do you know about it? Did he call you?"

Cutter climbed behind the wheel, waiting for Lola to shut her door before he continued. "Troopers can't seem to locate him."

"P O W is a big place," she said. "He could be on the other side of the island in some cove where there's no radio or phone coverage. You've been there."

"He's not on Prince of Wales," Cutter said, his forehead furrowed, working through some conundrum as he backed out of the parking lot and started for the airport. "AST had him on special assignment out of Talkeetna."

"Seriously? What's going on in little old Talkeetna?"

"Criminal Suppression Unit," Cutter said. "Smash-and-grab vehicle burglaries at remote parking lots. Sounds like he was patrolling the Parks Highway last night . . . and then went dark."

"That can't be good," Lola whispered, a pit in her gut.

"It's only been a few hours," Cutter said, as if trying to convince himself. "He's probably broken down on a back road with a dead battery and no phone reception."

"Did he check out on the radio?"

"No."

"Who was the last person to hear from him?"

Cutter glanced sideways as he drove. "That would be you."

CHAPTER 20

*T*he flight from Anchorage to Fairbanks was a quick forty-eight minutes. A strong westerly had blown away the clouds and Denali was out in force, showing off all snowcapped 20,310 feet off the left wing. The sight of "The Great One" on a clear day was nothing short of spectacular. Normally, Lola would have had her nose pressed to the window, but not today.

She tried Sam Benjamin's cell for the tenth time the moment the plane's wheels squawked on the tarmac. It went straight to voice mail. She left a message, begging him to call her back.

Cutter's mean mug had turned especially bleak. He did a lot of looking away, avoiding her eyes, which worried Lola all the more. For a time she thought he might send her home. There was a chance he still might, but with a Supreme inbound to Alaska, they needed all the eyes they could get for security.

"How you holding up?" he asked while they taxied to the gate.

"I'll be fine," Lola said. "Just worried."

He held up his phone, showing he had a text from the chief deputy. "Jill's offered us up to the Troopers to follow any tracks they find. She's calling in extra deputies from Washington and Oregon to help with the Morehouse detail if you and I get called away."

Lola perked up. "At least we'd be doing something—"

Cutter held up a hand. "AST doesn't have any place for us to start . . . yet."

"As long as there's a plan," Lola said. "This is so stuffed . . ."

They retrieved their bags and rented two vehicles, a Dodge Challenger and Subaru Legacy. Lola, or whoever replaced her, needed to be ready to split off the main detail and keep Ramona Morehouse entertained when her mother was busy hobnobbing with Alaska judges.

The conference venue was within spitting distance of the airport, nestled into a wide bend of the Chena River. Cutter gave Lola the Challenger and followed in the Subaru. They made the trip in less than five minutes.

The Alaska Bar Association held a yearly conference, usually alternating between Juneau, Anchorage, and Fairbanks. Virtually every attorney and judge in the state, including those from the US Attorney's Office and the federal bench, showed up, attending seminars, cocktail parties, and socializing with old friends. This year judges would arrive two days early for a series of events catered specifically to them. Judges were a mercurial bunch, to begin with, but put them all in the same room, add a little alcohol, and the situation could be a nightmare for the people tasked with protecting them.

To make matters worse, the event was advertised, giving any manifesto-writing crazy who'd ever wanted some face time with a member of the bench plenty of advance notice. Unlike a visit to the courthouse, there were no metal detectors or X-ray machines to contend with. Anyone could walk into the hotel like they were guests themselves, scope out their pet judge, and vent their spleen—or worse.

Alaska State Troopers investigated threats to state judges. They'd originally assigned four troopers, but two of those were leaving the parking lot at the same time as Lola and Cutter arrived, no doubt on their way to assist in the search for their missing coworker.

Cutter led the way inside, moving quickly, purposefully, intent on keeping Lola's mind on the duties at hand until they were relieved.

A Belgian Malinois explosive-detection K9 and his handler, Army Specialist Lopez from Fort Wainwright, stood inside the door, acting more as a psychological deterrent at the moment. By tradition the dog was one rank higher than the handler, making it a sergeant. The team wouldn't sweep the event room until a couple hours before Justice Morehouse's opening remarks later that evening. Cutter automatically gave Specialist Lopez a gruff "hooah" to show Army solidarity.

"Hooah, sir," the specialist said.

The dog cocked an ear his way, sizing Cutter up.

Most attending judges wouldn't arrive until that afternoon. Vendors from companies like Westlaw and LexisNexis were in the process of setting up displays in the foyer off the main event halls.

Supervisory Deputy Scott Keen was already on-site tasking his minions from the small first-floor side room the Bar Association had given them as a command post.

Lola began peppering him with questions the moment she and Cutter walked in.

"Any word on Sam?"

Keen looked up from the bank of radio chargers he was fiddling with.

"His cell pinged off a tower near Cantwell, a little after three a.m. Troopers are concentrating their search around there."

Rich Hooten poked a pasty head through the door of the CP. A defense attorney in Fairbanks, he'd done a stint as a part-time federal magistrate judge, and threw the title around like a battle-axe. He'd rolled the sleeves of his white shirt up to show off his new IWC Portugesier Perpetual Calendar watch. Anyone unlucky or foolish enough to talk to him longer than thirty seconds learned that the watch cost over forty thousand dollars. He never mentioned he'd made the purchase with his daddy's money. He spent an inordinate amount of time gazing at the watch, but rarely ever knew what time it was.

He didn't bother with waiting for a lull in the conversation.

"You guys talking about the missing trooper?" Hooten gave a low whistle. "I hear they can't find his patrol car either. That sucks mightily . . . My guess is they'll find it downriver. Bad deal all around."

"Yes, it is," Cutter said.

"So," Hooten said, continuing his original thought as if they'd been talking about the weather, "what do you think about taking the justice out to see the Pipeline?"

"I think we're in the middle of something," Lola said.

Cutter gave his partner a nudge, then eyed the former part-time magistrate.

Keen raised a hand before Cutter could speak. "We're bringing it up with the inspector."

"I'll talk to Judge Markham about it—"

"Outstanding," Cutter said. "Now, if you'll excuse us, we're kinda busy here, counselor."

"Hey," Hooten said, both hands up, palms open. "I'm sorry about the missing trooper, I truly am. But Justice Morehouse is coming to visit, no matter who happens to have driven into the river. She might as well have a good time—"

Lola wheeled on him. "Seriously?"

"I said go," Cutter said, inches from the man's face. "Now!"

"If you were in my court," Hooten sneered. "I'd—"

Cutter darkened. "Which court is that exactly?"

"You know what?" Hooten wagged his head. "Law enforcement, in general, has a serious image problem, but I've gotta say, you marshals are the surliest collection of assholes I've ever come across." He tossed his chin toward Cutter. "And you appear to be the head honcho."

"Nope," Cutter said, hooking a thumb over his shoulder at Keen. "That would be Scott."

Lola came up on tiptoe, glaring daggers. "I'm sure it hasn't occurred to you, but this surly bunch of assholes is stuck here protecting the likes of you, while others are out searching for one of our friends."

Hooten's hands came up again, surrendering. "Okay, I get it. You're worried. Sorry. But you don't have to be dicks about it."

Cutter raised his index finger. "Do yourself a favor and quit with 'sorry.'"

Both Lola and Cutter turned their backs on the attorney, who, with no one left to argue with, got bored and went to show someone else his watch.

Cutter took a look at the folders on Keen's desk.

"Need us to help with advances?"

Ideally, "advances" would be done well before Justice Morehouse arrived. This allowed deputies to find motorcade parking, alternate exits, and safe rooms in the event of an attack or medical emergency. More important, it gave them a chance to get a feel for the mood of the place.

Early in Cutter's career, the chief deputy in Miami had deemed him too intense to interact personally with any members of the judiciary and he was often assigned as advance. There were so many bigwigs visiting Miami that Cutter felt sure he'd spent half his early career checking out swanky restaurants or walking the bowels of conference hotels along the beach.

Keen shoved three folders across the desk toward Cutter.

"Take your pick. The Turtle Club restaurant in Fox, the university museum, or the Santa Claus House in North Pole."

Lola snatched up the folder that was marked *NP* on the tab. "Too early for prime rib at the Turtle Club," she said. "And I've seen the museum a half-dozen times."

"Knock yourself out." Keen checked his watch. "The justice's plane is wheels-down at two thirty-five. That gives you time to do a couple of stops. Her first event is here, tonight, but tomorrow night she's doing a Q and A at an intimate little theater in the woods, between here and North Pole. Check that out too."

"Sure," Lola said.

"Just do me a favor and make sure they've moved the dance cages outside."

Lola cocked a hip and flipped open the folder. "Dance cages?"

"Most nights of the week the place is a normal bar," Keen said. "Dance floor and a small stage for doing standup comedy, open-mic night, shit like that. But apparently, they have open-pole night every Tuesday. Management assures me the cages and poles are removable."

"Open-pole night," Lola muttered, as though it wasn't a half-bad idea. "That's rich."

Keen put a hand on the remaining two folders and glanced up at Cutter. "You going with your work wife, or do you want to help me out on one of these?"

Cutter took a deep breath. "Deputy Teariki, would you mind checking outside for witnesses?"

"Good idea," she said, but stayed put, glaring, eyes wide. "Wouldn't want anyone to see you put a boot up his ass."

Keen raised both hands. "Just yanking your chain, you guys. Lighten up."

Cutter eyed Keen like he was food. "I'll take the Museum of the North at UAF," he said, his jaw clenched, voice low and husky.

Keen slid him the file. "Seriously, Cutter, think about switching to decaf."

"You should try milk," Lola said.

"What are you talking about?" Keen scoffed. "Milk?"

"It's good for your teeth," Lola said. She put both hands on the desk and leaned across, peering down at Keen. "You know what else is good for your teeth, Scotty? Never calling me anybody's *work wife* again."

He outranked her, but she didn't care.

Cutter looked at his watch and then turned without another word.

"Hooten's right about one thing," Lola said once they were in the hall. "Keen is an asshole."

"Yep," Cutter said. "And that asshole could easily be our next chief."

CHAPTER 21

*C*utter had been to the Museum of the North three times before. Twice for work and once with Mim and the kids. He knew the layout well, so the advance took just long enough to give the curator his card, double-check the fire exits, and make sure nothing drastic had changed.

If he'd not had another pressing appointment, he might have spent some time looking at the huge fossilized skull of a cave bear that had canine teeth the size of his thumb. He liked to study fellow predators.

Advance completed, Cutter stood in the parking lot beside his rental car, phone to his ear.

Fairbanks and the rest of Interior Alaska often saw summer temperatures much warmer than Anchorage, sometimes even in the nineties. This summer hadn't gotten the message. A chilly wind blew in from the north, bringing the sticky sweet odor of birch trees. Intermittent drops of rain pecked his face with cold kisses.

Two months earlier, Officer Jan Hough of the North Slope Borough Police Department had given Cutter the information about one of Ethan's coworkers named Erica Bell. That meant sixty excruciating days of not being able to talk to someone who might have information on his brother's murder. Hough had also confided the rumors that both she and Bell had been involved in affairs with Ethan before his death. The rumors weren't true, Hough assured Cutter of that, but there had been some sort of relationship with Bell. She suspected Ethan was helping the young woman with some personal problem. It seemed more than one Cutter brother had a Tarzan complex—instinctively swinging in to save the day.

Cutter had attempted to meet with Bell four different times, but schedules, geography, and, Cutter suspected, something a little more sinister conspired to keep the meeting from happening. JBM Engineering had transferred her from Anchorage to Fairbanks and kept her on frequent trips to Deadhorse.

Now they were in the same town, at the same time.

Bell picked up just before the call went to voice mail. Her voice fell to a tentative whisper the moment Cutter introduced himself.

"I . . . I've been meaning to return your calls," she said. "I really have." Then, more forcefully to someone else, "Just a minute."

Horns honked in the background.

"It sounds like you're in traffic," Cutter said. "Are you okay?"

"You have the same voice as him," she said. "Same tone."

"We got that a lot," Cutter said.

"They're on their way," Bell snapped.

"Who?" Cutter said.

"Sorry," Bell said, softer again. "I was talking to someone else. The truth is, I've been in a fender bender. I can't reach my husband."

"Where are you?"

"Creamer's Field," she said. "Do you know it?"

"I know Google Maps," Cutter said, trying to lighten her mood—a skill better suited to Lola Teariki.

"Okay." She sighed, resigned. "I'll be the short woman in the blue Volkswagen accordion."

What was once the Creamer family dairy was now a waterfowl sanctuary, twenty-two hundred acres, a frequent stopover for thousands of sandhill cranes and other migrating birds. Cutter made the three-mile drive up College Avenue in a matter of minutes.

Erica Bell's VW Jetta was easy to spot, the front quarter caved in where she'd rear-ended an older-model Ford dually. The pickup had little damage, but the Jetta's radiator spewed a steady spray of steam. The driver's-side door was slightly ajar, canted downward like a broken wing.

Dressed in pressed jeans and a blue Patagonia rain jacket, Bell leaned against the pickup, chatting through the open window with the driver. Dark, shoulder-length hair was just beginning to grow damp from the drizzle. She hooked a thumb over her shoulder. The other driver, a bearded guy in a ballcap, leaned out of his pickup and eyed Cutter before driving away.

"I expected you to look different," Bell said after Cutter shook her hand. "I don't know, maybe darker, like Ethan."

Cutter tried the damaged car door, swinging it back and forth. It moved, but made a lot of noise in the process.

"Doesn't latch," he said. "You must have hit pretty hard. You sure you're okay?"

The woman shrugged. "Necks a little stiff," she said. "I'm sure I'll be sore tomorrow."

"You didn't call the police?"

"Oh, I called them," she said. "They were going to be a while. We just decided to exchange insurance information and do the report online. I thought my car was drivable . . ."

Cutter opened and closed the door again. "Wouldn't be a good idea."

"I see that now." She eyed the geyser of steam. "Wrecker's on the way . . ." She gave a sad chuckle. "*Wrecker* . . . that's what they called me on the Slope. Home-wrecker. I suppose that's what you want to talk to me about."

She'd been dodging his calls for weeks, but now she'd gotten straight to the point.

"You don't believe them, do you?" she said. "The rumors, I mean. Ethan was a good guy. He wasn't . . ."

"No," Cutter said. "I don't."

Bell sat back against her crumpled car, one arm across her chest while she gnawed on a fingernail. She gave a disgusted shrug. "There are some guys on the Slope . . . anywhere, really . . . who think the only possible reason you won't sleep with them is because you're getting it elsewhere. I guess that's just easier on their egos."

"And people thought you and Ethan—"

"They thought all kinds of shit." She nodded, tearing up. "That's what people do. But we were just friends. I swear. He was only helping me out . . ."

"Helping you how?" Cutter prodded.

She groaned, hugging herself tighter, staring up at the clouds. "A couple of the guys at one of the equipment companies were sending me some pretty intense texts. No dick pics or anything, but they were on the verge of explicit. My husband and I were already having problems and I didn't need that kind of crap."

"The person sending the texts," Cutter said. "He was on the Slope with you?"

"Yeah," she said. "They have safety protocols about that sort of thing and are usually pretty good. But you know what? One person's zero tolerance is another person's 'let's see if this blows over.' I mentioned it to Ethan, just in passing, mind you. Whoa! I did not expect his reaction. He swooped in and told the guy he'd cut his eggplant off if he didn't leave me alone. Word got out and everyone naturally assumed Ethan had claimed me for his own."

Cutter gave a disgusted shake of his head. "That's—"

"I know, right?" she said. "Neanderthal . . . and that's slandering Neanderthals. It wasn't like that at all."

"How was it, then?"

"Ethan treated me like a kid sister, especially when he thought I was in trouble." She looked up at Cutter, her face pinched with emotion. "I'm afraid I'm the one who got him killed."

Cutter waited for her to continue, but she just stood there, shuddering with pent-up sobs.

"You think the man sending you all those texts killed my brother?" he asked softly. It was a herculean effort not to sound threatening when he wanted to rip this guy's arm off and stab him to death with the bloody bone.

"No, no," she said. "Not him. I mean, I don't think so. I don't know for sure what happened. I mean, I thought I did, but that turned out to be nothing."

Cutter groaned, forcing himself to remain passive. This poor woman was wound tight enough to snap. "What turned out to be nothing?"

"The books," she said, like Cutter should have already known. "Accounting discrepancies. But they turned out to be nothing. A nonissue. Really."

"Every detail is important," Cutter said. "What kind of discrepancies?"

"Phantom accounts, you know, like shell companies, but Coop went over the numbers, line by line, with me later. There was a logical explanation for everything. Even Ethan said it was probably—"

"Just a minute," Cutter said. "Did you say *Coop*?"

"Cooper Daniels, yeah. He's an attorney in Anchorage. Most everybody calls him 'Coop.' He did some work for . . ." Her head suddenly snapped to the right. She maneuvered herself behind Cutter, using him as a shield.

"What is it?"

"My asshole husband," she said. "This is the last thing I need . . ."

CHAPTER 22

*C*utter turned to see a man in a gray hoodie bail out of a new-model Dodge pickup as if it were on fire. He was tall, at least six-three. Big hands clinched into tight fists. A blocky head sat on top of square shoulders—a Lego character come to life, and a frowny one at that.

Marty Bell gave his wife a sideways sneer and marched to the steaming Volkswagen. As he got closer, Cutter noticed the octagon logo of a Fairbanks mixed martial arts gym.

"What kind of horseshittery have you gotten us into now?"

Erica took a half step to one side, keeping Cutter between them. "There's a tow truck on the way."

Marty glared at Cutter. "You the other driver?"

"The other driver left," Erica said. "I have his information."

Marty kicked at the VW's front end, then spun toward his wife. "What do I have to do to get you to pull your head outta your ass—"

"Hey!" Cutter barked. "That is enough!"

Bell shook his head as if to clear blurry vision.

"Who are *you?*"

"Name's Cutter," he said. "I'm with the US Marshals."

"Well, Marshal, this is between me and my wife."

"And me," Cutter said, dead calm. "You need to step back."

Bell rolled his shoulders, posturing, like a bull moose showing he had the larger set of antlers.

"Okay, Marty," Erica said, sliding around Cutter. "Calm down. I'll take care of the insurance and—"

"Oh, you're right about that." Bell grabbed her arm, herding her toward the pickup. Erica jerked away.

"Knock it off!" Cutter barked.

Bell spun to face him, less than six feet away—kick-in-the-face distance. He stood there panting, nostrils flaring. His head began to shake with rage.

Cutter, his back to the damaged VW now, shooed the woman toward his rental car. Instead of complying, she rushed back to her husband's side and attempted to calm him. He loomed above her, rooted in place, staring at Cutter.

"Come on, Marty." She tugged on his elbow, pleading now. "You can go on back home. I'll wait for the tow—"

"Get in the truck!" Bell said through his teeth. He never took his eyes off Cutter. There was something about this guy . . .

Erica's voice became more childlike, pleading now. "Come on, Marty. Just leave it—"

"I said, Get. In. The. Truck!"

Cutter kept his weight centered. Ready. Men who bullied women were often thought of as weak. And they were. But that didn't mean they weren't dangerous. Pitiful? Yes. Void of morals? Sure. But anger, the real, palpable stuff that was boiling out of Marty Bell at the moment, combined with whatever he may have picked up in his mixed martial arts gym, needed to be taken seriously. All it took was a spark to set it off.

But Cutter was angry too, so he decided to light a match—and throw gasoline on it.

"She's not going with you," he said smugly, as if he'd already won. Then, hands hanging easy at his sides while the other man shook and fumed, Cutter gave him a little wink.

It was like flipping a switch.

Bell bowed his head and rushed forward, intent on taking Cutter down.

Ground fighting had its place, and real violence often ended up on the concrete or in the mud. But rolling on the ground could be problematic when you were carrying a gun, or, as in Cutter's case, two guns.

He'd known ahead of time Bell would charge him. He had that bum-rush look about him.

Cutter feinted to the right, like a matador, drawing the other man's attack in that direction. Then he jerked the VW's damaged door open as far as it would go. An inch to the left and Bell would have split his head against the edge, and frankly, Cutter would have been fine with that. But the man sailed past, as if he were diving into the driver's seat.

"Nope!" Cutter shoved the door, knocking Bell sideways.

He staggered out of the way, dazed. Panting, he raised his hands. "Okay . . . I'm done . . ."

Cutter knew better. The man's open hands said he'd given up, but his low shoulder and offset feet said he was about to throw a punch. His eyes zeroed in on a target, further telegraphing his intentions. Evidently, his martial arts coach hadn't gotten to that lesson yet.

Bell's shoulder dropped a hair, a split second before he brought a surprisingly quick left jab, hook combination. Cutter saw it coming and got his hands up, but the hook slipped in over his guard and rattled him in the temple.

Cutter had never considered himself a boxer. Oh, Grumpy had worked with him, but he was just as likely to pick up a stick or a book or grab a handful of hair. Ethan had called him a very angry man more than once.

Thinking he'd achieved the upper hand with the hook, Bell stepped back to assess. Cutter dropped his right hand a hair, exposing the same ear. Bell took the bait and tried the jab again. Cutter stepped to his right, letting the punch slip by as he came over the top of the other man's arm with a devastating right.

Bell staggered forward, slamming into the Volkswagen.

"Stop . . . You . . . win . . ." His hands shot up, open, surrendering for real this time. Blood poured from a deep gash over his eyebrow, where one of Cutter's rights had connected. "I'm . . . I'm leaving."

"A little late for that," Cutter said. "Get on your face."

Bell grimaced like he'd been hit again. "What?"

"You're under arrest."

Bell raised his fists. "You're not . . ."

Cutter sent another jab, followed by a quick uppercut that cracked like a rifle shot. Bell listed sideways, legs buckling.

"I can do this all day," Cutter whispered, resisting the urge to hit the asshole again as he fell. "On your face!"

Bell rolled onto his belly, bringing his hands behind his back, apparently familiar with the position.

His words came out tremulous, sounding like a pleading child. "Wh . . . what are you arresting me for?"

"Assault." Cutter put a knee against the man's ribs and ratcheted on a pair of bright red handcuffs he took from a case on his belt.

"This is bullshit!" Bell turned his head to the side, blood and bits of gravel embedded in his cheek and lips. "Assaulting who?"

"Your wife," Cutter said, "me . . . both."

A short siren blast caused Cutter to raise both hands. Now was not the time to reach for his badge or credentials.

He turned to see a female Fairbanks PD officer get out of her patrol car, pistol in hand. She stood behind the A pillar and her open door.

Erica or someone must have called 911.

A second patrol car skidded onto the scene a half second later.

"US Marshals," Cutter said, hands in the air.

He explained the situation and gave the officers his contact information for their case reports. Marty Bell turned out to be a frequent flier at Fairbanks Correctional and they were all too happy to take him back. The female officer slapped on her cuffs and returned the red pair to Cutter.

"I'll get you a copy of my use-of-force report," Cutter said, absent-mindedly rubbing his knuckles.

The officer gave him a slow nod. "Not saying he didn't deserve it. But you did quite a number on him."

"He was getting rough with his wife." Cutter shrugged. "I stepped in."

"Simple as that," the officer said.

"Simple as that."

"And you beat the hell out of him," the officer said. "That happen often?"

"More than you'd imagine," Cutter said.

"I don't know." The officer looked him up and down. "Lookin' at you, I can imagine a lot."

* * *

"Tell me more about Coop Daniels," Cutter said after the Fairbanks PD officers had gone.

Erica dabbed at her arm where her husband had grabbed her.

"What an asshole," she muttered; then she looked up at Cutter. "Thank you. For stepping in. Marty gets crazy about his vehicles. The wreck was my fault. I guess he kind of had a point."

"He did not have a point." Cutter closed his eyes and took a slow, cleansing breath. There was little reason to try and school this poor woman about what kind of man her husband was. If she didn't see it from his behavior, nothing Cutter could say would convince her.

"Tell me about Coop Daniels," he said again.

"Not much to tell," Bell said. "He's our traveling lawyer. For the firm, I mean."

"*Traveling* lawyer?"

"You know," Bell said. "He goes all over, the Slope, Fairbanks, lower forty-eight. We have a North Sea office. He takes lots of trips to Scotland, like the others."

"Cooper Daniels works for JBM?"

"On retainer," she said. "But yeah. He's definitely on the payroll."

CHAPTER 23

*T*he cabdriver swung by the whalebone arch on his way from the airport to the hospital—something he said he always did for first-timers to Utqiagvik. Mim recognized the ten-foot ribs immediately from posters and travel books—overlooking the Arctic Ocean like a portal to a prehistoric time. Ethan was the one who traveled. He had the adventures. She'd stayed home and raised the kids—where it was safe.

Mim hadn't admitted it to anyone—even herself—but this whole living-in-fear thing was getting on her nerves. She was tired of being afraid. There was plenty to worry over in the far north. She had no real statistics to back it up, but the chances of dying in this perpetually frozen place seemed exponentially greater than at home snug in her house.

Utqiagvik had reverted from the more familiar Barrow to its Iñupiat name, which meant "a place for digging roots." Ethan had spent almost as much time working out of JBM's small office in this town of around four thousand people as he had in Deadhorse. His friendly demeanor guaranteed that most everyone in town would be familiar with the Cutter name.

Mim felt especially pleased with herself for telling the lady in the hospital's personnel office to use her maiden name on her ID badge.

Miriam Miller had a nice ring to it.

Arliss would be proud. "PerSec," he called it, personal security, looking after your own skin.

Her supervising nurse practitioner's office was a short walk from HR. Samuel Simmonds Memorial had the new-paint-and-disinfectant smell common to every hospital, making her feel at home. Nurses and orderlies smiled politely as she passed them in the hall. A Native man in his late teens entered the back hallway from the lobby. He was dressed in civilian clothes, not scrubs like everyone else. A white patch the size of a silver dollar stood out above his ear in stark contrast to his otherwise coal-black hair.

Mim assumed he wanted directions and slowed to help as best she could, while, at the same time, a doctor stepped out of an adjacent door and nearly bowled her over.

When she looked up, the younger man was gone.

The doctor apologized and glanced at her badge. "Ah, you're Ethan's wife."

She felt the blood drain from her face. "You knew Ethan?"

"For years," the doc said. A somber nod. "Decades, really. He did an internship summer up here—"

"Before our last year of college," Mim said.

"That's right," the doc said. "I was fresh out of med school and paying back my time by working in the bush. I ended up just staying. So great he was able to spend so much time up here . . . Anyway, he was a terrific guy, your husband. I was so sorry to hear about what happened." The doctor looked at his watch, getting that bouncy look that came over physicians when they had to be somewhere and knew they would not quite make it on time. It was similar to how the twins looked when they needed to pee, but steadfastly refused to leave their video game.

"I'm Dr. Fleckenstein," he said, extending his hand. "But everyone calls me 'Dr. Rob.' I have to run, but I'll buy you dinner some evening during your rotation. That is, when we're both not up to our elbows in a ruptured appendix or something."

"I'd like that," Mim said, thinking it would be a good idea to make as many friends as possible at the edge of the world. Dr. Rob disappeared through a set of double doors and Mim continued down the polished corridor to report to the nurses' station. She decided not to mention anything to Arliss about the ID badge . . . or that she already had a date with Dr. Rob.

* * *

The morning was filled with paperwork and a tour of Samuel Simmonds Memorial. Mim's eventual focus as a nurse practitioner would be emergency medicine, but generalists were always at a premium in rural Alaska. She'd help out with the walk-in clinic and anywhere else they needed to put her during this short rotation. Stomachaches and eye infections had the potential to turn into emergencies fast when you were five hundred miles by air from Fairbanks.

Darika Khatri, the supervising nurse, was a few years older than Mim, maybe fifty. She was tall, built like a runner, with ramrod posture so perfect that it seemed judgmental. Then she spoke and her incredible kindness came out on a sort of purr that put Mim immediately at ease. Darika was from New York, but she'd been in Alaska for well over a decade, all of that time in Utqiagvik. Oddly enough, she'd been drawn northward when she'd discovered the vampire movie *30 Days of Night* that was set in a fictional Barrow-like town. Though they were close to the same age, Khatri's hero was an Indian-American astronaut named Sunita Williams, a former space shuttle commander and International Space Station veteran. With opportunities to go to space slim indeed, Khatri reasoned that a place where the sun was absent for months at a time would be like another planet.

"Coming somewhere so different is a great deal to absorb on your first day," she said, sounding motherly. "We'll hit the ground running bright and early tomorrow . . . Go on and get settled in your hotel tonight."

"But you'll call me if there's an emergency?"

"Of course." Khatri smiled, like she was explaining something to a child. "We are a very small community. If there's an emergency, you'll know, because everyone will likely know." She heaved a deep sigh. "I hope you'll consider coming back for a rotation with us in the winter."

Mim chuckled. "It's plenty chilly for me now."

"But it *is* light," Khatri said. "You should totally experience the Arctic during the dark time. The northern lights are beyond . . . well, anything."

"I'd like to see it," Mim said.

"Of course," Khatri said, giving a pensive shrug. "There are also polar bears . . . but you should keep an eye out for them at all times of the year."

"Even now?"

"You'll be just fine, so long as you don't stay out too late. The fewer people, the more likely you are to see a bear. Might be a few drunk souls wandering around. Even though it's light, better not to be out on the streets too late."

"Got it," Mim said, giving a cooperative smile. Staying out late was exactly what she planned to do.

Given the choice of a loaner pickup that she could get in two hours or an ATV she could have immediately, Mim chose the latter. The hospital custodian's eyes flashed in disbelief, then gave way to something Mim thought might have been respect at her willingness to brave the Arctic elements on an open four-wheeler. Five minutes after he'd given her the key, she realized the man's look hadn't been respect at all, but pity. The thermometer at the hospital, cruelly placed so you were forced to look at it before stepping out the door, had lied when it claimed thirty-seven degrees.

Her loaner was a dark blue Yamaha four-wheeler, the body of which was more duct tape than original parts. Tufts of yellow foam padding stuck out from what was left of the fake leather seat cover. The muffler had a crack that roared like an outlaw biker's ride. The front fenders were missing altogether. But it started right up, so she didn't care.

"Pretty is as pretty does," she said to herself.

The custodian called it a "Honda," but Mim had been in Alaska long enough to know bush residents referred to all ATVs as "Hondas," no matter what make or model—just as all soft drinks were "Cokes" where she came from, even Dr Pepper.

Her wool beanie low over her ears, head drawn into her parka, Mim hunched over the handlebars of her Yamaha Honda, and thumbed the throttle lever on the right handlebar. She instantly regretted her decision to bring gloves instead of winter mittens. A bitter sea wind ripped away her breath when she jagged north on Ahmaogak Avenue, knobby tires chattering over the muddy street.

The wind didn't come in gusts, but one long blow, like a humongous fan up on the North Pole. Low clouds fused sky and ice, so there was no horizon, only a great gray nothingness.

Thirty-seven degrees, my ass!

Her fingers cramped. Watering eyes sent half-frozen tears streaming along her cheeks. Her teeth began to ache and it took her a while to realize it was because of her ear-to-ear smile. She was *finally* doing something, moving forward instead of hiding at home spinning her wheels. Investigating Ethan's murder *should* hurt, or, at the very least, be uncomfortable.

Chilled and thrilled to the bone by the time she turned into the parking lot of the Top of the World Hotel, Mim decided she desperately needed to get some food in her stomach. The hotel's restaurant, Niggivikput—our place to eat, in Iñupiat—looked decent enough. She shucked off her hat and gloves and went straight in, ordered a cup of coffee, and hunched over it like it was a campfire.

The vast majority of bush villages had no restaurants or hotels. Most had some kind of store, though that might be milk crates stacked in the front room of someone's home. Travelers' meals often consisted of freeze-dried food cooked over a camp stove or a military-style MRE. In villages that did have a store, milk could cost fourteen dollars a gallon, a jar of peanut butter well over twenty bucks.

If there was a restaurant, burgers ranged from passable to school-lunch hockey pucks. Salads could be iffy, but Arliss said he'd never had a bad French dip, no matter where he was. It was hard to mess up a wet-bread sandwich.

Mim ordered, then leaned back in her booth, eyes closed, and considered her next move. The senior JBM engineer in Utqiagvik was Phil Hopkin. She'd only met him a couple of times at office parties, but Ethan always spoke highly of him. He'd been on the Slope when Ethan died. Whatever he knew, it was surely more than she did.

He sounded startled when she called, and quickly apologized, assuring her that while he didn't feel comfortable speaking over the phone, he would have loved to talk to her in person. Unfortunately, he was "working clear up in Utqiagvik at the moment" and was sadly unavailable. He promised to contact her the very next time he was in Anchorage.

She'd let him make his promises and then broke the news that she was right down the muddy street from him and she would love to get together at his earliest convenience. Trapped, he squirmed and stammered, trying to crawfish out of his agreement to meet. He was on a project out at Ilisagvik College, north of the lagoon, and didn't know how late he would be. She probably didn't have a car, anyway. Tomorrow would be better. On and on . . . one thing was sure, this guy was scared shitless about something. That was evidence in and of itself. Evidence of what remained to be seen. His fear should have bothered her, or, at the very least, made her more wary. It only made her more determined.

When pressed, Hopkin admitted there were people in his firm who would take a dim view of him talking with Ethan's widow, what with the previous litigation and all. They would have to be extremely discreet. He agreed to meet, but not until ten thirty that night. She would have to drive out to the high school football field away from any witnesses.

A quick look at Google Maps showed the Barrow High School field, covered in a startling blue artificial turf, was located along the coastal road north of Ilisagvik College, six miles from the end of the road. In this case the end of the road was just that, the terminus of the northernmost highway in the United States.

Arliss always said it was better to arrive at a meeting far earlier than your adversary did. While Phil Hopkin wasn't exactly an adversary, she had virtually forced him into meeting with her. On top of that, he'd picked one of the most out-of-the-way places in Utqiagvik, so she decided she'd get there with enough time to scope it out before he arrived—looking for what, she did not really know. She couldn't very well ask Arliss: *"Hey, I'm riding a four-wheeler out to meet some guy tonight. We'll probably be away from any witnesses. Anything in particular I should be watching for . . . ?"*

She groaned, beating her head softly against the back of her booth. Simply arriving early wasn't much of a plan . . .

She opened her eyes to find two men in tan Carhartt jackets and wool hats sitting in the booth diagonally across from her. One looked to be Native, the other was blond, shaggy like Arliss. Muddy clothes and windburned skin said they worked outside. Their faces appeared to be frozen into permanent scowls, but the beards and hats made it difficult to discern anything else about them. They'd been studying her. She was sure of that, but they both ignored her as soon as she looked up.

Were they just lonely guys, miles from their wives or girlfriends, scoping out the new nurse in town? Or were they thugs from JBM? She laughed at herself for the thought. That sounded like something Grumpy would have said: *"thugs from JBM."*

They ordered French dips, so if they were thugs, they were smart thugs.

Mim convinced herself she was being melodramatic and tucked into her sandwich, even scarfing down every last fry. Not a bad meal for twenty-six bucks, including the coffee. Exactly what she needed to get her warm for her ATV ride—that and the layer of merino wool long johns she put on before she went to her meeting at the end of the road.

It might as well be the end of the world.

CHAPTER 24

*L*ola badged her way through Fairbanks Airport security with Scott Keen and Dave Dillard an hour before wheels-down. Like everyone else on the Morehouse detail, Lola wore a clear silicone earpiece connected by a pigtail and beige wires to a small mic pinned to her collar and the Motorola radio on her belt. She felt a pang of pity for her friends in the Secret Service who had to be "on" all the time with their principal. Protective work was a nice change of pace, but she wasn't keen on doing it every day.

The motorcade vehicles idled curbside, staged near the Arrival doors. It wasn't every day that a justice of the United States Supreme Court ventured this far north, and a marked Fairbanks PD patrol car was at the front of the line. Behind the FPD unit, Paul Gutierrez, a Fairbanks suboffice deputy, waited in the blue Tahoe that had been designated as the "limo" for this protective detail. The Chevy was a new arrival from USMS Fleet Services. It still had a new-car smell and had yet to collect the spring squeaks and rock chips of an Alaska winter. More important for this event, it had not yet been used to haul prisoners. As the detail supervisor, Ninth Circuit Judicial Security Inspector Nicki Sloan would ride in the front passenger seat of the limo, within arm's reach of the justice.

Deputy Paige Hart stood on the sidewalk beside an older Tahoe that would serve as the "follow," carrying the bulk of the protection detail, at least two of whom would be armed with rifles.

Gutierrez had enough time with the Marshals Service to cloister himself inside the limo and let Deputy Hart deal with all the curious looky-loos demanding to know what celebrity was about to land in Fairbanks.

Keen, the big cheese until Sloan got off the plane, posted Gil Brady at the top of the escalator, where he'd have a bird's-eye view of the main floor below.

Cutter had the best gig. He could loiter near the rental car counters under the biplane suspended over the lower level of the terminal. His primary mission was to look outbound for threats, protecting the protectors while they focused on the safety of the justice and her daughter.

Upstairs, Keen flopped down in a chair with his back to the wall by Gate 1, where Morehouse's plane was supposed to arrive. He immediately opened Wordle on his phone. Dillard waited alongside the ticket counter, stretching his shoulders, and gazed out the windows as a Cessna 185 on amphibs settled onto the float pond on the far side of the runway. He turned suddenly, as if a thought had just occurred to him, and looked at Lola, head cocked quizzically to one side.

"You okay, kiddo?"

The term *kiddo* might have offended her, had someone else used it, but to Dave Dillard, everyone in the Marshals Service was a kid, even Cutter.

"I'm right-as," she lied. "Why? Was I whinging?"

"Whinge." Dillard chuckled. "My uncle married a girl from the UK. Somerset or some shit. Now, that girl was a whinger."

"Was I?" Lola asked again. "Whinging, I mean."

"Not at all," Dillard said. "You're a rock, Teariki. But every LEO in Alaska knows how close you are to that missing trooper. Stands to reason you'd be upset with him out of pocket."

"You're so sweet, Dave," she said, meaning it. Maddeningly, his concern made her throat convulse with emotion. "But I'm fine. Just worried."

"I'll bet a third of the troopers in AST are out there beating the bushes right now," Dillard said. "They've had an air force of planes doing grid searches all morning. They'll find him."

"I know," Lola said. "It's just stuffed that I can't help—"

Her phone buzzed in her vest pocket. "Thanks again, Dave," she said. "You're a solid dude."

He waved off the compliment, nodding for her to take the call. It was Joe Bill.

"Speaking of solid dudes," she said when she picked up. "A little dab of brightness in my otherwise shitty day."

"How you holding up?"

"Been better, I reckon." Her stomach fell, suddenly overcome with dread. "Why? Do you have news?"

"No, no, no," Brackett said. "Nothing like that. I talked to a friend of mine in the Palmer post a couple of minutes ago. Still no new developments. From what I hear, though, the Parks Highway is pretty much one big trooper parade."

"I just don't understand how an entire patrol car could just vanish."

Brackett gave a soft groan. "TIA. That's what my dad says. *This is Alaska.*' Weird shit happens in the North."

"Yeah." Lola sniffed back a tear. "I'll say."

"They'll find him."

"I know," she said. "It's just really wonderful that you would call and check on how whacked I am about a past boyfriend."

"Emphasis on *past*," Brackett said. "Anyway, Sam's one of us."

She caught movement out of the corner of her eye. "I need to run, lover boy," she said. "Scotty Keen just got off his ass. That can only mean our Supreme is wheels-down a bit early."

She ended the call with a smooch, as much to cheer herself as to flirt with Joe Bill, and stuffed the phone in the pocket of her fleece vest.

Dave Dillard closed a little notebook he'd been scribbling in and shoved it in the pocket of his sport coat.

"Showtime, Teariki," he said. "The ego has landed."

Alaska Airlines flight #1465 from Seattle touched down early, at five minutes past two p.m. Scott Keen's phone chimed moments after the gear squawked on the tarmac. He spoke for a moment, nodded, then ended the call.

"Sloan?" Lola asked.

"Yep," Keen said.

Dillard waited a beat, then ran a hand over his thinning hair. "You want to share with us what she said?"

Keen gave an exasperated groan. "Nothing to worry about. The justice likes her space. Doesn't want us to crowd her."

"Sounds good," Dillard said. "I'll drop back some. Lola can—"

"Lola's on the daughter," Keen said. "You go with the original plan."

"A tight diamond?" Dillard asked. "That's the opposite—"

"We're walking her through a crowded airport," Keen said. "Just do it."

Dillard gave a thumbs-up. "You make the big bucks," he said. "You make the decisions."

Ground traffic was light and the jet lumbered in quickly, rolling to a stop at Gate 1. Inspector Sloan exited the Jetway first, eyes up, scanning. Lola had never met the woman, but knew she'd been in Cutter's Basic Deputy class at the Academy. What little Cutter did say was overwhelmingly positive, but Lola couldn't shake the feeling that he was holding something back—not exactly a surprise.

Lola got a pretty good idea what that something was the moment she got a look at the inspector.

Sloan scanned the crowd of passengers milling around waiting to board the outbound flight. She wasn't much over forty, but her hair had gone prematurely silver. Lola thought it made her look like some sort of elven queen from a Tolkien novel. She'd traveled with the justice since DC, and her khaki slacks and cotton blouse had a rumpled, slept-in look. A light navy-blue vest concealed the gun and badge on her belt.

Scott Keen gave a flick of his hand to show he was her contact and stepped forward immediately. Sloan acknowledged him with a tip of her head—she knew who he was—but continued to search the crowd.

She was looking for Cutter.

Lola imagined a torrid Academy romance between her boss and the inspector back when they were both baby deputies. Sloan definitely had the robust farm-girl look he was attracted to. Lola stifled a chuckle. An affair with Arliss Cutter . . . no wonder Nicki Sloan's hair had gone gray.

Justice Morehouse strode off the Jetway next, long legs stretching out as if about to break into a sprint after the cramped flight. Ramona was next, wearing green corduroy overalls with the cuffs rolled above black converse high tops. She was almost as tall as her mother. Her dark hair was up on either side, in what Lola called mini buns. Neck pillow in one hand, she rubbed sleep from bewildered eyes with the other.

Lola leaned forward to get her attention. "Doesn't start looking like Alaska till we get downstairs."

Ramona acknowledged her with a silent smile.

Morehouse's Senate confirmation hearing had been a grueling one, with enough theater to garner a decent audience on C-SPAN. The flight was long enough that more than a few of her fellow passengers recognized her. A couple of women with daughters of their own in tow gave her fist pumps of solidarity. Some simply stood and gawked.

"Welcome to Alaska," Keen said.

Dillard held back a few steps, until Keen motioned him forward with a barely concealed wave, as if calling a disobedient child.

This drew a raised eyebrow from the justice, but she said nothing.

"If you'd follow me," Keen said. He led the way toward the exit. "You have time to get some rest before the welcome reception if you'd like. This four-hour time difference can be a little shocking."

Morehouse smiled, eyes sparkling with a glint of playful mischief. "That would be terrific."

Sloan fell a few steps behind, motioning for Dillard to do the same. Lola stayed with Ramona, who walked well behind her mother.

Morehouse was a fast walker, forcing Keen to hustle in order to stay ahead of her. He glanced over his shoulder as they approached the escalator and noticed Dillard's location, scowling like a kid who only got socks and underwear for Christmas.

Morehouse slowed, almost imperceptibly, allowing Keen to make it several steps down the escalator before she stopped in her tracks. His face flushed red when he turned to find the justice and the remainder of her detail still at the top.

"Nicki," the justice said. "Would you mind if we took the stairs?"

"Not at all, ma'am," Sloan said, brightening when she saw Cutter waiting in the terminal below, passively blocking anyone from coming up to meet the detail during their descent.

Lola thought she might have seen him crack a momentary smile.

Keen all but ran down the escalator to beat them to the bottom.

Ramona sighed. "Sorry," she whispered. "My mom has a real pas-sive-aggressive way of testing people."

Lola shrugged, not quite ready to admit to the girl how much she disliked Scotty Keen.

Ramona looked up in awe at the bush plane suspended from the ceiling. "I take it you're my babysitter."

Lola liked this kid. Direct. To the point, but not snide. "You're kind of old to have a sitter. How about we go with tour guide?"

Ramona nodded. "And protector."

"That works. I'm Lola, by the by."

"Hi, Lola. So, what if I don't feel like hanging out in the room while my mom naps?"

"That's why I'm here," Lola said. "You have a list of things you want to see?"

"Yes, I do!"

"Coolio," Lola said. "My car's at the hotel. We'll leave from there."

"I like your accent," Ramona said.

"Gift from my dad," Lola said.

Then, out of the blue, "You think someone's gonna try and mur-der my mom?"

"Well, don't we get right to the point."

"That's not really an answer."

"Then no," Lola said. "I'm not aware of any plot to hurt your mum. We're mostly here to stop attempted pies in the face, that sort of thing."

Ramona turned sideways, skip-hopping to keep up while getting a better look at the stuffed brown bear in a glass case next to bag-gage claim. "You'd tell me, though? If someone was trying to mur-der her, I mean."

"Oh yeah," Lola said. "I'll be dragging you to safety and shooting over my shoulder."

"Metaphorically."

"Metaphorically what?"

"Shooting over your shoulder."

"Nope," Lola said. "Someone attacks us and I'm definitely going to guns."

"You talk straight," Ramona said. "*With* me, not *at* me, like most people do. I like that."

"Righto," Lola said. "So let's you and me make a deal. I'll be honest with you, and you promise to follow my instructions."

"Instructions?"

The smell of moist earth rolled in as the exit doors whooshed open. Curbside, Deputies Gutierrez and Hart sat behind the wheels of their respective vehicles, ready to roll. Keen picked up his pace and opened the limo's rear passenger door.

Cutter leaned against a pillar thirty feet away, looking as relaxed as he ever could . . . which meant slightly less likely to pick his teeth with the bones of anyone who tried to cross him. Undercover work was not the man's strong suit. Lola was glad to have him here. If something was going to happen, this would be a likely spot.

Ramona slowed a hair as she approached the Tahoe, giving Lola time to finish her thought.

"Instructions?" she asked again.

"Ninety-nine percent of the time," Lola said, "I'll ask what *you* want to do. But if I tell you to get your head down, you get your head down. If I say to get in the car, you get in the car."

Ramona thought about it for a second, still walking sideways, bouncing like a puppy. "I can do that."

Lola gave a slow nod, feeling way too much like her own mother.

"Sweet as. Now get in the car."

CHAPTER 25

"*I* could have shot her in the face!"

Alex slid behind the wheel of the van and looked across the center console at his father.

Scouting inside the airport terminal with Gavrill and Ilia sounded exciting when he thought they might actually make a move. The new had worn off quickly. Stalking prey that had no idea it was being hunted was not especially difficult, or, for that matter, any fun. Too much standing around, watching, and taking mental notes.

"How many?" Maxim asked.

Alex grabbed the steering wheel with both hands, push-pulling back and forth to bleed off energy. "At least seven. Three women, four men."

"Plus, the drivers and the lacky who will stay behind to fetch the luggage," Maxim mused. "None of them paid you any mind?"

"We could have dressed like a Russian dance troupe and squat-kicked the hopak around the luggage carousel," Alex said. "No one would have given us a second glance."

Across the street the Fairbanks Police Department cruiser pulled away from the curb, leading the motorcade.

Alex exited parking and fell in with traffic behind them. "Killing her should be easy-peasy."

If he was hoping to impress his father with brave talk, it did not work.

Maxim gazed out the window. "Her daughter is with her?"

"She is," Alex said. "I could have blown her away too, *no problema.*"

"The girl may be useful," Maxim said. "A tool." He slumped lower in his seat, grimacing.

"Are you all right?"

Maxim's face twisted and then slowly relaxed as the pain bled away. He took a few panting breaths before regaining his composure.

Alex let off the accelerator, slowing as the marked police car led the motorcade off Airport Way into the parking lot of a small hotel along the banks of the Chena River. Alex started to turn, but Maxim flicked his fingers.

"Continue straight."

Alex passed the hotel, as did Lev in the SUV behind them.

"Should I make a block?"

"No." Maxim shook his head, deep in thought. "I need to rest. Take me to our hotel. We will return tonight for her speech."

"And kill her then?"

Maxim leaned his seat as far back as it would go and closed his eyes. "I will tell you this, Sashenka. When Charlotte Morehouse dies, the world will watch it happen." Still reclining, he let his head fall sideways so he was looking at Alex. "Gavrill and Ilia will go in and look over our options. They brought American clothing to help them blend in."

"*All* my clothes are American," the boy said. "Let me go, Papa."

Maxim's eyes fluttered. "Listen to me, Sasha. You are not to be directly involved in the violence."

"Then why did you—"

"I told you," Maxim said. "I am dying. You watch and learn. When this is over, you will return to Petropavlovsk and take over my business affairs. Your Russian will improve. Look to Uncle Oleg for guidance."

"But, Papa—"

Maxim stabbed the console with his finger. "Gavrill and Ilia will scout for us. Where do these protectors stand when they are with Morehouse? Do they place her on the right or the left? Do security personnel rely only on handguns, or do they have rifles? Machine pistols? Heavy weapons? Flashbangs? Gas? Are there other protectors whom we have not yet seen?"

"I understand," Alex said. "You want to know how many we have to kill to get to her."

"Ah, Sashenka," Maxim said. "Make no mistake. *I* am going to kill them all."

CHAPTER 26

*A*mong his grandfather's many credos, one of Cutter's favorites, and surely one to live by, was to *"never go anywhere for the first time."* Boiled down to the bones, this simply meant to locate the high ground *before* things went south—send scouts, talk to locals, do whatever was necessary to gather intel before a conflict.

To that end Cutter walked every inch of the hotel three times before Justice Morehouse began her speech. He knew where the cleaning staff took their meal breaks, the secret spots where they slinked away to smoke. He found the stairwell doors were difficult to open, and discovered which ones led to the roof. He learned that someone had stashed a mattress and scented candles for basement liaisons in a vacant storage closet behind a boiler that would not likely make it through another Fairbanks winter.

The lodge was a quaint log affair with high ceilings and varnished beams of honey-colored spruce. The ballroom, where Morehouse was giving her remarks, was separated from the main lobby by a bar and a small après-ski/reading area with a half-dozen tables and several overstuffed leather chairs in front of a stone fireplace. The ballroom itself had seating for eighty, enough for all the judges and their spouses. Two locked doors exited to the side parking lot, where two FPD officers would stand post during the event. It was a cardinal rule of protective work to never go through a door without knowing what was waiting on the other side.

The room was wider than it was deep, with three exterior walls and far too many windows for Cutter's taste. Another stone fireplace, larger than the one in the lounge, occupied the center of the long wall. Inspector Sloan had the hotel staff move the lectern in front of the hearth, giving the justice a decent place to stand without risking a threat from behind. It did put her in direct line with the doors to the lobby while she spoke. Not optimum from a protective standpoint, but the windows turned the rest of the room into a giant fishbowl. As often happened in protective work, it was chosen because it was the best-worst location.

Gavrill Pogodin snugged a ballcap over his dark hair and gave Alex a thumbs-up as he climbed out of the van to join Lipin. Despite his decade spent in prison, Lipin had retained his youthful swagger, carrying himself like a man closer to Gavrill's age rather than someone twenty-five years his senior. The men entered the hotel doors separately, dressed in faded jeans and polo shirts, loose like well-fed Americans, relaxed, as if they were guests.

"What if someone questions them?" Alex asked, drumming the wheel with his thumbs after they'd disappeared inside.

"Ilia's English is so good, one of the stooges in the US Embassy offered to replace his lost passport," Maxim said. "Gavrill's is nearly so. There is no reason for anyone to question them. But if they do . . ." He gave a little shrug.

"This is madness, Papa." Alex opened the van door a crack. "I'm going in to have a look—"

Maxim grabbed the boy's jacket and yanked him back, rattling his teeth. He was remarkably strong for a sick man. "Be still!" he snapped. "Each of us have mission! Yours is to watch. I have told you this! My men . . ." A malignant smile spread over his hatchet face. "*Our* men . . . will do what needs to be done."

Maxim smoothed his son's jacket and lovingly patted him on the shoulder; then he nestled deeper into his seat, groaning with fatigue. "Now is time to relax and learn. Ilia and Gavrill will let us know what to expect from those inside. We have come too far to fail because some overzealous policeman asks to see my papers."

"They do not do that here, Father," Alex said.

His head fell sideways again. "Are you certain about this, Alex?" he asked. "Because I am not."

Cutter stood post just outside the ballroom, hands low and relaxed, back to the wall. Sloan had ordered the doors shut to keep Morehouse out of view from the lobby, but a rubber wedge kept them slightly ajar.

Cutter was able to listen to a few minutes of the justice's speech and still keep an eye on the lobby.

The massive antlers of a bull moose cast a shadow over the reception desk. A stuffed polar bear peered down from a ledge above the alcove leading to the elevators. Everything on the walls was quintessentially Alaskan, from mounted waterfowl to fish. Fred Machetanz paintings of Eskimos and Arctic life stood out in brilliant whites and chilly blues, reminiscent of the ice pack itself. The rich aroma of coffee and freshly baked pies tamped back the musty hint of industrial carpet that had soaked up many winters of tramped-in snow.

Cutter shifted sideways a hair, bringing Nicki Sloan into view behind the justice. Her eyes shifted ever so slightly toward the door, as if she felt Cutter looking at her. They went back over a decade, to the beginning of their careers. The chemistry between them had been instantaneous and obvious. Half their Marshals Basic classmates believed they were sharing sheets through their entire Academy. A fair number were still under that impression more than a decade later. They'd certainly headed in that direction as soon as they had met.

Nicki Sloan was incredibly smart and not at all unpleasant to look at. She was even less prone to smile than Cutter. He was between marriages and she was on the rebound from a three-year relationship with an FBI agent—an unholy union that Cutter still teased her about. Many of their classmates at the Federal Law Enforcement Training Center were straight out of college, but Sloan and Cutter came aboard the Marshals Service in their thirties, him from the military, her with nine years as a Shreveport police officer. Long evening runs in the piney woods of southern Georgia helped them blow off steam.

They made a few halfhearted attempts at flirting—a double en-
tendre there, a good-game pat on the ass there, but they were both
too emotionally exhausted to pull the trigger. It turned out for the
best and their relationship blossomed into a diehard friendship
much deeper than any four-month FLETC romance. It was sure as
hell easier to look her in the eye now, without that gob of regret.

Sloan knew Cutter well enough to know the justice's speech
would interest him. She'd offered to let him stand post in the ballroom. He'd declined, joking that there wouldn't be enough air,
what with that many judges in the room.

Morehouse shared Thomas Jefferson's philosophy that the US
Constitution was a living document, meant by the Founding Fathers to change with the times. Dave Dillard lurked in the lobby,
doing his job, but staying as far away as he could from such heresy.

The justice quoted the Constitution from memory, channeling
her inner Jefferson, who, she admitted, was her "history boyfriend,"
despite his flaws. She came across as the kind of person Cutter might
like to have a drink with, but never want to face in a trivia contest
about Madison, Jefferson, the Constitution—or anything to do
with US History, for that matter.

Hooten slumped at a table toward the bar. As the vice president
of the Alaska Bar Association, and one of the planners of the conference, the former part-time magistrate had given up his seat at
the event to a couple of the chief judge's guests, hoping to garner
a little goodwill with the district court.

Cutter bristled a little when applause erupted in the ballroom.

Sloan's voice crackled in his earpiece.

"Detail, Detail, Sloan," she said in a pleasant Louisiana accent.
She used the more formal *"hey, you; you, it's me"* format to communicate over the radio. "We've got a fifteen-minute Q and A and
then the justice plans to call it a night."

Deputy Gutierrez and a uniformed trooper stood inside the ballroom flanking the main doors. Lola and Sloan sat at tables up
front, near the fireplace and within lunging distance of their two
principals. Scott Keen, who felt it crucial to his career to have as
much face time as possible with the judges, perched toward the
front, opposite the fireplace from Sloan.

Cutter went to advance the area around the elevator, leaving a female trooper named Montez and Deputy Hart chatting softly outside the ballroom door, scanning their surroundings between sentences. Brady and Dillard roamed between the lobby and the reading area.

A quick survey of the public areas showed two couples standing at reception with their bags, waiting to check in. Seven or eight people of various ages browsed in the gift shop. Another dozen lounged in the reading area, or talked at the bar. People came and went through the front doors, some with bags of food, others carrying wet gear from rainy outdoor adventures. Almost fifty unvetted strangers were within shooting distance of the justice. Sometimes . . . most of the time, really, it felt to Cutter as though they were half-assing protection. It was one of the rare times he actually envied the Secret Service. Those lucky bastards got to weld manhole covers shut and block off entire floors at their venues.

Sloan sang out again with a two-minute warning. Deputies responded with the status of their area of responsibility, giving the inspector a picture of what was going on outside the ballroom.

Everyone but Dillard.

"Anyone got eyes on Dave?" Sloan asked when she wasn't able to raise him.

"He was in the lobby two minutes ago," Cutter said. "I'll head that way—"

The radio "bonked," turning everything into garbled electronic nonsense as someone else keyed in to speak at the same time.

Cutter released the push-to-talk button, a lipstick-sized tube that ran from the radio on his belt up through his jacket sleeve and was held in place under his watchband.

The veteran deputy's whispered voice came over the net immediately.

"All good here," Dillard said, raspy, like he was whispering in a movie theater. "Just following a quirky guy down the east hall toward the saunas. Looked a little out of place, but I think he's all good."

Cutter knew better than to shrug off Dillard's gut instinct. Something had caught his eye.

"I'm coming your way, Dave," he said.

"Detail, this is Sloan," the inspector said. "We're breaking up here. Imminent departure. I say again, departure is imminent."

Cutter was halfway down the hall to Dillard when Hooten gave a startled shout, responding as if he'd been slapped.

Deputy Hart yelled, "Gun! Gun! Gun! North door!" keying her radio at the same time, so it came over the net, as well as down the hall.

Cutter spun on his heels and sprinted back the way he'd come— toward the sound of gunfire.

CHAPTER 27

*S*omeone at reception cried out in terror. A woman grabbed her two children and hustled them into the gift shop. General pandemonium broke loose as people fled the lobby in all directions. One of the FPD officers piped up with an all clear from outside, letting Sloan know it was safe to evacuate the justice out the exterior doors.

The radio squealed, bonking again as deputies attempted to transmit at once.

Cutter rounded the corner to find Paige Hart and Trooper Montez with their Glocks aimed in, standing over the prone body of a young man in a ballcap. Blood spread rapidly across the floor from a massive head wound. Hooten leaned against the edge of his table, cradling his arm.

"Hart?" Cutter barked, scanning for threats over the top of the Colt Python. "You good?"

"I am," Hart said. "He's down. Appears to be alone." Her first OIS, or officer-involved shooting, with the Marshals Service, the young deputy appeared locked into the last action that made any sense to her, pointing her weapon at the threat. To her credit, her index finger ran alongside the frame of her pistol, off the trigger.

"Justice is sheltering in place until you guys check the grounds," Sloan said over the radio. Cutter imagined the deputies in the ballroom ushering Morehouse and her daughter into a protected corner and forming a skirmish line around her, bristling with weapons.

"Dave," Cutter said into his mic. "Keep an eye on the lobby for other threats."

"Roger that," Dillard said, barking orders to someone nearby.

Cutter holstered the revolver and approached Hart and Trooper Montez.

"You both shoot?"

"Just me," Montez said.

"I would have," Hart said, "but my vantage point put the justice behind the threat."

"The son of a bitch tried to take my watch," Hooten said, picking himself up off the table.

Cutter frowned, incredulous. "He tried to rob you? In this venue?"

"Damn straight," Hooten said. "I was sitting right here, going over her itinerary. My Perpetual is new, so I had it off adjusting the bracelet when this guy—"

"That's bizarre," Cutter said. "This hotel is crawling with cops and you're telling me he—"

"Yes!" Hooten said, his voice tight like he might cry. "That's exactly what I'm saying. I had my watch off and that guy plowed right into me. The doors to the ballroom had just opened and judges were starting to come out, distracting—"

"Still." Cutter shook his head, continuing to scan for more threats. "It seems unlikely."

"I know what it feels like when somebody tries to lift a watch!"

Hart lowered her Glock, but was still locked in at the body. "There's a gun under him," she said, chancing a quick glance at Cutter. "He fell on it."

Cutter stooped near the man's shoulder, careful to avoid stepping in blood. Considering the size of the head wound, he wasn't surprised when he found no pulse. He rolled the body up enough to secure a small Kahr semiauto and pass it off to Hart. The troopers on-site would be unhappy that he moved it, but he wasn't about to leave a live weapon just hanging out on the floor with a Supreme Court justice only yards away.

Trooper Montez holstered her Glock as soon as the offending weapon was secure. She shuddered, tugging at the collar of her uniform. "You saw it too," she said to Hart. "Right? I mean, he was—"

Cutter stepped in front of the trooper, blocking her from the lobby. Several onlookers already had their cell phones out, grabbing video of the gruesome scene. He leaned close so as not to be heard by anyone but Hart and Montez. "I suggest it's time you two call your reps."

Montez nodded. "Right . . . yes. I should call my sergeant."

"Would that be Yates?" Cutter asked, grimacing when he said the name. While Cutter got along famously with ninety nine percent of the troopers in Alaska, he'd had more than a couple of run-ins with this particular AST sergeant. Grumpy would have called the man a shitbird, and he would not have been wrong.

"Yep," Montez said. "All of the other brass are out searching for Sam. We're stuck with Sergeant Yates."

"I'll call him," Cutter said. "You get ahold of your union rep or ombudsman or whoever Troopers call after an OIS." He glanced at Hart. "You a member of FLEOA?"

"I am. Dillard pretty much forced me to join."

"Kudos to Dillard," Cutter said, giving her a nod of approval.

Pronounced FLEA-OH-AH, FLEOA was the Federal Law Enforcement Officers Association. Yearly dues brought access to an on-call attorney after a use-of-force incident. Deputy Hart hadn't pulled the trigger, but she was close enough to the action that there was a better-than-average chance she'd be pulled into a civil suit.

"Looks like a lone threat," Cutter said over the radio. "As best we can see at the moment."

"Clear to move her to her room?" Sloan asked.

Brady piped up, "Third floor is secure. Good to go."

"I'm holding the elevator," Dillard said. "Ready when you are, boss."

"This is Sloan. Justice is moving to residence."

Montez remained beside the body while Page Hart helped Cutter make a hole through the crowd in advance of the scrum of deputies surrounding Morehouse and her daughter. Ramona tried to slow and catch a glimpse of the blood, but Lola cajoled her along. The look in Nicki Sloan's eye left no room for argument as she pushed the detail. Get out of the way or be trampled— or worse.

Sergeant Yates answered Cutter's call with a yawn. His attitude when he learned about Montez would have earned him an ass-whupping, had he been on-site. Fortunately for both men, Cutter would have time to calm down before he arrived.

CHAPTER 28

*I*lia Lipin shuffled out of the east doors, his movements jerky, constrained, a rabbit who desperately wanted to run, but knew quick movement would draw the attention of the wolf. Moments later, people began to pour from all the doors.

Alex grabbed the steering wheel, rocking forward and back, willing Gavrill to appear in the crowd.

Lipin made it across the road and slid open the van door, his face tight like plastic. Breathless, he looked over his shoulder as he hauled himself inside.

"Go!" He pounded on his armrest.

Alex turned in his seat. "Gavrill?"

Lipin gave a sad shake of his head.

Alex slammed on the brakes. "What happened?"

Lipin continued to look out, over his shoulder. He spoke in rapid Russian. Then, when Alex didn't move, he switched to English. "We need to go now," he said. "Gavrill is gone."

"Gone?"

Ilia told them what he knew. Gavrill had gone to take a photo of what he believed to be Morehouse's itinerary on the table, but had been confronted. One of the deputy marshals, a Black woman, had confronted him when he'd tried to run. Stupidly, he'd drawn his pistol.

Driving now, Alex pumped the brakes again. "And the bitch just shot him?"

"The marshal blocked his escape," Lipin said. "The lady trooper shot him."

"Then I will shoot her." Alex glared at his father. "I will shoot them both—and no one on this planet is going to stop me."

CHAPTER 29

*B*onnie Lynch looked for shape, color, and movement as they rode through the woods near the Parks Highway. The day before, she'd been rewarded with a glimpse of an incredibly beautiful cross fox.

The piney scent of Labrador tea hung on the air, moist and pungent, infusing every drop and drip of rain. Heavy moisture meant thick foliage. Winter vistas turned into green walls in summer, so she had to keep a sharp eye out if she wanted to spot any animals.

The six-wheeled Argo shot a rooster tail of soupy mud out the back as Bonnie's husband, Doug, braked the three wheels on the left side to skid-steer around a large stump. It had been his idea to buy the land a decade earlier. Tucked in the woods three miles off the Parks near Trapper Creek, the only improvement on the five-acre parcel was an outhouse. But that outhouse provided the most incredible view of a moose meadow while you did your business. The nearest cabin was a quarter mile away.

It took the Lynches four years, working on their days off to haul in load after load of building materials and equipment, but they were finally able to finish a cabin befitting of the moose-meadow throne room.

This was their first full summer with the cabin. The trails had turned to muck, but Doug bought a new Argo to float flooded creeks and power through muddy bogs. It worked beautifully, so much so that when Bonnie discovered they were out of mustard three days into their stay, she and Doug decided to make a quick supply run to the little store at Trapper Creek.

Doug drove. The Argo was his new toy, after all, and it used levers instead of the steering wheel or handlebars that Bonnie was accustomed to.

"This thing kicks ass," Doug said, skirting a stand of impenetrable white birch to link up with the East-West Express Trail that would take them back out to the Parks Highway.

A flash of something out of place caught her eye as Doug steered the Argo out of the trees and onto the gravel trail running alongside the Parks. He began to accelerate, but she patted his arm. He was used to her signals and turned around to see what she'd discovered this time.

Soaked with rain and almost invisible between the trail and the highway, tucked beneath a thick stand of willows, there was a blue Stetson hat.

Bonnie was inside the Trapper Creek store paying for a bottle of French's mustard and two Snickers bars when she glanced out the window. Two state troopers, both frowning like they meant business, flanked Doug at the gas pumps.

"I wonder what they want," Bonnie said, a flutter of worry in her chest.

The clerk, a woman about her age, gave a sad shake of her head. "Guess they still haven't found him."

"Found who?"

Bonnie's heart sank when the clerk filled her in on everything they'd missed during their brief stay at the cabin. By the time she finished paying and made it outside, a third trooper had rolled up. The new arrival, a bald sergeant who rivaled the Argo in size, clutched the wet Stetson in one hand and a cell phone in the other. He looked like he was about to cry.

CHAPTER 30

Secondary attacks were always a concern.

Inspector Sloan posted Brady and Gutierrez in the hall outside the justice's hotel suite. Brady had a Heckler & Koch UMP that shot two-round bursts of .45 ACP. Gutierrez carried a WitSec shorty 870 pump shotgun. Neither deputy made any attempt to conceal the weapons. This was the time to be loud and proud, to let the world know they were dead serious about protection. Fairbanks PD and the few troopers not involved with the search for Sam Benjamin had the hotel on virtual lockdown—a task made all the more difficult when the overwhelming majority of guests were judges who were certain the rules did not apply to them.

Astoundingly, or perhaps inevitably, none of the judges or lawyers appeared to have witnessed the actual shooting. Rich Hooten went on and on about how the guy tried to steal his watch, but swore he wasn't in the right position to see whether the would-be thief had actually been an immediate threat when Montez shot him. Paige Hart had a direct view of what happened and made it clear that if Montez hadn't shot, she would have. She gave Sergeant Yates a thumbnail sketch, but waited to give a written statement until someone with more juice showed up.

Cutter sent Lola to sit with Paige Hart and Trooper Montez. Law enforcement agencies, the Troopers and Marshals Service included, had a tendency to eat their own after an officer-involved shooting. Much of the post-OIS scrutiny was necessary, but some was unconscionable. Worst of all, Sergeant Yates was the first Trooper supervisor on the scene. A bully of the first order, it was all Cutter could do to keep from ripping his lungs out every time he spoke. He felt sure that the idiot would have thrown poor Trooper Montez into an active volcano, had there been one nearby, just to save himself the paperwork.

Inspector Sloan invited Cutter and Keen to join her while she made her case to Morehouse that the wisest move was to get the hell out of Dodge. Alaska Superior Court Judge Megan Reese and US District Judge Markham—the justice's Alaska hosts—did their best to downplay the threat. Reese sat relaxed, legs crossed, as if at a cocktail party and not a post-shooting threat assessment. Markham's signature bow tie hung loose from the collar of a crisply starched shirt. Hooten inserted himself into the meeting as the vice president of the ABA.

The justice's suite was twice the size of Cutter's room, but still filled to the gunnels by such a large entourage. Morehouse perched on the edge of the bed next to her daughter, dressed in the gaberdine slacks and a silk blouse from her speech. She listened attentively as Sloan ticked through the many reasons why it was better to be safe than sorry.

At length she looked up, seized by a sudden thought.

"That police officer who fired the shots," she said. "Is she all right?"

"That would be Trooper Montez," Cutter said when no one else answered. "She's just fine physically."

Morehouse sighed and hugged her daughter by the shoulders, comforting herself as much as the girl. "Good . . . That's good." Then to Sloan, "I feel sure there were dozens of witnesses to the shooting, considering it happened as all the judges were passing out of the ballroom, but please let the Alaska State Troopers know I had a clear view of the entire event through the open doors."

"Madam Justice," Hooten said. "Perhaps—"

Morehouse cut him off. "You saw it, didn't you? I mean, it happened almost in your lap."

"He knocked me down," Hooten said, staring at the floor. "I was just about to get to my feet and confront him, when I heard the shots."

Cutter bit his tongue, catching Sloan's eye roll at Hooten's I-was-just-about-to-grow-some-balls revision of history.

"Too bad," Morehouse said. "In any case, please tell the Alaska State Troopers that I very clearly saw the man in the baseball cap raise a handgun *before* the trooper fired."

Hooten kept digging. "Things were so frenetic down there, Madam Justice. Considering your position, perhaps you—"

"I'm going to stop you there, counselor," Morehouse said. "Before you embarrass yourself. Who I am should have no bearing whatsoever on what I saw."

"Thank you," Cutter said, deeply impressed. "I'm sure the AST, especially Trooper Montez, will appreciate your willingness to give a statement."

"Of course." The justice looked around the room. "Now, I suppose, we have some decisions to make."

Judge Reese lifted a hand, not so much asking permission to speak as making sure she had everyone's attention. She cleared her throat. "If I may. What happened is terrible, to be sure. That said, the Marshals Service has found nothing to suggest tonight was anything other than a random act."

Sloan chimed in. "The Marshals Service has found nothing to suggest anything either way."

"That guy was going for my watch," Hooten said. "This was a robbery gone bad, plain and simple."

Cutter started to speak, but caught himself. This was Sloan's show.

Accustomed to placating judges, Keen had no such compunction. "Magistrate Judge Hooten could well be right."

"Or he could be mistaken." Sloan gave Keen a what-the-hell side-eye. "I'd prefer not to come to quick conclusions regarding your safety. Judge Hooten's opinion notwithstanding."

"*Former part-time* Magistrate Judge Hooten," Markham corrected, as if to say, "This guy isn't one of us."

"May I say something?" Cutter asked.

Sloan looked to Morehouse.

"By all means," she said.

"Thieves . . . robbers generally look for easy marks," Cutter said. "This venue is crawling with bomb dogs, uniformed troopers, Fairbanks PD, not to mention a dozen deputy marshals with earpieces and sheep-killing dog looks on our faces. You've seen how we operate, Madam Justice. You'd prefer we were covert, but we can hardly help ourselves. Armed security was in this guy's face everywhere he turned. There are so many easier places in the world to steal a watch."

Processing, Morehouse looked to Markham. "Judge, what would you do if you were in my position?"

Markham spoke slowly, measuring his words. "For all practical purposes I am in your position. Yes, there's a chance the violence was aimed at you, or at one of us. I suppose that's always a risk when members of the judiciary flock together. We make people angry. That's part of our job description. Inspector Keen has already suggested that those of us on the federal bench should return home. I am inclined to agree with him. That said, Anchorage is four hundred miles away, almost twice as far as the distance between New York and Washington, DC. Violence in one location shouldn't hamper your actions in another."

"Inspector Sloan," Cutter said, unable to contain himself, "do you mind if I go into a little more detail about why we're reacting the way we are?"

Sloan flicked her hand, giving him the floor. "Go for it."

Cutter took a red grease pencil from his BattleBoard and stood in front of the full-length mirror on the wall across from Morehouse's bed. He made his case directly to the justice, toning down the goriest of details because of her teenage daughter, while keeping it graphic enough to make an impression.

"Recent violence is not isolated to Fairbanks. Two days ago, unknown people broke into a house in Voznesenka, small community of Russian Old Believers near Homer, two hundred miles south of Anchorage." Cutter used the grease pencil to draw a V at the bottom of the mirror, along with two hash marks. "Intruders murdered the homeowner with knives. The victim's twenty-two-year-old wife was also stabbed and remains in critical condition." Cutter drew another dot two inches to the right of the V. "A few hours later, the crabbing vessel *Esther Marie* was found half submerged across the bay from Homer. Initial reports indicate the boat was apparently scuttled . . . had been sunk on purpose on its way back from the Bering Sea. All six of the crew are missing." Cutter drew more hash marks halfway up the mirror. "That same evening nine people were stabbed and/or shot to death by unknown perpetrators during an attack on an illegal gaming operation in Anchorage. APD believes cash and several firearms were taken." He drew a circle star farther up. "Late last night Alaska State Trooper Sam Benjamin went missing on the Parks Highway between Fairbanks and Anchorage."

Morehouse frowned at that news. "Missing?"

"Yes, ma'am," Cutter said. "He and his patrol car seem to have vanished."

Ramona Morehouse looked at her mother. "How does a trooper *and* his car go missing?"

"Good question," Cutter said. "Alaska is a big place. Considering all that's happened—"

Sloan chimed in. "The botched robbery is particularly troubling because the perpetrator had no ID and no fingerprints in the system. He's a ghost. A clean-cut young guy his age should have a driver's license, something."

Cutter traced a line from the V at the bottom of the mirror through the other marks, all the way to the top where he drew an M. "One could call it coincidence." He circled the M. "But from a protective intelligence point of view, the pattern moves directly toward you."

Judge Reese paced the suite, chewing on a hangnail. "All due respect to the Marshals Service, Justice Morehouse, but you and I both know the human mind tends to grasp for patterns. It's our nature to try and soothe ourselves with explanations when there simply are no explanations to be found."

Cutter tapped the mirror with the tip of the grease pencil. "I know this is a bald analogy, but I have to tell you, Justice Morehouse, if I found this many tracks in one place, I'd follow the trail."

Reese closed her eyes, zoning.

Cutter raised both hands, palms out. "I know I can come off as aggressive, and that's the last thing I want to do with any of you. I'll say just one more thing and then I'll shut up. You are all experts in the law, but we're experts at keeping you safe."

"You mean you're experts in violence," Hooten said.

"Sometimes you need to be one to be the other," Sloan said.

Judge Markham blew out a full breath of air, slowly, the way every deputy in Alaska had seen him do when he was about to give his ruling.

"Justice Morehouse," he said. "I'd be remiss if I didn't confess that I have some personal experience with Deputy Cutter. As much as Judge Reese and I would love to show you around our great state, I tend to follow the Marshals' lead in these matters."

Cutter gave him a nod of thanks, but didn't say anything. It was best to keep his mouth shut and take the win.

"The alternative theory," Morehouse said, "is that you are both correct. The home invasion in Homer, the violence in Anchorage, even the missing trooper and the robbery, while each tragic, seem very different and removed from one another."

Both Hooten and Judge Reese brightened.

"But," Morehouse continued, "it *is* troubling that we know absolutely nothing about the dead man downstairs. Deputy Cutter is right. This hotel is a horrible choice of places to commit armed robbery. I believe we should err on the side of caution and cut this portion of the trip short."

Hooten slumped in defeat, but the two judges seized on the part of Morehouse's decision that she'd yet to explain.

"The judicial-specific portion of the conference winds down tomorrow, anyway," Markham said. "In light of what happened tonight, every judge here will completely understand why the Marshals whisked you away early. There's still much we can show you in Southcentral Alaska—fishing, a hike out by Eagle River Nature Center—"

Ramona yawned and turned to look directly at her mother. "We had the train trip scheduled for day after tomorrow. That looks like it would be pretty sick."

"The Alaska Railroad is magnificent, Ramona," Judge Reese said. Then, to the justice, "May I suggest this? The Marshals Service will transport you and your daughter safely to Anchorage tomorrow. If there is *any* indication of a credible threat, then by all means you and Miss Morehouse should return to Washington on the first available flight." Reese glanced at Scott Keen for approval. Keen ignored Cutter, but had enough sense to check with Sloan.

"It goes against my better judgment," Sloan said. "But if we see no credible threat, then I guess we'll all take a train ride."

Ramona nodded emphatically, clenching her mother's ruling.

Sloan stood. "It's after two in the morning on the East Coast," she said. "You've had a long day, Madam Justice. We should all let you get some rest."

The others nodded and shuffled toward the door, clucking as if it had been their idea to leave.

"As a reminder," Sloan said, "deputies will be posted outside your room throughout the night, as well as patrolling the halls and parking lot."

"We'll look after your floor as well," Keen said to Markham.

Morehouse tugged Ramona to her feet. "Thank you, all . . ." She used the back of her hand to cover an exhausted yawn. "And please don't forget to pass along to the Troopers that I'll be happy to provide my statement at their convenience."

"That won't happen until tomorrow morning, ma'am," Sloan said.

In the lead Cutter opened the door, running headlong into Lola Teariki, who was standing in the hall.

Her hair had escaped its customary bun and a frazzled black curl hung across bloodshot eyes. Her hand shot to her mouth when she saw Cutter.

"Arliss . . ." She collapsed against his chest, sobbing, completely defeated. "They . . . they found Sam."

CHAPTER 31

"*I* say we dump the bitch out on the ice," Sherman Billy grunted around the binoculars pressed to his good eye.

He and his partner lay on their bellies on an old carpet remnant, peering around the edge of a rusty shipping container. Low clouds couldn't decide if they wanted to spit rain or pelt sleet. A chain-link fence ran along the edge of the Barrow High School football field, meant to discourage polar bears from venturing onto the bright blue artificial turf. Someone had nailed strips of baleen from a bowhead whale to the top of some light posts along the chain-link fence, making them look like very sad palm trees. Locals called it the "Barrow National Forest."

Billy was tall, with a couple of extra chins and a thick gut. He wasn't exactly sure how old he was, but the couple who'd raised him reckoned he was about twenty-seven or maybe twenty-nine. He had a pretty good idea that his mother was a teacher's aide from Nuiqsut, a village to the east between Utqiagvik and Prudhoe Bay. She'd come to town once when he was eleven and bought him dinner, but she never mentioned anything about being his mom and he'd never asked. He'd heard later that she got killed by her boyfriend on a trip to Anchorage. He didn't know who his father was, and didn't much care to find out.

Billy's partner, a German named Karl Dittmar, roughnecked on the Slope for a little over a year before he'd knocked a coworker's nose off with a spanner wrench. He didn't bust the man's nose. He knocked it off. All the way. Evidently, noses got brittle in the cold. Short and skinny with a prominent Adam's apple, Dittmar was a hell of a lot stronger than he looked—and twice as nasty, which was saying something. The oil-and-gas company he'd been working for fired him on the spot after the nose incident, but his propensity for violence got the attention of people in the right places to make sure he was never at a loss for work.

The last two guys the boss had partnered with Sherman Billy had been level-ten pussies who panicked and lost their shit when things went sideways. None of them had ever knocked anybody's nose off. Dittmar was a weird little dude, but at least the bosses had finally found somebody with balls.

Billy lowered the binoculars and rolled half up on his side to look at his partner. "So, what do you think?"

"I think this old rug smells like rat piss."

"Right," Billy said. "So let's dump Ms. Miriam on the ice and be done with it."

"We're supposed to rough her up," Dittmar said. "Scare her off."

Sherman Billy pointed with his chin. "Dumpin' her in *that* will scare the shit outta her."

Across the gravel road beyond the blue turf field, the Arctic Ocean churned with bergy bits and chunks of pack ice large enough to park a truck on. The toothy slurry rolled and hissed on the tidal current.

Dittmar shuddered. "Yes, that would suck." He cocked his head, listening. "Sounds like a whispered scream."

"You're one weird son of a bitch," the Iñupiat man said.

"Maybe," Dittmar said. "In any case she must get here before we do anything. I'm surprised that she is not earlier. She is so eager for answers."

"She'll be here," Billy said, scanning again with his binoculars.

Dittmar sucked on his top teeth. "I do not like this light. We are much too exposed, whatever we decide to do."

A shadow, half a mile up the beach, caught Sherman Billy's eye. He scuttled forward on his toes and elbows, as if the extra few inches might improve his view. It was probably just a mirage, the warmth of the day shimmering off the gravel. The wind and rain could play hell with your eyes. He took a deep breath and braced himself on the pissy carpet, steadying the binoculars to get a clearer look.

Then the shadow stood up on its hind legs and sniffed the air with a black nose. Sherman Billy grinned from ear to ear and began to sing to himself. "She's back. She's back. She. Is. Back."

Dittmar rolled his eyes. "And you call me the weird son of a bitch."

Billy passed the binoculars to his partner and glanced instinctively over his shoulder, checking the distance to their truck, which was hidden between another set of shipping containers. "We are not the only ones here."

Dittmar threw the binoculars to his eyes and adjusted the focus. "I don't see any . . . Wait. She has cubs."

"Yep," Billy said. "She's comin' for the *a vi luaq*." The K sound of the Q made a guttural click in the back of his throat.

"I wish you'd speak English," Dittmar said without looking up from the binoculars.

"And I wish you'd learn Iñupiaq," Billy said. He snapped his fingers, demanding his binoculars back. "*A vi luaq*—gray whale. That dead calf that washed up on shore a couple weeks ago."

Dittmar turned up his nose. "You mean that twenty-five-foot pile of rotten flesh? I can't believe you guys ate that shit."

Sherman Billy shrugged. "You eat aged cheese," he said. "Anyway, it wasn't all that rotten. Little bit fermented maybe, but the muktuk had a pretty good flavor. Nutty—"

"I'll take your word for it," Dittmar said. "It's a moot point. Between you guys and the bears, there's nothing left but bones and gravel."

"The bear don't know that." Billy swung the binoculars to the south. He couldn't help but chuckle at how well this was turning out. "And here comes our nosey bitch, right on schedule."

"Maybe Mama will get pissed if she thinks this woman is trying to take her food."

"This is a polar bear, dude," Sherman Billy said. "Miriam Cutter is the food."

Fifteen minutes earlier

Mim spent the evening watching self-defense videos on YouTube, worrying that Arliss would call and ask what she was up to. She had her lies all planned out, rehearsed. That was worse than a lie concocted on the spot. Wasn't it? Premeditated. Lying in the first degree.

She decided to leave early, enduring cold rain on the back of a biting wind. She could wallow in her own deceit on the move.

The weather app on her phone said outside temps hovered around thirty-four degrees. Judging from the chill on her ride home from the hospital, she thought that was being generous. She bundled up in merino wool thermals, a hooded sweatshirt, a puffy down sweater, and a heavy-duty rain jacket from Patagonia that Constance called her "Pata-Gucci."

Ethan had had this thing about rain gear, harping on the axiom that there was no bad weather, only bad clothes. The Patagonia was one of the last gifts he had bought her. Arliss focused on footwear. She supposed it was the tracker in him. The first Christmas after he moved to Alaska, he'd noticed she could use a new pair of cold-weather boots and bought her a pair of Danners, which were working out very nicely for this trip to the Arctic.

She topped off her wardrobe with a wool beanie and a pair of insulated Mechanix gloves Arliss had given her, along with the Danners. It seemed ludicrous to wear so many clothes in June, even in Alaska.

Dressed, she tipped up the barrel of a little Beretta Tomcat to make sure it was loaded. Ethan had never served in the military or been a cop like Arliss, but Grumpy was his grandfather too. No wife of his was going to go through life without knowing how to use a pistol. The .32 ACP was admittedly a mouse gun, minimal for defense, but Mim shot it well, and it was better than teeth and fingernails.

She flicked on the safety and stuffed it under the rain jacket in the pocket of her down sweater—though she seriously doubted she'd even remember to use it if push came to shove.

The seat on the little four-wheeler had seen better days. The exposed foam padding soaked the seat of Mim's pants the moment she sat down, promising an extremely air-conditioned ride. She kicked herself for not bringing the bottom half of her rain gear.

Her penance for lying to Arliss.

The city of Utqiagvik was divided into three parts by a series of lagoons. The Barrow side, with the airport and many of the businesses, was to the south. Browerville, with the hospital, was in the center. Farther up a narrow gravel road between South Salt Lagoon and Imikpuk Lake, Ilisagvik College and the high school football field were located. The original site of the Naval Arctic Research Lab, this lonesome northern section was nicknamed NARL, based on the lab's acronym.

Mim's meeting with Phil Hopkin would happen there.

Having a few minutes to spare, she decided to take the scenic route, which essentially meant jagging a block out of the way to the whalebone arch.

A gang of kids about the twins' age followed her on bikes for half a block, recognizing her as someone new.

"Whatcha doin'?" they called, grinning, waving. Most of them wore nothing more than thin jeans and a sweatshirt or light hoodie. This was their summer and they didn't intend to let a little wind and rain slow them down.

Ethan had called it tundra tough.

She passed weathered houses, their yards, such as they were, littered with the rusted hulks of old trucks and snow machines that had been cannibalized for parts. Here and there a sealskin or some other green hide flapped over a porch rail or fish-drying rack.

The wind barreled in from the north, straight off the Arctic, piling acres of slushy sea ice against the beach. The nearest chunks lodged against the gravel, but a few yards out, jagged bergs sailed past like a hissing train.

Mim horsed the little ATV into the gravel lot and rolled to a stop beneath the arch. There were other bones too, the weathered skull of a juvenile bowhead, scattered ribs, a broken vertebra as big as her ATV tire. Some, she thought, might be giant wristbones from a whale's pectoral flipper. The wooden skeletons of two umiaks, hunting skiffs that needed only sewn walrus hide skins to make them seaworthy, rested on sawhorses, bookends on either side of the little boneyard.

Mim had never been the selfie-taking type. She lingered a few moments to absorb the Arctic scene and then threw a leg over the damp ATV, and headed north along the coast on Stevenson Street.

She had the road to herself. Surprising, until she remembered that despite the constant daylight, it was almost eleven o'clock at night. And this wasn't exactly the best weather to go for a joyride.

Utqiagvik, Alaska, had twenty-eight miles of road, and every one of them was a dead end. Stevenson ran northeast for nine miles, through NARL, past Ilisagvik College and a series of salt lagoons until it reached the spit and finally Point Barrow, the farthest north spot in the United States.

The wind intensified as she rode, stinging her eyes and creeping steadily through all her layers. A sudden gust blew her hood against the side of her face, whipping the snap at the collar over and over against her throat. Memories of riding behind Ethan on his old Triumph Scrambler flooded back, making her smile. They'd been so young then, before Constance or the boys, when life didn't suck. She wondered if she'd ever feel like that again. Arliss had shipped up his Harley, but she'd yet to ride with him. It seemed too personal to get on a bike behind him, or at least it had.

She adjusted the snap on the move, shaking off the nostalgia.

A lone bull caribou nibbled at lichens on the roadside, raising its head at the sound of her approach. It trotted alongside her for a time before veering suddenly inland toward the tundra. Scenes like this were commonplace on the North Slope, but they were new to Mim and she couldn't help but imagine a David Attenborough narration.

As cold and miserable as the weather was, she preferred it to the bugs of biblical proportions that the Arctic was famous for.

Shortly after Ethan had moved the family to Alaska, a Slope worker came into the hospital complaining of pain and odd sensations in the back of his neck. A Florida girl, Mim was accustomed to creepy-crawlies, but she'd been horrified to learn that the Slope worker had a warble fly larvae tunneling under his skin. In nature the persistent flies laid their eggs on a caribou's legs, where the larvae burrowed in and migrated upward under the animal's skin to a spot along its spine. There they gouged another hole through the hide and spent a cozy winter breathing through their ass and chowing down on caribou backstrap. In the spring the little buggers chewed their way out, dropped to the ground to start the cycle over again. In the rare cases where humans were infected, the larvae migrated to the scalp. They'd been able to treat the Slope worker, but Mim had never been able to get the images out of her mind.

The blue turf of the Barrow Whalers' football field hove into view up ahead, startlingly bright against the otherwise gray backdrop of gravel and ice and clouds. Mim stood up on the pegs, catching a face full of wind as she looked for Phil Hopkin. She felt like an idiot for not finding out what kind of car he drove, but consoled herself that it didn't matter. She was completely alone.

She chuckled at the whale baleen "palm trees" as she putted slowly along the road, paralleling the chain-link fence. To her left the rolling ice shrieked and spewed, like ten thousand soda cans opening in concert. Scattered outbuildings and a dozen scattered shipping containers lay off the end of the football field. They were out of the wind, but dark and lonely and way too creepy to make a good place to meet when Hopkin showed up. No. It was far better to meet in the open. She reached in her pocket and touched the little Beretta, reassuring herself.

There were more bones on the beach. Figured. The North was proud of her bone piles—as if everyone needed to be reminded how precarious life was in the Arctic. Mim gave the ATV more gas, riding closer to investigate. Unlike the weathered specimens at the arch, these were shiny and pink, only recently stripped of flesh. Deep tooth marks creased nearly every surface. Oily gore soaked the rocks and gravel in an oval thirty feet long and half as wide. The sand and gravel were black as tar.

Mesmerized, Mim rolled even closer. By chance, she approached from upwind, so the smell didn't hit her until she was almost on top of the scene. Arliss said the ground told a story and she found herself wondering what this mess might tell her if she could only understand the signs—

Frantic honking jerked her out of her stupor. The boom of a shotgun shook the air.

She ducked at the noise, flattening herself against the handlebars, trying to figure out which way to go.

A brown pickup barreled up the beach toward her, honking, swerving back and forth like the driver was drunk.

Had Phil Hopkin come to murder her?

Her hand dropped to the pistol in her pocket.

The truck skidded to a stop fifty yards away. An Iñupiat man Mim didn't recognize bailed out of the passenger door with a shotgun in his hand. He fired twice into the air and then pointed frantically to something up the beach.

Mim turned to find the biggest bear she'd ever seen loping directly toward her, nose up, white fur rippling in the wind. Two cubs, each big enough to kill and eat her without any assistance from their mother, loped alongside their larger mom.

The man with the shotgun scrambled back into the truck and it resumed its wild ride, honking and swerving as it sped past a cowering Mim.

All three bears stopped just twenty yards away. The two youngsters wheeled and trotted off a few steps, looking over their shoulders as if they didn't quite know what to do. The big female rose up on her hind legs, great paws up like a prizefighter. Towering at least seven feet tall, she cocked her head, looking back and forth between Mim and the truck, as if deciding which to eat first.

The truck skidded to a stop ten yards from the bear. In what seemed like slow motion, the passenger door flew open and the Iñupiat man bailed out again. He looked so puny silhouetted against the massive wall of white fur. The shotgun boomed again, and the bear flinched, struck square in the brisket by a rubber bullet.

That appeared to do the trick . . . for the moment. The bear dropped to all fours and then, as if disgusted by the men, turned slowly and ambled away. The man popped her again, slapping her rump with another rubber bullet. This one caused her to tuck her butt and sent her loping up the beach toward the end of the road.

The truck made a quick 180 on the beach, throwing gravel as it came around behind Mim, to turn once again so as not to leave their backs toward the bear.

Both the driver and the passenger turned out to be Iñupiat. Bear patrol.

The oncoming truck, the threat of the approaching bear—it had all happened so fast that Mim's fear lagged behind reality. She had to grab the handlebars and squeeze to keep from shaking uncontrollably.

"New in town," the driver said. It was more pronouncement than question, but Mim answered, anyway.

"I'm a visiting nurse," she said. "A friend of mine said I should meet him out here."

The passenger, still clutching his shotgun and keeping one eye on the bear, leaned across the cab and spoke over the driver's lap through the open window. "This friend of yours a local?"

She nodded. "He works in town."

The driver crinkled his nose. "Then he shoulda known better than to send you out here. Them bears'll eat your guts." He used his chin to point at the bones scattered on the gore-soaked gravel. "People been comin' to this stretch of beach for a week to watch 'em eat a gray whale calf that washed up. I've seen as many as three big males at one time. They finished it a couple days ago. Bears all went off to find something else to eat and the people stopped coming out, especially this time of night." He wiped his face as if trying to wake himself up. "A few bears show up to check out the smell from time to time. We come out here and run 'em off."

Mim pressed a hand flat to her chest, willing her racing heart to slow down. "Okay," she said, panting. "So she was after the smell of dead whale. Maybe she didn't even see me."

"Oh no, ma'am," the driver said, slowly shaking his head like he was disappointed in a small child. "Polar bears, they see as good as you or me. This one probably saw you and thought, 'Look at that delicious seal standing there all by herself. I think I'll go eat her guts.'"

The passenger leaned across again. "Nanook can run faster than that old Honda. We'll follow you back to town."

"Awful damned dangerous," the driver muttered. "Your friend tellin' you to meet you way out here . . . is like he wanted you to get yourself eaten."

CHAPTER 32

Sloan offered to send Lola home after the news about Sam Benjamin, but she wouldn't hear of it. Cutter walked her to her room and waited until she got Joe Bill Brackett on the phone before he told her good night.

Back in his own room, Cutter dug a fresh white shirt out of his suitcase and hung it up, letting the wrinkles fall out. The soldier in him said he should iron it, but it was late, and the time would be better spent talking to Mim. Sloan had assigned him airport advance, which meant he needed to be up by four thirty a.m. Not too far from his normal wake-up-and-stew time.

Mim called on FaceTime while he was staging his gear for the morning. She sat on the hotel bed, propped up, as usual, on every pillow she could find.

"Thought you might have already conked out for the night," he said, feeling the familiar rush that came over him each time he saw her face or heard her voice.

"Won't be long," she said. "It's been a day."

Her face was flushed, like she'd been in the weather. He started to say something, but caught himself. Instead, he brought her up to speed on the finding of Sam Benjamin's hat and then his body. She sat up a little straighter at the news, free hand to her lips.

"That's just awful," she whispered. "How's Lola?"

"She's taking it hard," Cutter said. "Understandably. Brackett offered to fly up and be with her, but we're heading home tomorrow."

"That kid's a keeper," Mim said. "Wait. You're already done."

Cutter caught her up on the evening's events, toning it down a hair from his briefing to the justice.

"How's the hospital?" he asked.

"All good," she said. "They're treating me great. Loaned me a little Honda to get around on while I'm here."

A disapproving eyebrow shot up in spite of himself. "That's got to be cold."

"I'm fine," she said, looking away just like Constance did when she was hiding something. Instead of pressing it, he told her what he learned from Erica Bell.

It was her turn to raise an eyebrow. "So," she said, lips set in a tight line, "you're accusing Coop now."

"I didn't say that." He knew she was processing.

"Arliss!" She threw her head back, exasperated. "Cooper Daniels has done nothing but offer his help from day one."

"But was he helping or keeping tabs?" It was dangerous territory, but it needed to be said.

"You know he gave me a shoulder to cry on," she said. "After Ethan died. Is that why you're so set on finding something wrong with him?"

"I'm not set on anything," Cutter said. "Except the truth. We have to keep an open mind. Especially with you—"

"With me what?" she snapped. "What were you going to say? With me traipsing all over the North Slope like an idiot."

"Mim," Cutter whispered. "I'd never—"

"I'm not an idiot, Arliss. So, what if Coop did occasional work for JBM? Does that necessarily mean he's complicit in Ethan's death?"

"No," Cutter admitted. "It does not. But it does mean he's been less than forthcoming. He did pro bono legal work for you, filing court documents against the same company that had him on their payroll. That's a monumental conflict of interest. Holding back on the truth is the same as a lie, and if somebody's going to do it, they better have a damn fine rea—"

"Save your Grumpy rules for the twins," Mim fumed.

"Mim," Cutter said. "I'm—"

She softened. "I know, Arliss. It's just . . . I've got a lot to process. We both have to get up early."

"Right," Cutter said. "Anyway . . . you getting anywhere on your end?"

"What do you mean?"

"Leads," he said.

"No," she said. "Not really. Nothing."

Had Cutter been interrogating her, he would have called so many denials what they were. A *yes.*

Instead, he heaved a deep sigh.

"Mim—"

"I know, Arliss," she said. "Me too."

She ended the call, leaving Cutter alone in the screaming silence of his hotel room.

He had all of twenty seconds to think before his phone buzzed again.

It was Jill Phillips.

He yawned. "Hey, boss."

"Just talked to Nicki Sloan," the chief said.

Cutter rubbed a hand over his face, thinking he needed to shave. "Sorry. We tried to get the justice to go home. Not everyone sees the patterns we do."

"Exactly what Nicki said. But that's not why I'm calling you. Captain Krieger from ABI has asked for our help looking over the scene around Trooper Benjamin's body."

"That's a surprise," Cutter said. "It's not like Alaska Bureau of Investigation to ask an outside agency to poke around their crime scene."

"True enough," Phillips said. "State techs are on their way out now, but Captain Krieger asked if you'd see if you can glean anything from any tracks."

Cutter swung his feet off the edge of the bed, resting his elbows on his knees while he spoke.

"You know I'd be glad to help," he said, unconsciously shaking his head. "But I won't be much good if they've already trampled the ground."

"That's exactly what I told Krieger," Phillips said. "He assures me that up to this point, only three troopers have approached Sam's vehicle. They've checked his body for signs of life as soon as they got there . . . and then backed off."

"Hang on," Cutter said. "They're actually holding the scene?"

"Not just for you," Phillips said. "They don't trust us that much. They're waiting for daylight so they don't screw it up. Captain Krieger wants to take advantage of the stall and get you there before they start—if you can get away."

"Of course," Cutter said. "I'll let Nicki know."

"I just asked her if she could do without you," Phillips said. "Got a weird response until she figured out what I was talking about. You two must have a history—"

"Anyway," Cutter said.

"Right," the chief said, moving on. "Sunrise is a touch after four a.m., but it'll be light enough to see well before that. Krieger's sending a chopper to their hangar on the civil aviation side of the airport. ETA one hour from . . . three minutes ago."

"And Lola?" Cutter asked.

"What do you mean?"

"I'd like to take her with me," Cutter said. "She's got a hell of an aptitude for seeing tracks."

"I don't know about that," Phillips said, her soft Kentucky drawl coming out on the back of her fatigue. "If she chooses to stay on the detail, Sloan will want her watching Ramona Morehouse."

"Nicki's folding Ramona in with the justice's detail. They're not separating at this point. She's fine with Lola coming with me."

"She and Sam Benjamin were a serious item for months," the chief said. "As far as I know, they remained close. That friendship could cloud her judgment."

"Or steel her resolve," Cutter said. "The Troopers are a small organization, Chief. Something like four hundred in the entire state. Sam Benjamin was a well-respected hard worker. If friendship is a disqualifying factor, then half the troopers going to the scene tonight shouldn't be there. Law enforcement is too close-knit in Alaska to only work cases where you have no personal connection."

"Fair enough," Phillips said. A baby cried in the background. "I'll leave it up to you. Keep in mind, though, Lola can be an unguided missile—"

"So can I," he said.

"That's not true at all." Phillips groaned, as if from the sheer weight of supervising someone like Arliss Cutter. "Your guidance system works perfectly, 'Big Iron.' Your problem is the collateral damage your missiles leave in their wake."

Cutter couldn't exactly argue that point.

"Chief, something like this . . . guts us all."

"It does indeed, my friend." Phillips groaned again. "And you need to remember that, when some distraught trooper takes his misplaced anger out on you for intruding on his turf."

Mim filled the tub with hot water as soon as she ended the call with Arliss. Then she thought better of it, and crawled into bed in her long johns to stare at the ceiling and brood while she listened to the clock radio.

KBRW, the local station, aired a public service announcement about a polar bear being spotted north of town.

Not exactly breaking news . . .

This stuff about Coop Daniels was nonsense. It had to be. He'd seen her through some of the darkest moments of her life. There was no way he was taking advantage of her. Was there? He was Ethan's friend. At least that's what he'd told her. Now that she thought about it, Ethan had only ever mentioned Coop Daniels in passing. They'd never had him over for dinner or seen him socially. Everything she knew about Cooper Daniels was what he'd told her during the aftermath of Ethan's death. And she had to admit, he'd been noticeably absent since Arliss moved north. Her dear brother-in-law had that effect on people. There was always the possibility that Erica Bell was lying. Maybe she was just spreading hate and discontent. She was the one who'd been avoiding Arliss for months.

Mim trusted her husband, but . . . was it possible she hadn't known him as well as she'd thought? Every time she turned on the television, there was a documentary about some dude's secret life—and a poor shattered, astonished spouse who could not believe what she was learning.

Ethan rarely talked about his coworkers. He'd become quieter the weeks before he died, distant. Where there was smoke . . .

She pulled a pillow over her face and screamed into it. Entertaining such doubts, even for a microsecond, made her feel dirty.

Ethan was dead. That was the only thing she knew for sure. Well, that, and that Arliss was likely going to prison if he learned who killed his brother. She could almost hear Grumpy calling this whole thing a "soup sandwich." It wouldn't be long before everyone in Utqiagvik knew that Ethan Cutter's widow was on the ground stirring up trouble. And what about those two thuggy-looking dudes who kept staring at her in the restaurant? The thought of them made her crawl out of bed and wedge a chair against the door.

The Beretta Tomcat was still in the nightstand drawer resting on the folded washcloth—like Ethan had taught her to do when they traveled.

She ran what-ifs in her head. The flimsy chair wouldn't stop an intruder, but it would give her time to go for the pistol. Then what? She never got past opening the drawer and looking at the gun. Arliss would know what to do.

Arliss . . .

He didn't deserve any of this. Sometimes, between moments of self-pity, Mim could almost catch a glimpse of a future where they were together, a future that would never be until she learned what really had happened to Ethan.

She pulled the sheet to her chin and closed her eyes.

Even then . . .

CHAPTER 33

Never in his life had Alex felt such rage, made even more unbearable by the fact that his father had yet to lift a finger. He'd lost count of the number of people they'd killed over the past three days, all in preparation for avenging an ex-wife. Now that one of their own had been gunned down, they sat on their asses in a stinking Fairbanks hotel gnashing their teeth and blubbering like a bunch of old grandmas.

Details of what happened to Gavrill were sketchy at best. He'd seen Morehouse's written schedule, and then texted a photo, but it was blurry, barely readable. Fishing. Flights to see bears. And a sightseeing trip by train in two days' time.

Ilia Lipin's laptop illuminated his face. "Sorry, boss," he said. "No seats left on the train from Anchorage."

Volkov pounded a fist against his knee. "We will take her as she nears the fishing boat."

Yegon Zhuk sat on the floor against the baseboard heater. He spoke without looking up. "Better to kill her on the street. It does not matter, so long as she is dead."

Lev Rudenko stood by the television, muscular arms folded across his chest, flexing, looking for a neck to crush. "It is strange they did not move her tonight."

"My son is dead," Oleg Pogodin said. The poor man seethed, stricken with sorrow, unable to sit or stand still. "I will kill her here. Burn the hotel to the ground!"

"I agree," Alex whispered. "I want the bitch who did this."

"My son," Volkov said, "you must—"

Pogodin spun on his heels. "And what of *my* son, Maxim? Should he not be avenged? Or is it only your dear departed ex-wife who deserves such things?"

Maxim closed his eyes. The tips of his fingers brushed the grip of the pistol in his waistband.

Ilia Lipin spoke, looking to the others in hopes of enlisting them to avert a looming disaster. "The woman who shot our Gavrill was a trooper," he said. "I did not see her pull the trigger, but I know it was her. The Black woman is the marshal. She blocked his path, kept him from getting away."

Pogodin sniffed back a tear. "Then she is also to blame for the death of my son. I will kill them both."

"Not here," Volkov said. "Not yet. They are fortified too well. Any attempt on the trooper will only raise alarms."

Rudenko looked up from his phone. "You're right, boss. Fishing charters leave early in the morning. The docks will make a good choke point, but it could be a problem—"

Lipin looked up suddenly from his laptop. "The sightseeing train is called *Glacier Discovery*. It is an out-and-back journey into an extremely remote area of mountains and glaciers. Much like Petropavlovsk."

Volkov gave a contemplative nod. "She would be trapped on board the train—as would her security personnel."

"As would we," Lev Rudenko pointed out.

"What does it matter?" Alex said. "He already said there are no seats."

Lipin tapped the top of his computer. "None departing from Anchorage. More than two dozen people get off when the train reaches Whittier. We simply drive through the tunnel and board the train when it departs Whittier at twelve forty-five."

Volkov began to bounce slightly where he sat on the edge of the bed, animated. "Get the tickets from Whittier."

Lipin tapped the keys, talking to himself. "Seven . . ."

"Six," Oleg Pogodin whispered, his face a mix of anger and sorrow. "We are . . . only six."

Lipin gave his friend a solemn nod before turning to Volkov. "The train goes into the mountains after that. Very remote, but we should have signal as we leave the highway."

"Then five of us will take the train there." Volkov looked imploringly at Yegon Zhuk. "And you will help me with the video, my friend? We should have service until we reach the mountains. The world needs to see what happens to this heartless woman."

"That has always been the plan," Zhuk said. "My sister is dead because of her."

"I am all in, boss," Rudenko said. "You know that. Whatever you decide. But it is my duty to point out that the things that make the train a good target also make it a good trap—for us. Forgive me for saying, but Morehouse's security has already shown the will not to hesitate to use force to protect her. We must also consider something like a hundred fifty other passengers, some of whom are not likely to simply stand by and watch us do what we have come to do."

"Pshh!" Yegon Zhuk scoffed. "Americans dream they are all action heroes . . . until it is time to be one. Mark my words. They will piss themselves."

Rudenko shrugged. He was in no way tentative, but was simply being practical. "I suppose. Depending on where we make the move, escape could be a problem."

"I do not expect to get away," Volkov said.

"Nor do I," Pogodin said. "There is no reason."

Volkov closed his eyes and groaned. "Alex, my son, you will stay—"

"I'm coming too," Alex said. It was all he could do to keep from smashing the television or driving his fist through a wall.

Volkov shook his head. "No. We must stay with the original plan. This changes nothing!"

"Oh, Papa," Alex said, wiping away tears of anger and frustration. "Don't you see? They murdered Gavrill. This changes everything."

CHAPTER 34

*H*elo-3, the Alaska State Trooper A-Star 350 helicopter, lifted to spitting rain. The clouds added a brooding texture to the Arctic summer twilight, making it just possible to make out the spruce forests of the Tanana River Valley below. Lola sat across from Cutter, staring mutely out the window. The pilot flew in silence, concentrating on navigating around pockets of low weather. Cutter and Lola were his only passengers.

The chopper drummed southward, dropping lower to follow the Parks Highway through the Alaska Range. They made the 180-mile trip in seventy minutes. Five Trooper patrol vehicles cast their headlights across the landing zone, a wide woodlot off the Parks Highway, a scant mile north of Trapper Creek.

Captain Will Krieger waited in a drizzling rain in front of an unmarked Dodge Durango, hand pressed to his blue Stetson against the rotor wash of the approaching chopper.

In his early fifties, with a soft-spoken demeanor, Krieger was Alaska Native, primarily of Iñupiat and Tsimshian heritage. He'd been raised in the village of Unalakleet and attended Mt. Edgecumbe High School in Sitka, a stone's throw from the Alaska State Trooper Academy. He'd served as a Village Public Safety officer in his hometown, a police officer in Dillingham, and then joined the ranks of AST when he was twenty-four. Cutter had run across a fair number of troopers who were experts on rural policing. Will Krieger was a master.

"Cutter, Teariki," the captain said. He shook their hands in turn. "I appreciate this."

"Of course," Cutter said.

Krieger held on to Lola's hand a hair longer. "I understand you and Trooper Benjamin were close."

"We were," Lola said, her voice catching. "Very."

Krieger swallowed hard. "I was a Trooper pilot back in the day," he said. "Met Sam when he was just a kid and I landed my Super Cub at his family's hunting camp." He sniffed and wiped a tear from his eye. "I gotta warn ya, this is a hard thing to see."

The drive from the helicopter landing area to Sam's vehicle was a short one, less than three miles. A dozen AST SUVs along the shoulder of the Parks Highway marked the spot. The sun was still a few minutes from making an appearance, but Cutter could already make out the pale lines of an ATV trail disappearing into the dense spruce forest on the west side of the road. Everyone had taken care to park on the east side, and well north and south of the apparent entry point, so as not to disturb the crime scene.

The hum of a generator carried over the constant patter of rain against foliage as Cutter climbed out of Captain Krieger's Durango. Construction lights glowed through the trees.

Lola stretched a pair of blue nitrile gloves over her hands while she marched straight toward the trailhead without waiting for Cutter or Krieger. To her credit, she stopped the moment she reached the ruts where someone had apparently driven the SUV into the woods. Whoever drove it in would have had to walk out.

Two somber uniformed troopers stood guard at the tree line. Seeing the captain, they didn't bother to challenge the two deputies.

Krieger gave the men a nod. "These are the trackers I mentioned earlier." He turned back to Cutter. "It'll be light enough to see anytime now."

Cutter glanced at the glowing orange line below the clouds to the east. "This is good. The low angle of the light this early will be helpful." He noted a half-dozen numbered yellow evidence placards in the muck alongside what looked to be identifiable tracks.

"Our techs will start casting impressions with dental stone as soon as you've had a look," Krieger said. "I'm not sure about your process, but if it's all the same to you, I wouldn't mind if you'd start with the vehicle and work outward. That way we can do what we need to do to get that poor young man out of there."

"Of course," Cutter said.

Lola and Krieger lined up single file behind Cutter in an effort to keep from tramping on any more ground than they had to. They stayed to the trees, well clear of the established ATV trail on their way in. It wasn't far. Four uniformed troopers, and half again as many plainclothes troopers and crime scene techs, stood at the edge of a muddy trail, twenty yards from a white SUV that was wedged under a thick canopy of alder and birch, stark and lonesome in the gathering light. Even the golden bear on the AST badge decal affixed to the door looked forlorn in the gathering light.

A heavyset sergeant that Cutter didn't recognize scowled under the low brim of his Stetson, puffing up when he saw the two Feds intruding on what he viewed as sacred ground.

"Stow it, Sergeant Bowden," Krieger said before the man could voice a concern. "I got no time for turf wars. The Feds know how to track, so we're going to let them track. Are we clear?"

"Yes, Captain," the sergeant said, the if-you-say-so attitude was implied on his face.

Krieger was not having it. "You don't have the corner on being pissed, Sergeant. Everyone here is heartbroken. If you can't throttle your attitude, then you may consider yourself relieved."

"Apologies," Bowden said, almost meaning it.

Death, especially the death of a friend, tended to make people feel fragile. Staring one's own mortality in the face was uncomfortable and some compensated by lashing out at anyone and everyone around them.

"No worries," Lola said.

The sergeant's eyes softened when he realized who Lola was. "You're . . . Teariki . . ."

"I am."

"Sam talked about you all the time," Bowden said. "He said you're 'damn good people.'"

Lola opened her mouth to speak, but couldn't muster the words. Tears ran freely down her cheeks. She was finally able to say, "Let's . . . let's get to work" and started for the SUV.

Cutter stopped ten feet out, raising his hand to keep Lola from moving any closer. Sam Benjamin slumped, chin to chest, in the front passenger seat, held away from the steering wheel by a seat belt.

"You don't need to see this," Cutter said. "How about you cut sign outward, ten yards or so from the vehicle. Tell me what—"

Lola followed Cutter's suggestion and strode forward to study significant damage to the fender over the rear driver's-side wheel. She gestured to the mud and scratches along the entire SUV. "Somebody pitted him," she said, jaw clenched, the muscles in her neck tensing. "You think he spun around, flipped onto the driver's side, and"—she looked at the smeared mud—"slid backward?"

"That's what it looks like," Krieger said, taking care to watch where he put his feet.

"Driver's window is intact," Cutter said, thinking out loud, as he peered into the vehicle. "Passenger window is shattered, but all the glass is on the driver's side." He played his flashlight around the interior. "Glass all over the door frame, in the armrests . . ."

Lola had made her way around the SUV and now stood mere inches from her dead friend. She took a deep breath, steeling herself. "Boot prints on the front fender," she noted.

Cutter joined her, shaking his head at the awful scene. "You good?"

"Hell no, I'm not good." She sniffed. "This whole thing is stuffed beyond measure. Let's just get it done."

"Right." Cutter pointed to the fender damage. "So the car's on its side, like you said, sliding . . ."

"Sam's behind the wheel, stunned," Lola said, stoic, clinical. "Before he even realized what's happening, at least one of the killers climbs up the side and jumps in on top of him, shattering the window and keeping Sam from going for his gun."

"Maybe the bad guy just shot through the window," Sergeant Bowden offered.

"Mountain View mineral," Lola said under her breath, shining her flashlight around the interior of the SUV. She groaned. "No, the killer jumped down on the window . . . like he was hopping into the water feetfirst. Probably had to fold his arms to fit through the window." Her light hovered over the blood and gore on Sam Benjamin's head. She took a couple of deep breaths. "See that partial boot print and the tiny squares of green glass embedded in his forehead . . ." Her throat convulsed. "They jumped down on him . . . and then they shot him."

Cutter caught something out of place at the edge of her light, clinging to the collar of the trooper's uniform. He leaned in to get a better look.

Lola noticed it too.

"A flower?" she observed.

Cutter chewed the inside of his cheek, turning to scan the ground around the SUV.

"I'm seeing fireweed and Nootka lupine around here," he said.

"I don't think this is either one of those." Lola held her light on the flower. "It's wilted, but it looks purple to me."

"Agreed," Cutter said. "I'm thinking it's monkshood."

"Wolfsbane." Captain Krieger nodded in agreement, using another well-known name for the plant. "I've heard stories about Iñupiat using monkshood as a poison."

"A lot of cultures did," Cutter said. "Some dipped arrowheads in it. Nazis added it to experimental bullets."

"Bastards," Lola muttered.

"I don't get it," Bowden said, barely concealing his disgust. "Are you suggesting that Sam was poisoned? That's the biggest crock of shit I—"

"No, Sergeant," Lola said, a picture of calm. "He's suggesting there isn't any monkshood growing at the scene. It was transferred here."

The sneer stayed put on Bowden's face. "What does that even mean?"

"It means that whoever stomped Sam, also stomped on a monkshood blossom. You see any purple flowers in this clearing?"

Bowden took a look around and then shook his head, more sheepish now.

"No. Just fireweed and lupine, like you said."

"That's right," Lola said. "It's worth supposing that there's at least one monkshood plant in or around the place where Sam was run off the road."

Cutter gave his partner a friendly pat on the shoulder, to show her he approved of her assessment, then took the chief's advice and followed up with the sergeant to show he meant no ill will. "Do y'all have that scene located?"

"Not yet," Bowden said. "All this rain and heavy ATV traffic along the roadside . . . it's been impossible to pin it down."

"What about his hat?" Lola asked.

"We were concentrating thirty miles to the north," Krieger said. "Nearer the tower where his cell last pinged. It was already dark by the time we moved our efforts down to where the Stetson was found. That gave us a starting point, but the wind can be brutal coming off the mountains. And every trooper knows, these damned hats can travel once they start rolling. Frankly, we were lucky we found this place."

Sergeant Bowden was already on his handheld, dispatching troopers to start looking for patches of purple flowers along the road. They'd been up and down that stretch of highway so many times, most had it memorized. It took less than ten minutes to locate the exact spot where Sam Benjamin had been run off the road.

Cutter and Lola spent another hour poring over the clearing around the SUV. They diagramed pitch, straddle, and stride of two sets of boot prints, building profiles in case the AST ran into the same track makers later. The ground was predominately spongy moss and muck, and gave up little specific information on tread or boot design.

Lola waited quietly by the passenger door of the SUV while Cutter finished up. He gave her a nod when he was ready.

"See ya, Sam," she whispered, choking back another sob before turning to follow the boot prints of his killer toward the road.

Krieger drove them straight to the crash site—the initial crime scene, the spot where Sam Benjamin was presumed to have been murdered.

"No broken glass," Cutter said, combing the willow scrub on the side of the road. "Not even so much as a piece of taillight. Whoever did this, they're either extremely good or extremely lucky."

"I can't believe this," Krieger said. "You'd think a Tahoe sliding along on its side would leave more of a trail."

Cutter stood off the gravel shoulder, rocking on the balls of his feet, burning off energy. "This whole place is more water than land. Those willows have spent the past five months buried under four feet of snow. They're used to bending out of the way." He stooped, pointing out the green of bruised bark, where the trooper vehicle had slid over the top.

Lola piped up, waving the men over. "I've got the monkshood he stepped on. It's growing here, along the ditch." She took out her phone and stooped to snap a couple of photos of the bruised plants. "Take a look at this, boss."

Cutter and the captain hunkered down to get Lola's angle of view in the thick bed of purple flowers.

"A cough drop wrapper," Captain Krieger said, "Halls. We're ten yards from the ATV trail." He scanned the patch of monkshood. "Would I be wrong if I said no other pedestrians have walked through here?"

"That would be my assessment," Cutter said. "And this wrapper's too clean to have been here long. There's a good chance it came out of the killer's pocket. My grandfather was forever leaving cough drop or hard-candy wrappers in his wake every time he fished something else out of his pocket." Cutter stood up, turned in a tight 360 to survey the entire area, reading the story told by the scuffs and scrapes on the ground, imagining the event. "This all happened fast."

"Size-twelve, or size-thirteen, boot," Krieger said, reviewing what

Cutter had told him. "Probably a lug sole, stride indicates someone over six feet tall . . . with a cough."

"I know," Cutter said. "It's not much."

The captain took out his cell phone and shrugged. "Well, it ain't nothing."

Five minutes later, *Helo-3* lifted off, rising out of the clearing. Lola's eyes were shut, but Cutter could tell she was awake. He leaned against his window and peered north, letting his mind drift beyond dense spruce forests, two mountain ranges, and miles of tundra, and wondered what kind of trouble Mim was getting into.

CHAPTER 35

A life of uncertain schedules had trained Cutter to grab sleep whenever the opportunity presented itself—most of the time. The house was unbearably quiet now; worse than that, it was his brother's house. Mim's house. No matter how hard he tried or how long he stayed, he was a guest in this place.

Grumpy, a widower since before Ethan or Arliss came into the picture, had often told stories of "talking matters over" with Nana Cutter. The boys had grown up thinking their grandmother had made frequent visits from beyond the grave to counsel with the old man on important things. As he grew up, Arliss came to assume the talks were more figurative—Grumpy chatting with the memory of his best friend. But there were times that made him wonder. Things the old man said and the way he said them . . .

Now, alone in the stillness of his dead brother's house, Cutter half expected Grumpy to appear and sit on the edge of the bed to offer up some sage advice. Or, if ghosts were capable of such things, Ethan to come and kick his ass for getting serious with Mim.

With a nap not in the cards, Cutter got up and used the alone time to fix a broken rain gutter and install a new garbage disposal, which had been sitting in a box under the sink for two weeks. It was well after six in the evening before he realized he'd forgotten to eat.

He considered checking in with Mim, but thought better of it. His natural inclination was to smother—definitely something he needed to work on. Cooking helped him think. He had the kitchen to himself, so he whipped up Grumpy's go-to meal. The boys called it "hot-and-brown"; it was a pan-fried pork chop, thin cut and lightly dusted with flour and spices. Diced potatoes went into the same grease after the chop came out. He mixed a diced onion in the frying potatoes when they were about done—something he'd not liked as a boy, but now saw as crucial.

Like most things, Cutter had learned to cook from his grandfather. He'd never known his grandmother. Most memories of his mother had been repressed and he had little recollection of his father other than that he was a very sad man. But even with all the loss, his childhood had been idyllic. Life with Grumpy and Ethan was something to be envied—fishing, hunting, overnight trips out to the blue water or deep in the glades. Grumpy had turned over the controls to his Boston Whaler for the first time when Arliss was only nine years old. It was heady stuff for a boy to know the man he idolized trusted him with the boat.

Vivid memories of sound and smell drifted up on the sizzling grease. A couple of spoons of the leftover frying fat and the spiced flour he'd used to dust the chop made for a milk gravy, smooth as silk. Hot and brown indeed.

He put his phone on speaker and called Nicki Sloan while he ate. Like Cutter, she harbored serious reservations about stuffing their protectee on a rolling metal tube full of unvetted strangers, none of whom had to pass through any kind of security beyond the scrutinizing eyes of a half-dozen deputy US marshals. She planned to get the justice buttoned up for an early night and then do a walk-through of the train. He might as well invite himself along for the ride.

CHAPTER 36

*M*im leaned over her grocery cart, resting on her forearms, and browsed her way down the aisle. Blondie's "Heart of Glass" poured over the store's sound system, oddly in time with the rhythm of the cart's squeaking wheels. So far, she'd loaded up with roughly thirty bucks' worth of groceries—a loaf of bread and a jar of peanut butter. There was a red Igloo cooler in the cart too, but she'd brought that in for safekeeping. Darika had tasked her with stopping by North Slope Borough Search and Rescue to give a few vaccinations after work. Mim hadn't wanted to leave vials of whooping cough and tetanus vaccine strapped to the back of her Honda while she made a quick stop at the Stuaqpak in the center section of town known as Browerville.

As a bush-community hub, Utqiagvik served a large enough population to have a couple of decent grocery stores that sold everything from frozen pizzas to fishing line. Canned green beans at one end, brand-new ATVs in the back by the boat anchors. There were deep freezers too, and a rack with assorted hoodies. She looked for mittens, but as chilly as she was, this wasn't mitten season.

A man in a ballcap and heavy Carhartt jacket almost ran into her when she popped out of the frozen-food aisle. He was empty-handed—no cart or basket—and slightly flushed as if he'd been caught in the middle of something. He looked older, maybe sixty. She'd never seen him before, but something about him instantly put Mim on edge. He paused when he saw her and took a step back, gesturing with an open hand.

"Please . . . after you."

Mim forced a smile, wondering if this guy was a shoplifter. She'd been around Arliss so long, she expected to find criminal activity under every rock and leaf.

"You have the right of way," she said.

He didn't move. "I insist."

Something about his eyes put her off.

"I don't care," she said, rooted in place. It wasn't in her nature to be rude, but her gut said she didn't want this guy behind her.

They stood in a silent impasse for another fifteen or twenty seconds—an eternity to spend locking eyes with a stranger at the end of the frozen-food aisle. Finally he shrugged and walked toward the back of the store without another word.

Mim hurried to check out, eager to get out of there while the creepo was still in the store.

The few evening shoppers in the parking lot seemed busy with their own personal lives and didn't appear to have any interest in Mim at all. She strapped the red cooler down on the back of her Honda, along with her reusable shopping bag of bread and peanut butter, and headed south. It was finally time to do some rural nursing.

The rain had cleared off and there was more traffic out, but she couldn't shake the feeling that she might run into another bear, or meet up with a caribou warble fly.

The hangar was pretty much a straight trip down a lonesome gravel street past Isatkoak Lagoon to the east end of the airport—on the Barrow side.

The abrupt buzz of her cell phone in her scrubs pocket brought images of vicious warble flies as she rode across North Star Street, nearly sending her into a panic. She pulled to the side of the otherwise deserted road and fished out the phone to make sure it wasn't Arliss or one of the kids. The caller ID said JBM.

Johnson, Benham, and Murphy Engineering.

She'd been leaving messages for Phil Hopkin all day, ready to unload on him about standing her up, not to mention sending her into the jaws of Nanook. Not surprisingly, he wasn't answering his phone. She tried to leave a message, but his voice mail was full. By noon, after six attempts, she called JBM's main North Slope number. She was able to leave a voice mail, but never expected a call back.

Mim whipped into an empty lot behind the Heritage Center and answered, panting, worried the caller would hang up.

"Johnson, Benham, and Murphy Engineering," a female voice said. "You left a message earlier that you needed to speak with someone."

"I did," Mim said. "I'm trying to get in touch with Phil Hopkin. It's very important that I speak with him."

"I'm so sorry, hon," the woman said, sounding like a bored Southern belle. "Phil's been transferred."

Mim's mouth fell open. "Overnight? I just talked to him yesterday."

"I'm sure the move was scheduled."

"We were supposed to have a meeting," Mim said. "Has he gone to Anchorage?"

"No, no, hon. Our North Sea offices," she said. "Scotland. He took a company charter out last night."

"Scotland? Are you—"

A pickup truck rattled up alongside her, pulling her attention away from the call. Her stomach fell when she recognized the blond driver as one of the two roustabouts from the restaurant the day before. A big Native man jumped out of the passenger side. Both "Blond" and "Big" seemed laser-focused on her, and neither was smiling.

There was no one else to be seen. It was obvious the men were there for her.

She shoved her free hand into her pocket, grabbing the pistol, accidentally ending the call in the process.

"Can I help you with something?" she asked, angry with the quaver in her voice.

"Maybe we can help you." Blond laughed and raised his eyebrows up and down, Groucho Marx style.

Big paused at the fender of the pickup, eyes on Mim's hand in her pocket.

"I'm all good," Mim said.

"Phil Hopkin's a friend of ours," Blond said. "He's sorry about the mix-up last night. He asked us to give you a ride if we found you."

"A ride to Scotland?" Mim said, wishing, the moment the words left her mouth, that she hadn't tipped her hand.

"No," Big said, stone-faced. "Not Scotland." He tossed a glance at the truck. "You're lookin' for answers, we got answers."

For the first time Mim realized she could see neither of the men's hands.

"I'm good," she said. "Tell Phil to give me a call. He's got my number."

The Iñupiat frowned and started to say something, but the blond man cut him off.

"We don't wish to frighten you—"

"Well, you are," she snapped back. Inside her pocket her finger found the Beretta's trigger. "You're scaring the shit outta me. I'm not going anywhere with you."

Big took a step toward her, right hand hidden behind his back. "Let's talk here, then."

A horn blared to Mim's left and she took her eye off Big long enough to chance a look, hand still gripping the pistol. A surge of adrenaline shot down both legs. She let go of the gun and pressed the starter on the ATV. Big and Blond both saw it too and scrambled to jump back in their truck.

Meanwhile, across Ahkovak Street, the driver of a dark blue Chevy Blazer sat on his horn, clutching the wheel with both hands as he barreled directly toward them.

CHAPTER 37

*C*utter picked up Inspector Nicki Sloan and Deputy Dave Dillard at the downtown Marriott a little after nine p.m.

Morehouse and her daughter had turned in early for the night with deputies posted outside their door.

Sloan gave Cutter a wink. "You smell good."

"Thanks."

She snapped on her seat belt and settled in. "I mean you smell like food. You've always smelled like food, for as long as I've known you." She laughed. "Remember how your jacket smelled like hamburgers and a campfire when you showed up at the Academy?"

"I drove up from home." Cutter shrugged. "Caught a lot of shit for stopping at a campground off I-95 to cook some lunch."

"Oh, don't get me wrong," Sloan said. "I liked it. Still do—"

Dillard spoke up from the back seat. "Is this gonna turn into one of those *Tom Jones* food-porn-type deals? Because if it is, you can let me out here."

Cutter chuckled, glancing in the rearview mirror. "I knew you were old, Dave, but damn, *Tom Jones?*"

A light drizzle fell when they pulled into the parking lot across from the Alaska Railroad station near Ship Creek. Cutter grabbed an extra fleece and his rain jacket from the back seat beside Dillard. It seemed like he'd not truly been warm since his last trip to Florida.

Sloan gave a long, stretching yawn as she climbed out of the

SUV. "I can't get over how light it is at nine thirty at night. Don't get me wrong . . . it's nice—"

"Like Arliss's yummy food stench?" Dillard said.

She gave him a don't-forget-I'm-your-boss glare.

He laughed. "Sorry. Couldn't help myself."

A train whistle sounded, causing the deputy's head to snap around, an old hunting dog catching the chatter of a distant squirrel. The five-car *Glacier Discovery* rolled in on the tracks behind the station. Dillard clapped his hands together and made a beeline for the building without another word.

Cutter wasn't averse to the concept of trains. They were interesting enough, but Dillard, a self-confessed rail buff, was a savant.

According to him, he'd taken the Amtrak *Empire Builder* from Seattle to Chicago to visit his daughter so many times, he was on a first-name basis with many of the porters. Flying was for people with no patience, he said. He and his wife had ridden the Trans-Canadian twice and spent their vacations traveling with Eurail or Japan Rail Passes. His wife's gift for his pending retirement was for them take the once-in-a-lifetime trip from Paris to Istanbul on the *Orient Express*. The six-day train ride for two would cost the equivalent of their yearly mortgage payment, but he did not care. Trains were in his blood.

"I'll chat with the staff," Sloan said to Cutter. "If you want to make a quick sketch of the cars, you know passenger compartments, restrooms, control security, that kind of shit."

"Copy." Cutter held up the BattleBoard to show he'd come prepared to do just that.

Sloan gave a nod toward an extremely excited Dave Dillard. He'd already badged his way onto the platform and was hanging off the engine catwalk.

"I guess Dave's just going to play on the train."

"He'll be good to have around," Cutter said. "A solid deputy. I'm pretty sure he could drive the locomotive if he had to—"

"And he's old enough to know about *Tom Jones*." Sloan grinned. "My grandmother loved that movie."

CHAPTER 38

Mim's ATV was still warm and started on the first push of the button—then promptly died.

Big had left the pickup running. He threw it into gear and stomped on the gas, throwing up a shower of gravel. The tires finally grabbed and he shot forward, narrowly missing Mim's right knee, but spinning the little ATV like a rodeo bull. She flew off, sliding on her butt across the gravel. She rolled, scrambling to get out of the way as the blue Blazer smashed into the pickup, snapping the rear wheel.

Dazed and crawling on all fours, Mim heard the whoop of a siren. A Native man she'd seen somewhere before climbed out of the Blazer and walked toward the pickup. He looked to be in his teens . . . with a white shock of hair. The hospital! She'd seen him there on her first day.

Big came out of his truck, cursing. Blond screamed something in German.

The young man turned and ran back the way he'd come, abandoning the steaming Blazer.

The siren sounded again, earsplitting, and a white Tahoe slid to a stop within inches of the pickup. A woman in the dark blue uniform of the North Slope Borough Police Department bailed out, gun drawn.

"Sherman Billy!" the officer barked. "How you doing?" She spoke into her radio, "We got a runner."

Big raised both hands, glaring at his partner.

The German froze for a moment, then raised his hands as well.

"Good, good, good," the officer said. Her voice was direct and clear, absent even a hint of ambiguity. "Now, I see the gun in your waistband, Mr. Billy. Do not touch it. You armed, Mr. Dittmar?"

Another North Slope patrol vehicle rolled up behind the white Tahoe in the parking lot. The second officer, who looked like he was barely out of high school, stood at his car to provide backup. He had drawn his weapon too.

Dittmar shook his head. "A revolver for polar bears," he said. "All legal."

"For you, maybe," the female officer said. "Mr. Sherman Billy happens to be a felon. That's a problem."

"Hey," the one called Dittmar said, "we were just asking if the lady needs help. That other kid's the one that caused all this. We meant no harm."

"I saw exactly what happened." The officer gave a wary side-eye. "If this lady is who I think she is, you two are in serious danger of an ass kicking from her brother-in-law."

Sherman Billy kept his hands raised, but turned to glare over his shoulder. "That a threat?"

The officer laughed. "An observation," she said. "And, if you want to get down to it, a pretty damned serious warning. For your own good."

She ordered both men on their knees and then nodded for the backup officer to handcuff them. "Officer Lorenz will get you booked. I'll be down shortly to settle you in."

"Lawyer," Billy said.

Dittmar shrugged. "Lawyer."

"Good deal," the officer said. "Have a chat with your attorneys and see who wants to rat on the other one first."

"Janice Hough," the officer said, shaking Mim's hand as her partner drove away with the two prisoners. "My friends call me Jan."

Mim calmed a notch and took a moment to look at the woman for the first time. Blond curls and a splash of freckles added to the gleam in her eye, giving the impression she was smiling, though she'd yet to do so.

"Jan," Mim said, as if trying on the name for size. "I guess my husband was one of those friends who called you that."

"He was," Hough said. "And I'm happy to get into it, but first things first. Are you okay? You didn't exactly nail the dismount coming off that Honda."

"I'm fine," Mim said. Meaning it. "I nearly got eaten by a polar bear last night, so this was nothing. Honestly, these guys probably should have scared the shit out of me, at least more than they did."

"Eaten by a polar bear," Hough said. "That's a lot to unpack."

"True," Mim said. "I'd say you and I have a great deal to . . . as you say, unpack."

"Fair enough," Hough said.

"Who was that kid driving the Blazer?"

"No idea," Hough said. "I have people looking for him. Should be easy to find with that white birthmark."

Mim tapped her jacket pocket. "I think I'm supposed to inform you that I have a handgun."

"Good," Hough said. "I'd expect anyone related to Arliss and Ethan to be packing around here."

"Those two guys," Mim said. "Who are they?"

"The Native guy is a local named Sherman Billy. A real village terrorist. Always in, beating on his wife or girlfriend or both. The other guy is new. From Sweden or . . . no, Germany, I think. Karl Dittmar. Smart, but not smart enough. I mean, he's thrown in with Sherman Billy. It's only a matter of time before he steps on his own dick. Anyway, I'll pass along their names to Arliss and see what he can come up with."

Mim gasped. "Arliss will kill them. Or at the very least, rough them up."

"That's kind of up to them, isn't it?" Hough said. "I mean, they could tell him what they know."

"No," Mim said. "If Arliss finds out they hit me with their truck, he's likely to beat them to death. I'm not kidding."

"Oh, I believe you," Hough said. "We'll keep that part close to the vest for a bit . . . if we can."

"They knew about Phil Hopkin," Mim said. "Said they would take me to him."

"That'd be a long trip," Hough said. "I heard he flew out early this morning."

"Does everyone know everything about everyone in this town?"

"Pretty much," Hough said. "That's how I rolled up on you here. Your administrator told me what kind of Honda you were riding." She hooked a thumb over her shoulder at the SUV. "You want to get in my rig, where it's warm?"

"I'm expected at the Search and Rescue Hangar to give DTP shots."

"Search and Rescue?" Hough said, sounding spooked. "Don't want to make them mad. We better get you over there, then." She hitched up her gun belt. "I guess Arliss told you what we talked about . . ."

Mim gave a slow nod. It felt good to hold at least some of the cards. "He said you felt Ethan's death was more than the official report."

"Nothing else?"

"You mean that everybody thought you were sleeping with my husband?"

Hough groaned. "So he did."

"Arliss always says if you keep a secret, you better have a damned good reason."

"Fair enough," Hough said. "And sometimes the reason to keep a secret is to protect people from vicious, untrue rumors. Which these were, vicious and untrue, I mean. You knew your husband."

"I think I did," Mim said.

"You did," Hough said. "I promise you that. Tell you what. My husband is out of town. I have to work tonight, but I get off at five a.m. What time do you get up?"

"My shift starts at nine a.m.," Mim said. "But I'm a nurse. I get up whenever."

"Good," Hough said. "Come over to my house around six, to-morrow morning, and I'll make us some steak and eggs. We can talk. Compare notes." She opened the Tahoe door. "Wind's kicking

up. You want a ride to the SAR Hangar? I'll get someone with the
Borough to get your Honda back to the hospital."

"You know," Mim said. "I'd appreciate that."

She climbed in beside her husband's former confidant and settled into the soft seat, out of the cold wind, safe at last from polar
bears, idiots who wanted to run her over . . . and warble flies.

CHAPTER 39

*T*he night before, Cutter had thrown the US MARSHALS OFFICIAL BUSINESS placard on the dash during their advance visit to the station in order to save the taxpayer a few pennies. Today he put the parking fee on his government credit card, not wanting to advertise to any would-be smash-and-grab artists that they were dealing with a car full of gadgets and goodies.

Just like the previous evening, Dillard clamored out of the back seat like an excited puppy.

Cutter and Sloan walked a few steps behind the charging deputy. He liked to look around. Sloan was just a slow walker. Cutter had met the detail for breakfast before heading over early. It was just before eight. A night of heavy rain had tapered to intermittent sprinkles. Breaks in the clouds left the streets and sidewalks of downtown Anchorage chilled and shining. The train wouldn't depart for another two hours, but a handful of early arrivals milled outside the station, some puffing away to stock up their systems with nicotine, most just waiting for the doors to open and give them access to the coffee stand.

Scotty Keen would bring the remainder of the detail moments before the train rolled away.

Cutter made a quick call and one of the ticket agents unlocked the double doors long enough for them to squeeze past the smokers.

"Andy'll meet you on the platform," the uniformed agent said, blinking sleepy eyes and returning to her counter.

The smell of coffee and a hint of diesel exhaust drifted through the cavernous station. It was empty for the next fifteen minutes, after which they would open the doors for the gift shop.

Cutter flashed his badge and a railroad employee wearing a bright yellow vest motioned them through the open doors onto the outside platform.

Storage buildings and assorted freight cars provided a backdrop for the *Glacier Discovery*. The dark-blue-and-yellow Alaska Railroad colors popped under the summer light.

"This thing is a postcard wherever she is," Dillard said. "Just wait until you see her along the ocean. Absolutely gorgeous!"

Sloan leaned sideways, whispering to Cutter. "You'd think he was describing his girlfriend."

"He kind of is," Cutter said.

A smiling man who looked to be in his mid twenties stepped off the car behind the massive blue-and-yellow engine, hopping down to the platform. He wore dark slacks and a matching vest over a blue shirt and tie. Black leather coach's shoes were well-worn, but polished to a high gloss, a detail that Cutter noticed immediately.

The young man hadn't been on duty the evening before, but he must have done his homework, because he extended his hand toward Nicki Sloan first.

"Andrew Franks," he said. "Please call me Andy."

"Inspector Sloan." She took his hand. "I was told the conductor was Ms. Washington—"

"Absolutely," Andy said, peppy and exuberant, like he might go bouncing down the platform at any moment. "And she remains so. We have a full train, so she'll be pretty busy. You'll deal mostly with me. I'm the onboard supervisor—a made-up title as far as railroad terms go, basically a combination of assistant conductor, brakeman, and tour guide."

"And stand-up comic," Dillard said.

Andy gave him a finger-gun thumbs-up. "You must have ridden with us before."

"A time or two," Dillard said.

"I understand you guys saw the train last night?"

"We did," Sloan said. "But I wouldn't mind if you walked us through it again."

"Absolutely," Andy said. "I was hoping you'd say that." He waved his arm toward the train with a broad flourish. "As you can see, the *Glacier Discovery* whistle-stop service is configured of five cars. The locomotive, commonly called the engine, is in the head of the train when we leave Anchorage. There we have two extremely competent engineers on board today."

"As opposed to the days with the incompetent ones driving," Dillard said.

Andy raised his eyebrows, up and down conspiratorially, and plowed ahead, walking along the platform as he spoke. "Behind the locomotive is that baggage car. Today that will be filled with rafting equipment and camping gear for those of our guests who plan to hop off at Spencer Glacier or Grandview. Next in line are the two passenger cars, affectionately called 'A' and 'B' on this trip. Each car has seating for seventy-eight passengers."

"A full train?" Cutter asked.

"There may be a vacant seat or two out of Anchorage," Andy said. "A fair number of the 'Q-tips' will get off in Whittier for glacier cruises and such, but we pick up almost as many at that same stop."

Cutter shot a glance at Sloan. *"Q-tips?"*

Andy grinned. "Sorry. You know, the white-hair, white-sneaker crowd. Cotton on both ends. Q-tips."

He stopped at a double-level car at the end of the line.

"And this is our Diesel Multiple Unit self-propelled railcar."

Sloan gave Dillard a nudge with her elbow. "Close your mouth, David. You're slobbering."

"The DMU," Dillard said, a reverent whisper, like he was in church. "The only one in the country."

"The only one in the world," Andy corrected. "That's operating at least. It is pretty cool. Cab section is up front on the lower level, secured like a commercial airline cockpit, the same as the locomotive. Behind that is the galley, with a café selling snacks, soft drinks, and that sort of thing."

He put his hands on a metal rail and led the way up a set of stairs.

"This takes us to the upper level. Twenty-four tables, with four seats each. Sounds like we've held the entire top deck for your group."

"Correct," Sloan said, surveying the car. "I'd hate all these windows if we were in the city. Too much of a fishbowl. But they'll be fine for this trip." She made her way up and down the aisle, running her fingers along the tables and the backs of the upholstered seats around them, four each like restaurant booths. They'd checked it all the night before. Now she'd had time to think over her plan. She motioned Cutter to the tables forward of the stairwell. "I still like this area up here for Morehouse and the other judges. We'll give them a vacant row for privacy and then post here, so we can cover the stairs."

Andy stood by, waiting for any questions. When none came his way, he said, "We certainly don't anticipate any problems, but in my opinion, this is the safest place on the train."

He took an old boarding pass out of his vest pocket and read from scribbled notes. "As far as staff on board, we have the two engineers, our conductor, myself, another tour guide, a porter, and a server in the café car. The US Forest Service has two tour guides aboard and there are always some rafting guides too. The Placer River can be pretty turbulent, what with all this rain."

"And they're all dressed in uniforms similar to yours?" Sloan asked.

"The Alaska Railroad staff are. Tour guides will be in red polos or Forest Service uniforms. I'll introduce you to everyone before your VIP arrives."

Dillard walked to the end of the car and knelt on a small padded bench to gaze out the large window. "And this becomes the front of the train at some point? Right?"

"Absolutely," Andy said, putting on his tour guide hat. "The DMU has two six-hundred-horsepower diesels and can be completely self-propelled. The locomotive pulls the train out of Anchorage, taking us south along the Turnagain Arm and through the mountain into Whittier. From Whittier the DMU pulls the train back through the tunnel and then cuts south all the way to Grand-view, turning the locomotive into a sort of caboose. Instead of turning around in Grandview, the engineers pick up and walk to the locomotive, which again becomes the front of the train. You don't notice any difference when you're on board."

"Cool," Dillard said, then more quietly, "Cool, cool."

CHAPTER 40

*D*eputy Paige Hart drove the limo again—in this case boss's Tahoe. As the presidentially appointed executive for the district, the US Marshal had the newest and nicest vehicle. Alaska Railroad law enforcement let the motorcade in through a side gate a block away, allowing the justice to board without passing through the packed station. Alaska Superior Court Judge Megan Reese rode with Judge Markham, who had forgone his customary bow tie and French-cuff shirt for Filson wool and an English tweed driving cap.

The Marshal was away in DC. Chief Phillips showed up to represent district management and see the train off. She planned to join Morehouse for a late dinner when the *Glacier Discovery* rolled back into the station a little before ten p.m.

Sloan and Lola got the justice and the other two judges settled upstairs in the DMU as the train pulled away, to the blast of a steam whistle and the rumble and squawk of wheels over steel track. Deputy Brady volunteered for the first stint as rover. Cutter accompanied him, wanting to get a feel for the passengers' mood.

As Andy Franks had predicted, a good many of those on board were older couples, likely on an Inside Passage cruise or other tour. Visitors to Alaska were a cosmopolitan lot and Cutter heard snippets of conversation in Japanese, Chinese, Russian, and Spanish as he and Gutierrez made their way up the aisle toward the baggage car and engine. The need for translators meant ethnic groups tended to stay together.

The train picked up speed slowly, swaying enough that Cutter needed to touch a seat back, now and again, to keep his balance.

"Seeing any untrustworthy types?" Brady asked on their walk back to the DMU.

"Yep." Cutter nodded. "About one hundred sixty of them."

Cutter left Brady and Hart at the base of the stairs near the café. With a supply of hot coffee and soft chairs, it was a plum posting for a deputy US marshal.

Upstairs, Cutter found Justice Morehouse chatting amiably with Judges Reese and Markham. The two Alaskans were beyond giddy to show off their state, pointing out a bald eagle soaring over a moose that stood in water up to its hocks in Potter Marsh, south of Anchorage. It was a scene straight out of a guidebook, but Alaskans were treated to that sort of thing so often, it was easy to become numb to it.

Teariki and Ramona sat together two tables away from the justice, both stifling laughter over some joke, probably crude, judging from the look on Lola's face. Sloan and Dillard sat one table forward so they were between their protectee and the stairs, but had eyes on anyone coming up.

Keen, whose primary responsibility was Judge Markham, sat alone at a table on the left side of the train.

Cutter glanced at Sloan, raising his eyebrows and tipping his hand toward his mouth in the universal pantomime for coffee. Sloan shook her head and patted the table. "Sit first," she said. "Take a load off. We're all set. Trooper helicopter on standby. Gutierrez is staged at Portage, if something goes down and we find ourselves in need of emergency egress. And you and Brady are tactical medics."

"Brady's your man when it comes to field medicine," Cutter said. "He's been to pig lab with Air Force pararescue."

"Arms up to your elbows in a wounded pig is one thing," Sloan said. "But you've been . . . you know . . ."

Cutter watched out the window as the mountains zipped by. "Yep."

Morehouse called out to her daughter as they turned away from the ocean and into the Kenai Mountains, nearing the Anton Anderson Memorial Tunnel through the mountain to the seaside town of Whittier.

"It looks as though Alaska is just a few miles out of Anchorage," the justice said.

Ramona pressed her nose to the window, fogging the glass with her breath. "Amazing," she said.

"Those two are getting along like schoolgirls," Morehouse said to the other judges, loud enough that the deputies could hear.

"Except one of those schoolgirls has a gun and pepper spray," Judge Reese said.

"I have personal experience with Deputy Teariki," Markham said. "I trust her completely. As a matter of fact, we arrested a violent felon together." His voice trailed off as he presumably regaled the justice with tales of his derring-do in bush Alaska.

Keen looked up from his lone table, dyspeptic that the bigwigs were shining their light on someone other than him.

Cutter posted himself at the base of the stairs during the two and a half miles of darkness and noise of the Anton Anderson Tunnel. Rain pelted the windows like a car wash the moment they popped out on the other side, into the busy seaside fishing village. The train clacked slowly along a deep green-water fjord overlooked by craggy mountains and crystalline blue glaciers.

Deputy Hart had come up the stairs with Cutter, getting a peek at the ground from the higher windows of the DMU.

"This is beautiful," she said. "What's that quote? Something about rain making the scenery seem like we're looking through our tears . . ."

Dillard chuckled, his voice low. "In the words of another great poet, 'The weather is always shittier in Whittier . . .'"

CHAPTER 41

Maxim Volkov tapped his stick against the wet concrete as the train thumped into Whittier. The pain in his stomach was worse today, twisting his face into a perpetual grimace. In truth, he would not have gotten out of bed, had this not been the day. The notion that he would finally look Charlotte Morehouse in her face set his nerves twitching like a live wire.

On the platform beside him, Lev Rudenko cleared his throat, stifling a cough.

"Boss," he said, heavy with phlegm and foreboding, "he is on the train."

"No riddles," Volkov snaped. "Who is on the tr . . ." His fist tightened around his walking stick when he saw the answer to his question.

Alex's sallow face peered back at him through the window of the rear car, absurdly defiant.

Volkov loosed a string of sputtered curses. His face flushed crimson. How could the boy defy him like this? When Maxim Volkov gave an order, no one went against it. No. One.

"He is upset, boss," Rudenko whispered.

"We are all upset," Volkov snapped.

A searing pain shot up his spine, stooping the Russian as surely as if he'd been struck in the back of the head. He put his weight on the heavy stick, relying on it to keep his feet. It faded along with the blast of the train whistle, leaving only the ache in his gut, dull and persistent, like the churning of the nearby waterfall.

"What do you want me to do?" Rudenko asked.

Volkov stabbed at the concrete platform with his stick, fuming. "My friend," he whispered, "I fear we will have to break this boy's legs just to save his life."

CHAPTER 42

*J*anice Hough insisted on making breakfast alone, leaving Mim to snoop the knickknacks and photos in the apartment's living room. Police housing was spartan but neat, provided by North Slope Borough and shared with other officers who rotated through every two weeks. Photographs of caribou and close-ups of tundra berry bushes hung on off-white walls. Past occupants had inserted colorful pushpins into various locations across a framed map of the United States.

"You have your own pin on here?" Mim raised her voice enough that it carried from around the corner and into the small kitchen.

"I do," Hough said amid the sound of clanging pans. "Mesquite, Nevada. Wide spot on the highway north of Vegas. Golf courses, a couple of casinos, and miles of gorgeous red-rock desert. Populated mostly by retired Mormons who don't want to pay state taxes up in St. George."

"You're a long way from home," Mim said. "Were you in law enforcement down there?"

"Geez," Jan said from the kitchen. "That seems like another life. Truth be told, I was a dancer on the Vegas Strip for a couple of years. It paid okay, but I gotta tell you, police work is a hell of a lot safer."

"I'll just bet you danced in Vegas," Mim muttered under her breath, then, louder, she said, "That's cool."

Mim had seen enough cops come into the emergency room to know ballistic vests and police duty belts didn't do any favors for a woman's figure, but it was still surprising to witness Jan Hough's transformation into civilian clothes. Even in a cowl-neck sweater and faded jeans, she looked like a stand-in for Marilyn Monroe. Mim was no slouch in the full-figure department, and though she hated to admit it, the women could have been sisters. If Ethan had had a type, Hough definitely fell into that category.

The smell of searing meat rolled out of the kitchen.

"How do you like your steak?" Hough called.

"Medium rare's fine," Mim said.

"Shit," Hough said to herself. Then, "I'm afraid the medium-rare ship has sailed. How's medium well?"

"I'm good with whatever." Mim tapped a framed photo of Hough on a beach beside a stout man with thinning blond hair. "Is this your husband?"

Hough leaned around the corner, fanning the smoke detector in the hall with a paper plate to keep it from going off. "That guy? No, that's some dude in Kona I was stealing from another woman."

Mim cocked her head, frowning.

"I'm kidding," Hough said. "Yes. That's my husband. He's an accountant. Works on a contract basis for several oil field supply companies on the Slope. Travels more than I do."

"Did he know Ethan?"

"He did," Hough said. "But . . . he . . ."

"He believed the nasty rumors?"

"Oh no," Hough said quickly. "I mean, not really. But he had to put up with all the talk. People can be real shits, you know? It was awkward."

"I'm sure," Mim said. "I have to admit, I would have been the same way, had I been in his shoes."

Hough released a pent-up sigh. "So, you trust me?"

"I'm not even sure I like you," Mim said, straight-faced.

"Mim, hand to God—"

"I'm kidding," Mim said. "I get the impression you're kind of a flirt, but you seem to be an honest flirt. I suppose I can live with that."

"I swear," Hough said. "Ethan never even stepped up to the line, let alone crossed it." She leaned forward, confiding a secret. "In my experience the Cutter brothers were, and are, both beyond devoted to only one woman, and that, my dear, is *you*."

"I don't know—"

"Yeah," Hough said. "I think you do."

"Let's talk about Cooper Daniels," Mim said, changing the subject. For all practical purposes Janice Hough had probably saved her life. She could be trusted. Couldn't she?

Hough shrugged. "Okay. Let's see . . . Coop Daniels. At first blush he seems like a good dude."

"And after that blush wears off?"

"How should I put this?" Hough said. "Once you get to know him . . . he's kind of a dick."

Mim gave a nervous laugh.

"I think so too. I just don't want to admit it to Arliss. He thinks Coop might know something about Ethan's death."

"I've heard stranger ideas," Hough said. "I feel like I've talked to anyone and everyone who could have possibly had information about what happened to Ethan. Coop went down to Anchorage to look after you right after the incident. We spoke later, but, now that I think of it, he's kind of weaseled out of an actual sit-down interview."

Hough motioned her into the kitchen. "Come on, I plot better on a full stomach."

"Plot what?"

"How we're going to put Coop Daniel's balls in a vise he can't squirm out of—"

A phone on the counter began to buzz, dancing across the Formica. Hough snatched it up.

"This is Jan."

She listened for a moment, a bewildered slack falling over her face. "I'm putting you on speaker," she said. "Say that again."

"We found the kid from last night."

"You're sure it's him?"

"Yep," the officer said. "Same white birthmark in his hair. He's nineteen, so we can hold him."

"He have a name?" Hough asked.

"He says his name's Cutter," the officer said. "Max Cutter."

CHAPTER 43

Volkov considered shooting Morehouse and her entourage of US marshals the moment they stepped off the train, but his son's sudden appearance added a new wrinkle—tar in the honey. Had they been in Anchorage or virtually any other city, Alex could have watched and then slipped away with the crowd. But Whittier was locked off, reachable—and thus, escapable—only through the same tunnel they'd come in on, or via boat. The death of a Supreme Court justice would cause the sky to rain law enforcement. Everyone in town would become a possible witness. Volkov hated the American FBI with a white-hot passion, but he had to admit their expertise. It would not take them long to connect Alex to him, once they began to look—and look they would.

"You will not get back on board," Volkov spat when Rudenko ushered his son to the end of the platform where their group waited to board. "I forbid it!"

"I love you, Papa," Alex said. "I truly do. But I have every right to be—"

"Do not—" Volkov boomed, and then lowered his voice to a vehement whisper. "Do not presume to tell me about what is your right. I am your father. It is because of me you are on this operation at all. I decide your rights! I will tell you when you are to ride a train or car or airplane—"

"Will you also tell me when I may mourn my dead cousin?" Alex snapped.

"What?"

"Gavrill is dead, Papa," Alex said. "Murdered at the hands of people on this very train. You said you want me to watch and learn. Well, I have been, watching and learning since I was old enough to understand. You have every right to avenge the death of your ex-wife, so then I assert my right to avenge the death of my dear cousin—your nephew."

Oleg Pogodin did not speak, but the look on his face made it clear he agreed with the foolish boy. His son should be avenged.

"Gavrill's death was a tragedy," Maxim said to Alex. "But I need you alive when this is over."

"I do not intend to die," Alex said. "But you have told me a thousand times to be audacious. And that is exactly what I intend to be. I have been on this train for the past two hours, watching the marshals and the railroad staff's movements and behaviors. I have a plan, if you'd care to hear it, Papa. But make no mistake. You will have to kill me to keep me off."

The boy spun on his heels and stalked away, flashing his ticket stub to a uniformed conductor before hauling himself up the steps and onto the train.

"The fool makes a show of disobeying me in front of my brothers," Volkov hissed.

"Boss," Lev Rudenko said, "I have been with you a long time. Forever, I think. Alexander is very much like his father."

"Are you saying I am impetuous and stupid?"

"I am saying you take what you want when you want it," he said. "You made him part of this. He is correct about that. You were right to do so, but you must not forget that he is your blood. You have raised the boy to be a bear, no?"

Volkov groaned, nodded. "I suppose I have."

"'If you invite a bear to dance,'" Rudenko said, quoting an oft-used proverb, "'it is not you who decides when the dance is over,' boss."

Volkov closed his eyes and gave a nod of resignation.

"'It is the bear.'"

CHAPTER 44

*O*fficer Joe Bill Brackett threw out an arm, checking for Lola in bed beside him, waking from a deep sleep. She wasn't there, dammit—and he'd forgotten to turn off the ringer on his cell.

He reached for the phone, knocking his watch and a pair of earplugs onto the floor before finding it. He answered with a groggy mumble.

Trooper Ian Rose roused him with a chipper "Good morning, brother!" Rose, a fellow University of Alaska Anchorage criminal justice graduate, had been in the same cohort as Brackett. He and Montez had gone on to the Alaska State Troopers, while Joe Bill had accepted a position with APD. Rose was a former Marine. Level-headed to the extreme when the shit hit the fan. Brackett and Montez had formed an easy alliance while in school, often hitting the gym together. Rose was a beast, benching more than Brackett could squat. There was no doubt he'd end up on the Troopers' Special Emergency Reaction Team, or SERT, when they had another class. Until then, the smart sergeants invited him to join in on the tactical stuff whenever he was nearby.

"I thought you might want an update," Trooper Rose said. "Since you're up to your nuts in all this mess."

"Mess?" Brackett blinked sleep out of his eyes and scooted into a sitting position against the headboard.

"You know what I mean," Rose said. "All this Alaska turning into Murderville, shit."

"What's up?" Brackett said. "Are you in Murdervi . . . Anchorage?"

"No, man," Rose said. "My ass is with an ad hoc team in Homer getting ready to jump on a plane across the bay to Seldovia. Remember that Russian chick from the Old Believers?"

"Did you die?" Brackett said, still half asleep.

"What? No. Dude. Wake up!"

"You know what I mean. Did *she* die?"

"Negative," Rose said. "Victim's still critical, but holding on. I'm talking about the kid sister. The witness."

"Okay . . ." That would wake him up.

"She came in and amended her statement. Seems she saw a hell of a lot more than she let on at first. The killers were, get this, Russian mob. She got a look at their tattoos. Her dad's pissed about her coming forward, but he's talking now too, hoping for some protection for his family."

"Are y'all giving it to him?"

"Above my pay grade," Rose said. "Probably. According to her daddy, this blade man was some mighty big cheese in the mob, just across the Bering over in Kamchatka. He came to Alaska about five years ago. Goes by the name of Lev Russel, but we believe his real name is Rudenko. We've got no operator's license on file, but there's a photo from last year's halibut derby. Big dude. Bigger than me even. He's got a place somewhere in the woods off Seldovia Slough. Feebs are sending a couple of guys to go across with us."

"By plane," Brackett said, to show his friend he'd been groggy but listening.

"That's the plan," Rose said. "I'm not the decider. Anyway, the asshole's probably in the wind already."

"Probably," Brackett said. He yawned again, thinking. A muffled conversation erupted in the background.

"Speaking of deciders," Rose said, "my boss is telling me it's about go time."

"Can you send a copy of that halibut derby photo?"

"Check your in-box," Rose said. "Be safe, brother."

Brackett opened the attachment as soon as Rose ended the call.

Russian fugitive. Old Believers victims. Someone speaking Russian at the scene of the game-room murders . . . a dead trooper, and an unidentified dead guy in Fairbanks.

Brackett tried Lola's cell, but it went straight to voice mail.

Rather than thumb-typing a text, he rolled out of bed and grabbed the laptop from the desk. He'd be a hell of a lot less likely to pepper his message with undecipherable typos if he sent an email. Yawning, he banged out a quick note that outlined the information on Lev Rudenko and the Voznesenka murder, which Trooper Rose had given him, then attached the photo of the giant Russian. The dude was huge, almost as big as the 422-pound halibut hanging beside him on the Homer docks.

Brackett waited for the *whoosh* signaling the email had been sent, then closed the computer and pushed it to the other side of the bed—Lola's side, if he didn't manage to screw things up.

CHAPTER 45

*L*ola's phone pinged the moment the *Glacier Discovery* rolled out of the tunnel, the DMU now at the head of the train. Dave Dillard had gone into the cab downstairs for a tour of the controls while they'd been stopped in Whittier and was now telling anyone who would listen about this "exceptional, one-of-a-kind, piece of railroad machinery." A wide grin spread across Lola's face when she saw the email.

Ramona Morehouse gave her a sly side-eye. "Your boyfriend?"

"You're going to go far with that kind of perception," Lola said. "I wouldn't normally be scrolling my phone while I'm on duty, but a bunch of emails just came through. One of them looks especially important." She glanced up, giving the girl a wink. "And it does happen to be from my boyfriend, but it's relevant to work."

The subject line said **Voznesenka Murder Suspect**, but the body of the email hadn't yet downloaded from the server. She waited, opened and closed her email, but nothing worked. She tried to call him back, but the phone went to voice mail. Made sense. She'd seen him sleep through a car alarm outside his apartment window after he'd worked a long shift.

She waved a hand at Cutter, who was blushing while he listened to Sloan reminisce about their time at the Academy.

"Boss," she said, "I need to jump the chain of command while I've got a phone signal."

"By all means," Cutter said. Both he and Sloan moved forward a table so they could hear.

"What's up?" Cutter asked.

Lola pointed to the phone which was in the process of connecting.

"We're on speaker."

Chief Phillips answered on the second ring.

"It's probably nothing," Lola said after she'd explained the cryptic email from Brackett. "But considering our circumstances, I thought we should check in to see if there were any developments we need to know about."

"None that I've been told," Phillips said. "I'll make some calls. How long will you have service?"

"Not long," Lola said. "We'll be in the mountains, so the angle could make the satellite phone touch and go. Terrain opens up some when we stop in Grandview. I'll try you on the sat phone there . . ."

"What do you think?" Lola asked after she ended the call.

Sloan looked from Ramona to Lola and then smiled. "Like you said, probably nothing. But it's worth checking back with the chief."

Ramona raised a hand. "Like my dad used to say, 'not for nothing,'" but I'm going to go to the restroom so you guys can talk about whatever it is you don't want to say in front of me."

Lola chuckled, at once amused and relieved. "There you go again with those powers of perception."

Sloan nodded at Hart, who accompanied Ramona to post outside the restroom.

"What do you really think?" Lola asked after the girl was gone.

"Voznesenka is a Russian village?" Sloan asked.

"It is," Lola said.

"Not really sure what that has to do with us," Sloan said. "Hopefully, the chief will turn up something, if there is anything to turn up. Until then, I'm thinking we keep our heads down and eyes open." She turned to Cutter. "Unless you have a better idea."

"Nope," Cutter said. "I know the justice wants us to give her space, but we need to press this. We should be glued to her heels whenever she moves. All of us if she'll allow it."

"Which she won't," Sloan said. "Lola, you keep doing what you're doing with Ramona. Arliss, you and I will work together when we can, and switch off when forced. You know what that means . . ."

"Yep," Cutter said. "It means it's my turn next."

CHAPTER 46

*T*he sliding door on the vestibule that connected A car and B car did not latch automatically, leaving it to bang annoyingly with the movement of the car, unless it was manually shut when a passenger went through. The conductor made several announcements asking passengers to be aware of this, but people, being mainly idiots, ignored her. Seated nearest the door, Yegon Zhuk took the brunt of the noise, getting up to shut and latch the door no less than a dozen times, every twenty minutes. A somber man, to begin with, he was ready to explode by the time they headed into the mountains.

"You stupid cow!" he yelled at a woman who left the door to bang away each time the train swayed. "Pull that ugly face out of your ass and do as you have been instructed—"

"Can you throw this guy off the train?" Scott Keen asked. He'd come down to the café car for a cup of coffee and a short change of scenery. Andy Franks, the onboard supervisor, had met him at the base of the stairs and told him about having to step in between two aggravated passengers. One of them had a Russian accent.

"Absolutely," Franks said. "The conductor can and will, if it comes to that. It gets a little problematic the farther we get into the mountains. Can't say as I blame him for getting mad, though. It pisses me off when the same people forget to latch the door, over and over and over. It's all handled for now. I just thought you'd like to know he was about to make an ass of himself in the next car back from your VIPs. Pretty sure he's Russian."

Keen sipped his coffee. "Better point him out to—"

Judge Markham appeared at the bottom of the stairs. "Scott, Judge Reese and I were wondering if they have anything stronger than coffee."

Andy Franks nodded. "Alaskan Amber and a nice IPA from Denali Brewing."

Markham brightened and hustled down the steps. He ordered one of each.

Franks waited for the judge to collect his beers and return upstairs before catching Keen's eye. He tossed a glance over his shoulder toward the next car. "Shall we?"

"I think I'll go up to make sure the judge is settled." Keen checked his watch. "Point the guy out when we get to Grandview."

"Absolutely," Franks said, spinning on his heels.

Ilia Lipin watched the bars on his phone, noting where he lost service completely as the train left the highway and headed deep into the Chugach Mountains. He followed their progress with a handheld GPS he kept beside the window, comparing it to a map he'd picked up at the station the evening before.

Alex had watched the operation of the train all the way from Anchorage. He'd listened to the guides describe the upcoming tunnels, how rafters would get off at the Spencer Glacier whistle-stop, and their ultimate destination of Grandview, where the train would stop for almost an hour. It was here at the terminus that the engineers/train drivers would leave their cab compartment in the DMU, which was secured much like the cockpit of an airplane, and walk to the engine, which would again become the front of the train.

"Most of, if not all, the passengers will be off the train hiking around, taking in the sights," Alex said. "The engineers will necessarily board the train to get ready for departure, while everyone else is still walking around. My guess is that the marshals will move the justice on board prior to everyone else."

Lev Rudenko looked at Volkov and gave a somber nod. "The young boss is right," he said. "That would be as good a time as any. If we do it right—"

"Very well." Maxim Volkov pounded his walking stick on the floor and whispered to his son, "We take the train in Grandview."

CHAPTER 47

*C*utter felt his body sway forward as the train slowed.

They were starting up a long grade prior to a series of five tunnels.

"Looks like we're up," Sloan whispered from across the table, nodding toward the front of the car.

Cutter turned to see Justice Morehouse slide out of her seat and stand in the aisle, rising up and down on her toes.

A consummate gentleman, Judge Markham stood when she did, but she motioned for him to stay put.

"You two finish your beers," Morehouse said. "I just need to stretch my legs."

Cutter and Sloan both got to their feet.

"Where would you like to go?" Sloan asked.

Morehouse gave a wry chuckle. "Do I really have a choice?"

"I suppose not," Sloan said.

"No need for an entourage," Morehouse said. "I'm sure you have deputies up and down the train."

"Mind if I join you, then," Cutter said.

Morehouse frowned, looked Cutter over. "Really? I told you, I'm just going for a short walk to clear my head."

Cutter conjured up what he hoped was a genial smile. "I'm starting to feel a little cooped up myself."

"Then 'lay on, Macduff,'" Morehouse said, motioning toward the stairs. "Let's you and I explore the train." She turned to her daughter. "Pay attention to the deputies while I'm gone."

"Like you do, Mom?"

"Touché."

Onboard supervisor and king of dad jokes, Andy Franks stood in a vestibule at the back of the A car, speaking over the PA system, in the middle of a story about seeing "bare tracks" out the window. Passengers heard "bear tracks" and rushed to the window, to find that instead of a grizzly they'd been duped with an empty section of "bare" railroad siding.

"She needs to stretch her legs," Cutter said. "Mind if we walk to the end of the baggage car?"

"Everybody knows who you guys are," Andy said. "Nobody will challenge you."

Cutter put Morehouse in the lead as they walked, reasoning that although it meant she would reach any threat before he did, at least he'd be able to keep her in sight.

Along with the couplings, the passenger and baggage cars gave them slightly less than a football field of length for their stroll. Cutter would never say it out loud, but Charlotte Morehouse had a serious pair of legs on her and she used them to great effect, striding out like there was some kind of prize waiting at the back of the train.

They found the door to the baggage car unlocked and stepped into the dim surroundings. A small blond woman was already there, smoking a cigarette next to an open cargo door. Stacks of camping gear and deflated river rafts hid their approach until they were almost on top of her. Wind in her hair and the clatter of tracks in her ears, the poor kid nearly fell out of the train when she finally noticed Cutter and the justice behind her.

She stooped forward, hand to her chest, cigarette clenched between trembling lips. "You . . . you scared the shit outta me! You know you're not supposed to be in here."

Cutter started to say something, but Morehouse raised a hand to stop him. "I'm so sorry," she said. "Andy told us it was okay to walk the train."

All the color drained from the girl's face. "Wait. You're that judge . . . I mean *justice*. I apologize. I'm the one who shouldn't . . . Here, these doors aren't supposed to be . . . I'll shut—"

Morehouse raised her hand again. "Please," she said, "leave them open. It's nice to feel the wind. What's your name?"

The poor kid looked like she might jump to escape the scrutiny. "Jacinda."

"Do you have another one of those cigarettes, Jacinda?"

The girl's face went slack. "What? I mean, yeah, sure." She fished a pack of Marlboros out of her vest pocket and shook one out for the justice. The action appeared to calm her at once. "We're gonna be heading through some tunnels," she said. "Pretty cool to see how close the rocks are when the doors are open."

"I'll bet," Morehouse said. She turned to Cutter, holding up the cigarette. "You look like the kind of man who would carry a match . . . or maybe flint and steel."

Cutter took out his orange Zippo.

"Well," Jacinda stammered, "I . . . I should get back to work. We're really not supposed to smoke on the train, but I won't say anything."

"Nor will I." Morehouse smiled, cigarette inches from her lips.

Cutter flicked open the lighter. Jacinda ducked out and hustled away toward the front of the train.

"Is she gone?"

"Yes, ma'am," Cutter said.

Morehouse nudged the lighter away and tucked the unlit cigarette behind a stack of folded packrafts.

"So," Cutter mused, "you don't actually smoke on trains."

"I don't smoke at all," Morehouse said. "But it seemed like the best way to keep poor Jacinda from having a heart attack."

Cutter shook his head, eyeing her.

"What?" Morehouse said.

"Impressive," Cutter said.

The justice chuckled. "I get the feeling that's quite a compliment coming from you."

The stink of Charlotte Morehouse's passing still lingered in the aisle when Volkov turned and hissed the order to Rudenko. "Go see what they are doing!"

"Probably getting some exercise, boss," Lev Rudenko muttered, coughing into his sleeve.

"Then you get exercise," Volkov whispered.

Everyone but Rudenko had gone to the next car forward to the café. They'd surely seen Morehouse walk past them, but, to their credit, had not followed her. Volkov had tasked them with identifying all the deputy marshals on the train prior to their stop at Grandview. Killing could be indiscriminate, but the marshals would be shooting back. They would need to be dealt with first.

The big Russian leaned forward, grabbing the back of the seat in front of him to haul himself to his feet.

"Yes, boss," Rudenko said.

Volkov put a hand on the man's arm. "If I finish this now, Alex might still slip away."

"Maybe," Rudenko said. "But I doubt he would go."

Volkov began to tremble in his seat, energized from the thought of finally wrapping his hands around Charlotte Morehouse's neck. He threw a quick glance over his shoulder. "There may be other marshals in the crowd. Sleepers. Follow her. See if the shaggy blond one makes eye contact with any other passengers. If they are truly alone, I will take her when she passes this row. You see to the marshal."

Rudenko sighed, then fell into a blackhearted scowl, his murder face. "Of course, boss."

CHAPTER 48

As was his custom on a protection detail, Cutter stood quietly with his hands clasped loosely at his waist, eyes up, scanning. The natural inclination was to focus on the principal, but threats didn't come from there—usually. At the moment there was a very real danger that Justice Morehouse might fall out of the open cargo door on the side of the baggage car.

Deep in the Chugach Mountains now, the train chugged steadily up a steep grade along a deep ravine. Rocks rose up to their right, a wild river lay to their left—visible out the open cargo door, some 150 feet below at the bottom of a narrow gorge. Steady rains over recent weeks combined with melting glaciers to turn the water into a chalky white torrent.

Cutter reminded the justice to brace herself as the train slowed even more. The *clack-thump* sound of steel wheels over track joints came further and further apart. Piled baggage on either side of the car shifted and settled with the swaying of the train.

The clattering suddenly grew louder as the front of the train entered the first of five tunnels. "Madam Justice," Cutter said, raising his voice above the noise of roaring wind and squealing metal. "Wouldn't hurt my feelings if you took a step back from the portal of death."

She chuckled, but complied.

"Takes your breath a—"

Her head snapped up midsentence, looking toward the door.

Cutter turned to find an extremely large man peeking in the car as if looking for someone. Baggage racks and the darkness of the tunnel had hidden their presence, and the door closed behind the man before he realized they were there.

"Help you?" Cutter barked above the noise.

The man coughed, covered his mouth, and mumbled something into a huge hand. Scars and scabs covered knobby knuckles, a man who made his living outside—or a fighter. Likely both. He was easily three inches taller than Cutter and every bit of three hundred pounds. Judging from the forearms sticking out from rolled sleeves, those pounds were predominately muscle.

"This car's off limits," Cutter said.

"You are here," the man said. "Not so off limits."

Cutter took a half step to the side, blading his body and blocking access to the justice. "We were just leaving."

There was something about this guy that Cutter couldn't put a finger on, something beyond the fact that he'd come snooping in an out-of-bounds car where they just happened to be.

He'd barely said a word, but there was definitely an accent. Russian?

"Enjoying your train ride?" Cutter asked, hoping to elicit further conversation.

"Is good," the man said, more stoic even than Cutter.

Yep. Russian.

Cutter motioned toward the front of the train. "After you."

"As you wish."

And then Cutter saw it, the flash of light off a piece of glass embedded in the man's heavy work boots. Blue glass. The kind of glass from a shattered windshield. Lola's Mountain View mineral . . .

The hulking Russian followed Cutter's gaze to his boot. His eyes went wide and he rushed forward with surprising speed, slamming Cutter backward against the upright post of a baggage rack. Cutter careened sideways, to bounce off a much softer bundle of pack-rafts.

Stunned from the three-hundred-pound hammer, Cutter heard Justice Morehouse shout something unintelligible, muffled, as if through a thick fog.

Massive fists dealt blow after blow. The Russian was head-hunting, intent on braining Cutter. Cutter slipped and rolled, letting most of, but not all, the punches slip past.

Staggered, he got his forearm up to his ear just in time to block the worst of an oncoming haymaker. He countered instinctively, driving his raised elbow forward into his opponent's face, finally stunning the man long enough to catch a breath.

Behind Cutter, Morehouse's fevered shouts sent a chill up his back.

The Russian was monstrous, and, as such, had probably done more beating than actually fighting someone who fought back. Cutter dropped the forearm, inviting another hook to his unprotected head. The Russian obliged, swinging wide and giving Cutter time to bring his arm back up, while, at the same time, countering with a left hook of his own as the Russian dropped his guard. Cutter's punch caught the much larger man behind his ear, wobbling him, but nowhere close to ending the fight.

The Russian roared, lashing out at the same moment the train entered the next tunnel, throwing the car into relative darkness. Cutter avoided the worst of the blows, but found himself trapped between the open door and the giant. A black wall of rock clacked by mere inches away from his head. The Russian pressed forward, laughing now, jabbing at Cutter in an attempt to shove him between the immovable rock and fifty tons of train.

Cutter spun, slapping the man on the ear as he went by. He followed with an elbow from the same arm. The big man doubled over, meeting Cutter's knee with his face on the way down, bellowing in pain and surprise. If anything, Cutter's attack only made the Russian angrier, more determined to grind him into hamburger on the chattering rocks.

The train popped out of the tunnel. Cutter had been anticipating this and brought a hammer fist up into the other man's groin when his attention shifted momentarily. Cutter followed with a double ear slap, cupping his hands for greater effect. The Russian staggered forward, teetering in place on the swaying train. Cutter stepped off-line to draw his Colt, but the Russian kept coming, flailing.

"Arliss!" the justice shouted. "Company!"

The connecting door slid open and another man appeared, barking something in Russian.

The giant pressed in, gathering Cutter in a great bear hug and planting a brutal headbutt into the bridge of his nose.

Blue lights arced behind Cutter's eyes, fireworks, lava, and sickening pain. He fell backward, clawing at the air. He was vaguely aware of falling, of leaving the train, spinning, twisting, caught in a tornado with a bag of hammers.

With Cutter gone, Charlotte Morehouse, associate justice of the highest court in the land, found herself alone and unprotected against the two Russians. One of them was battered and bleeding, but the other sneered at her as he held a gun in his hand. Both looked like they wanted her dead. She'd rushed to the door when Cutter fell, crying out when she saw him go over the lip of the mountain, sliding on the loose rock, upended by shrubs and deadfall—toward the swollen river below.

The train was going slow, to negotiate the tunnels, but not nearly slow enough to make it safe to jump off. Trapped, and with nowhere else to go, Morehouse chose the best of her terrible options and jumped from the moving train an instant before they reached the next tunnel. Rolling when she hit the gravel, and powerless to stop her descent, she followed Cutter over the edge, sliding down the mountain in a mini avalanche of her own making—toward the raging white water below.

Lev Rudenko had to hold on to the baggage rack to stay upright. His ears rang. His balls were killing him.

Yegon Zhuk rushed to the open cargo door, holding on to lean out when they exited the short tunnel. He cursed, smacking himself in the forehead and then cursed again.

"She has escaped!" Zhuk paced the car, clutching his hair, ranting to himself. At length he dragged a plastic valise off the shelf and then snatched a collapsible kayak paddle from the stack of gear behind it.

Rudenko blinked to clear bloodshot eyes, still holding on to the baggage rack. "What are you doing?"

"Do you not remember why we are here?" Zhuk said. "That bitch let my sister die. I will not allow her to get away."

Rudenko dabbed at the cut over his left eye. "She is dead," he said. "She is lying at the bottom of this mountain with a broken neck."

"Then I want to put my boot on that neck," Zhuk said. He first threw out the bag containing the raft, then the paddle, before jumping without another word.

"My brother," Rudenko whispered. "You are an idiot. Breaking your own neck does nothing to avenge your sister."

Rudenko shut the baggage car door and the train continued down the track toward Grandview. They still had the daughter—Maxim would have someone kill.

CHAPTER 49

*M*urder wasn't a federal crime, per se, but the FBI often got involved for just cause—i.e., just 'cause they wanted to.

In this case the fact that this suspect was a Russian national living off the grid across Kachemak Bay in the tiny seaside village of Seldovia gave the Bureau all the nexus they needed.

Even in a relatively wild posting like Alaska, Special Agent Heston Smith of the Anchorage FBI Field Office had a pleasantly mundane schedule. He had six years with the Bureau focusing mainly on white-collar investigations that dragged on for months or even years. Smith had plenty of leftover fingers when he counted the arrests where he'd been hands-on. Bringing in someone suspected of knifing a man to death in his sleep was bound to give Smith the street experience he lacked.

Smith felt sure the only reason they hadn't called in the FBI's regional SWAT team was that the Troopers, tasting blood in the water after losing one of their own, insisted on going in, ASAP. The FBI was a powerful machine, but it took a minute to spool up. The Troopers were already rolling.

And they had immediate access to a plane.

Smith hated airplanes. Alaska bush planes were the worst. He didn't much care for the water either. Now he found himself crammed into a Cessna Caravan on amphib floats with six dour state troopers and a senior FBI agent, whose name was Griggs but may as well have been nicknamed Rambo. The flight from Homer was only minutes, almost bearable, but the pilot appeared to be lining up to dive bomb the choppy waves of Seldovia Bay. Rocky beaches and thick hemlock and spruce forests surrounded the bay, giving the plane nowhere to go but the ocean if anything went wrong in the approach. Worse yet, no one else on board appeared bothered by the gut-churning maneuver. Smith would have grabbed his armrest, but the removable seats in the Cessna didn't have one.

Across the narrow aisle, Special Agent Griggs, who could be a real asshole, feigned a British accent and spoke into the tiny boom mic on his headset.

"About time to saddle up, Heston-Smythe," he said over the intercom. This bastard was going to have everyone thinking Smith had a hyphenated name.

To Smith's surprise, the aircraft settled in smoothly, throwing up tails of spray as the huge floats cut into the waves. The pilot turned, and gunned the engine, bringing the Cessna alongside the docks.

"Grab your shit, Heston-Smythe," Griggs said when the pilot killed the engine. The senior agent was already up, hunched over in the low cabin, and making his way aft to grab his rifle.

The Christmas before, Smith's dad, a detective with the NYPD, had given him a covert-carry briefcase for his H&K MP10. He'd never used the thing, other than going to the range, and thought this might be the perfect time to break it out.

Griggs laughed when he saw it. "Just the gun, kid," he said. "You're in Alaska. Business suits and briefcases get more stares than a submachine gun."

The Seldovia police chief—the city's only officer—and one state trooper met the arrest team at the float docks. A commercial fisherman in a previous life, Chief Hayes was a longtime resident and the most familiar with the geography and players in the area.

Lev and Margo Russel had a small clapboard cabin in the woods behind the school, not far from a trail that the locals called "the Otterbahn." They had dogs, big chows that were particularly attached to Margo. Hayes hadn't seen Lev in several days, but Margo was around. They'd exchanged pleasantries at the town's only grocery store the day before. She'd been carrying a pistol, which, while not unusual in Alaska, was not the norm for her.

The team threw their rifles and daypacks in the two SUVs and piled in.

Locals and salmon fishermen took immediate notice at the eight strangers who'd arrived with no fishing gear. Katherine Fortenberry had seen more than one of them with a rifle. She immediately called her friends to see if they knew what was going down. None of them were aware of anything, but they would see what they could find out.

Twenty-six minutes after the AST caravan motored to the float dock, Margo Russel chained both her dogs so they didn't get shot, left her Ruger GP100 .357 revolver in the nightstand by her bed, and walked out to greet the small army of grumps bailing out of the two SUVs that had barreled up her gravel driveway.

The troopers called her back to the vehicles. The dogs lunged on their chains, going bonkers to see the frowning men crowd around Margo.

She told them her husband had left a couple of nights before to meet a friend and she hadn't seen him since. They searched the house, anyway. She wasn't happy about it, but gave her permission. Resistance, as "they" say, was futile.

Trooper Ian Rose stood back and watched, listening. The senior guys did the talking, more specifically, Special Agent Griggs with the FBI.

They'd seated Ms. Russel on her tattered love seat after first searching the cushions for hidden weapons. The thing sagged so much she'd have to be a gymnast to get out of it with any speed. Nearing fifty with the case-hardened look of a woman who'd spent years splitting her own firewood and gutting her own fish, she was handsome if not classically beautiful. The years of backbreaking work had slowed and stooped her and she settled into the deep, soft cushions of the couch with a low groan, as if glad for the forced rest.

She admitted from the start that though she and Lev Rudenko were married in the eyes of God, satisfying Alaska law was tricky, since Lev hadn't exactly checked in with Immigration when he came across the Bering. As a result he'd adopted her maiden name of Russel.

Special Agent Griggs rubbed his face, swaggering to the window to look out, facing away from the woman. "Were you aware your husband was connected to Russian organized crime?"

Margo Russel screwed up her nose, mimicking the agent's slightly nasal voice. "'Were you aware your husband . . .'" She smirked. "Hell yes, I was aware. The eight-pointed stars and onion-domed church spires tattooed on his chest might have been a clue. Yeah, I figured that out pretty quickly."

"Did you know he was still involved?" the agent asked, struggling to regain control of the conversation. "With organized crime?"

The woman's shoulders slumped.

"Lev's tried to move on. I swear it. He works hard. Rarely drinks. It's that other guy. He's the problem. Lev owes him a debt he'll never be able to get out from under."

"What guy?" the AST sergeant asked. "What debt?"

"A guy named Volkov. Lev says it *Wolkov*. They were in prison together. Now, there's the guy who's hooked up with the Russian mob. To hear Lev tell it, he runs the entire Kamchatka Peninsula."

"And this debt?" the younger FBI agent asked. "Financial?"

"No," Ms. Russel said. "Nothing like that. Wolkov donated one of his kidneys."

"Are you saying your husband would kill someone for Volkov?" Griggs asked.

"Hon," Russel said, "Lev would chop me up and feed me to the crabs if Wolkov ordered him to. It would make him sad, but he'd do it."

"Where would he be now?" the AST sergeant asked.

"No idea."

"When was the last time he called?"

"A couple of nights ago," she said without hesitation.

"I find it hard to believe he didn't tell you where he was."

"Really?" Ms. Russel said, not bothering to hide her smirk. "You do? Because if that's the case, I find it hard to believe you've ever dealt with the Russian mob . . . or anyone from Russia, for that matter. They sort of expect you guys to be all up their ass, to barge in and smack us around to get information on them. Hell, if this was Russia, you might be holding me off a balcony to find out where he's hiding." Her brow furrowed, lips pursed, like she might spit. Instead, she said, "Lev didn't tell me shit."

The younger agent crowded in a half step. "Would you mind if we looked at your phone?" he asked.

"Take the damned thing," the woman said. "I got nobody to call anymore." She took a deep breath, head up, looking inches taller than she had just moments before. Trooper Rose thought she looked like his seventh-grade English teacher whenever she got righteously pissed about something.

"Now look," Russel said. "Lucky for me, we ain't in Russia. The way I see it, I've chained up my dogs, voluntarily let you come in my house with your boots on, and answered all your questions. For cryin' out loud, boys, I just gave you my damned cell phone, which I know you will use to try and find my Lev."

"We could have gotten a warrant," Special Agent Griggs said.

"And now we don't have to," the younger agent said, looking especially pleased with himself.

Chief Hayes escorted Ms. Russel outside, while the team loaded up into the two SUVs in a steady rain. She rubbed her wrists when he took off her handcuffs.

"No hard feelings, Margo," he said.

"Sure."

"See you at the spaghetti feed at the school tonight?"

"You coulda just called me." She stood and stared at the chief, hands balled into fists so tight they shook. For a moment Trooper Rose thought he might have to jump out of the SUV and pull her off the guy. At length she spat into the mud. "I imagine you and your boys will be out there now looking to gun down my husband. To be honest, Hayes, I don't give a shit if I ever see your face again."

If the FBI was good for anything, it was greasing the skids when it came to records subpoenas. Smith, the young agent, had the contacts with the phone company to get the dump on Margo Russel's cell in less than an hour. There was no way to know the contents of the call, but they knew when it came in and where it came from—a tower on the George Parks Highway, south of Talkeetna, three hours before Trooper Sam Benjamin went dark.

Trooper Rose called his friend Joe Bill Brackett and passed on everything they'd learned, off the record. Brackett had a contact in the Marshals Service. With the justice in town, they'd want to know. The FEEBs would get around to passing them the info . . . eventually . . . maybe. Griggs was awfully butt-hurt after his junior partner got the key piece of evidence. It might take a minute for him to figure out how to spin this so he was the hero.

CHAPTER 50

*C*utter slammed into the icy water, his muscles knotting at the sudden shock. The current grabbed him immediately, rolling him under. He flailed and kicked, but it didn't matter. Rivers always won if you took them head-on. Spume and froth enveloped him, leaving him unable to breathe even during the rare moments when he managed to get his head above the waves. Something had to change, or he was doomed.

Air. He had to have air.

His shoulder struck a submerged boulder and flipped him half out of the water, like a salmon leaping a set of falls. Half a breath, then he was jerked under again by some unseen hand. Spinning, tumbling, completely out of control, he hit another rock, big, dark, like a hidden grizzly. Slowed momentarily by the impact, he had a fleeting moment of counterfeit control before the current piled up behind him and shoved him over the top. His back raked against the rough stone.

Another quick breath and he plunged into a deep hole on the downriver side of the rock. Roiling turbulence held him under for an eternity, amid a cloud of silver bubbles and black shadows. He willed himself to relax and let the water have him—and spit him out the other side of the hole.

Another breath, then back into the spin cycle.

It took all he had left to get his legs ahead of him, pointed downstream as he raced along with the current. His hands focused on little more than keeping his head away from the rocks. He hit an eddy, slowing long enough to take two gulping breaths before the river grabbed him again.

Movement in the rapids to his left caught his eye. *Morehouse? What was she doing here? How did she—*

Cutter slammed against something hard, rattling his teeth and sending a shock up his spine. The weight of the river bore down on him, holding him against . . . something. It took him a moment to realize he was pinned against the limbs of a half-sunken tree that lay across the water, root ball still lodged on the bank. Cutter got his head up for a quick breath before the tree dragged him under. He clawed blindly at the broken limbs, desperately trying to free himself. The tree moved and he thought that it was rolling, ready to pin him to the bottom of the river. Instead, it bobbed three times with the rhythm of the current. It rose slightly higher on every fourth tumbling wave. Cutter had a mere half second to breathe before it yanked him under again. He rode the cycle, knowing the tree could shift or sink or roll at any moment, taking him with it. On the third lift, he noticed a decrease in pressure. He went under a fourth time, conserving his energy for an all-out burst that got him high enough in the broken branches to keep his head and shoulders above water. He hung there for a long moment, oblivious to the bone-numbing cold, thinking only of sweet air. But oxygen brought back more clarity.

Legs still underwater, blood from countless cuts and gashes running down his face and arms, Cutter realized Morehouse clung to the crown of the same thirty-foot tree that skimmed the surface of the raging river.

He began to work his way to her, hand over hand, gingerly, testing each branch. If he dislodged the tree and it rolled, he'd kill them both.

"Are you stuck?" he yelled when he was less than ten feet away.

Her head jerked up, surprised to see him.

"Holy shit!" She scrambled, kicking against the waves, struggling to retain her grip. "Thought . . . you . . . were . . . dead . . ."

"All good," Cutter lied. "Can you get free?"

"I . . . think so!" she yelled. "But that would just put me in the current again."

Cutter pointed to an eddy of relatively smooth water some thirty yards downstream. "Swim at an angle!"

She looked wide-eyed. *"Angel?"*

"Angle!" he yelled again, pantomiming the route. "Feetfirst! Steer with your arms. Don't fight the river!"

"You say so!" She stayed put, her body wrapped around the tree at her waist by water pressure.

Cutter inched closer until he didn't have to yell quite as loud. "This water was a glacier a few minutes ago. We'll freeze to death if we stay here."

She nodded. Her hair plastered her cheeks; bits of flotsam speckled her forehead. A trickle of blood oozed from a split lip, blue with cold.

"I'm fr . . . frozen already," she said, teeth chattering. Cutter suspected that was more from shock than cold—for now.

"I'm with you," he said. "We should go. Now."

"Now?"

"Now!" Cutter crowded in beside her as the branches thinned near the crown.

She launched herself into the current. Cutter waited until she popped to the surface a moment later—then followed her in.

"Always . . . I . . . always thought . . . I was . . . a strong swimmer," Morehouse gasped. Cutter held her by the elbow, helping her out of the water and up the steep bank. She fell against him.

The relative safety of the bank gave her brain time to think about other horrors.

"Ramona! She's still on that train!"

"I know," Cutter said. "Along with a small army of deputy marshals. Lola will look out for her."

She lifted her head. "Like you looked out for me?"

Cutter bit his lip.

"I apologize," Morehouse said quickly. She dabbed a bloody spot above her ear. "This isn't your fault."

"I should have seen it coming," Cutter said.

The justice pulled at the tail of her shredded fleece jacket, dazed and shivering, like she was trying to figure out how she'd gotten where she was. Cutter couldn't blame her. He shrugged off his own jacket and wrang out the water before putting it back on. It was still damp and clammy, but no longer dripping. She followed suit.

"I swam in college," she said. "That . . . should have been easier for me."

"That wasn't swimming," Cutter scoffed. "That was war with water. This river is swollen to three times its normal size."

"Whatever it was," Morehouse said, "thanks for dragging me out of it."

"May I?" Cutter asked, tilting Morehouse's head gently so he could get a better look at the growing purple bruise over her ear. "Could just as easily been you dragging me out," he said. "I'm lucky I didn't run headfirst into a boulder. How's your vision? You still seeing okay?" He touched the area around the bruise.

She winced, jerking away.

"I guess," she said. "Look, thanks for your concern, but I need to know what we're doing about Ramona."

"Lola will take care of her. I promise."

She shuddered, started to sob, then shook her head, catching herself, sniffing back tears.

"What happened back there? Did we stumble into something?"

"I'm afraid so," Cutter said. "A plot to kill you."

She looked up at him, blinking, now unable to keep her jaw from trembling as she spoke. "So, what do we do?"

Cutter swung his arms and rocked back and forth on his feet to keep the blood flowing. She watched him and copied.

"I still have my guns," he said. "The radio and phone are toast. We need to get warm . . . except . . ."

"Except what?"

"Hang on," Cutter said. "This cold is making me stupid."

He left the justice where she was and scrambled up the loose scree toward the tracks. Already sapped, he panted heavily by the time he reached the top. It didn't surprise him at all to see a red packraft pop through a slot in the canyon a quarter mile up river, negotiating the white water—straight for them. When no other rafts emerged, Cutter slid down the hill as quickly as he could without losing control.

"We have company."

"Rescue?"

Cutter shook his head. "Bad company. The second Russian at our little party. He must have jumped off the train with a raft. He had to inflate it or he'd already be on top of us."

Morehouse looked up and down the river, her breath quickening into short bursts of white vapor on the mountain air. "What now?"

"Hang your jacket on those willows so he'll see it," Cutter said. "And then get down behind that boulder. Lay flat if you can."

"Okay." Morehouse started to peel off her jacket, then stopped. "Are you going to arrest him?"

"If I can," Cutter said, though he knew that would not be the case. "Odds are, there's more of them behind this one."

He took the Glock out of its holster and pushed it toward her, grip-first. "You know how to use this?"

She nodded. "It's been a while, but I can manage."

She kept the muzzle toward the ground and her finger off the trigger. At least she wouldn't shoot herself.

"Where are you going?" she asked.

Cutter groaned. "Back in the water."

CHAPTER 51

North Slope PD personnel figured out the boy's real name by the time Jan Hough drove Mim to the office.

"Max Tunik . . ."

Mim rolled the name around on her tongue as she stared in stunned silence at a black-and-white image on the CCTV screen. The young Iñupiat man seated in the next room. Try as she might, she found it impossible to get her head wrapped around this new information. "How old is he?"

Tunik's knee bounced like a sewing machine. He looked tall, with a strong chin . . . but was it Ethan's chin?

"Nineteen years of age," Hough said, scrolling the screen on a laptop to read her partner's report. "I hate to ask, but does that timing fit with Ethan's past?"

Mim did the math in her head and then exhaled sharply through her mouth.

"Yeah," she said. "I'm afraid it does. He did an internship up here the summer before our senior year of college. Not that it matters, but we weren't married yet. That trip is one of the main reasons he eventually brought us north." She teetered on her feet. "I think I need to sit down."

Hough rubbed her face with both hands, exhausted.

"You feel up to talking to him?"

"He's been trying to talk to me since I first got to the hospital," Mim said. "Let's see what he has to say."

Hough gave a nod and pushed open the door.

Tunik stood when the two women walked into the room. His hands were cuffed in front of him, secured to a metal ring on a wide leather belt.

"Have a seat, Max Tunik," Hough said. "Am I saying that correctly?"

He locked onto Mim the moment she entered the room.

Hough snapped her fingers. "Max, over here. I asked you a question."

"Yes, ma'am," he said. "Am I under arrest?" There was an earnest look about the young man that took Mim's breath away.

"You are," Hough said. "Leaving the scene of an accident."

"I didn't . . . I mean, it was those other guys," he said. "I hit their truck to keep them from hurting her." He nodded at Mim. "Just ask her."

"They say you knocked them into her ATV."

"That's not true," Tunik said, restrained, almost a whisper.

"You told the officer who arrested you that your name is Max Cutter," Hough said. "Why does your ID say Tunik?"

He stared at the floor.

"Okay," Hough said. "Let's try this. Why have you been following Ms. Cutter around? It's pretty damned creepy."

"I just wanted to talk to her."

"Then talk," Mim blurted out. She was surprisingly calm. "You told the officers that my late husband was your father. I'd like to talk about that."

Tunik gave an emphatic nod and scooted to the edge of his chair. "Ethan used to come to our village a lot," he said, "when I was little. He always brought my mom groceries. You know, oranges, peanut butter, stuff from Anchorage. He knew I liked apples, so he always had Fujis or Honeycrisps. The good ones we never get in the bush."

"Your mom lives in Wainwright?" Hough asked.

"She passed four months ago, tomorrow," Tunik said.

"Sorry to hear that," Hough said.

Mim put a hand to her chest. "Me too."

"Thank you," Tunik said. "Anyway, Ethan stopped coming for a long time, like four or five years. My mom just told me to be patient. She said he'd come back. Then the oil companies started doin' some studies on the tundra outside our village and he just showed up one day. It was like the old times, you know. Like when I was a kid. He and his crew stayed in the school, so I'd go over there and we'd play basketball every evening. He helped me with math, worked on my Honda with me, you know—"

"You pretty good at math?" Mim asked.

He shrugged. "Ethan always said I shouldn't brag, but I guess I am good at math. Anyway, it was that summer when my mom told me he was my real dad." He looked up at Mim, brown eyes brimming with tears. "I really miss him, you know."

"I do know," she whispered before she turned to Hough. "He's right. Max arrived *after* those other guys ran into me."

Hough covered a yawn and then leaned against the wall by the door—verboten during an interrogation because it reminded the subject there was a way out, no matter how slim.

"Did Ethan Cutter ever actually tell you he was your father?"

"No," Tunik said. "Not in those words, but he *was* my dad. I'm sure of it. Anyway, my mom made me swear not to talk to him about it."

"Okay." Hough dug a key from the pocket of her jeans and took off his handcuffs. "You can go. But if I call your phone, you need to answer. Understand?"

"Yes, ma'am." He looked to Mim again. "Do you think somebody killed him?"

Startled, she shot a glance at Hough. "I don't know."

"I think somebody killed him," Tunik said.

Hough eyed him suspiciously. "Any idea who?"

"I don't know yet," he said. "Maybe those two guys who tried to run her down. I mean, why else would they?"

"Other than those two," Hough said. "Or . . . even them. What's the motive?"

"I'm not sure," Tunik said. "What I do know is that Ethan was really quiet the last time he came over. He was usually so happy, but this time he was . . . I don't know . . . broody, like somethin' was really heavy on his mind." He sighed. "I get like that sometimes."

"When was this?" Mim asked.

"Two days before he died. I remember what he said to me when he was leaving. 'Watch your heading, Max.' That's what he said. 'Watch your heading.' It was like he knew something bad was going to happen."

"Shit," Hough whispered, coughing to cover a sob. It was clear everyone in the room loved Ethan. "You think he talked to your mother about whatever was bothering him?"

"Probably," he said. "Not while I was around."

Hough put a hand on the door. "You're staying in Utqiagvik for a bit?"

"I was flyin' back to Wainwright on Friday."

"In the meantime," Hough said, "I'll get you a notepad. I want you to write down all your thoughts on who might have killed Ethan Cutter—"

"My father," Tunik prodded.

"Okay," Hough said. "Don't worry about spelling or neatness, just write down anything and everything that comes to mind. Will you do that?"

"Of course." He looked at Mim, biting his lip.

"Was there something else?" Hough asked.

"I just . . ." He took a deep breath, and then released it all at once, eyes closed, reaching some conclusion. "I want to give you something before I change my mind."

"Okay."

"It's probably nothing," Tunik said, "but I'm sure he'd want you to have it. Can I bring it by the hospital?"

They set up a general time to meet and Tunik left, carrying the new notepad Hough grabbed from her desk drawer.

"That was one of the more bizzarro things I've ever heard," Hough said as soon as he'd gone.

"Maybe," Mim said.

"Do you really think—"

"I'm not sure who that boy's father is," Mim said. "But he quotes Grumpy. And who stands up anymore when a woman comes into the room? There is no doubt in my mind that Ethan had a hand in raising him."

CHAPTER 52

Dave Dillard's voice squawked over the radio, filling Lola's earpiece. She'd been trying to raise Cutter for the past ten minutes, to no avail. Dillard had just walked the train.

"No sign of him or the justice," he said.

Paige Hart chimed in, "How about restrooms?"

"Negative," Dillard said. "Arliss would be waiting outside if Her Honor was hitting the head. My bet is that they're in the DMU chatting up the engineers, lucky bastards. I tried the radio, but it must be tits up."

Keen spoke next. "If they passed me, I didn't see them."

"I'm coming forward now," Dillard said. "If anyone runs into Andy, have him radio the engineers and check."

"Andy might be on a break somewhere," Brady said. "We're pulling into Grandview in a couple of minutes."

"Balls!" Dillard said. "I was just in the baggage car. There was no sign of 'em. Maybe Andy's showing them the engine. I wouldn't mind having a little peek at that myself."

"Listen up," Sloan said. "If someone would be so kind as to find the conductor or someone with a radio, I'd sure as hell like to locate our Supreme!"

CHAPTER 53

*C*utter willed himself into the icy water just downstream of the fallen spruce. Rafters called such a tree a "strainer" because it was halfway submerged in the water. (A "sweeper" extended over the top of the water.) This strainer hadn't been here long. Most of the boughs were still thick with green foliage. Cutter suspected it had come down the mountain during breakup.

He gasped when the water reached his belly, and he slowed momentarily from the shock. Numbness came on quickly and he trudged ahead, pulling himself toward the middle of the river with the aid of protruding branches. The tree broke the current, but he had to concentrate to keep his balance negotiating the rocky bottom with wooden legs.

A flash of red through the tree told him the packraft was close. He hunkered lower, keeping his hands out of the water as best he could. He needed them nimble, able to hold a weapon.

Cutter chanced another look upstream, behind the oncoming raft. There was value in taking this guy alive and getting the information in his head about what was going on. But did it outweigh the danger to the justice if another threat came along?

The decision, Cutter decided, would be up to the man in the raft.

As Cutter had hoped, the Russian saw Morehouse's fleece jacket. He paddled furiously toward the eddy, coming around the spruce five feet out.

Cutter launched himself into the current, aiming well ahead of the passing raft. His inclination was to simply shoot the man and drag him to shore, but with the justice surely watching his every move . . . she wouldn't be keen on what he actually planned to do, but he'd argue the finer points later, probably in court—or maybe from prison.

The Russian fell sideways, startled by the sudden onslaught, nearly toppling out of the little boat. Packrafts were small, like inflatable bathtubs with just enough room to stretch out your legs and lay a backpack across your lap—a combination kayak and inner tube made of sealed nylon. Light. Packable. Quick and easy to inflate.

Cutter deflated this one with a single stroke of his blade. The Russian sank immediately in a tangle of nylon rags. He swung the double-bladed paddle at Cutter's face as he went down, trying vainly to tread water with only his legs. His head went below the surface. Cutter snatched away the paddle with his left hand, attempting to hold the other man under long enough to tenderize him and make him more compliant, less dangerous. But they were both being carried downriver and it was impossible to get any leverage in the rolling current.

The Russian attempted one futile chop at Cutter before surrendering the paddle to the river. Seconds later, the barrel of his pistol rose above the surface. Cutter saw the flash, felt the pressure as the round flew past his ear, but he never heard the shot over the roaring water.

The Russian had just changed the rules of engagement for him.

Cutter dove under the roiling surface, knife in hand, zipping the razor-sharp blade upward with the same motion he'd used to deflate the raft.

Numbed by the frigid water, the Russian likely felt no more than a bump. He had no idea he was open from navel to breast. Cutter rolled, trapping the hand with the gun under his left armpit. He drove the weakening man backward, essentially lying on top of him and riding him like a raft, while the effects of the knife wound caught up with him.

The Russian clung to life, miraculously getting two more convulsive shots off before finally losing his grip on the pistol. Cutter felt the body go limp beneath him, but held it under for another few seconds. Then, feeling like he might slide under himself at any moment, he pushed away. The Russian bobbed and rolled in the white water, a piece of limp trash floating downriver, bouncing off the rocks.

Morehouse ran forward and offered Cutter a hand as he dragged himself into the eddy. She bounced on her feet, looking frantically from Cutter to the Russian and then back to Cutter again.

"What if he swims to shore?" she asked.

"He won't," Cutter said, bent forward with his hands on his knees.

"How can you be—"

Cutter collapsed in the gravel, rolling over so he faced skyward. His brother's MAK blade slid from his hand, still bloody around the mammoth-tooth handle even after the swim.

"Oh," Morehouse said. "I see."

He reached out his hand, working to slow his breath. "Madam Justice, if you wouldn't mind helping me up, I need to see if anyone else got off the train."

She grabbed the hand and pulled. "You think . . . we might d . . . d . . . die out here?"

Cutter clamored up the incline, zombie-like now, to get a look upriver. He took far less care to remain hidden than the last time. If he saw anyone now, he would simply shoot them—if he could steady his hand long enough.

"We're clear . . . so far," he yelled.

"You really k . . . killed him with your knife?" she asked when he slid back down the hill to her.

Cutter put his hands under his arms, shivering uncontrollably now.

"I did."

She pulled him close to her, enveloping him in a great hug. "Not sure how much warmth I have to spare, but—"

"You . . . shouldn't . . ." Cutter stammered. "I sh . . . should . . . be taking care of—"

"Horseshit!" Morehouse said. "I need you warm. W . . . we have to . . . to save my daughter."

Cutter leaned into the warmth. He'd come off a motorcycle at speed once and slid on his back for thirty feet down on a gravel road—and his body hadn't hurt this bad.

"Th . . . thank you, Madam—"

"Shhhh," she whispered. "It's t . . . time you called me Charlotte." Her lips brushed his ear. "Considering."

Cutter nodded awkwardly. "Okay . . . Charlotte. C . . . can I ask why you're here? Did they throw you off the train?"

"No," Morehouse said. "You were gone and they didn't look friendly . . . so I jumped."

Cutter blinked stupidly, trying to make sense of all this. "Okay," he said. "Smart . . . I guess."

"It was moronic," Morehouse said. She pulled back just enough to look him in the eye. "I left my little girl on that train. They'll look for us, right?"

"They will," Cutter said, slowly warming enough that he could speak without breaking a tooth. "Inspector Sloan will give us some latitude because she knows I'm with you. She's figured out we're missing by now, though. Freight moves on this line as well, so the engineers can't just stop the train or reverse course on a whim."

"But . . . they'll call the Troopers? Right?"

"If they can," Cutter said. He rubbed her shoulders to get the blood flowing. It was an extremely intimate thing to do, but at this point survival trumped convention. "These mountains have a lot of dead zones," he said. "Angles this far north make sat phones iffy. There's a Trooper helicopter on standby . . . S . . . Sloan will call them as soon as she can. The timing has to be right. They could be back inside of two hours, m . . . maybe less, depending."

Shared warmth notwithstanding, Morehouse now trembled so badly she couldn't keep her head still. "De . . . depending on . . . wh . . . what?"

Cutter ran through the possibilities in his head. Few of them looked good.

"On who has control of the train."

CHAPTER 54

*P*assengers clapped and cheered when the *Glacier Discovery* rolled into the whistle-stop. The place was called Grandview for a reason. Rugged mountains loomed over a lush glacial valley. Trees and rock glinted in the sunshine, dazzling after the recent rains. Expansive snowfields, stark white to the hanging glaciers' blue, turned greens greener and blacks blacker. Inside the train noses pressed against windows, fogging glass. Expensive cameras swung around would-be nature photographers' necks. Elderly couples sniped at each other for forgetting their jacket or hat or phone charger, chiding their own forgetfulness by proxy. The clouds had parted, the sun was out, and everyone wanted off the train to take part in the bluebird moment.

Inspector Sloan broke squelch.

"Listen up," she said. "Something's not right here. Keen's sticking tight with Judge Markham. Teariki needs to make a call on the sat phone. Brady, keep your eyes on Ramona while she takes care of that. Hart, find someone to get you in every closet and hidey-hole. See if Cutter and the justice are playing canasta or something. Dillard, you help her."

"I can do that," Dillard said. "Andy's talking to someone between A and B cars. I'll get his radio."

Hart responded immediately. "I'm in the baggage car now. Something's off in here. Like—"

The brakes squealed and they all rocked forward as the train came to a complete stop.

"Dave," Sloan said. "Yes! Get with Andy. Hart, stand by where you are. I'm headed your way. Everyone's in the aisle, so I'll get off and walk back to you outside."

Lola followed Sloan to the stairs, out of Ramona's earshot.

"Do you think it's possible they fell off?" Sloan whispered.

"Very possible," Lola said. "Cutter would have jumped if she fell for some reason."

Sloan's face screwed into a worried frown. "That's the truth. Make your call. Get us some help. I'll have train staff get in touch with their Dispatch. I'd love to see a chopper flying the line, ASAP."

"Copy that," Lola said. She turned to Ramona and clapped her hands in front of her. "Hey! Ready to see Alaska?"

"What?" Ramona eyed her suspiciously.

"'What'? What do you mean, 'what'?"

"You're too chipper," Ramona said. "Like the time my mom told me how much she loved me, right before she told me my cat died."

"Come on," Lola said. "Let's get some air."

"You said you wouldn't lie to me."

"You hear me lying?" Lola said. "Because I don't hear me lying. I hear me asking you to come outside with me so I can make a phone call."

The girl balked. "Hey, I haven't seen my mom. Is she okay?"

"She's with Cutter."

"That's not an answer."

"We're looking for them both," Lola whispered. "Now, please, let's go make this call."

Judges Reese and Markham both pretended to grouse about not getting off the train, but agreed with Scotty Keen when he practically begged them to remain on board until the justice was located.

Lola hoped to find Cutter and the justice walking up the tracks from the other end.

No joy.

Heaps of sunshine and air so crisp it pinched her nose—but no Cutter.

"Shit," she whispered.

"Lola . . ." Ramona bounced on the balls of her feet, arms tight across her chest, growing more jittery by the second.

"One of the railroad staff is probably just showing them around," Lola said, sounding less convincing than she'd hoped she would.

Lola canted the antenna and began to turn in half steps, watching for the bars that should show her the best signal.

Miraculously, the phone beeped, showing it had connected to a satellite—and began to ring.

The sun shone overhead, but black clouds rolled over the mountains to the east and a misty rain began to drift in. A sun shower, or "monkey's wedding." It was breathtaking under different circumstances, but Lola worried the clouds might make her drop the call.

Railroad staff and the Forest Service tour guides had warned passengers ad nauseam about Alaska's fickle weather. Most had listened and the whistle-stop was instantly transformed into a sea of glistening raincoats.

Still hoping against hope to see Cutter, Lola caught a glimpse of a man with a cane walking with the two engineers as they made their way toward the locomotive.

"My jacket!" Ramona said, glancing toward the train, grimacing. "I'm so worried about my mom, I forgot—"

Lola held up her index finger. "Hang on."

"I'll go with her," Deputy Brady said.

Lola was going to tell him to wait, but her call connected. "Joe Bill—"

He began talking immediately, intent on filling her in on information from Trooper Rose that he felt was vital. She tried to break in and tell him they needed help, but the spotty connection rendered him unable to hear her.

"This is an emergency, Joe Bill!" Lola said.

"Sorry . . . what was that?"

"We can't find the justice," Lola said.

"I'm get . . . ev . . . oth . . . word," Brackett said.

Sloan's voice came across Lola's earpiece. "Anything?"

"Andy hasn't seen them either," Dillard came back, grim. "They're not on the train."

Joe Bill was still going on and on about Russians. Lola blurted into her radio mic, "On the phone with Anchorage PD."

"Get us some help!" Sloan said.

Lola cupped her hand over the phone and cut to the chase. "Emergency! Emergency! Grandview! Grandview! Help!"

Brackett would have to suss out the details, but if he was getting every other word, at least he'd know they were in trouble.

The sat phone beeped three times and dropped the call, leaving Lola to wonder if he'd heard anything at all.

She jumped on the radio again while she redialed, pivoting to try and find a satellite.

"Russians," she said, bonking Dillard who tried to speak at the same moment. She groaned, stifling the urge to hurl the radio and satellite phone into a rock. "We need to keep an eye open for Russians." She trotted toward the train as she spoke, wanting to reach Ramona. "Big guy. Possibly Russian mob—"

Something out of place drew Lola's attention to the damp gravel. She stooped quickly to grab it. A scrap of paper. The wrapper from a . . . cough drop. Her head snapped up to find the giant of a man who'd likely dropped it less than twenty feet away. He was moving toward Ramona. The side of his face was covered in an ugly bruise. The sun caught the ground around him and glinted off something shiny embedded in his boots—glass.

Lola screamed for Ramona to stop.

The man swept his shirt and went for a gun in his waistband, wheeling.

Lola, half a breath ahead in her decision making, drew her Glock and shot him.

CHAPTER 55

Volkov and the engineers reached the locomotive at the first crack of gunfire. He drew his own pistol and shot the taller of the two engineers in the face. The other man crouched instinctively, trying to make sense of what was going on, and then, as they always did, raised his hands to ward off any oncoming bullet.

"Idiot," Volkov snapped. "You would only have hole in your hand and your head. Open the door!"

Volkov knew Morehouse had jumped from the train and pictured her now limping down the tracks, attempting to get away and save herself. So pitiful. He wanted to put his stick against her neck and stomp, but he would accept running her down with a train as consolation if such an opportunity presented itself. He would kill the girl to make his point—as soon as they reached a place with a signal. He could not have planned this to work out more perfectly.

The surviving engineer's chin trembled as if he might break into tears. "Why did you have to kill him?"

"Mathematics," Volkov scoffed. "I need only one of you to drive the train."

"But why?"

Always the same question.

Volkov prodded with the pistol. "Get in!" He gritted his teeth at the fresh pain cramping his belly. He waited for the worst of it to pass and then struck the engineer across the back with his stick as if the pain were his fault.

Gunfire echoed off the mountains, cracking and popping up and down the length of the train. Passengers screamed. Some fled into the woods. Others fell as they ran, legs tangled in their terror. Some squatted behind whatever bush or rock they happened to be near, unable to believe the scene unfolding before their eyes.

Volkov beamed as one of the marshals fell at the other end of the train. The battle had moved on board now. His men were experienced and ruthless. And Alex . . . that boy was his father's son. They would easily neutralize a handful of policemen, surely none of whom would know violence like his trusted brothers!

The engineer opened the door and then balked, turning slowly. He clenched his fists and dug in, his courage finally catching up to the situation. He was older than Volkov, balding, thick glasses. Someone's grandfather. "You bastard! W . . . what the hell are you up to?"

"That sound you hear," Volkov said, "is my men killing every last US marshal on board this train—"

"But why?"

"Move!" Volkov spat. "I do not need you that bad."

CHAPTER 56

*C*utter and Morehouse scrambled up the loose scree, slid backward, and then climbed some more, clawing their way to the top of the steep incline to the tracks.

They walked along the right of way without speaking. Shaking with cold and fatigue, each locked in their own cloudy thoughts trying to get warm. By Marshals Service policy, Cutter should have been taking her north—away from danger—but Morehouse threatened to revolt if he even hinted at the notion.

They'd been in the river about a mile and would make it back to the tunnels soon if they kept up this pace. Cutter had no idea what he would do when they got there, but he needed to think, and walking helped pump blood to his brain.

Morehouse walked beside him, coherent but shaking badly—which was actually a good sign, all things considered. Her body was still working to keep itself warm. If she had appeared calm and sleepy, it meant her core had given up on itself, surrendering to the cold.

For a time the only sounds were the distant hiss of the river below, the wind in the trees above, and the rhythmic crunch of their boots on the gravel rail bed.

"I'm s . . . sorry," Cutter said out of the blue. "I . . . should have seen that guy . . . Let him get too close. Wasn't ready."

Morehouse stopped abruptly. "Knock it off! I c . . . can't think of anything but Ramona—"

Cutter tapped his forehead with a forefinger. He knew it looked foolish even as he was doing it, but he was too loopy to stop himself. "Working on a p . . . plan."

"A plan I will help with." It wasn't a question.

"No," Cutter said. "Not a chance. I c . . . can't let you—"

"What would you do"—Morehouse shuddered, blowing a cloud vapor—"to save the most important person in the world?"

"What wouldn't I do?" Cutter admitted. "But right now, from my perspective, that person is you."

"You know that's not what I—"

"L . . . listen," Cutter said, warmed by frustration and anger at their predicament. "My partner's on that train. I love Lola T . . . Teariki like she was my little sister—but she is not my responsibility at the m . . . moment. You are."

"I understand your job, Marshal," Morehouse said. "But s . . . say it was *your* daughter on the train?"

"I don't do hypotheticals," Cutter said. "I have to—"

Morehouse clutched a handful of hair on either side of her face, exasperated. A sob caught in her chest and made her wince. "If I am your responsibility, then you have got to help me."

"Ah," Cutter said. "But do I help you do something that might get you killed?"

Morehouse started to walk again, steeling her resolve. "Think you c . . . can stop me?"

"Oh," Cutter said. "I could stop you. I'm pretty good at stuff like that."

Cold and exhausted and beaten half to death, he rubbed a hand across the stubble on his face and groaned. There was not a doubt in his mind that Charlotte Morehouse was easily twice as smart as he was on a good day. Debating her now was out of the question.

"We . . . we need to get warm," Cutter said.

Morehouse dug in her pocket and came out with three Werther's butterscotch hard candies. "We should s . . . split these."

"You eat th—"

"Would you j . . . just stop!" Morehouse said. "I n . . . need you alive, so shut up and . . . and . . . eat this."

She gave him one of the soggy candies and ate one herself. He chewed it quickly. She bit the third one in two and passed him the larger half.

"We could alternate licks," she said. "But I figured this was simpler."

He ate it, knowing she wouldn't take no for an answer.

"What if we could do both," Morehouse said, hoarse from crying and the sudden sweetness of the candy.

"Both?"

"Save my daughter and your partner?"

Cutter gave a sardonic chuckle. "That's not *both*," he said. "'Both' means saving your daughter and not getting you killed."

"That too, then."

"Okay," Cutter said. "I'm g . . . game. What's your plan?"

Morehouse shrugged. "Plans are your department. I'm just here to tell you they have to be made. Truth be told, I'm pretty used to g . . . getting my own way."

She tripped, staggering drunkenly in the gravel.

Cutter reached out and grabbed her, and nearly went down himself.

"That does it." He rubbed her hands between his, as much to assess them as warm them up. "We'll figure out a strategy, but at the moment we have more pressing problems."

"There is nothing more important than—"

"Your daughter is job one," he said. "I agree w . . . with you. But we h . . . have t . . . to get warm." He pressed on her thumbnail, which had turned a chalky purple blue. No change. "Slow c . . . capillary refill."

"W . . . w . . . well," she said, teeth chattering, "you're not looking too ch . . . chipper yourself."

Cutter gave a nod toward the heavy clouds over the mountains, low and gray. "Something like thirty percent of the Chugach is glaciers. Cold wind on wet clothes is gonna k . . . kill us. We get warm . . . or we die."

"Strip d . . . down and sh . . . share body heat?" Morehouse moved her jaw back and forth. "I've s . . . seen those movies."

"It may . . . come to that," Cutter said. "B . . . but I have an . . .

other idea." He forced a smile, feeling like his face might crack in the process.

"What?" Morehouse asked.

"A f . . . fire," Cutter said. "My lighter's soaking wet . . . but I have a ferro rod."

Morehouse cocked her head and looked him up and down, swaying amid her shivers.

"Of course, you do," she muttered. "But the train's coming back. You said it yourself. They'll see a fire."

"Maybe not." Cutter nodded at the layers of mist and fog hanging along the rocky cliffs. "Growing up, my brother and I built a lot of fires."

CHAPTER 57

*L*ola rushed her shot and missed center mass, but she was sure at least one of her rounds had hit the big Russian. He grabbed Ramona with his free hand and shoved her toward the open door at the end of B car, directly behind the DMU.

Deputy Gil Brady, snapping to the sudden threat, lunged to pull Ramona away. He was two steps away when a new player, young and ghostly pale, leaned out of the door and shot him twice.

Lola flinched at the gunfire, as if she had been hit too. Brady was facing away from her, so she couldn't see where the shots had landed. He slumped immediately, falling sideways as one leg gave out before the other. A supremely bad sign. Lola had no time to grieve or even check on the downed deputy. Rounds from the big Russian's pistol zipped past her head. Ramona screamed as the pale blond figure leaned out and pulled her into the B car.

Shots cracked to Lola's right, sending her diving for conceal-ment if not protective cover behind a wooden awning at the Grandview trailhead. She fired as she moved, cognizant of the fact that she was in the middle of nowhere with a finite supply of ammunition. Two young women in OHIO STATE jackets lay flat on their bellies in the gravel, hands pressed tight to their ears. They screamed when Lola slid in beside them, cowering at the sight of her Glock.

"US Marshal," she said. "Stay here!"

The women gave tight nods, eyes clinched.

Situated alongside the train, the big Russian half turned and dragged himself aboard, firing blindly in an attempt to suppress Lola's attack.

Brady lay on his side, with one arm trailing behind him.

"Gil!" Lola shouted when the Russian disappeared.

He didn't move.

She gathered herself up to run to him, but rounds slapped the ground around her.

She dropped, pressing herself against the gravel.

A tour guide wearing a red shirt bolted for the willows in a hail of bullets. Gravel crunched as he fell, but Lola remained focused on the train. There was nothing she could do for him now.

Sporadic shots came from her left now, probably inside the baggage car. Sloan had been heading that way, just before this shitshow blew up.

The radio erupted in a mass of garbled static as several people attempted to speak at once. Gunfire erupted inside the DMU. Peering around the base of a wooden post at the trailhead, Lola saw faint flashes through the windows of the bottom level. The firing stopped for a beat, long enough for Lola to take advantage of the silence.

"Scott," Lola said. "Status?"

Keen came back, remarkably calm. "Taking fire from below. Stairs are defendable . . . for now. So far, no rounds coming through the floor."

"Have you got eyes on Ramona?" Lola asked.

"Negative."

Automatic gunfire rattled the DMU. Keen's H&K.

Hart spoke next. "Sloan's down," she said. "I'm with her in the baggage car."

"Wounded," Sloan added, her voice almost transparent, it was so frail. She was clearly hurt.

"Any sign of Morehouse?" Lola didn't ask about Cutter. If he wasn't with the justice . . .

"Negative," Sloan said.

"These guys pulled Ramona on board," Lola said. "She's either in B car or on the lower level of the DMU. I counted at least two."

She described them, including the fact that she'd wounded the big one, then bit her lip, fighting the urge to give orders. Every deputy on the detail was a type A.

Sloan filled the silence immediately. "Dave," she said, "fall back to B car. Push through with Lola and Gil. Get Ramona out of—"

A sudden volley of gunfire covered her transmission, crackling over Lola's earpiece.

"Dave's taking fire," Sloan said. Her voice was muffled. Lola imagined her crouching lower behind a stack of luggage.

"Shots coming from the north end of A," Dillard snapped. "The vestibule between you and me, Sloan—"

More gunfire, close enough to Dillard's mic that the *ping* of bullets slapping metal was sickeningly clear.

"Two shooters," Dillard said, dead calm. A garbled voice spoke in the background, and then Dillard continued. "Andy's with me. Nobody shoot him."

"Gil." Sloan went on with her orders. "You and Lola get Ramona. Paige and I will help Dave!"

"Gil's down," Lola said. "I'm looking at him now. He's not moving."

"Shit!" Sloan said. "It's up to you then."

"Copy," Lola said. She popped the magazine out of her Glock—six rounds left—then swapped it for a fresh one from her belt. That gave her fifteen, plus the one in the chamber. With the mag and a half remaining on her belt, she had a grand total of thirty-seven rounds. Plus, the five-shot Ruger SP101 get-off-me gun in the small of her back, a Benchmade automatic folding knife in the pocket of her khakis—and, if it came down to it, teeth and fingernails.

"Scott," she said, "can you draw their fire from the stairs? Cover my move?"

"I can try," Keen snapped back.

Lola drew crazed looks from the two Ohio women as she crouched like a sprinter off the line. "Okay," she said. "I'll get Ramona—"

Then a diesel engine belched—and the train began to roll.

* * *

Volkov banged his wooden stick against a metal support. "When will we get a cell signal?"

"I have a radio right here," the engineer said, reaching for the mic.

Volkov swatted the hand away. "That is not what I asked."

The engineer's face twitched with rage and indignation, looking like he might explode. There reached a point in a man's life when the threat of death did not outweigh what he had to lose. Volkov knew that all too well.

He would have to watch this one.

"Cell service?" Volkov asked again.

"Not until we're closer to Portage."

"Speed up!" Volkov spat. "We are no longer looking at sights."

"Mister," the engineer said, "the sum total of all the things that can kill us on this section would astound you—"

Volkov raised his stick. "And I am one of those things—"

"Yeah," the engineer said, a scoff barely hidden in the tremor of his voice. "I suppose you are. But if I go too fast, you won't get the chance. Dangerous curves, rocks in our path, too much sway in the tunnels. Hell, a moose standing in the wrong spot could derail us."

"It appears that I shot the wrong conductor."

"Engineer," the man corrected, then hastily added, "Don't forget, you need me to operate the train."

Volkov turned to stare out the rain-flecked windows. The ache in his stomach burned when he envisioned Charlotte Morehouse.

"I said more speed!" he said. "As fast as possible without derailing."

The engineer nudged the throttle forward. "You're the boss."

Volkov swung the thick mahogany so it impacted the engineer's forearm with a sickening thud. The man fell against the far wall, sinking on his knees from the staggering pain.

Volkov swung the stick, again and again, crushing the cowering engineer's fingers where they clutched the injured arm.

"You are correct," Volkov said. Sweat dripped from the end of his nose as he caught his breath after administering the beating. He used his sleeve to wipe a bit of blood from his stick. "I am the boss.

It would serve you well to remember that. I need only one engineer to operate this train—and you need only one hand." He struck the console with his stick, the sound of it eliciting a satisfying flinch from the terrified engineer.

Volkov took a deep, cleansing breath and waited for the pain of exertion to subside in his belly.

"Now," he said, "give me more speed."

CHAPTER 58

"**M**y grandfather c . . . called this a 'Seven Council Fire,'"
Cutter said, scraping gravel and muck from a hole in the ground.
He wanted something roughly eighteen inches deep and a foot
across, but the topsoil was scarce in these glacial valleys, making
any hole collapse on itself almost as soon as it was dug. At his direction Morehouse scraped out a second, slightly smaller spot,
about a foot away from his. They worked feverishly, talking to
keep their thoughts from drifting away on the chill. Muscles
shook with cold and abject fatigue.

They'd found a likely spot, not far from the tunnel entrance,
where centuries of deadfall and erosion had made a passable layer
of topsoil over silt and gravel left behind by retreating glaciers.
Rather than getting two simple holes as he would have done with
better ground, Cutter connected both their work and made do
with a natural trench, scraping it out as best he could and then
using flat stones to reinforce it.

Morehouse glanced up, on her knees and still bent forward,
both hands clawing at the gravel. She turned her head, attempting
to brush a smudge off her face by rubbing it against her shoulder—a bird preening her wing.

"Se . . . Seven . . . C . . . Council F . . . F . . . Fire . . . " She repeated the words, as if to keep herself on track with Cutter's story.

"After the friend who taught him to build it," Cutter said. "He
was Dakota, one of the Sioux Nations of the Great Plains."

"Your . . . grandfather was S . . . Sioux?" Morehouse sat back on her haunches, muddy hands in her lap.

"S . . . sorry," Cutter said. "No. I mean his friend was Sioux. Most people call what we're building a 'Dakota firepit.' Two holes connected by a small tunnel underground." He pointed to the larger end of what was supposed to be two holes, but was essentially a figure eight bridged in the middle by a flat rock and piled dirt to form a space beneath that connected the two fat ends of the eight. "F . . . fuel goes here. Heat rises, drawing fresh air from the tunnel . . . p . . . pulling it from this smaller hole. The flames are low, out of sight, and the c . . . constant air flow works like a forge. Burns hot . . . not much smoke."

Cutter worked as quickly as his chilled brain would allow, his mind on autopilot as he went about the various tasks to complete to build a fire without matches or his sodden Zippo. He found a likely birch tree and peeled off a curl of white bark, about eight inches square. Using this curl as a receptacle, he raked the spine of his knife blade down the bark of another birch, scraping the papery white outer layer until he had a pile of dust, about a quarter and a half inch deep. Morehouse gathered bits of standing dead spruce, twigs at first and then working her way up to limbs slightly smaller than her wrist—easy enough to break without the need of an axe.

Cutter next built a nest out of the smallest of the twigs, wrapped it in feathered curls of paper-thin birch bark and then set it on the ground beside the larger hole. He placed the tip of the ferrocerium rod tight against the birch bark square and ran the spine of the MAK knife sharply downward, like peeling a stubborn potato. A shower of sparks sizzled onto the bark, a few of them igniting the birch dust. Bark square in one hand, Cutter lifted the twig nest with the other and placed it gingerly on the bark beside the tiny flame, close enough to catch when he blew on it. He lowered the bundle into the bottom of the hole, gradually adding sicks. The heat rose quickly, pulling air and fanning the flames.

Cutter and Morehouse crowded close, leaning over the hole, giddy at the constant blast of heat on their hands and faces. Overcome, Morehouse began to sob. Cutter wasn't far behind her.

*   *   *

"I almost feel human again," she said a short time later.

"We're lucky," Cutter said. "Much longer and our core temps wouldn't have come back up with just a fire."

She rolled her shoulders and moved her neck from side to side. "Is hypothermia supposed to make you this sore?"

"Falling off a train makes you sore," Cutter said.

"Yeah." Morehouse stared into the flames between them. "There's that, I guess."

"I really am sorry," Cutter said. "I should have seen that guy in the baggage car. Frankly, I shouldn't have taken you back there, to begin with. Only one way in and out. Stupid—"

"Stop beating yourself up, Cutter—"

"Arliss," he corrected. "If I have to call you Charlotte—"

"Touché," she said. "Anyway, if you think about it, women are prey animals. We get used to looking for threats early in life. At least the ones who survive very long do."

"Makes sense," Cutter said.

"I suppose that sort of thing doesn't happen to you very often."

"Being prey?" Cutter dabbed at the bruising along the bridge of his nose where the enormous Russian had used him for a punching bag. "You might be surprised."

He checked his watch.

"What's next?" Morehouse asked. It was clear she wasn't going to sit back and let Cutter go with this. She wanted to be informed every step of the way. He couldn't blame her. Her kid was on the train.

"A remote run like this," Cutter said. "There's a better than average chance they planned to take over the train in Grandview and . . ."

"And murder me," Morehouse said.

Hands open flat over the fire, Cutter glanced up, meeting the justice's eye. "About the size of it, ma'am."

"You warned me something like this might be on the horizon." Her voice was steadier now. Somber. "You drew me a map, for crying out loud."

"Okay, now," Cutter said. "I don't do hypotheticals *or* I-told-you-so sermons." He gave her a wink. "There's a good chance my part-

CHAPTER 68

*L*ola pitched abruptly forward, slamming into Blondie's knees and knocking him onto his face. She scrambled sideways, shoving herself away. The little revolver flew out of her hand in the process. It rattled along the top of the car for a moment, dancing like a drop of water on a hot skillet before disappearing over the edge.

"Shit!"

Barely stable herself, she turned her attention back to Blondie, who was just now pushing himself to his knees. She put a boot between his shoulder blades and put him down again, hopping to keep her balance.

When she looked up, Cutter was gone.

Blondie roared with laughter.

"He's gone! It's just me and you now!"

The train was still rolling, slower, like in the tunnels, but fast enough that the swaying of the cars amplified every step and turn, as if trying to shake her off.

Lola screamed. Not the shallow, frenzied scream of fear or shock, but a visceral bellow that boiled up from deep inside her. Sam Benjamin was dead. Gil Brady, dead. Hell, for all she knew, the child she was charged with protecting was dead. And now . . . Cutter . . . It was too much to comprehend, too much to bear—so she didn't try.

The only way to stop this man was to kill him—and that would kill her too.

Blondie rolled onto his back, scooting sideways to stay center on the car. He didn't intend to get up, but to shoot her from where he lay.

Lola fell on him like a feral cat, intent on ripping away his throat. They could roll off the train together. She didn't give a shit, so long as he was dead. She led with her knee as she dropped, crushing his groin against the metal roof. He gasped, tried to cry out, but she clawed her way up his body, grabbing, clawing with stunning ferocity. Her body pressed against the AK pistol, trapping it between them.

He bucked his hips, over and over, pitching, all while trying to stay in the center on the centerline of the railcar. The distressed metal wasn't meant to take such abuse and popped and twanged like a bent saw blade under the pressure. Instinctively, Lola wrapped her heels between and behind his legs, getting her hooks. Groin to groin, chest to chest, it would have been supremely intimate, had they not been trying to kill each other.

Lola rarely did much thinking during a fight, relying instead on ingrained muscle memory. If a target presented itself, she exploited it. This man was taller, stronger, and armed. It was only a matter of time before he shot her or simply rolled her over the edge. Each buck of his hips tossed her violently upward. She inched forward, her heels still hooked behind his knees, transferring pressure from his groin to put the bulk of her mass directly against his chest. Robbed of his ability to throw her, he twisted sharply, inadvertently smashing her broken wrist. He hadn't meant to, probably didn't even realize it was a target. Nausea grabbed her gut. She jerked away from the searing pain, covering a yelp with a war cry.

He was onto her and twisted in earnest now, chuckling as if he'd already won, while he slammed against the injury.

Her right hand was useless. There was no "fighting through the pain." The fingers just wouldn't obey her commands. Her arm was a different story, however, and Lola knew how to fight dirty.

Staying low, she used the weight of her body to rake the bony ridge of her uninjured forearm across his nose, twisting his neck so his cheek pressed against the roof. She bored down hard, as if trying to shove his teeth through the roof of the railcar.

He kicked and thrashed. Muffled curses buzzed against her arm.

Driven by heartbreak and fury, she capitalized on the strength of her legs and lower center of gravity to hang on as she sank her teeth into the exposed flesh under his right eye.

He broke loose in a curdled screech of shock and terror, throwing himself to the side.

Lola took advantage of his upward shift in energy and snaked her left hand into the scant gap between their bodies, clawing at flesh and clothing until her fingers curled around his knuckles, where they gripped the AK pistol. Rather than attempting to wrest the weapon away from him, she trapped his finger inside the trigger guard.

Sharp edges of the stamped metal firearm gouged Lola's hand, torquing her knuckles until she was sure the bones would snap. She held fast, ignored the pain, and yanked the butt of the little AK pistol upward, toward her, driving the short barrel into his solar plexus.

Blondie's cries grew louder as he realized what was happening. He struggled in vain to move his finger—but there was only one way for it to go. A volley of lead ripped through his abdomen, destroying bowel and spine in a breath. He convulsed, then gasped once, before going limp, as if a switch had been flipped.

Lola remained frozen on top of him, as if fused. She'd thrown so much energy into the fight, she was unable to relax her cramping muscles even if she'd wanted. Their bodies had muffled the noise, absorbing shock and most of the muzzle flash, but a searing pain made her wonder if she had been shot too.

A deep voice resonated in front of her, extremely close. She would have fallen off the train, had she not been so spent. Sobs swelled in her chest when she looked up and saw who it was.

"Cutter!" Her mouth could hardly form the words. "Where? Wha . . . ?"

He dropped to his knees and pulled her into a great bear hug. She sobbed uncontrollably, dizzy.

His voice was calm, steady against her ear.

"You did good."

"Oh, Arliss." She fought the urge to be sick. "I . . . I thought you . . ." She buried her face against his chest.

Still holding her tight, he scooted sideways to reach for the Draco pistol, where it lay on what was left of the dead man's belly. Even going slowly, the train rocked and swayed, threatening to toss them into the rocks. He draped the AK over her neck, and then grabbed the Glock 19 from the dead man's waistband.

Lola's mouth fell open in shock when she saw his empty holster. "Your Colt!"

"I know where it went over," he said dismissively, but was clearly unhappy to be separated from his grandfather's sidearm. She checked the AK's magazine, out of habit. It still had visible rounds, but she couldn't be sure how many. She watched him press-check the Glock. Nodding, he shoved the gun into his holster. It was meant for a revolver, but secured the medium-sized semiauto better than carrying it in his hand. The entire process took seconds.

Cutter gave Lola's shoulders an urgent tug. "Ramona?"

She sniffed, composing herself. The wind off the mountain, and from the movement of the train, whipped her hair across her swollen face.

"She was in the DMU," she said. "With the Big Guy."

"A Russian?"

Lola clawed the hair out of her eyes with a shaky hand and nodded.

"We've met," Cutter said. "Pretty sure he killed Sam."

Another impatient pull toward the DMU.

"Me too." Lola grimaced—a mix of pain and anger. "Name's Rudenko, according to Joe Bill."

Cutter checked the mountainside to their left, and the river to their right, before glancing up the tracks as if getting his bearings.

"We need to get down now." He all but dragged Lola toward the DMU. "Any second now, this train is going to brake. Hard."

CHAPTER 69

*F*inding Lola Teariki on top of a moving train in the middle of a fight for her life wasn't the most startling thing that had ever happened to Arliss Cutter, but it ranked in the top three. It was like walking into a movie that was already half over. He'd been in the process of shooting when he fell, landing on the accordion vestibule that connected two railcars. It took both hands to keep from sliding into the rocks, forcing him to sacrifice his revolver to hang on. By the time he clamored back to the roof, Lola had stomped her own snakes.

Dizzy with fatigue and borderline hypothermia, he had only a vague idea of what was going on. Lola briefed him on the fly. They moved in a sliding shuffle, lending support to each other in a train-top tango, where they kept both feet in contact with the roof.

"So only one more bad guy," he confirmed when they reached the vestibule connecting the two-story DMU.

"Correct!" Lola said. "Not counting whoever's driving this damned thing." She'd regained some of her swagger, but the fight with the blond kid had taken a tremendous toll, physically and mentally. She babied her wrist and hunched sideways to protect injured ribs. Cutter rarely saw her cry, even then never from physical pain, but this was grinding her to the bone . . . literally.

And still, she moved with singular focus toward danger.

Judges Markham and Reese stood with their noses pressed to the upper-floor DMU window, mouths agape. They'd evidently watched the entire battle. Scotty Keen was just visible behind them in the shadows, near the top of the stairwell. He held the stubby black Heckler & Koch UMP at low ready—his Alamo.

"Hold on!" Cutter yelled, pointing with an open hand to the metal lip on the leading face of the DMU. Lola followed his lead and leaned across the vestibule, bracing her feet on the back of the B car, their faces only inches from the two judges on the other side of the window.

"Can you shoot?" Cutter yelled over the noise.

She nodded, the wind whipping her hair again. "Yis!"

"This is going to happen fast," he said. "Here's what I want you to do . . ."

Steel screamed against steel as the train lurched to a stop. Momentum shoved Cutter and Lola toward the engine, but they hung on by boot and fingertip, Lola gritting her teeth from her broken wrist.

Cutter had to use both hands to go over the edge in even a semi-controlled descent. Even then, he hit the ground hard, landing on the river-facing side of the tracks, jamming his knees and hips in the process.

Rolling to his feet, Cutter worked the latch on the door at the rear of the B car, shoving it inward. He drew the Glock and hauled himself up the steps. Rudenko's head snapped up at the noise and he turned, sending a short burst from his AK pistol into the vestibule, shattering the thick glass. Cutter ducked out of sight, using the reinforced thresholds around the doors as cover.

The Russian roared, eyes wide that Cutter was still alive after falling out of the baggage car. He stooped behind the counter and came up holding Ramona by the hair. He shoved her toward the door, firing well-controlled bursts as he moved. Lead pinged and clanked off and through metal and glass. Ramona screamed, an agonized, infantile cry that sent bile rising in Cutter's throat.

He backed down the train car steps to the gravel, wanting desperately to beat the larger man to death, but knowing he'd do Ramona no good if he caught a gutful of AK rounds.

Rudenko barked commands in wet, phlegmy Russian, sounding drunk, out of his mind. Ramona continued to wail, no matter how much he shook her or yanked at her hair.

Cutter moved sideways, working his way toward the rear, but staying tight against the railcar, with a vague idea he'd dive under it if he had to.

Ramona appeared at the door first, her head arched cruelly backward so her face canted skyward. Her hands were bound in front with silver duct tape. She attempted to jerk away. Rudenko screamed and slammed her head against the doorway. Stunned, she staggered, her knees buckling. He gave a vigorous shake and she straightened up. Her wails died down to a pitiful keening.

Exhausted from the exertion, the Russian listed to his left, using the door for support. A rust-brown blossom of blood covered the front of his shirt in sharp contrast to his ashen skin. His breaths came in short, uneven gasps, like tearless sobs. He was bleeding out . . . just not fast enough.

Using Ramona as a shield, he did a quick peek, up and down the train. A pitiless sneer perked his lips when he saw Cutter was alone.

"Put down gun!" he barked. "Or I kill girl!" Dried spit crusted white at the corners of his mouth.

"You'll kill her, anyway," Cutter said, continuing to back away.

"Stop moving! I kill her. I swear it!" He shoved Ramona to the bottom step, leaning out to peer around her and get a bead on Cutter.

Lola, waiting above, put a bullet straight down through the top of his head.

Ramona stumbled away from the dead Russian, spattered in blood and gore. Cutter rushed to her side, turning her head away. Lola was on the ground in a heartbeat, the AK slung around her neck.

"Let's get her on board," Cutter said. "I don't like her out in the open—"

A shout drew his attention up the tracks. His fear, his nightmare scenario, unfolded before his eyes. Beyond the engine Justice Charlotte Morehouse, who was supposed to stay hidden, burst out of the willows the moment she saw her daughter.

She called out, mistakenly thinking that since Cutter and Lola had shot the man holding Ramona, there was no further threat.

A muffled *whoomph* from the locomotive sent a chill up Cutter's back. He cursed under his breath. Gunfire in the cab.

"Get her inside!" He pushed Ramona and Lola toward the door before turning his attention toward Morehouse and the small man who'd just fallen out of the locomotive. He clamored to his feet, a walking stick in one hand, and a pistol in the other—a football field away.

Morehouse froze in place beside the tracks, entranced by the sight of her daughter. Cutter broke into a run, waving at her to hide. He shouted, hoping to draw the man's attention to him, away from the justice.

Undeterred, the man began to shout at Morehouse in Russian, seemingly oblivious to everything else. He dropped the walking stick and raised the gun as he limped toward her.

The *thump* of an approaching helicopter came from up the valley.

Cutter had just passed the midpoint of the A car, when Dave Dillard stepped down from the baggage car. Listing badly, he braced himself on the rear of the locomotive, took careful aim with his pistol, and shot the slender Russian in the small of his back.

Morehouse took a half step toward the bushes and then froze again.

The Russian pitched forward, still clutching the pistol.

"US Marshals!" Cutter barked, a hundred feet away. "Don't you move!"

The Russian did and Dillard shot him again.

CHAPTER 70

"*H*ell of a shot!" Cutter said as he passed Dave Dillard at a limping run, Glock shoved back in the ill-fitting holster. He paused only long enough to scoop up the dead Russian's pistol, and make sure he was no longer a threat, before racing to intercept Morehouse, who was walking unsteadily toward him.

He put an arm around her shoulder, stationing himself between her and Dave Dillard, who was in the process of handcuffing the dead Russian behind his back. Scott Keen had come out and done the same for Rudenko—though he'd taken a rifle round from stem to stern. These guys had caused enough trouble, and no one was taking any chances.

"Ramona?" Morehouse said, picking up speed as they walked.

"She's fine," Cutter said. "Lola's inside with her now."

"Arliss . . ." She looked at him, and then shook her head.

"We'll talk after you see your daughter," Cutter said. "I'm at your disposal."

Satisfied the threats to Morehouse had been taken care of for the moment, Cutter went immediately to check on his old friend. Lola and Scotty Keen remained in the DMU, just in case.

Nicki Sloan winced when Cutter raised the tail of her shirt and assessed the bullet wound in her side. It was an ugly purple thing that had shattered a floating rib and may have clipped her lung.

Paige Hart stayed put, keeping steady pressure on the wound in Sloan's shoulder until help arrived. As soon as he'd secured the dead Russian, Dave Dillard had dragged himself out of the spattering rain and now leaned against a pile of dry bags that campers had never had the chance to off-load at Grandview.

Sloan's eyes fluttered sleepily. "Hey, buddy . . ." Her pulse raced, her skin was cool to the touch. Not a good sign.

"Hey, yourself," Cutter said, forcing a smile.

Sloan's forehead wrinkled. "How did you get the train to stop? Tell me you didn't use the justice as bait."

"Nope," Cutter said. "Well, sort of."

"I can't wait to hear about it," Sloan groused. Her head lolled and she drifted back and forth from angry to sleepy with alarming speed.

Cutter explained what had happened as he checked for undiscovered wounds, exits, spallings, or through-and-throughs that might be hiding beneath the greater pain of her known injuries.

"Our justice has some legs on her," he said. "She ran up the track as fast and far as she could, while I climbed up to jump on the train. Made it well over a mile and then hung her fleece on some willows. The Russian knew she'd gone off the train, so her jacket was all the incentive we needed to get the engineer to stop."

"I guess that doesn't sound so bad," Sloan said.

A helicopter thundered overhead.

Sloan shuddered.

"Troopers are here," Cutter said. He patted the back of her hand. "Medics will get you set up shortly."

She crinkled her nose. "Is it my imagination or do you smell like barbecue? Maybe butterscotch . . ."

"Geesh!" Dillard said. "More of your food flirtation. You two need to get a room."

Deputy Hart looked back and forth from Cutter to Dillard, confused.

"Hell of a shot you made back there, Dave," Cutter said again, changing the subject. "I know we shouldn't discuss it until after you give your debrief, but there is no doubt in my mind you saved the justice's life. It was at least thirty yards."

Dillard shrugged, like he did that sort of thing every day. "I'm not bad if I have time to turn my glasses upside down."

"What about Gil?" Hart asked.

Cutter shook his head. "Lola's on the radio with the Troopers. They're counting casualties now. I'm afraid Brady's one of them."

Two Air Force PJs entered the baggage car with trauma kits. In Alaska it was not at all uncommon for Air Force pararescue to assist the state.

"We were tasked with checking on the justice," one of them said, "but she ordered us to come check on . . ."

The PJ saw Sloan before he finished speaking and dropped to his knees beside her. Two minutes later, he'd shot an eighteen-gauge needle into her thighbone and started an IO fluid drip.

Now he was just in the way, so Cutter patted Sloan on the knee and excused himself to limp to the other end of the train and check on Morehouse.

Cutter arrived in the DMU to churchlike silence. Keen stood at the back window with the SMG slung around his neck. Judge Reese slumped over the table, her head buried in crossed arms. Beside her, Markham talked in hushed tones, obviously trying to offer some comfort.

It was difficult to tell if Ramona was clinging to the justice or vice versa. They huddled together under a shared blanket, with More-house cooing softly to her daughter. Ramona appeared to be trying to assure her mother that she was okay, but the justice remained unconvinced.

Lola sat at the next table, spinning the AK magazine on the table. The gun was out of sight, on her seat. She was smart enough to know it would soon be taken by investigators as evidence, but for now, it was all she had to defend herself and Ramona, so she wasn't going to give it up until she was properly relieved. For the first time he noticed the dried blood and swelling on her purple upper lip. She brightened when she saw him and patted the seat beside her.

"That engineer's a tough bird," she said. "Took one through the knee and still had the wherewithal to kick the Russian asshole out of the locomotive."

"Good thing," Cutter said. "Probably slowed our guy down long enough Dillard could take him."

Probably." Lola looked up, meeting Cutter's eye. "You okay?"

"I'm fine," Cutter lied. "Are *you* okay?"

"Chief's on her way," Lola said.

"I'm not surprised."

"Because Gil's down and three of us had to use deadly force?"

"Because leadership is about being there," Cutter said. "We could do worse than copying her. I'd lay odds the only reason she's not here already is that she didn't want to bump a medic off a flight."

Lola rubbed her eyes with a thumb and forefinger. "Can I ask you something?"

"Of course."

She lay both hands flat on the table and heaved a long sigh. "Is it bad that I don't feel sad for blowing that Russian asshole's brains all over the tracks?"

"We should probably wait until—"

"Just tell me," Lola said. "Cutter, am I a sociopath? I mean, I would have arrested him if he'd given me the chance . . . But I have to be honest, I'm glad he didn't."

"That feeling may come and go," Cutter said.

Lola sighed, wincing from the mere effort of breathing. "I just worry that . . . I don't know . . . I should maybe feel worse."

"Don't do that to yourself," Cutter said. "A shooting doesn't necessarily mean you need counseling." He tapped the table with his index finger to make sure she was listening. "But it doesn't mean you won't either. Everybody's different, Lola. No two events are the same."

"I know . . ."

She yawned and leaned forward on the table, deep in thought, and began to spin the AK magazine flat, like a top. "I only have three rounds left." She glanced up at him, chin still resting on her arm. "How about you? How many rounds did you have when you lit out for the justice?"

Cutter shrugged.

Her eyes narrowed.

"Come on," she prodded. "How much ammo did you have left?"

"Enough," Cutter said.

"You were empty, weren't you? You ran forward with an empty gun?" She clutched her hair and rocked to and fro in her seat. "You have got to be kidding me—"

Morehouse came around the table and saved him from having to answer.

Cutter pushed off the table with a stifled groan, getting to his feet. Lola started to do the same, but Morehouse waved her down.

"Could Ramona join you for a moment, Deputy Teariki? I'd like to borrow Arliss if you don't mind."

"Of course, Madam Justice," Lola said, then, leaning into Cutter, whispered, *"Arliss?"*

"Are you all right?" Morehouse asked when they'd walked to the far end of the DMU.

"I'm fine," Cutter said, startled by the question. "Do I act as though something is—"

"I'm sore as hell," she said, "and I basically stepped off a very slow-moving train. I'm pretty sure you landed on your head."

"My shoulder," Cutter said, grimacing when he attempted to roll it. "Yes, ma'am. We'll all be sore tomorrow. Once the adrenaline wears off."

She motioned to one of the tables. "Speaking of sore, do you mind if we sit down? My hip is killing me."

Cutter turned to go. "I'll get one of the Air Force PJs up here—"

"No, no, no," she said. "I'm fine. Just a little beat up."

They sat, facing each other. She folded her arms on top of the table and leaned forward, shivering. Draped in her blanket, face flushed and damp hair sticking every which way, she looked like she'd just gotten out of bed. Her voice dropped to a low whisper.

"Are you going to be okay after all this?"

"I'll be fine," Cutter said.

"That man in the river . . . wasn't your first, was he?"

"Madam Justice . . ."

She grimaced. "I'm sorry. That was a horrible thing to ask. I'm not trying to . . . I just want you to know you have my support."

Another helicopter flew above the train. Cutter pointed upward. "We'll get you and Ramona out of here very soon, straight to a hospital and then back to DC. I'm sure my chief is working it all out as we speak."

"All right." She sat back in her seat, deflated. "I'm sorry if I offended you."

"I'm hard to offend."

"At least not on your own behalf," she said. "I get the feeling you go a little bonkers if someone else is in the crosshairs."

"Fair assessment, ma'am" he said.

She touched him on the shoulder gently, like an old friend. "I thought we agreed you'd call me Charlotte."

"May I say something?"

Her hand stayed on his shoulder.

"By all means."

"You and I both are more than a little giddy just to still be alive. Any second now, all that cold and hunger and fear will catch up with you. You won't be able to keep your eyes open."

"Arliss," she protested, but stifled a yawn.

"Don't fight it when it comes," he said. "Grab sleep when you can. The most difficult thing to do after something like this is go back to normal. You'll replay everything, over and over, in your head. You might try and take the blame, dream up a million things that you could have done or said differently, second-guess every choice, even the future ones. Don't do that. You might even start to hate me because I'm part of the memory—"

"I would never," Morehouse said, her eyelids drooping, as he knew they would.

"You might," Cutter said. "And that's okay."

"And that's okay, *Charlotte* . . ." She gave his shoulder a friendly pat. "We've shared body heat and butterscotch candy covered in my spit. You saved my life, Arliss Cutter. Take the win."

CHAPTER 71

*T*he wounded went out on the first choppers—Sloan, Dillard, and seven passengers—two of whom Cutter thought might not survive the flight to Anchorage. Two more had injured themselves running, one badly hitting her head on a rock. The surviving engineer would probably lose his leg from the massive bullet wound to his knee, but he insisted on being one of the last of the wounded to be transported out. Justice Morehouse and her daughter were taken next in the Trooper helicopter. Chief Phillips and two deputies accompanied them, all armed with rifles. An ad hoc team of Anchorage PD officers, and special agents from the FBI, waited for them at the hospital in Anchorage.

Protection details didn't just stop because someone was killed. If anything, they grew more robust.

Chief Phillips peeled away as soon as they touched down and went to break the news to Gil Brady's wife.

Dave Dillard was treated for a through-and-through bullet wound that had, in the surgeon's words, missed his femoral artery by a whisper. His wife advised him in no uncertain terms that though the government set his mandatory retirement date in seven months, she had decided his papers were going in today.

Cutter should have been flown out with the wounded, but had grown skilled over the years at hiding his pain. He and Lola came out of the valley on the train with the remaining passengers, rolling into the Anchorage station just before two in the morning.

Joe Bill Brackett drove them both to Providence Hospital, where

Nicki Sloan had just gotten out of a four-hour surgery. Cutter found it hard to put weight on his left leg by the time they reached the hospital. Lola winced every time she breathed.

In addition to bruised kidneys and at least three cracked ribs, she'd broken a front tooth during her first jump from train car to train car.

Cutter had torn something in his knee, and his shoulder was badly sprained, probably worse.

The doctor seemed most concerned about the bruises on his head, paying special attention to his pupils. He found it impossible to believe anyone could fall off a train and tumble down a mountain without getting some kind of concussion. Like Grumpy, the doc warned him to avoid getting hit in the head in the future, and then admitted him for a CT scan and observation.

Jill Phillips was waiting when they wheeled him to his room, looking nearly as beaten up as he felt. She leaned against the wall as the nurse checked his IV and made certain all the wires were attached to the monitor beside his bed.

He raised his arm toward the chief when the nurse left, lifting the IV line. "I'd get up, but . . ."

Phillips just shook her head.

"You okay?" he asked.

"That's rich," she said. "You checking on me."

"Guessing you went to tell Gil's wife she's a widow."

"Yep," Phillips said. "Her sister's with her now. I'll check with her again tomorrow."

"Nicki?"

"Resting," Phillips said. "Dillard too. Paige is asleep in a chair outside his room."

"Figures." Cutter yawned. "We're lucky to have her."

"They gave Lola some pain meds for her tooth and released her. Joe Bill took her home."

"Lola," Cutter whispered. "I'm going to have to talk to her about decision making."

"Really?" the chief said. "Because you found her on top of a train . . . when you jumped on top of a train?"

"I had a plan," Cutter said. "Anyway, how's Scotty?"

"Keen?" Phillips said. "He's shaken up, but okay. To be honest, I think he's upset he didn't get some superficial wound."

Cutter chuckled, wincing when he tried to move his neck. "He can have mine. Seriously, he did good."

"He said the same thing about you."

"Did the justice make it out?"

"On a direct flight to Reagan as we speak," Phillips said. "Gutierrez and Billings are with her—along with four FBI agents the SAC loaned me. Speaking of the Feebs, they identified the man Dillard shot as Maxim Volkov, a bigwig in the Russian mob. They're running down his associates over here now."

Cutter yawned. "Outstanding."

Mim knocked on the door frame.

Phillips waved her in, gathering her in a quick hug. "We've got to stop meeting like this."

She rushed to Cutter's side, out of breath.

"Sorry it took me so long. I got the last seat on a charter from Utqiagvik as soon as I heard. Then the flight from Fairbanks had mechanical—"

"It's okay," Cutter said. "I'm glad you're here." He didn't bother to hide his smile.

"I was just going to go check on Nicki," Phillips said. "I'll see you kids tomorrow."

Mim hovered over him. "Are you all right?"

He gave a sardonic chuckle. "I wish people would stop asking me that."

She took his hand in hers and began to stroke the back of it. The numbers on his heart monitor began to rise.

"I've been thinking," he said, more than a little breathless. "We should—"

"Yes, we should," she said, and bent to kiss him hard on the lips. Beside the bed the heart monitor went berserk.

She drew back, her lips just inches from his, close enough he could taste the peppermint she'd eaten before she came in.

"You still okay?"

Cutter's throat convulsed. He wracked his brain for the right words, anything that wouldn't sound sappy or desperate or just plain crazy. He'd been waiting for this kiss since he was sixteen years old.

In the end he simply smiled up at her and said, "Yep."

Two days later

Nine-year-old Matthew looked up from the picnic table, peeled potato in one hand, knife in the other. Carrots, onions, caribou kielbasa, and cabbage leaves were arranged for an assembly line beside his cutting board. He'd thrown a dish towel cavalierly over his shoulder, as he'd seen Cutter do dozens of times.

Michael, the older twin by twelve minutes, tended the fire in the backyard ring. Tongue out to help with his concentration, he worked meticulously to arrange a bed of glowing coals for their tinfoil dinners. Even Constance had joined in with the prep, whipping up a batch of dessert beans and chips to eat while they waited.

Sunlight and bluebird sky sifted through a thick birch canopy, giving the backyard a cathedral-like feel. It was almost seven in the evening, but it wouldn't be dusk for another six hours. A redheaded woodpecker was hard at work wrecking the neighbor's eaves, the machine-gun rattle echoing off the trees.

Cutter and Mim sat in reclining deck chairs, feet toward the fire, watching the kids work. They'd been given an ultimatum—relax or else. Both of them were beat down, exhausted to the point of passing out.

"You think Lola's going to be okay?" Mim asked.

"I imagine so," Cutter said. "A lot to process. The director is coming up for Gil Brady's funeral. Not sure when it is. They're waiting for some of his family to arrive from the lower forty-eight. Sam Benjamin's service is this weekend. I'd like to go to that . . . for Lola."

"I'm with you there." Mim stared at the sky and slowly shook her head. "It's all just so senseless."

"Uncle Arliss," Matthew asked, gesturing wildly with the knife and earning a brutal side-eye from his sister. "Did you really run on top of a train after a bad guy?" He spoke with such exuberance he sounded like he had a mouthful of spit.

Mim's chair was close enough that Cutter could hear the sudden change in her breathing. She let her head loll sideways and gave him a what-are-you-going-to-do-about-this look. There was a fine line between inspiration and dangerous example.

Michael stared into the flames, nodding slowly as if he knew the answer to his brother's question.

"They said online that deputy marshals ran on top of a train to go after a bad guy."

Constance raised a wary brow and joined her mother in waiting for Cutter's response.

"Well, men," he said, "you can't believe everything you read online."

Michael looked up from tending the fire, face twisted into a picture of concern.

"So, you didn't go on top of a train to get a bad guy?"

"I did," Cutter said. "But I didn't run. I was walking . . . very slowly."

Matthew made a harsh buzzer noise.

"Wrong!" he said. "You don't *walk* after bad guys. You run. That's a Grumpy Man-Rule."

"Nice try," Cutter said. "But nope."

"Sounds like it should be a Grumpy Man-Rule," Michael mused.

"Generally true," Cutter said. "But sometimes . . ."

"How about some of those dessert beans, Constance," Mim said, coming to Cutter's rescue.

"Dessert Beans!" the boys crowed.

Grumpy's version of refried beans had been their favorite since they were babies. Cutter couldn't blame them.

He leaned back in his deck chair and gazed up at the sun-dazzled canopy of leaves, hands folded on his chest. There were very few places on Cutter's body that didn't hurt, but he didn't care.

Woodsmoke, the kids jabbering while they cooked dinner for their mom—it was the closest he'd ever come to a family of his own.

"I'm glad you found Grumpy's gun," Constance said.

She took the lead helping the boys assemble the foil dinners, doing a little too much of the work herself.

"Me too," Cutter said. "Troopers found it in a clump of willows, about to tumble over the edge."

Matthew gave him a knowing side-eye. "From when you were running on top of the train after a bad guy?"

Cutter chuckled. "It has a few more scratches, but still in working order."

Mim held up a crumpled paper sack.

"I brought y'all something."

The boys abandoned their half-made foil dinners and crowded around her.

"You too, Constance," Mim said.

"A friend of your dad's gave them to me on this trip. He said they were meant for you."

Constance let the boys go first.

"Fossils," Michael said.

"Cooool!" Matthew held up his fossilized tooth next to his brother's, to make sure he hadn't been cheated. "Oreo . . ."

"Oreo." Michael nodded. "Nice."

It made sense that Ethan would get something like that for his kids. Grumpy's pockets had often been stuffed with interesting shells and fossilized shark teeth when he came home.

"Why 'Oreo'? Like the cookie?" Cutter asked. "What does that mean?"

Matthew held up his specimen. "This is an oreodont tooth."

Mim nodded. "Max said it was a kind of mammoth."

"Max would be wrong," Michael said with the certitude of a nine-year-old boy who knew stuff. "Oreodonts weren't mammoths. They were kinda like pigs or tapirs. Dad said oreodont means mountain tooth. His knife handle is made out of the same thing."

"I thought his knife was mammoth tooth," Mim said.

"Oh yeah," Michael said. "It's that too. Fossilized mammoth tooth from Alaska and oreo from South Dakota."

Cutter's stomach dropped. He swung his legs over the side of the chair. "South Dakota? Not here in Alaska?"

"Nope," Michael said. He held his fossilized tooth up in his thumb and forefinger like a prize diamond. "Dad said these little puppies come from somebody's ranch near the Badlands." He grinned. "I like that word, *Badlands*."

"Badland oreo," Matthew said around his mouthful of spit.

Cutter shot a glance at Mim, who caught his meaning without a word. "Y'all," she said, "would you mind if I hang on to those rocks for a couple of days? I need to check something out."

The boys finished eating and went inside to have their showers and watch *Jurassic Park*—inspired by the fossils from their dad. Constance sat in her camp chair, arms folded, staring at her mother and uncle. She'd added a couple of fresh pieces of split spruce to the fire. The heat from the flames knocked down the smoke and added a pleasant show of crackling sparks that spun into the air.

"I've decided not to be so mad anymore," Constance said out of the blue. Her eyes were locked on the fire, the sullen flap of hair covering half her face. "For the time being anyhow."

Cutter and Mim shot tentative glances at each other, but said nothing.

"It's too exhausting," Constance said. "It's just that . . . Uncle Arliss, I have to make sure my memories of my dad don't get all muddled up with you."

"Your dad was a far better man than I ever was."

"No one's arguing that," Constance said.

"So," Mim said, "not mad, just mean."

"I'm just kidding, Mom." Constance got to her feet and wrapped her arms around Cutter, tight, the way she'd hugged him before. "I love you, Uncle Arliss. Really. But right now, you smell like wood-smoke and dessert beans. That just reminds me of Dad. It's gonna take me a while to deal with that."

Mim started to say something, but Constance shook her head.

"I'm going inside. You guys be good."

Mim frowned, taken aback. "What are you—"

"Just remember, there's moose poop on the grass if you decide to go that route."

"Constance!"

She shrugged and gave a little smile, a real smile, the first one in . . . years.

"Just sayin' . . ."

* * *

They were quiet for a time. Then Cutter got up from his chair to stoke the fire, even though it didn't need it.

"Coop Daniels made trips to—"

"South Dakota." Mim cut him off. "I'm aware. You've hated him since you first got to Alaska. Sure, he took me to dinner a couple of times. According to you and Constance, that makes him the devil incarnate. You forget he did hours of free legal work when those bastards at Johnson, Benham, and Murphy were holding up the insurance payout."

Cutter kept his voice low, calm, belying the fact that he spent a good portion of each day willing himself *not* to hunt down Coop Daniels and beat him to death with whatever was handy.

"He may not have been involved, but that guy knew Ethan's death might not have been an accident. That seems like something an attorney representing your interests would have told you."

She swung her feet to the side of the camp chair and stood. For a moment Cutter worried she might go inside. Instead, she joined him at the fire.

"Did you ever think he might be trying to protect me?"

"At first, maybe," Cutter said. "But not now. A lawyer can't rep you and fly to South Dakota on behalf of the company he's helping you battle in court. No way. You can't trust him to tell you the truth. That much is clear."

"I know." She gave a low groan. "It just pisses me off when you rub my nose in it."

"Mim," Cutter said. "I'm not trying to—"

"Again, I know." She warmed her hands over the fire and looked sideways at Cutter. "What's the deal with these fossils?"

"Not sure," Cutter said. "Did Ethan ever make trips to South Dakota?"

"If he did, he didn't tell me."

They stood together, looking into the flames.

Cutter broke the silence. "Do you really believe Max Tunik . . ."

". . . is Ethan's son?" Mim finished his thought. "I mean, I don't think so, but Max believes it, and that makes him happy. All he seems to want is the memory. I'm fine giving him that."

"Listen," Cutter said, "we'll work on this together. And not because I don't trust you to be safe, but because we'll be more efficient that way."

"I'd like that," Mim said. "I'd like that a lot." She leaned sideways, letting her shoulder brush his arm. "What do we do now?"

Cutter knew what he wanted to do, but instead of admitting it, he said, "Talk to Coop Daniels."

"That goes without saying." Mim turned suddenly, looking him dead in the eye. "I mean, what do *we* do? You and me."

"What do you think we should do?"

She leaned closer, kissing him. The tip of her nose exhilaratingly cold against his skin. She lingered there, in no hurry to stop, then pulled away slightly, still close enough he was enveloped in the vapor of her breath when she spoke.

"I'll tell you what we're *not* going to do," she said. "Because, you know, there's moose poop in the grass . . ."

They stood and watched the fire for a time, shoulder to shoulder, together, really together for the first time, but locked in their individual thoughts.

Mim broke the silence. "And about Ethan? What's our first move there?"

Cutter's jaw tensed. "I have some ideas."

She took a half step away, serious now. "Okay . . ."

"We're taking a trip to the Bad Land," Cutter said.

"You mean Badlands?"

"Maybe." He paused for a beat, picturing his brother's face, then spoke softly. "If someone killed Ethan, wherever they are, when I find them, it's going to be *bad*."

Grumpy's Dessert Beans

A savory dish, but when Ethan and Arliss were young, they craved them like a dessert

2 cups dried pinto beans
1 Tablespoon lard or vegetable oil
1 onion chopped
1-3 cloves garlic, chopped
Small handful of cilantro (optional—but Arliss hates cilantro)
8 cups water

   Cook on stove until tender
   Or pressure cook 35 minutes

   Drain and retain liquid.
   Blend beans in blender or food processor, adding liquid back little by little until beans are creamy—or the consistency you want.
   Salt to taste.
   Salsa can be added as well.
   Eat with tortilla chips, fajitas, or . . .

Ritz Cracker Fried Halibut

Halibut filets (or any other white meat fish)—not frozen
2-3 eggs (depending on how much halibut you prepare, you may
need more)
¼ cup of milk
1- 2 rolls of *Ritz* crackers (depending on how much halibut you
prepare, you may need more)
Oil for deep frying—enough for 3" deep in the pan you plan to
use

Remove skin from halibut. Cut halibut fillet into 1½ inch square
chunks depending on the thickness of the fillet.

*Expect that the chunks will end up in a variety of sizes and
shapes that are not uniform.

Using a rolling pin, crush the Ritz crackers into fine crumbs in a
plastic bag, one roll at a time.

*Use only one roll at a time and refresh the crumbs from the sec-
ond roll as they get soggy and become clumped in the plastic bag.

Heat oil to between 350 and 370 degrees F.
While the oil heats up, mix eggs and milk together in a bowl.
Dip the halibut chunks into the egg mixture and then coat with
the crackers by dropping them a few at a time into the bag.
When the oil is ready, drop a few halibut chunks into the oil to
cook.
Cook until golden brown, flipping them in the oil to brown both
sides if needed.
Cooking time is approximately 1½ minutes.
*Smaller or thinner pieces will cook faster.
Remove fish pieces and allow them to drain on a paper towel.
Check for doneness by breaking one open. It should be white
and flakey throughout.

ACKNOWLEDGMENTS

For me at least, writing is a solitary endeavor—finding me cloistered away with my favorite Blackwing 602 pencils and notepad or pecking away on the computer. I need quiet and time for creative boredom to set in.

Even so, I've been incredibly fortunate to have enjoyed the help and collaboration of many talented people over the decades I've been doing this.

As I write this, my wife and I are driving down the Alaska Highway through the startlingly bright fall colors of Canada's Yukon Territory. This is a journey of thousands of miles, so we have time to talk plot, as we often do. I pitch a scenario I've been mulling, then she comes back with some cool counterpoint or plot twist. These are some of my favorite moments in the process.

Arliss Cutter and Lola Teariki are deputy US marshals, and I lean heavily on my time with the United States Marshals Service. I've been retired for a decade, and still, not a day goes by that I don't miss the people and the mission. Being a deputy US marshal was, in my estimation, the best job in the world, and it is my hope that the pages of these Cutter stories reflect what a tremendous group of people carry that circle-star badge.

Friends from Anchorage Police Department, Alaska State Troopers, Village Public Safety Officers, Fairbanks PD, Air Force Pararescue, and countless other agencies have helped me out with my former job as a deputy and continue to do so as I work my way through these Alaska stories.

The team of researchers and contacts has grown over the years, and, to my good fortune, continues to do so.

Ty Cunningham, jujitsu master, tracking mentor, Marshals Service partner, and friend of three decades, walks through virtually every fight and tracking scene I write, offering insight and ideas.

Joe Huston of Bear Mountain Air is a heck of a bush pilot. I've seen a significant portion of the state out the window of his Cessna 185—including the remote set of Alaska Railroad tracks and stretch of river that appear in this book.

Dear friends, Rob and Michelle Heun of High Lake Lodge offer one of the most peaceful places in Alaska (or anywhere) to get away from it all and write . . . or just be.

Brian Weed, of Juneau's Hidden History, is a wealth of knowledge and, after helping me explore miles of underground mine tunnels for Bone Rattle, continues to be a valuable resource about all things Alaska in subsequent books.

Brian Krosschell has taught school all over bush Alaska, knows the people and the waterways, and, in addition to being a friend, never seems to tire of showing me around and answering my endless questions.

Mike and Lori and the rest of the gang at Northern Knives in Anchorage continue to give me a place talk all things bladed—for research and just to decompress. And, of course, Jericho Quinn and Arliss Cutter both carry 3 Dog Knives.

Anyone who knows me at all knows that my wife and I are frequent visitors to Rarotonga in the Cook Islands. Dear friends, Bill, Amber, Jaret, Peter, Jolene, Mii, Rod, Lilly, and countless others help define what makes Lola Teariki who she is.

I took several trips on the Alaska Railroad while researching this book—north to Fairbanks in summer and winter, and, of course, out to Spencer Glacier and Grandview, where this book is set. Alaska Railroad personnel were beyond helpful on each and every trip, helping me turn a kernel of an idea "I want to set an adventure on a train in some remote place in Alaska" into a story. David Graboski, Lauren Wynn, and Daniel Fretwell were great resources during those trips. Andrew Lyon went out of his way to provide me with maps of routes and sketches of train layout. I am grateful to them all.

Speaking of teams, by the time this book comes out, Robin Rue of Writers House Literary Agency will have been my agent for twenty years. She and her assistant, Beth Miller, have mentored my wife and I through the ups and downs of publishing, and we are forever grateful to them.

Gary Goldstein has been my editor at Kensington for almost as long as Robin has been my agent. We've become good friends over the years, and I count myself fortunate to have him and all the folks at Kensington in my corner.

My three kids and their spouses, who have all grown into stellar adults, offer endless insights into the world and their generation that I frequently miss.

My grandkids provide terrific inspiration for Arliss's nephews— as anyone who follows me on social media can plainly see.

Above all, the most important member of this team is my bride, Victoria. She reads everything I write, wielding her red pen while giving me encouragement and ideas. Even now, I'm writing, she's mulling over a section of another story that was giving me problems . . .

and she just came up with a brilliant idea I need to write down . . .

DISCUSSION QUESTIONS

1. Arliss Cutter has strengths and flaws. How do his strengths redeem his character as a protagonist? What are his weaknesses and how do they contribute to the story?

2. Marc Cameron writes strong female characters, including Lola Teariki, Chief Jill Phillips, Mim Cutter, Constance Cutter , Justice Morehouse, and Winnie Tomaganuk. How does the author reveal these strengths? Is there one character you particularly admire or relate to and why?

3. The rural settings in Alaska play an important part in moving the plot forward. If Alaska were a character, do you think it would be a protagonist or an antagonist and why? Does this book make you want to visit Alaska or avoid it and why?

4. As readers, we are getting to know Mim better when she takes a more active role by investigating her husband's death. What do you think of the risks she takes, and why might she be taking them now?

5. Justice Morehouse is fiercely protective of her daughter when she feels the girl might be in danger. Based on the circumstances and acknowledging her good intentions, evaluate Justice Morehouse's actions as she tries to rescue her daughter. Do you agree or disagree with her choices? How might you have acted in the same situation?

6. Arliss and Mim's relationship has taken a more personal step forward. How might they be challenged as their relationship tries to progress? How would you envision their future together?

7. Before reading this book, what was your understanding of the mission of the US Marshal Service? Has your understanding changed now that you've read this book and to what extent?

8. Have you ever found yourself in a position similar to Efrosinia Basenkov, the younger sister of the Russian woman who was attacked, when she was faced with being a witness or endan-

gering her family? How did you handle it? If not, how do you think you would handle it?

9. A reoccurring theme in this book is loyalty. What does loyalty mean to you? How important is it in your hierarchy of values? Compare how the members of the law enforcement community and the Russian Volkov family relate to and act on that theme? How is loyalty valued in Cutter's family?

10. Grandparents can play an important part in a child's life. What kind of influence does Grumpy have on Arliss and Ethan? What kind of influence has a grandparent had on you and your life?

11. Part of the plot is driven along due to the US Marshals protecting of the visiting Supreme Court Justice. What's your opinion on the amount of security measures that are taken to protect members of our judiciary?

12. Rudenko recites this Russian quote: "If you invite a bear to dance, it is not you who decides when the dance is over. It is the bear." What does this quote mean to you?

13. The book cover art depicts the massive bones from a bowhead whale that actually exists in Utqiagvik to welcome folks to town. The remote wildness of this town with its whale carcass and wandering polar bears highlights the danger that can exist when nature collides with people and civilization. Have you had a close or dangerous encounter with nature? How did it affect you: your choices, opinions or behavior?

14. Eating together in a social setting bonds people together. Family cooking and eating time are depicted in this series regularly. A recipe used in the story is usually given at the end of the book. How have these scenes helped to create a vision of the family? What do you think of the recipes? Have you tried one, and, if yes, what did you think of it? Do you have a special family recipe that seems to bring your family together?